All That Swagger

Miles Franklin

S.H. Prior Memorial Prize Winner, 1936

ANGUS & ROBERTSON PUBLISHERS

All characters in this novel are fictitious, and
have no relation to any living person.

ANGUS & ROBERTSON PUBLISHERS
London • Sydney • Melbourne • Singapore • Manila

First published by Angus & Robertson Publishers, Australia, 1936
This Arkon paperback edition 1979

© Miles Franklin estate 1954

National Library of Australia
card number and ISBN 0 207 14394 3

Printed in Australia by Hedges & Bell Pty Ltd

CHAPTER I

MEMORY recaptures a song or two echoing wistfully through the generations of Delacy in the voice of old Fearless Danny. He was wont to rune to himself as he sat alone, thrust aside by his sons as childish, his eyes glazed with absence—that retreat of the aged when time has wrung the colours from the present and left the rose and green only on the distant fields of youth.

"Oh, moi! Oh, moi!" he would ejaculate, conversing to himself. Rarely was there an understanding listener. When there was, he would gaze backward into what long ago had been the future, and belatedly indulge in nostalgia. He would linger on the picture of his mother taking her farewell of him, and his father lacking the courage to see young Danny being picked up by the coach that was to bear him away for ever.

The wild Murrumbidgee sinking into the bunyip hole, and tumbling therefrom into Delacy's Crossing, would vanish, the Shannon take its place, graciously traversing its ancient plain by Limerick, the beauteous city. The road ran by Sarsfield Bridge to old Ennis in County Clare, to the ruined Abbey where the boys played, and to Clare Castle. The day would be in May with the whinchats merry in the furze, the larks high in the air, such a day as the Isle of Destiny knows, a cajoling day, a day to caress the heart of a youth to water in the presence of a maid, and to turn a maid's heart to a man; and the era was a hundred years from now, for young Daniel Brian Robert M. Delacy, born in the year of Waterloo, was stretching towards eighteen.

His home was on the rise by Ennis that looks north-east to the Slieve Aughty Mountains, and north-west to the Aran Isles and the Atlantic, which had expatriated or swallowed entirely so many Clare and Galway lads. He stood in the road, not that he was at that date given to meditation, but the ancient legendry of the scene, the acknowledged presence of the fairies in the glens and raths, was as saturating to his inner consciousness as the sun to his outer. The sunshine spread a benediction full away to Kilrush and Liscannor Bay, to Kilkee and Killaloe, to lilting Kildare and hilarious Kilkenny and Tipperary, to Ennistymon and Crusheen, and Rathdrum and Carrickmore, to Enniskillen, and Trillick and

Letterkenny and Ballysodare, and Tara, and Tralee, and Mallow, and Bantry, and Bandon. The darling loves and doves of names that swell in the heart of Erin's inheritor, until he is thrappled! A presence grown palpable through centuries of articulate myth and poesy had nurtured young Delacy's spirit. He loved the open view of the thatched white cabins on the treeless hillsides with the sociable roads across them. Roads excited him, packed as they were with history, glamorous with fable, with chivalry and romance and liberation in the way they ran through the winds and rains of all the seasons of all the generations, a foe to stagnation, a hostage to adventure.

He had a sense of deprivation that none of the green land was his. The only soil he could dig his spade into was the paltry acreage of his father's college, where there were prior rights of a playground for the scholars, and a plot for the goat.

There was a legend that the Delacys had crossed the English Channel with the Conqueror, and the Irish Sea with Strongbow. Whatever, the Delacys had followed clerical pursuits and had never been rooted in the 'soil as were the families of the reverberating cognomens and Firbolgian descent, whose bones and brains had fertilized the soil and culture of Eire long before culture or agriculture began in Albion. So Gaelic lore and archaeological research would have it; but perhaps only pride, put on its mettle by presumptuous usurpers, could reconstruct so gratifying a prospect from the records of the savage and bloody procedure of all factions in past days. At any rate, among the whole boiling of Delacys was never a Kevin, a Patrick, nor an Aloysius, which showed they had lost their chances in epochs later than the Tuatha de Danaan and Milesian.

Danny's father was principal of a preparatory college for boys. His curriculum was limited, but he transmitted with his canings something invaluable to his third son in his after life in the Antipodes—character unflinching and resourceful. In the dislocation which accompanied Continental military glory and the local agitation against oppression, Schoolmaster Delacy, who was classified with the petty gentry loyal to the Union, could not provide careers for three sons. One in due time would step into his father's shoes, but it is debilitating to camp for an old man's shoes, and no one knows what became of Robert Delacy. No doubt he and the school petered out together. The second son, William, was engulfed by India. It is known that he rose—or sank—to be a major in the army there, but nothing more.

Danny's hunger for land was a crying for the moon in so far as his father could help him. There was, however, an opening to appeal to the lad. Poverty following the Napoleonic wars had driven thousands across the Atlantic. Now the Colony of New South Wales was greedy for settlers. Tales of rosy prospects for free men penetrated to Ennis, though Mrs Delacy suppressed any talk of this.

Danny went often to the Cooleys, of Cooley Hall, over the hill, a name pretentious for the farm, but the Cooleys remembered that they were of one of the ancient and powerful clans. Mrs Cooley was a Francallew. The patronymic, as found in an antique missal, had been written Franc-Alleu, and signified freefield. The first Franc-Alleu had also been a follower of the Bastard of Normandy. Thus the Cooleys and Francallews, as the Delacys, had claims to a gentility characterized by loss of the Gaelic tongue and the acceptance of the decree that Irish nationality was synonymous with treason.

Danny enjoyed walking around with old Cooley, looking at the turnips, discussing the bull in the meadow or the pigs in the sty, and was always ready to help for love of work on the land. Old Cooley thought him an obliging gossoon and sometimes lent him a nag to appear in the hunts. The acuter Honoria had lately opened her husband's eyes.

"Helping you, is it! Have ye seen his eyes light on our Johanna?" Pretty Johanna was mistress of the dairy, and could turn the heel of a sock with the best.

* "The devil mend him! I'll break the young spalpeen's back."

"Father O'Fogarty shall say a special word to her on her duty."

"A Prodestan', and him with nothing to his back—will have to go for a soldier belike."

"He talks more of going to the Antipodes."

"The sooner the better! Kevin O'Gorman with a phroperty near as good as me own, waiting for her to say the word."

"An old widow-man with big childre, not to touch the heart of a young girl."

"I'll touch her back with a stout ashplant if she shows anny nonsense."

Thereafter Danny was frigidly met, and found it difficult to see Johanna alone. She confessed to undergoing penances. "Sure, 'twas worth it," she said, tossing her head.

---

* The aim is merely to indicate the rhythm and poetic and philosophic idiom of the speech of the Irish characters, not to make a pedantic exhibition of Irish pronunciation word by word. Those acquainted with the deeply-placed voices, and rich unorthodox vowel sounds which distinguish much of Irish-English, despite disclaimers by those who adopt the haw-haw, flat-vowelled Public School English, are independent of phonetic reproduction, and to read dialect is a wearying and frequently an impossible exercise to all but those who specialize in linguistics.

This made Danny feel like a king. He, too, had been taken to task. The unpleasantness suffered by love's young dreamers on opposite sides of a sectarian fence was theirs, though the elders had kindly dispositions and were among the enlightened and less bigoted. There was, too, an endearing story about the Delacys. In bad past days when the land had been parcelled among the usurpers, a Delacy had accepted in name only and permitted the rightful inheritor to occupy. In the recent agitation for Catholic Emancipation, Schoolmaster Delacy had allowed the use of his class-room. These things were not forgotten. Also, Danny's emigration was becoming practical, and both sets of parents looked upon this as a way out of the danger. The Cooleys welcomed it with relief, the Delacys with sorrow, but also as the lesser of two evils.

Danny was taking his head with a precocity and enterprise natural to one who was as Danny was, who did what Danny did when he became known by half a dozen nicknames, all tributes to character and courage. On the intoxicating day of his recollection he was scanning the landscape for a handkerchief on a gorse bush at the back of Cooley's barn. On that day old Cooley went to market, and Danny had something to read to his Johanna.

Scarcely waiting to take precautions against discovery, he pulled a paper from his shirt and cried: "Johanna, Mavourneen! Listen to this. I've got it all laid out in me moind."

Johanna had rather he noted her dainty shoes and trim kirtle. What satisfaction was there in virtue without opportunity to win its spurs? Kevin O'Gorman—nasty widow-man of the advanced age of thirty-five—was over-ready to test her, but she resisted his attempts with loathing, while she doubted that Danny could be provoked out of his respect for women by any tactics possible to an inviolable maiden.

Danny liked to read. He had more facility than Johanna, the victim of an inferior governess. "Out there, sure there are new developments at every turning of the moon. Listen, will you?—

"The short space of little more than four decades has converted the horrid and trackless wilderness—the transient hunting field of some migratory tribe of naked and unidead savages—into the busy mart of civilized and enlightened intercourse where there is yearly exported to the mother-country produce of many kinds, and where the tastes, the pursuits, the comforts, and even elegancies of English Society, are valued and enjoyed to a far more substantial extent than in many of the large towns of Great Britain itself."

"It reads like a grand story," commented Johanna.

" 'Tis actual fact. There are towns like Limerick, and fine establishments like your aunt's already there."

"Can that be true?" exclaimed Johanna, her eyes dancing with excitement. "I'm wanting to hear of the elegancies."

"True, why true! You can depend on the printed word as if 'twas from the book of Ballymote. Listen to their aims:

"To induce respectable and virtuous families among the industrious ranks of society at home, to transfer their capital and labour from an arena where the whirl of competition stands formidably in the way of successful exertion, to a field where not competency alone, but certain fortune can hardly fail to reward the efforts of careful, persevering and honourable toil.

"Certain fortune! A man would be driving his carriage, with high-steppers like the Thomonds', before you could turn round."

"Ah, 'twould take too long!" said Johanna, dubiously. "Me Aunt Della had a letter that came from Shamus O'Tooley, who wint out after the rebellion, and it was full of terrible hardships, and convicts, and nothing to eat. I saw it meself. 'Tis kept in the old book."

"Och! Johanna, I have trouble getting things into your head, and then they come out again. The rebellion was a generation ago, and sure, they were rebels and convicts."

"They were noble heroes foighting for freedom."

"Maybe they were, too, but they were treated as felons and transported. 'Tis all dealt with here. It says that Sydney Cove was a repository of national crime, a vast territorial jail inhabited only by felons and their overseers. 'Even the Governors themselves scarcely exceeded, either in dignity or importance, anything but superintendents of houses of correction.' Sure, what could that generate but a superfluity of naughtiness? That was at the beginning, but since 1820, 'a tide of respectable immigration has been diluting that deplorable state of affairs at the furthest extremity of the globe'."

"It sounds desperate to be so far away."

"Lo, and behold ye! 'Twould be the centre of the universe if you were there with me, Johanna," said Danny, boldly.

"And what put such a notion in ye'r skull?" demanded Johanna with mounting interest.

" 'Tis natural, Johanna, and there is no escape from Nature."

"And what do ye mean by me being at the centre of the universe out there? Me father and mother would never emigrate to the furthest ends of the globe, and them with this fine place."

"Then are you going to remain unmarried? That would be difficult for the prettiest girl in County Clare."

"It would that same, with O'Gorman never giving me a moment's peace. Sure, his eye would be on me now, but for his going to market a pig."

"Arrah! O'Gorman, an old grandfather like a gorilla, with grown-up children."

"He could give his wife everything, Danny Delacy."

"He could never give her the advinture of going over the seas to a splendid new country. I could soon give you a carriage and pair like the Marchioness of Sligo. They give a free man 130 or 150 acres, and a few acres to each child, and you can get Government men assigned to labour for you."

"It doesn't sound rational."

"At anny rate, I'm off the day I'm eighteen. Will you wait for me?"

"How long, Danny-boy?"

"Maybe two years. Time is consumed with the voyage."

"I could never hold out two years against O'Gorman's importunities, and me feyther all for getting me set up with such a property. I'm a full year and a trifle more than ye, Danny-boy. 'Tis only a dream."

"Everything is a dream till it is made come true. Come make this true with me, Johanna."

He stood before her, not yet eighteen, and the meagre stature of five-feet-seven-and-a-half-inches wherewith to attack the wilds of the Antipodes in bravura days of convicts and aborigines, before the explorers had finished their surveys. Neither had he the features of the classic heroes; a small pointed nose, a stubborn mouth, now full of ugly teeth, and later to be ambushed in an unmolested beard. But Johanna doted on his eyes, as blue as the heavens on the days when the salmon wait to go up; his hair with the raven sheen and as soft as floss silk; his forehead broad and full; his voice as deep and brave as a stag hound's.

As the Isle of Destiny animated the early Milesians with the expectation of refuge and plenty, so did the Continent of Australia inspire young Danny. His hunger for land and need for action banished indecision. He dreamed of wide acres like those of County Clare, running away for square miles, all his own.

"Moi, oh, moi! What a prospect," he would exclaim.

The district was combed for families with members in New South Wales, and, no matter what the nature of the information, it fanned the enthusiasm of Danny Delacy. The schoolmaster aided the lad, as far as small means allowed, to escape from restricting circumstances to spacious opportunities baited with adventure. The eyes of Mrs Delacy reflected her bereavement. Industrious and cheerful, his ready wit with never a barb in it, and cowardice and lies unknown to him, Danny was his mother's bright spot in life, her baby. Now he was to go. She would be old and deserted. Her eyes reflected her bereavement.

Otherwise, the situation was eased for neighbours who feared a mixed marriage. Danny confessed that he had asked Johanna to come out to him. Danny not quite eighteen! His parents hid their smiles. The difficulties of communication guaranteed the defeat of young love. The widow Cassidy once had had a paper with a mark beside the title which meant that her daughter was living, but not another line in all the years. It would take more than a year to receive a reply to a letter. A little tact until Danny departed was all that was necessary.

Mrs Cooley was likewise sensible, and also sympathetic. Cooley had been foisted on her as a safe match when her imagination hungered for something more knightly. She was a steady woman and true to her faith; she was firmly for establishing Johanna but, "Be aisy," she would advise. "Danny Delacy is a nice boy, for all he's a heretic. He's as fearless as a game cock."

"It's a bantam he is."

"And with the lively word for young and old, and all his foine book-learning and conversation from his feyther; it is not to be wondered that Johanna is a bit touched; but sure, he's but half-fledged—not a pluck of beard on him yet. Whin he's gone, and no sign for a full year, then O'Gorman can be tender, and it's snugly settled she'll be before the second year."

"O'Gorman may be a little coorse in the horn beside young Danny, but he has a tidy phropery, and with twinty years more on her, 'tis glad she'll be that she was saved from a come-day-go-day Prodestan'."

"Maybe, and maybe not," said Honoria, with recollections of herself at Johanna's age. "At anny rate, let her have a rich good-bye to him. Sure, she was crying all night."

"Women can turn the taps on for annything."

"All the same, O'Gorman should not be too pressing for a while. She has been teasing to go stay by me sister Kate Thomond. She need not come back till Danny has gone for good and all."

Cooley left the matter to her. She was his second wife. He had never been able finally to get the better of either; women were unfathomable. New dresses were necessary for the visit to Mrs Thomond, whose husband throve in the law in Limerick, but Honoria pointed out that they would do for the wedding later. Honoria was plotting for Johanna's escape from the widow-man.

There would be promising sprigs of the law about the Thomonds. Johanna could seize her chance to mate in accordance with youthful taste as well as in her own religion.

She and Danny had their final meeting in the coomb, reached by the stile out of the barley paddock behind the Cooley Hall barn.

"I could never hold out for two years, Danny-boy," sobbed Johanna. "As soon as ye'r back is turned, they'll put on the clampers. Besides, it's out of sight, out of mind with min. The minute ye don't see me, ye'll forget me."

"Be all the pipers in Paradise!" shouted Danny, his eyes flashing blue flame. "We can put the comehither on it in a twinkling. Come with me, Johanna, and see to it that I do not change me moind, nor yours neither."

Johanna baulked momentarily. She accused Danny of his youth, which he said would quickly improve. There was the dread obstruction of creed, like black magic, but Danny was inclined to pooh-pooh all religions as superstition. In this issue his lissom young form and fair skin outweighed the swarthy hairy O'Gorman, with a breath which made kisses a persecution; and not for nothing was Johanna given a nose like an Emperor's, and black eyes to go with it, and a mouth as beautiful as those that the Greeks sculptured in marble, and as firmly set.

She lacked Danny's love of the soil and open spaces. Her cravings were for town graces as found with her aunt, Kate Thomond; and the O'Gorman farm had fewer amenities and uglier furniture than Cooley Hall. She could see what was ahead of her in County Clare. She did not share Danny's visions, but was it not in print that the people of Sydney Cove "enjoyed to a far more substantial extent than in many of the large towns of Great Britain itself, the tastes, the pursuits, the comforts and even the elegancies of English Society"? Johanna adored elegancies. Better the hope of elegancies at the "furthest extremity of the globe" than the certainty of inelegancies on O'Gorman's farm. She swallowed the camel of faith in the delusion of brides that husbands can be reformed. The susceptible Danny, who could not meet her eyes without flushing and collapsing into self-consciousness, would be easily managed when she had him all alone. His conversion would reflect glory on her.

That pretty day they sat side by side upon the stile overlooking the ripening barley, their troth plighted, and considering, with the high-heartedness of youth and inexperience, the stratagems necessary.

She packed her box that night and put in her best bits, collected against marriage. Her mother wondered at the weight of it at the time. She was to travel with a Sister from the convent.

"Just supposing that ye'r Danny never comes back?"

"Then I'll be a nun, but I'll never marry O'Gorman. Don't say I have not warned ye."

It was certainly better that she should have her chance at Kate Thomond's fine parties and not be plagued by the hairy O'Gorman for the present.

The wrench of departure remained unrecorded by Danny except in the final perspective of memory. When years had taken the strength—though never the courage—from Daniel's spirit, the old eyes would rest upon that poignant drama. He could be seen with all his worldly goods in a box on his shoulder, walking away from his home to take the coach where the lane met the highway to Limerick. He had few goods: a tool or two, a new suit, a second pair of boots, several pairs of socks, some shirts, a Bible, and a book of poems. All the currency that his parents could collect was in his belt, but there was a fortune in his sound stomach and high heart.

"Sure, me father kissed me—the only time he ever did, that I remember. He handed me his own frieze over-coat, and went into his schoolroom and shut the door. . . . Me mother sat on a milestone and flung her apron over her head and buried her head in her arms. That's how she remained as I looked back—all the way to the turn of the road. That's how I remember her always. . . . All those years, and I never saw her again . . . dead a lifetime ago . . . but in me moind I can see her sitting there still . . . The moind! The moind!"

On that summer day, when the heavens matched his eyes in sparkle and colour, he glanced blithely toward the coomb, with the stile at its feet, where he and Johanna had sealed their plan of action with sacred promises. He took the parting from his family lightly—going to Johanna as he was, and full of impatience to be accumulating that fortune which would bring him back to them or them to him—but it deepened in his memory as the road lengthened. Later he found a song to voice his emotions, and this he would rune over and over, forgetting his listener—if any—his fading eyes on the sweet distance of old County Clare:

I'm sitting on the stile, Mary, where we sat side by side,
On a bright May morning long ago, when first you were my bride.
The corn was springing fresh and green and the lark sang loud and high,
And the red was on your lip, Mary, and the lovelight in your eye.

The young man's consciousness was instinct with the comprehended soul of Ireland, a tangible entity wrought by countless generations to a nourishing cloak for the ego. Stored for sustenance later was the spiritual grace of concrete places, that supra mundane presence which gave reality to the musical names, the long-trodden ways of Eire. His heart and eyes were ahead on adventure. Away, away, from his native environment so rich in mystic lore, to a land purged of history since before Etruscan Ides or Babylonian orgies were calendared, his spirit of an independence to further the artificing of a new culture and of legends distinctive of places whose names at that date were scarcely taken down from the aborigines.

There was wild dismay at Cooley Hall when it was discovered that Johanna would never more return to superintend her dairy or help the younger children with their lessons. One Cooley blamed the other. O'Gorman blamed them both, having held his horses for two years for this reluctant girl. With the aid of a cousin— herself bent on eloping with an English officer—Johanna had made her escape forty-eight hours before it was suspected. A letter came some days later stating that she was off to Belfast to be married to Danny Delacy and emigrate to the Antipodes.

"Marry a Prodestan'—to travel without marriage and be rooned— and in that scoundrelly northern town!" Mrs Cooley keened affrightingly and set out to attack Mrs Delacy. Both women said things that they could neither forgive nor forget.

There came in time a letter from young Delacy to old Cooley reporting that the absconders were married and on board the good ship *Jane* bound for Sydney Cove. Honoria Cooley preserved the document as the certificate of her daughter's rectitude, but old Cooley never felt that it was a real marriage. His bitter denunci- ation followed his Johanna—once his delight. He disowned her as part of his flesh, and prayed that she would rue the vile sorrow and shame she had put on him and her mother.

Johanna accepted excommunication cheerfully. Maledictions could not travel so far as she and Danny were going, and all would be repealed when Danny was brought into the true fold. She was full of excitement in sailing with the personal effects she had col- lected, ostensibly as the bride of the odious O'Gorman; and had she not her own rights of being? The Cooleys claimed descent from the princes of Ith or Heremon. Were there not legends of Queen Maeve and the great cattle spoil of Cooley?

Moyna Thomond, Johanna's accomplice, a generous and romantic girl, was distressed by Johanna's going so far away, and insisted upon giving as many of her own things as the two girls could smuggle out of the house. Among these was a cedar work-box with drawers, set on a tripod pedestal, which had to be lashed on to the deck and tended all the way to Sydney Cove. There was also a little chair with carved back and curved legs with claw-and-ball feet, a pair of china ornaments and a set of three Waterford lustres. The cousins parted with promises of eternal fealty and the hope of reunion in Sydney. Every possibility dangles before the nose of adventurous youth.

They never met again. Nor did old Cooley ever rescind his curses. That, perhaps, is why the Delacys know so little of their ancestry in Ireland. Mrs Daniel Brian Robert M. Delacy rarely mentioned her family, except abstractly, even to her sons and daughters. Danny lost account of his because his mother died shortly after his departure, and he disregarded letter-writing. Also, His Majesty's mails were not so cheap, swift and dependable a hundred years ago as to-day.

A later Mrs Delacy wrote home to the parish priest, who could find only an aunt on the Cooley side, and her memory was gone. A hundred years from the date of Danny's embarkation, a great-grandson of his name alighted out of the sky near Ennis. He was hospitably received by the Bishop of Killaloe, and entertained at St Flannahan's College, but not a trace of a Cooley or a Delacy could he find. Nevertheless, in the indestructible archives of imagination, Mrs Delacy still sits upon the milestone with her head bowed upon her arms. By the further aid of an old song, Danny and his Johanna remain for ever in the sunlight on the stile, he young and brave, and listening to the words she now for ever speaks, the lovelight in her eyes, the red upon her cheeks.

CHAPTER II

THE *Jane*, 374 tons, entered Port Jackson, "the beautiful land-locked marine lake", and anchored in Sydney Cove, seven miles from the Heads, six months from the day she had sailed from Southampton. The arrival of the Delacys was chronicled in the *Australian* of the date:—"Mr George Moore, of Ballyshannon, Co. Donegal; Mr and Mrs Daniel Delacy, of Ennis, Co. Clare, as well as 20 steerage passengers, principally mechanics and their families. All the passengers spoke in high terms of the gentlemanly treatment afforded them by Capt. Jas. Riddell."

Mr George Moore of Ballyshannon had a promising estate in the Colony at Bandalong and at Quebarra on the Morumbidgee. He had been out for some years, driven from Ireland by the death of his wife, and had returned to Dublin only to place his son at Trinity College. On the *Jane* he had shown a warm interest in the immigrant bride of nineteen-and-a-bit with her groom of eighteen, and his kindness and generosity had mitigated some of the hardships of the voyage for Johanna. To conserve his currency Danny had taken a steerage passage for himself and put his wife in the between accommodation. Mr Moore had had them both removed to berths near his own so that his young countrywoman could have the company of the ladies in the cuddy. From his ample stores he had coaxed her appetite and exerted himself for her comfort in other ways as well as by cheering and sustaining her during the trying months of their passage. He also offered Danny the position of overseer, and invited Johanna to take up her residence as lady-housekeeper at his station. For the moment Danny had other ideas.

Mr Moore was an esteemed patron of Petty's grand new hotel for the gentry on Church Hill, and, on landing, took the young pair to a select boarding establishment near by, which the proprietor had "the distinguished honour to announce is recommended by ladies of the first respectability, that his dinners are got up in the first style with change of soups daily and mock turtle three times a week". This gentleman also pointed out that his hostelry had a fine view of Port Jackson and Darling Harbour, and that his clients could hear the strains of the military band from the Fort near at hand.

Those elegancies which Johanna had expected, were, as elsewhere, for the privileged. She saw little of them at her boarding establishment, where the cark of funds running low and the discomfort of approaching motherhood depressed her. She was not at that date susceptible to the swagger of the military bucks, nor was she concerned with the lady, who desired, for a consideration, to undertake "the preservation of the complexion from the burning pernicious influence of the solar beams of the Antipodes". She was delighted with orange blossoms, water-melons, guavas, and pomegranates. Grapes and peaches were to her taste, but the clouds of flies and mosquitoes and the heat distressed her. A "brick-fielder" frightened and prostrated her. Danny demanded her enthusiasm for the lively harbour with a forest of masts like a deciduous wood, and shouted in her ear that there were twenty-two whalers at sea, in addition to all those in port, and that their capacity was from 70 to 700 barrels.

"Moi! Think of that wealth. Sure, a boat with 800 barrels of sperm oil put in the same day as ourselves because ten of the crew refused duty. They've been a year away in the Antarctic."

It was a blow to Danny to learn that land grants had ceased in 'thirty-one. The information imparted to Johanna in the coomb had been out of date. There were no special prizes for a young man because he was free and honest. He had to acquire by toil. Without a trade or any special influence there was a stiff prospect ahead of the little pair in the Colony, thrusting beyond its garde-major days, but still hampered by bedraggled swaddling clothes of convictism.

Danny was out every hour of the day seeking an opening. Johanna was left much to herself. Mr Moore had too much business demanding attention to pay her any but a short call. A lady—especially one in her "delicate" state of health—did not walk abroad alone when the quarterly muster of ticket-of-leavers was proceeding at the post office, when prisoners were marched about in gangs under guard, when misdemeanants were sent aboard the hulks as a respite from severer punishment, or were sentenced to days on the treadmill. Danny would burst in to declare that the cattle market had excellent beasts, but that he saw a rubbishing lot of ewe-necked horses. "Och, the field for breeding horses that's here—the uses for them!" Or he would tell of the cricket match for £50 a side.

Johanna read the newspapers and learnt that bread was 4 lb., 7d.; bacon, 6d. lb.; beef, 3d.; butter, 1/2; cheese, 4d. to 8d.; and candles, 6½d. Salted hides were 2d. per lb.; horns, 10/- per 100; guinea fowls, 6/6 per pair, and turkeys, 5/- each.

Danny was determined to own land, but how was he to clear and
work it without capital, and in competition with established and
favoured men who could command all the Government labour
they needed? He had not arrived early enough. The big fellows,
with parents to provide capital and influence, frequently dishonestly
exercised in official circles, had already pegged their claims and
were squatting on them west, north, and south, to the full extent
of the Nineteen Counties.

Danny said he would be doomed if he had travelled thirteen
thousand miles for land, then to sit down like a hen in a town
as a servant to any man. At length, when funds ran out, he consented to go up country with Mr Moore until he could set-up on
his own land. That she was to be with Mr Moore was to Johanna
the only factor to temper the strangeness and uncongeniality of her
new environment. Had Mr Moore been situated near Sydney, she
could have been comparatively happy, but what elegancies or ease
could there be in the untamed bush from which came blood-
curdling tales of bushrangers and aborigines.

The size and height of the trees frightened her. "Sure, they'd
make gallows posts big enough for the devil to collect his own,"
she cried, and withdrew her eyes from those standing stark and
dead early on the route; and she never forgot the gibbeted form
she saw along the way.

The trees inspired Danny. "They're giants, bedad! From the top
of them you could slip into heaven itself, me brave Johanna."

"There's nothing that would be called grass at home—nothing
that affords a full bite."

"But if it provides a full belly, it is the same thing."

"At anny rate the whole world is a forest. There is ne'er a
meadow at all," said Johanna, disconsolately.

"They're for me to make," maintained the undefeatable Daniel.

"Och! Live horse till ye get grass!" murmured Johanna.

They travelled in two drays, with only a few yoke of oxen in
each vehicle, and progress was retarded by the necessity of double-
banking at stiff pinches. They had assigned men to attend them,
men glad to be going to Mr Moore, who had a good name.

The Goulburn Plains were already held by families, which, in
some instances, hold them still with prestige and comfort. Lake
George was gone, likewise Gounderu. Limestone Plains was in the
hands of first families, there to remain, in imitation of the English
squirearchy, until dispossessed by an imperative democracy in
favour of an ideally modelled city.

They reached Bandalong, one of the farthest-out stations, not

far from Mount Bowning, which a year later was declared the
official limit for settlement. The holding was large and watered by
the Bandalong, a short tributary of the Morumbidgee. Mount
Bowning's round blue head was a sentinel from every direction.

For Johanna's sake Danny was relieved to anchor, but he was
emphatic. "It's only till I can foind meself."

Johanna's child did not live long, but it was only a girl, and
Johanna had a reverence for producing males that was descended
from a racial era when an adulteress, with sons, could wear a bolder
face than an honest wife with nothing but daughters.

"The poor little thing would have been a help in manny ways,"
observed Danny, having in mind that family labour with which
men of various designations made their way on the land.

Danny pegged away with Mr Moore, with little adventure but
that of a strange environment. Johanna was weak and fretful. This
fact and the unwelcome attentions of Walter Moore prevented
Danny from going with Major Mitchell in 1835. Lack of capital
kept him from joining the overlanders who rushed along the
Major's Line in the years following, years during which the squatters
extended their occupancy of the land from the Morumbidgee to
the Darling, and changed the social and economic composition
of the Colony. The sheep owners within the Nineteen Counties
authorized for land settlement, had, under existing policies, been
able to secure most of the grazing areas. Later arrivals coveted
holdings beyond the jurisdiction of the area delimited for the
maintaining of law and order, and soon spread like a bursting
dam in disregard of an Act declaring squatters to be unauthorized
trespassers on the Crown. The mere name did not wound the
hardy and mostly unscrupulous adventurers, there beyond the
application of law, in millions of acres of inland grass country to
be had for the seizing. The Governor preserved Governmental
prestige by sanctioning what was too strong to suppress, and
licensed the squatters to trespass by the payment of a small yearly
fee, or rental, for vast stations. "Squatter" acquired an antipodean
connotation approximating that of manorial lord as the graziers
entrenched themselves in parody of English County Families. Conditions have ensured that they remain a parody to this day.

There were no coolies, Zulus, nor abducted negroes here. In the
serf class were only British prisoners, and transportation was soon
to cease. Thenceforward for several generations, Australian men
were to establish their homes, if not by the sweat of their brows,
then in saddle galls and the physical hardihood of an existence
which demanded the pluck to ride colts that had run ungentled

until mature. Women had had to give birth to their families in the same way since Eve, but in Australia, the highest type and breed of white woman had to add to that fundamental travail the secondary labour, which in more populous lands is delegated to the disinherited and servile classes, or to the backward races.

Though he was hobbled by domesticity plus lack of capital, Danny never settled as an underling at Bandalong. He disliked his relation to the convicts as overseer, and abhorred theirs to the lash. Though of invulnerable integrity himself, no man was more merciful to transgressors. Decency abode in him as melody in music and without any sense of superiority. There was little of either the bully or the servant in him; he was ineradicably a free man, an individualist. His father was a Trinity College man; Danny himself at least knew of the classics when only "betters" could read or write. Old Cooley, too, had the status of a fox-hunting squire, and Johanna had not forsaken her country and forsworn her faith to sink in the social scale.

Each time that Danny reached the plateau that lay between Bandalong and another holding of Mr Moore's on the Murrumbidgee—as it was later to be spelt—he was bewitched by the spectacle of the heavens prinked with a necklace of ranges beautiful as opals and sapphires. There it lay, land in plenty beyond County Murray. No one had penetrated its gorges since Hume and Hovell had skirted them in reaching the Doomut ten years earlier. This domain was guarded by natural ramparts and dismissed as inaccessible while there was ample open country. The high blue ranges were the wall of a fountain province beyond which the Colony sloped down and away to droughty plains of heat and mirage, already held in lively cattle runs from the Lachlan to the Murray, and from whence came news of desperate encounters with inhabitants who resisted invasion, or who executed summary justice upon men who upheld white prestige in desecrating black women. The Out Back had no allure for Danny. He babbled of the cool endearing mountains in a way that filled Johanna with apprehension. On the other hand, Walter Moore, a waster and libertine, laid her under continual siege so that she longed for some way of escape. Mr Moore voiced the opinion, volubly upheld by Walter, that native dogs would destroy all young or weak stock in winter in the gorges. In summer, the aborigines, who migrated there for their initiation ceremonies and to feast on the boogongs,* would spear or frighten away what animals escaped the dogs.

"Maybe we had better stay where we are well-off," sighed Johanna.

* Large edible moths.

"Well-off, by damn!" was all that Danny said.

Finally Johanna had to complain of Walter, and she begged his father to assist Danny to a place of his own. Mr Moore had seen dubious incidents, and regretfully acceded to Johanna's plea. He had for the handsome young woman the affection of a parent, and would miss her, as the society of any women, and especially of ladies, was highly prized. The Commissioner—the all-powerful of the period—was Mr Moore's friend, and through him Moore obtained a sliver of land on the Morumbidgee, adjoining the Moore property, Quebarra.

Some time earlier it had been a grant to a convict who had saved an official's life. The man, given his freedom, had married and settled there. For the birth of his child he took his wife to Mrs Fullwood, of Heulong, eight miles away across the river. He brought wife and child home on Mrs Fullwood's horse at dusk when the river was a little high, so that he had to give all his energy to guiding the horse and keeping him on his feet. When the horse rushed up the bank past him out of the water, the saddle was empty. The bodies were found days after and buried near by. The man abandoned his land and disappeared. It remained unoccupied because of a legend that the ghost of the woman and child wailed in the crossing when the water was shoulder-high at the dark of the moon.

Danny "arrahed" at ghosts. They raised no fear in his valiant flesh, and the river frontage secured the gorges behind it. Currency being scarce, Mr Moore paid Delacy in live stock, which were allowed to run on the skirts at Bandalong. Now he advanced labourers to fell timber and put up a hut.

Johanna regretted her comfortable quarters and lady's life, with assigned labour for all purposes, including a nurse for the baby, and prepared to accompany Danny into the wilderness once more. She moved to Quebarra to be safe from young Moore and nearer to Danny while he was erecting their shelter.

The new place was called Bewuck by the blacks for the hauls of cod they caught in the fish hole, almost in front of the homestead. It was a reservoir from which the water issued in a slight fall and ran wide on a stony bed that made one of the few safe crossings in a day's ride. While at Quebarra, Johanna was told of the ghosts by the stockman's wife, and that the bottomless waterhole was the home of the bunyip, most mysterious of all the fantastic Australian animals.

Johanna soon moved to her home with her belongings on a slide. The early settler's heart sank as she struggled down the declivity to the rough spot without a road, and far from neighbours. Terror invaded her when she saw the wild river rushing past so near her door. She clasped her toddler against the mesmeric danger. The river had a long, harsh name and was lined with uncanny trees, strangely called oaks, and clothed in green hair that was tormented by the breeze to the melancholy cadence of the banshee.

The new home was a wooden shell. The cracks let in the sun. Johanna found no bar on the door, and when Danny went out of her sight in the gathering dusk, she wailed that the bunyip would devour her and the child.

"You've been listening to some nullity with an empty skull so that stories rattle in it," said Danny, with scorn. "The bunyip will be all to the good to scare the child from the river. No wan has ever heard of the bunyip away from the water. Sure, I wish I could capture the beast. I'd be clearing up a mystery that disturbs the zoologists and gaining renown for meself."

The brown and the black, and even the deadly tiger snakes were thick about the river banks—an added torture to an exile from the sacred Isle of Inisfail from which the blessed St Patrick himself had banished the reptiles. Danny did not minimize the danger from snakes, though he could break their backs by cracking them like a whip, a performance which made Johanna tremble for his safety. He was more than occupied as the founder of one of the first families on the Morumbidgee, and was as full of satisfaction as though his frontage had put him among the landed gentry of Ireland. His gunyah of shrinking slabs, covered with bark, elated him; but the drips spoiled Johanna's bed curtains and made it necessary to hide her few linen treasures, and thus defeated the elegancy dear to her heart.

Day or night there was no relief from the Morumbidgee, so lone and dark and far, with the voice of a ravening wind—thousands of miles of it until it met an unknown sea. Johanna felt that here indeed was the furthest extremity of the globe from the placid Shannon in its park-like plain. The contrast between this stream and that golden mirror in the westering sun, when the gentry's salmon waited head to tail to go up, was so gruelling that her father's curse seemed to have overtaken her. Here, at length, she felt the punishment of her name being tabu in her family, and that never again would she see Cooley Hall in old County Clare.

CHAPTER III

GUARDING the illusive land were throngs of giants—the stateliest trees on the globe. Delacy was like an ant in the aisles of box trees and towering river gums, but he attacked them as an army, grunting with effort, sweat dripping from him. His slight form grew as wiry as steel; his hands were corneous and scarred with the work of felling and grubbing.

"Mother of God!" little Johanna cried, as she saw the columns toppling. She was sick with terror lest her world of Danny and the child and the animals should be crushed there by the lorn river, with none to come to the rescue. It resembled the destruction of a universe, as in fact it was. A world of unexcelled, unrealized wealth had to go up in smoke that a small patch might be cleared to grow bread, and a hut have safety. Felled, the timber encumbered more ground than standing, until, with the help of men supplied through Mr Moore, Danny rolled the smaller logs into fences, and burned the remainder. He was out before daylight. He could scarcely desist for meals. Johanna brought him food and drink at intervals. The burning-off kept him until midnight, his pillars of fire licking the starry heavens low above his gorges.

In the evening Johanna would put her child to sleep, and help by gathering up the sticks. This work relieved her loneliness, intensified by the moaning of the river oaks, and the noise of the queer grey birds that threw laughter back and forth for miles, until dark and after. Their lusty guffawing, upon the smallest provocation or upon none, had a brow-beating effect, and she was mortally afraid that the bunyip would rear his undescribed form from the fish hole, or that the ghosts would cry in the crossing. These fears festered; she dared not confess them to Danny. He had none of the cruelty of the cowardly, but he had an inability to estimate the torments of the timid, which is sometimes a part of fearlessness. He had the heritage of his Irish temperament, which had enabled his exiled compatriots to turn desperate plights to brilliant victories, though Danny himself was free from swashbuckling taint. He despised belligerence. He disregarded firearms. His warrior prowess was thus freed to assault the continent of Australia, and he did not grizzle because he was unarmed and single-handed.

Though not at Bewuck until November, he was ready for the autumn ploughing. One of Moore's men, named Hannon, and trusted by both Delacys, was left to guard the new home. Danny borrowed the stockman's daughter, aged eight, from Quebarra for company for Johanna. The arms were also left with her—a broken cutlass and a flint-lock musket. Should the fire die out, a greasy rag, ignited by firing it from the gun, could be applied to punk. Danny with his sledge and the second man set out to forage for seed and provisions at Bandalong, thirty miles distant. Drays were scarce in the district of some fifty square miles, but two belonged to Danny's protector.

Danny's courage was as inexhaustible as his energy. Johanna therefore merited extra consideration, as her fortitude was cold and stricken. Her unborn child depressed her and made her a prisoner in the gorges with the river's banshee trees and bunyip hole. Endurance born of necessity kept her from breaking down during those breaking-in days. Danny scarcely realized her heroism in remaining there. She did not realize it herself. Danny did not recognize himself as heroic, and had no *vis* to spare from the combat to worship other heroes. Martyrs he would have overlooked as hypochondriacs or malingerers.

"Now, you're all set, Johanna, Mavourneen," he observed, when ready to depart. "Hannon will look after you like a father, and what could hurt you here at all, annyway? The bushrangers have died out, and would not come for so little. If they do, let them have it. It's the fighting and defence that makes all the trouble."

"But it's a queer man who does not defind himself."

"The trouble with defence is that the few it saves are nothing to the danger it brings upon innocent people by provocation. And now tell me, you'll be all right, me brave Johanna; who has come over the seas with me."

"Would there be anny good in telling ye annything else? Get on with ye, and waste no time in returning."

"You may be a little lonesome now, but this is to be a greater place than Cooley Hall, with a finer town than old Ennis on top of us."

"Ye'll be too old to enjoy that whin it comes."

"Och! You must look to the future. 'Tis only the beasts and nullities have no foresight."

Johanna suffered keenly during his absence. Hannon slept at a distance from the house. When the jackasses ceased, the dark fitted over the tree-tops like a night-cap, and the boobooks hooted, or the native dogs howled, or the little booraby bears wailed like tortured children. It was the dark of the moon, and the river more than girth deep, so Johanna was sure it was a ghost that screamed there. She went to bed at dusk, gathering Florry—the visitor—and her own child with her, and shuddering at every sound. Sometimes she wept, but empires are not wrought, nor won, without the tears of the weak, aye, and of the strong. "Tears wash the eye", as the young Delacys later wrote in their copy-books; and Johanna had fine, flashing eyes, independent of spectacles, to the end.

When the sunlight left the gorge she would climb with the children and an old dog up the track where the sun still shone across the plateau, and there watch for Danny's return.

"He can't be here yet, Misthress," Hannon would say.

" 'Tis an excursion away from the dungeons of me castle," Johanna would reply.

At length a party approached among the more open timber. Mr Moore had lent Danny a dray and four bullocks. There was the horse slide and a third horse farther away. Danny hurried forward.

"Sure, Mr Moore is a white man if ever there was wan. I've got a power of potatoes and pumpkins and all manner of seed wheat and barley, and suckers from fruit trees, and flowers for a garden in me spare time, me brave Johanna."

Spare time among settlers was a rare elegancy.

"And Johanna, will you believe me, they have a township laid out by Moore's. There's to be a store and a lock-up; and churches and schools and a post office will come. Sure, the teamsters congregate there from three directions, and there's a power of traffic already. People are buying blocks for farms."

The stir of Danny's returns compensated for his absences. His booty was sometimes inutile but always entertaining. This time he had beads—as for the Island trade—but there were also two Dutch toys for the children, a roll of dowlas, twine and sail needles, raisins, writing paper, powder for ink, and a keg of tobacco. Sperm candles were a contribution to Johanna's elegancies.

"I'd rather a roll of flannel for your underclothes than so much dowlas."

"Sure, I'll be warm working in dowlas. I have wan kag of chisel-pointed lath nails and another of green paint. The paint is your own. A place can be made a palace with a dab of paint and a lick of plaster."

The recital progressed before the homy log fire while Johanna and Florry prepared the meal.

"But now, Johanna, can you guess what more I've got?"

"A newspaper!"

"Och, I have a dozen of them!"

"A letter from Ennis?"

"Not this time, but 'twill come."

"Mr Moore has lent ye some books."

"I have wan, but there will be no time to read, so I resisted more."

"Did ye bring me anny burrds, Danny-boy?"

"Och!" It was a shout of triumph. "As fine a pair of turkeys as ever you saw, and thim 16/- the pair in Sydney this mortal minute; and a little cock and two hins."

"I'll go see they are not smothered," exclaimed Johanna.

"Leave them be. You haven't guessed what more it is I've brought."

"I'd like it to be a cask for a tub."

"I've wan big enough for a bath, and a little wan to make pails beside it; but what more have I?"

"Ye'r so full of wonders, Danny-boy, that ye might have the Brown Bull of Cooley himself hid along the track."

Danny loosed a shout of triumph. "You've almost said it. I have the next thing to the Bull of Cooley or the Shan Van Voght captured. I've got a fine lump of a colt—the brown entire."

Johanna strove to be impressed, though the poultry were more to her understanding than a crippled horse.

The colt had been the hope of Mr Moore's stud. Eyes of men, dulled by the "System", had brightened at sight of the animal who combined all the virtues and graces. Then, about a year since, the groom had been galloping him in sight of the household, when he put his foot in a hole, and crack!—with a sound like a pistol, the off fore fetlock was clean snapped. The jockey was killed, and put a gloomy seal on the fate of the Singer, son of Skeleton.

" 'Tis a pity not to give him a chance of his life," said Danny, who loved a good horse for his beauty and usefulness, though he had as great a contempt for horse-racing and all that went with it, as he had for army swagger.

His idea of a stringy-bark stocking for the fetlock was carried out by a surgeon guest. Danny slung the animal and tended him constantly for weeks. That was his way, with no purpose other than absorption in the enterprise for its own sake. The horse had grown dangerous after Danny's departure, but was so calm when handled by his old friend again that Moore said: "You've earned that horse, Delacy."

Thus Johanna saw the animal in the twilight. He was in poor

condition and unkempt after his journey on three legs, but his eyes were wide and wise, and he had the stance of an emperor.

"Is he really such a grand beast and all?"

Doubt impelled speech from Dunn, the dour man holding the halter.

"Sure, ye'r honour, there's not his aquil in the Colony this day, beggin' ye'r pardon for spakin'. He's own son of Skeleton and by a mare of the purest blood herself. And Skeleton himself was owned by the Marquis of Sligo himself at first; and he sowld him to none but a prince, him wid the name of Ester Hazy. It sounds loike a faymale and all, but 'tis a man, as Oi've been towld by thim that's seen him at the great race meetings.

"Sure, he was the bist horse of the year whin Lord Sligo purchased him, and the bist horse of the year in owld Oireland is the bist horse in the world, beggin' ye'r honour's pardon, for mintioning it to wan from the owld place herself. By the Calendars can be seen Skeleton's manny successful performances. He was considered in ivery way superior to Arrogance, who won the King's Plate at Doncaster in as short a toime as iver before or since. But Skeleton was superior. And Master Robert was decidedly the best of his year before him. Master Robert was the dad of Skeleton and was got by Buffer. His dam was Spinster by Shuttle, and his great-dam by Sir Robert, great-granddam by Bordeaux, great-great-granddam was Speranza, own sister of Saltrom, by Eclipse."

Johanna retired. Refinement decreed that ladies should feign ignorance of the presence and purpose of stud animals.

This information had been read to Dunn from the newspapers by a lettered fellow-lag, and Dunn had committed it to memory as a poem. "Sure," he added, "Skeleton as a two-year-old ran at the Curragh of Kildare and came second to horses he afterwards beat to smithereens."

"By damn!" said Delacy. "We're in the presence of royalty. Me fortune's made entirely. What is more, Dunn, I go by the dam. This fellow's dam was a thoroughbred, and a perfect lady to boot. The nullities think anny old dam will do. Observation shows that the mother is equally impoortant—more so, to judge by human beings."

There were now free immigrants arriving under the new policy of assistance with funds derived from the sale of Crown Lands, but the towns and the big men had the pick of these, and Delacy, short of capital, was dependent upon ex-ticket-of-leavers, who sometimes imposed upon him because of their grey hairs. His personal industry continued unabated. He robbed from the nights by working in the light of log fires in the barn, called the kitchen, and used as the men's hut. There took place the grinding of wheat in the hand mill, the making of halters, hobbles and ropes of greenhide, and the construction of big saddle-bags employed for transport over an ordinary saddle. The useful pack-saddle had not then come into use.

Hannon and Danny ploughed with two steady bullocks lent by Mr Moore, and a pair of milkers' calves. It was part of the day's work to pursue the bolting team around the paddock, Hannon trying to "whoa" them while Danny clung to the precious borrowed plough. Palings were split for Johanna's garden. Land was set aside for fruit trees and vegetables. The jackasses followed plough or spade for the fat blue-and-ivory grannie grubs that popped from the gleaming furrows. Danny found them entertaining companions and mingled his laughter with theirs. The brown colt became a member of the family and helped to shape its fortunes—all in the trend of the times.

Johanna had been startled on the morning after his arrival when she saw her husband sitting on the ground with the entire's foot in his arms as he refitted the splint.

"The Saints preserve us! He could batter ye to pieces."

"Arrah, he's as gentle as a lamb. You've only to treat him like a Christian."

Dunn had the congenial task of groom, and many a feed of sprouting barley was filched for the horse.

Mrs Wade left Florry at Bewuck to help Johanna, and later came herself. Mrs Fullwood was cut off by the river's winter level. The infant settler was one of few arrivals during the cold months. The Delacys were remote from roads. A man or two came, having heard of the colt, and there was a messenger from one of the big stations towards The Plains to borrow salt and a bag of flour.

There were floods of marsupial visitors, some of whose species have since been extirpated. One of the men had to be on duty all night to save the crops. Gentle furry things fell into simple traps or to Rover and his colleagues. Their flesh fed the poultry and pigs, and scores of their skins were pegged out to dry. Pelts of kangaroos and wallaroos were marketable. Kangaroos were also eaten. Cattle were too precious to be made into beef at the beginning.

Spring came and ripened towards summer and Christmas. The waters of the Murrumbidgee subsided, and Delacy's tenancy was contested by the Fullwoods and Butlers. One morning Heulong cattle supplanted the Bewuck herd right to the fence of the cow paddock, and not far away were Butler cattle from Glenties. The little man was to be squeezed out by the bigger squatters on either side.

Danny summoned his dogs and rode to contest this. In charge of the Heulong stock was a man named O'Neill, on a good horse. He had his instructions, and rode belligerently at Danny, pulling a pistol from his holster. Fullwood and Butler were cronies of the Commissioner, Danny was a penniless immigrant wedging his way on to the river.

The pistol was so enraging to him that he rode straight at it, ordering O'Neill to drop it, "before I skelp the eyes out of your head, you scoundrel, doing the dirty work of some cowardly crawler, who's bought you for a plug of tobacco and a taggeen of rum."

O'Neill shouted. "Take back ye'r durrty words, ye little shrivelled bastard Prodestan' heretic! Get off of ye'r horse and meet me man to man."

"Impty the charge from your pistol and I will," said Danny, "Though it's thim that's above you I should be meeting."

O'Neill, surprised, obediently discharged his pistol and replaced it in the holster. He had been a bruiser and smiled to think how he would dispose of Delacy and get the reward from Butler and Fullwood. The men dismounted, tied up their horses and took off their coats. Butler's man, who had been in the offing to report, now rode up. Butler himself halted at a distance behind the trees, and there were Danny's two assigned men from Mr Moore.

None of the Delacys had the physique of boxers. They were as slight as reeds, with delicate hands. Danny's only chance was to rush his opponent. O'Neill waited for him, parried him easily, and with one blow brought the blood from Danny's nose; a second closed one of his eyes, a third, on the point of the jaw, laid him out. It was over in a minute. Butler came from ambush with contemptuous mien. Danny's men gloated to see one of their own fraternity as capable as O'Neill. They despised Danny, insignificant and unable to shake a fist in self-defence.

"Pour a drop of water on him and take him home to his wife," ordered Butler, and rode away with his man. The victor mounted his horse and drove the Heulong cattle towards Bewuck homestead. Danny lay winded for some time, then he sat up, went to the river, and soused his head in the clear cold water. His men hung about currishly, without contesting the encroachments of O'Neill. Charles Fullwood, who had watched from across the river, rode out of sight well satisfied.

O'Neill had not punished Delacy too heavily. But for the closed eye and a slight dizziness he was quickly himself. He made no remark to his men, but mounted his horse, and with his long heavy stockwhip in hand, rode towards O'Neill.

"You've beaten me at that noble art," he said mildly. "I met you because otherwise I would have been open to the insinuation of cowardice, but I fear no man in heaven or hell, and I'm no man's servant but me own. Me brave gladiator with the pistol and fists, acting for another, who's too craven to represent himself, now it's for the second round. The first was to your pattern, the second is to me own. Your horse is better than mine, and you have a whip the same, and I hereby give notice that I'll skelp you off me premises. Arrah! Begin!"

O'Neill took up the duel. Delacy was on him with a yell, getting the first stroke at the horse's flank and sending him rearing and plunging. O'Neill had as little chance when agility was demanded as Delacy when it was weight. The little man got in two cuts for the big man's one. O'Neill's shoulders had not so stung since he had been on the triangle. As Delacy gained the ascendancy, he ordered his men to round-up the trespassing cattle, and with dogs barking and biting, they were driven into the river, to the consternation of Butler and Fullwood.

Danny had earned the men's respect. He gave instructions as to where the cattle were to be pastured, and rode home.

He explained his eye to Johanna as the result of fly bite, then prevalent, took a meal and rode away to Mr Moore, who used his influence with the Commissioner for Crown Lands. Delacy was allowed to add to his holding land to which those already settled wanted the right without payment. Seeing that he had a protector, Butler and Fullwood desisted from open hostilities. They feared they had gone too far in setting a lag to attack a freeman.

The tale spread from the Heulong and Glenties men to the stockmen of Quebarra, and returned to Johanna from Florry's mother. Mrs Fullwood was perhaps the only one who did not know of the encounter and she did not withdraw her neighbourliness from Johanna. Gossip was that Fullwood discarded O'Neill for exceeding his duty in carrying the issue to a physical fight.

"Time will test the whole pack of them—which are min and which are crawlers!" grunted Danny.

The next stir was the approach of blacks. A man from Glenties reported to Quebarra that Bewuck was their objective. The fish hole was their feasting and camping ground. Two tame aborigines came to herald the tribe and to inform Danny that he was on their territory.

"God help us! What's to become of me and the childre?"
exclaimed Johanna, terrified.

"Sure, we have taken their ground," said Danny. "But these have
never hurt a hair of the settlers from here to The Plains. I'll go
meet them like a Christian and see what can be done."

One of the Moore bullocks had developed lumpy-jaw and had
been left to Danny for disposal, so he rode to meet the dispossessed
with the oppressed servitor as a peace offering. One of the envoys
was with him, and introduced him and explained the bullock. It
was accepted as a princely gift. The unarmed Danny was received
as a brother, and guffawed in concert with the men. When he got
on his horse, one of the envoys brought a girl piccaninny and
signified that she was to be taken on the pommel. Danny was
elated, but Johanna received the child with mingled feelings.

"They'll be after ye with spears, taking ye for an abductor." Her
elder child, now three, was terrified of the girl's dark skin and asked
would she eat the baby. The Australian was not alarmed but full
of curiosity about the white babies and their clothes.

"Dayvil if ever I met pleasanter people, smiling from ear to ear,
they were so pleased with Bally. It wrung me heart, the poor old
fellow walking along with me so friendly and intelligent, but he
is only a beast after all. The child reminds me of a wild turkey, but
as you see, not wan bit uneasy."

"Murra me, that ever I was born and came roaming to the wilds!
They've given the child to ye for fosterage, and that's why she is
so easy."

"Be the powers! That would be an honour to you, me brave
Johanna."

She saw the adventure. "If it wouldn't bring hordes of murdering
savages upon us. In anny case I must put a shimmy on her, not to
let her be a shame before me and a bedivilmint to the min."

Late that night shadows stole between Johanna and the moon
on her tiny window. Danny sprang forth and called on the prowlers
to halt. They were petrified by his booming tones. He lit a candle
and invited the visitors to investigate the fate of the piccaninny.
They were impressed to see her already in white man's garb in a
bed beside the cot of the toddler, from whom she refused to part.

"That one sit down longa white pfella—all same as white pfella,"
they said. The child's account must have been satisfactory for she
was left where she was—adopted. Only Danny tasted the roasted
boogongs brought as a present, which, he recorded, reminded him
of dried plums.

Her people camped at the bunyip hole, on the other side of the

river, which gave some safety from the mangy curs. Otherwise, as
Danny pointed out, they were far less destructive than a company
of whites would have been. "And me having taken the heart of
their ground! Sure, they're the most generous and forgiving
Christians," he exclaimed. "They make a contrast to old Butler
and Fullwood, trying to batter me up."

Peace was aided by abundance of cod and bream. One or two
cod weighed more than a hundred pounds each. Danny strutted
among the bucks with the enjoyment of a boy, and they taught
him how to use for fish-bait the big casuarina grubs without
puncturing them, lest they leak away in a milky fluid. One of the
men had been with Major Mitchell, and came to the home. He
was interested in the colt's wooden stocking and called him nullah-
mundoey—wooden leg or boot. Johanna was amused by the half-
tamed gins, and set them to wash for her in return for a garment
or two.

At the end of a fortnight they moved farther south to the
mountains that beckoned Danny as the Lorelei, and where there
remained undisturbed by whites a hundred or more square miles
teeming with fish, waterfowl, turkeys, marsupials, emus, snakes,
lizards, boogongs and other food. In the retreats near Numba
Nanga the aborigines held their ceremonies safe from intrusion.

The little girl made no attempt to leave with them. " 'Tis
romantic, Johanna. She is left with us like an ancient chief's
daughter to rear up in civilization."

They were not clever enough to extract her name. As a gesture
to Johanna, Danny christened her Maeve, after the chieftainess who
had had such an inordinate desire to possess the Brown Bull of
Cooley. The child was lovable and willing, and Johanna's first
native-born servant, though in Danny's commonwealth she ranked
as a daughter of the house.

Delacy, as the Colony at large, was completely the grazier and
little the farmer. He could never ascend from his gorges to the
higher land of Quebarra or Glenties without exalted emotion. He
would gaze towards the Australian Alps and collaterals, extending
for eighty or a hundred miles around the translucent horizon, and
feel as a poet drinking from the fountain of inspiration. There lay
a land to be wrought to his heart's desire. With this attitude of the
visionary was interwoven the need for energetic action. In the rare
moments when he sat with Johanna before retiring he talked of
going up the Murrumbidgee with his surplus stock and settling in
a valley that the blacks called Burrabinga.

"Utterly inaccessible," Johanna would say with failing heart.

"Wasn't Australia inaccessible till Cook found it, and America out of bounds till the Puritan Fathers settled it? No place is inaccessible if you have the moind to go there."

What Johanna really felt was that the mountains were all too accessible to Danny.

"Sure, we must look ahead. 'Tis only the beasts and nullities have no foresight. I'll need territory for me sons."

"And thim not born yet! Counting chickers before they are hatched."

"You'll have more luck with time," said Danny cheerfully. "I'll be too late again if I don't look out. There's Urquhart at Keebah these five years, and him building a fine house by Government min, near as good as Moore's."

Danny had already been in the coveted territory in pursuit of bushrangers that had stuck up Moore's stables. He had also helped a late explorer to follow the Hume-Hovell line to the Murray; when, according to Johanna, he had better have been minding his own business. But what is the business of an adventurous dreamer but to penetrate the forest and traverse the untrodden plain and establish outposts.

"It would be more sinse to wait till there is more population," Johanna would say.

She could not understand his urge to go first, his exaltation in reaching beyond roads and fences. 'Someone must first make the road, me brave Johanna," he would chant. "Have you never considered that every road was no road wanst? 'Tis amazing to consider the min away back in the immensity of time who went first—even in old Ireland."

"But there's no call for ye—a man with childre—to be that wan. There's reason in all things, and there's little in rushing ahead to the backward places to be lost and to starve."

After the second harvest there was no restraining him. He had his holding ring-barked and fenced in paddocks near to the house, and a relatively large portion under cultivation. He had a house and garden and a sprouting orchard; he was overstocked, and Heulong and Glenties harried him whenever possible without coming into the open.

Hannon, blacksmith by trade, carpenter by natural gift, was a treasure. That he should ever have been a lag was, Danny said, a reflection on the "System". Danny had no hesitation in leaving him in charge of the place and of Johanna. Johanna had confidence in Hannon, but she hated to be left at Bewuck. Maeve, fat and sonsy, was merry company and helpful. Wade, with a wife and children, was still at Quebarra, only nine miles distant, so Delacy felt that the country was thickly populated. He would not be commendable to common sense, the crown of which was profit if he confessed that there was a compulsion on him to push farther out, to do, to be, to put something into life and country, without envy of those who might pillage fortunes in his tracks. And without such as Delacy whence would come wealth for harvesting by the sane self-seekers? Why should not he himself seek gain? But it is in a man's stars whether he is a giver or a getter, and the two are separate as marble and mud.

Johanna became resigned as the enterprise took shape. Danny's eyes had the light that had shone in them seven years before, when he talked of emigrating.

CHAPTER IV

IT was a wide morning in the New Year, with the summer braver than ever it is where the Shannon flows, when Delacy started farther out with fifty head of mixed horned cattle and a dozen horses. With him was the dour Dunn, a carpenter of sorts, who could build a hut. They had four horses loaded with provisions and gear, and the old musket and ammunition, with which to supplement their larder.

"Come with me, Johanna, up to the top. You can wish me luck."

From the day of her advent, Maeve could be trusted to keep her foster sisters from harm, so Johanna walked beside Danny, who led the mare with the elder child astride her, to the crest of the ascent.

"Ah, me brave Johanna, look at that!" he exclaimed, his eyes enlarging and darkening with emotion. "With that before me I could lepp over the moon."

"It was the owld grey mare that was waiting till me back was turned to lepp into me lettuce plot," said Johanna, whose heart and body were heavy.

The cattle lowed questioningly at this disturbance of their habits. The dogs—brave heelers and intrepid kangaroo chasers—yelped and whined and rolled on their backs in impatience to be gone. Danny took the pipe from his mouth to kiss his family good-bye. This weapon did not look so big with a beard around it. His beard at twenty-five was sleek and fine, and had the goatee contour of the whiskers of the great Earl of Cork, to whose portrait, by Paul Van Somers, Danny bore a resemblance.

"If you get lonesome, shut the house and away to Mrs Wade. You and the children are more important than all the country."

He mounted and took off his hat and looked back, while the mare pranced and spluttered to overtake her company.

"The woild blacks up there maybe will eat ye," called Johanna.

"Why put such a calumny on quiet people," he laughed, and rode into the boundless day with the ancient enchantment upon it.

Johanna took her child's hand and watched the path against snakes. Their despatch with a stringy-bark sucker with a knob remained an ordeal to her. Maeve was her mainstay in this. The flicker to be seen in the dark people's eyes lit in hers at the sport, and she had to be trained to forgo such rich food.

Danny travelled with a paean in his heart, his eyes towards the ramparts that swept southwards to Brisbane Plains—the Monaro of to-day. The dazzling clarified atmosphere imposed no border on distance but eternity, and had a liberating effect. Nearer lay Limestone Plains, where to-day is the parliamentary city, conceived and planned in a spate of democratic idealism.

The tourist, succeeding the traveller, who early followed the explorer, may look across that view to-day, and see, still undefaced by man, the haunting beauty of the ranges wearing the ages down tenaciously. He can choose for himself where across them was the way of Daniel Brian Robert M. Delacy. Delacy's Gap and Delacy's Peaks sentinel the distance, though the old name is wearing faint with the passing of living memory, and new names are being substituted in compliment to petty officials. Where Danny raised his first hut may be known by the abrupt gorge, like the cleft keep of an ancient fortress, through which the river winds. The spot was familiar to the blacks as Burrabinga, or the jump, where a giant once leaped across with thunder and lightning in his spears. The homestead, an agglomeration of the years and the generations of Delacy, was for long one of the best known in the southern district.

A stockman going towards Ginninginninderra crossed Danny's track at noon with the news that the tribes of Monaro and those from lower down the Murrumbidgee had been mustering for a week. They had arrived lean and mangy from Riverina, but several weeks' feasting, topped off with boogongs, had put a gloss on their hides and filled them with virility, which in all tongues is synonymous with fight. A battle was expected.

"Be the poipers, 'twill be an exhilarating spectacle," exclaimed Delacy.

The cattle, who could sense the approach of aborigines two or three days distant, had to be driven in a northerly direction from the smoke signals. Two days pressed travelling brought them to Keebah, where there was a good crossing. Delacy was welcomed by Urquhart and his wife, two young settlers with three infants. Urquhart was Danny's age, and his wife five years younger.

The house was the farthest-out convict-built house in its direction. The third generation of Urquharts used to exhibit the staples in the cellar—to which delinquents had been chained—as the patent of their own gentility, until the Federal authorities shore their outer runs from the home paddocks like the belly from a fleece lest the inhabitants should pollute the watershed of the new city, and

thus dislodged a number of early settlers and endowed them with
bitter views on Government resumption of land.

At the end of a pleasant visit, Delacy pushed on for another
twenty miles, where the horses and cattle drew together baulking
on the edge of the precipices which guarded his valley.

"Sure, ye'r honour, 'tis impassable," said Dunn.

"Impassable, by damn!" shouted Danny. "I have the intintion
of breeding horses that could manipulate a steeple. This mare can
be the pioneer. I'll go first. Rouse them up to follow."

With an "arrah" or two, the long-suffering brood mare was urged
forward, and nervously sought the safest place to set her hooves,
where later her progeny romped with the assurance of goats. The
man on her back forced his flesh to the dictates of his mind, and
horseflesh had to conform. Down she went, snorting, sliding, sitting,
scraping the hide off her hocks, and with Dunn compelling the
packed animals pinch by pinch in her wake. The dogs heeled the
cattle and horses between Dunn and their leader and they came
to the foot of the descent without loss.

The cattle settled for the night. Snow was falling in defiance of
the calendar and had purged the air of the disturbing aborigines.
The men made fires for warmth and to scare the dingoes. The dogs
drew attention to an object which Danny found to be a native boy
of ten or twelve years in the ashes of a dead fire. He was in a
pitiable condition: the front of his torso was deeply burned: he
made no movement.

Delacy carried the suffering creature to his camp and wrapped
him in his own blanket. The charred body was softened with grease,
protected from the weather, and had a few drops of rum forced
down its throat. Later Danny tried to feed his patient on a morsel
of bandicoot, taken from the dogs and roasted, but he could not
swallow.

Next day Danny and Dunn had to carry the boy in a blanket. He
lay motionless and on the brink of death during the difficult transit.
The dogs worked among the stock and at dusk the men rigged a
canvas shelter.

"Sure, 'twould be aisier for ye'rself and him, ye'r honour, if you
finished him now," said Dunn. "I've seen them shoot down manny
a fine buck on the north coast whin I was serving me turrn. They
do be saying that they're not human, but only animals."

"What haythen promulgated that idea? Am I a murderer to
choose between the colour of a skin? I show aquil respect to
humanity whether it is black, white or yellow, bond or free."

He wrapped his invalid against frost-bite, while Dunn rode

around the cattle and returned to report that a couple of blacks
were spearing a heifer.

"And you to be letting them," yelled Danny, seizing Dunn's nag.
Later it was well-known from the Yackandandah to Yass that
Daniel Delacy had no fear of anything—a surer protection than
the old musket.

He galloped up to the aggressors—if that were the right term—
dismounted and made signs of friendliness in the manner of
Governor Davey's proclamation, and he bellowed—simply bellowed.
It was said that in middle life he could sit on his verandas and
converse with stockmen miles out on the run, so powerful his lungs,
so resonant his voice, produced in the deep-chested Irish way,
which is rarely muted by self-consciousness. He tried to convey
that he gave the speared beast, but that the warriors were to touch
no others. The fervour of his utterance, his blue eyes glinting
conspicuously in the tan, impressed them. They made signs of
peace. Danny rode around his cattle all night, but there were no
further depredations.

On the day following, other blacks appeared, among them some
who had feasted on the lumpy-jawed beast at Bewuck. Danny
gathered from the pantomime that the story of the fosterage of
Maeve was being told. They traced the burned boy to Danny's
camp—possibly coming to bury him—and were impressed by seeing
him alive and cherished. Danny had established himself as a super-
man, a big pfella chief, a popular corroboree theme. He had not
embroiled himself by defence.

The boy's name was Doogoolook. He was left with Danny, and
as soon as the beast was devoured, the tribe moved towards the
black rock of prehistoric ages which still guards their borah rings.

Danny was safe to "tail" his cattle so that they would home in
the valleys. He and Dunn made a hut of logs with a lean-to called
a "skilling" and a roof of stringy-bark.

"A prodigious country, Dunn, to provide a roof for the skinning
of it from the trees. A fine thing too to be killing a few trees in
the process."

For weeks, the eyes alone showed that Danny's patient lived.
Danny did not flag in greasing him, and fed him on skilligalee
procured from the blood of wild animals. He talked to him in loud
and cheerful tones, but no response came from the emaciated half-
cooked frame. A bitch, brought to supply successors to casualties
from snake-bite or kangaroo maulings, kept the sores as clean as
anything science could devise, and one day when Danny was eating
his own meal of duck, his charge reached for a discarded bone.

"Be the poipers! We shall have ye as strong as the Bull of Cooley or the *cervus giganticus* before long."

Dunn was unable to endure the stench of the fat on the creature in the blanket, but Danny's ardour for results rendered him superior to bad smells. He contributed a shirt as bandages for the sores, and a pair of trousers cut off at the knees. The remnants of moleskin made a comforting breastplate. The boy began to walk. His limbs were sound.

"Why does he never make a sound?" Danny would demand.

"Maybe he's dumb, ye'r honour."

Danny thereupon yelled behind the child but he gave no sign of hearing. "There's deaf and dumb whites, and sure, this is a black wan. Doesn't that show that he is human and aquil with us? How shall we teach him anything at all?" After pondering Danny decided, "I'll have to keep him as a pet. He'll be an astonishment to me wife."

The cattle settled in the valleys contiguous to the hut. Danny warred against the trees with ring-barking—the new aid to destruction—added to fire. The weeks disappeared like quicksilver. Only two callers penetrated to the fastnesses—a man who helped to hump provisions from Keebah, and an adventurer from Limestone Plains. Danny had had but one chance of sending a message to Johanna. The heavy frosts of May brought him to a sense of the calendar. One day he brought the mare back on her haunches with a yell. "Be the poipers, the youngster must have arrived, and me not to have remembered!"

He could not be sure to a few weeks in the months, nor a day or so in the week, where he was. He returned to the hut as if pursued. "Give me a bit to eat. I'm off to Bewuck. There's important business I should have been there a month past for. You give an eye to the stock," he ordered Dunn. "If you want rations, you can make out to Keebah."

Doogoolook ran after his master like a dog, so he had to stop and catch a second horse and furnish it with an improvised bridle and a piece of bag for a saddle, with greenhide loops for stirrups.

"Maybe I'll be back within a week, and maybe not till ye see me," Delacy shouted, his horses on the run.

His intention of riding night and day had to be abandoned because of Doogoolook, whose body was not all healed. They reached Bewuck three days later, the dogs announcing their arrival. Johanna took her second child, little Della, and sat on the verandah facing the river.

Hannon came forward for the horses through a gate painted green, and Doogoolook, at a sign, went with him. Kathleen Moyna was so shy that she ran from her father and clung to the leg of Hannon, the ex-lag. Danny went inside with fear in his heart because Johanna had not come to meet him.

"Good day, is me wife well?" he asked of the strange woman who met him at the threshold.

"Quite well, sir."

"Johanna, me brave Johanna, where are you?" he called. He sought in every room for her. "Johanna, I've come home." She turned her head away and looked so thin and frail that he was startled. "The child that was coming," he murmured.

Her eyes flashed scornfully. "Ye might well ask! Ye to stay away all that toime without wan flick of proper affection as husband or father!" Danny was smitten mute, shamed that he had forgotten his impending fatherhood.

"The foinest boy ye ever saw, and him to be born dead by all I underwint. Lonesomeness and fright! The trees everlastingly moaning like banshees, and the bunyip screaming like wan murdered, night after night. Sure, Maeve and Hannon both tracked him as plain as bull beef on the flat rocks around the hole."

Danny did not scoff at the bunyip. "I'm sorry, Johanna. Sure, there are things that can't be explained."

"There are plinty of them with ye, Daniel Delacy."

"I'm glad you have a woman with you, Johanna."

"Was I to be alone here with Hannon, a scandal for all the world, and Walter Moore another? I wrote to Mr Moore and he took pity on me and sent the woman."

"Sure, Hannon is a quiet, harmless man."

"Ye need to be more rational."

"So a boy, and it dead," repeated Danny, subdued. "I'll need maybe to recast me operations."

"Ye'll need to mind ye'r ways. I can stand no more. It's nothing but a snake killer in a territorial prison ye've reduced me to."

He dared not caress her. He retreated for the present.

He noted the rough chairs made elegant with paint, and was touched by the efforts towards refinement. Everything seemed prosperous and ship-shape, so really and comfortably a home to be proud of, that he was convicted of dereliction as a husband.

He made friends with Maeve and Kathleen Moyna. "Sure a brother for you, Maeve." Maeve smiled at Doogoolook and quickly discovered his disability. He clung to Danny, who returned to Johanna with him and the girls.

Johanna refused to look at him. "Ye can run after every black and Tom cat, and let ye'r own die forgotten," she said.

Danny had to go to the kitchen and eat with Doogoolook, and he persuaded him to sleep there until a "skilling" could be erected for him. Danny was cheered by the sight of his yearlings, the nucleus of the Delacy walers.

He had to dismount from the charger of adventure and propitiate Johanna, not without fear that he might lose Burrabinga. Having retired from the field of gallantry at eighteen, he was rusty in its graces, but he was urgent to revive Johanna's affection. He devoted himself to her throughout the winter, the more so because Walter Moore quartered himself at Bewuck for weeks. He was a lascivious fellow and had long been the bane of Johanna's life. Danny, who thought no evil, was at length convinced of Walter's wicked intentions. "Sure, 'tis a grief that he is the son of the best friend we ever can have. Otherwise I'd scald him with a kettle of hot water without anny compunction whatever. Come with me away to Burrabinga, Johanna, and you'll escape him and be with me to build up our fortune."

Such was the burden of his lay, until Johanna knew that further resistance would be useless, though her melancholy heart would not rise. In Danny's eyes was the light that had lit them in the far days of Ennis, when, as a way to escape O'Gorman and have her love, she had consented to flee to New South Wales—a cataclysmic experience to one whose dream was an orthodox home with good carpets, china and napery. Hardship, suffering and loneliness had been her portion. Childbearing—four children and only two surviving—had weakened her for marital combat. In the intoxication of passion she had chosen Danny against her family, her country and her God, and could not now rebel. She had no one behind her. Marriage was inviolable in her world, divorce a scandalous phenomenon, a woman who deserted her husband a social outcast. Johanna had to cleave unto Danny now though the allure was no longer potent. The thrilling enfranchisement of her husband's early conjugal behaviour had degenerated to that sheepishness and self-consciousness irritating to a wife.

CHAPTER V

ON another grand long day Danny set off once more for the hills. Four children and Johanna had to be transported this time. The ravines between Keebah and Burrabinga were impassable for vehicles. Doogoolook, quick at understanding and making signs, was free from the venial sins of white boys. He and Maeve shared one nag. Johanna had another and a side-saddle to herself. Kathleen Moyna had a quiet old mare and Della clung on behind her sister. Dunn had lately ridden down to find out what had become of his master, and was now in charge of a string of pack-horses.

Hannon had married the woman sent by Mr Moore, and they were left to keep Bewuck in order.

Johanna stayed two days at Keebah with Janet Urquhart, and from the amenities of this home drew fresh courage to advance beyond the surveyors, beyond the security of roads and fences.

During the descent, Danny had to go beside Johanna, while Dunn had the children. Urquhart and Doogoolook guarded the pack-horses against the fate of the Biblical swine. Dusk fell before the last lap, so Danny camped at his spring where the clearest, coldest water in Australia bubbled straight from the earth amid tree-ferns and maiden-hair. The children had their foster relatives to introduce them to wonderland. Johanna was weary and busy with the meal, while the men took off the packs and prepared the bedding.

Danny had brought the colt, named Nullah-Mundoey by the blacks, and went back to fetch him up to the company.

"He'll never go down the precipices, ye'r honour," said Dunn.

"What is there to prevent him, if I make up me moind?"

The animal, through being left behind, was heady. Danny admonished him. "On with you! You'll soon be in the valley, and then a gentleman's career among the ladies ever after, strutting about with a mug of consequence on you."

The second day was a repetition of the first and Johanna grew more depressed by the prison-like features of her retreat. Nearing dusk, the hut was reached. Johanna could have wept with weariness and despair, but Danny felt the elation of a conqueror. He could envision his domain denuded of the native standing armies, a place worthy of many sons to be.

"Come in, me brave Johanna. Here's your second home, all ready waiting for you. In another twenty years think what it will be, and us still in our prime."

" 'Tis Bunratty Castle* itself," she sighed, "and ye not contint with *seeing* it. Surely, Danny Delacy, this is the furthest extremity of the globe, and there is no further place to drag me, but Purgatory itself."

Johanna was repelled by the grime and uncouthness of her hut. It had been a dreadful drop from Moore's to Bewuck; now she was at the end of a much longer fall from amenities, friends, music, books and every elegancy, even those attainable by green paint, and mortar of chopped horsehair and cow dung to fill cracks. The children could nearly run between the slabs of Burrabinga walls. More birds riotously guffawing, and higher precipices than at Bewuck hastened the night. Doogoolook had already exhibited a snake. The situation was too depolarizing for tears.

However, when hunger was satisfied, retreat to bed by the light of the fire in the big hearth was a relief from fatigue. All were soon asleep but Johanna, who turned over the realization that never again would she see the soft green plains of County Clare with its old homesteads nestling amid pet trees and friendly shrubs. Out on the flats, amid the tussocks and the thickets of tea-tree, the plovers were almost as plentiful as the ducks. More curlews than elsewhere—for these be solitaries—came as night deepened, and their chorale arose above that of the dingoes. Curlews were the banshee birds of Johanna's childhood, but these in the swamps of Burrabinga wailed the same melody as those in the sedges of Clare, and the homesick immigrant fell asleep comforted by a familiar voice in a strange lost land.

If ever woman earned an inheritance for her sons in Australia it was Johanna, but that night she was conscious only of the bruising of those impossible descents where it was too rough to sit on a horse, where a false step would have sent her crashing over the precipice. Now the mountain was a mighty bastion to imprison her among fearsome trees so high that they shut out the heavens—a frightening land of endless forests far from the gentle Shannon.

In the morning she found that the river had none of the mourning trees of the Murrumbidgee, and was lined with ferns more beautiful than those in the hot-houses of the gentry in

* Bunratty was a castle in County Clare "so strong that besiegers often had to content themselves with viewing it from a distance."

Limerick. The children found the blossoming grevillea (rosmarini-folia) and adored it as ducks and drakes, and plucked the chookies of the banksia—misnamed honeysuckle. The valley was white as Ireland's May with tea-tree, and blue with mint shrub, a paradise replete with flowers for the children. Doogoolook and Maeve were conjurors as well as reliable guardians. The girl laughed with the jackasses and cawed with the crows, and reproduced the heavenly warbling of the magpies; they had wild things' eggs for toys, their young for pets.

All importation had to be on pack-horses that negotiated the worst pinches on their hocks. Everything possible was manufactured on the spot. With axe and adze Dunn quarried tables and stools from green wood as heavy as lead. Mattresses of sacking filled with grass were placed on stringy-bark on pegs sunk in the floor. The shutters were of greenhide.

"The peasants around Ennis would be surprised to see our bothy in the glen," observed Johanna.

"Moi, woman, the peasant's crib is a crumb begrudged from the overlord's spoils in an effete civilization. Our shortcomings must be endured only till the population advances."

" 'Twould be rational to wait till the population had advanced."

"Och, you have no reason at you. We waited till the population was out of bounds."

Pelts of dingoes, wallaroos and beautiful possums were to be had for little effort. Those of half a dozen subsidiary species were not worth garnering. Fur rugs replaced blankets, skins cushioned the rough chairs. Johanna, tenacious in gentility, never surrendered her napery, though a special pack-horse had to import Russian sheeting. The earthen floor was carpeted by the hide of a pack-horse, who had lost his life in pioneering at Delacy's Cutting. For ornaments there were emu eggs and lyre birds' tails, bullock horns and the skin of the speckled echidna, but Johanna craved china, pictures and cross-stitch mats, and vases with glass dangles like those which decorated the withdrawing room of her aunt in Limerick. And, oh, for the sideboard at Cooley Hall with its carved foxes' heads, and the stand in the hall with its ashplants and blackthorn sticks!

In time she had a garden meagrely furnished with immigrant plants. She struggled to extirpate anything native as a weed. She lacked originality to knead unfamiliar products into the dough of culture. She taught Maeve and Kathleen Moyna their letters. She instructed Maeve in her own catechism as she remembered it with-out the text, left at Cooley Hall, and forbidden by Danny. If she

had not been excommunicated she could have found ease in
describing her surroundings to her home folks, but she had no
one with whom to correspond. She was starved by the spiritual
emptiness of her days, but she grew reconciled in homemaking.
She never had Danny's luminous satisfaction in pioneering. He
was a torch of purpose; she had to step as well as she could in the
rugged pathway lighted by that torch.

The blacks did not trouble them. They stopped on the far side
of Numba Nanga, distant some days' ride. Danny gave them a
beast or two each season. His live stock were prolific. He grew
wheat, potatoes, maize, pumpkins and other vegetables.

Two winters slipped around and Johanna had a male infant in
her arms. Janet Urquhart had come up from Keebah to attend
her. She was a stiff, fattish woman and found the journey down
the pinches almost as arduous as parturition.

With this son Johanna recovered her pluck, and Danny his desire
for expansion. He had not dared to go farther than Keebah all
this time, and had managed Bewuck by sending Dunn down at
intervals. This was a tribute to his consideration for Johanna, as
he lacked ability to delegate, a weakness which kept him from
multiplying his own man power.

He was short of money to entice labour. In the Colony, farm
labourers and grooms buried their avocations in the general term
of rouseabout, and added the work of carpenter, builder, blacksmith, butcher or other trades according to their capabilities. Those
were the years of the tussle between Wentworth, patriotic native
son, and Gipps, ablest of Governors. The Governor had to support
the Crown against Wentworth's claim for local control of immigration, land sales, police, education and so on, and among the cross
currents, speculation in land and general mismanagement bore
their usual fruits.

The nadir year of 'forty-three was reached. Banks failed, many
people were bankrupted and there were more than a thousand
unemployed in Sydney. No one had money to employ labour or
buy land. Fine bullocks brought only ten or fifteen shillings per
head. Boiling-down establishments were rendering them for 5/-
each. In the bad 'forties tallow was one of the Colony's chief exports.

Delacy mustered cattle in the hope of disposing of them at
Goulburn, where there was a boiling-down establishment. Johanna
was willing to remain alone with Maeve, while Doogoolook, as
well as Dunn, helped to steady the cattle beyond the Murrumbidgee.

"Good-bye, me brave Johanna," said Danny on the morning of

departure. He was now such a part of the pipe that he did not remove it. His family used his brow for kissing. "You won't be alone for more than four days, barring accident. Nothing could harm you here. The bushrangers are a thing of the past."

"I might be glad of their company," said Johanna, brave indeed, tossing her head.

Danny was riding a "foine lump of a colt", which required a breaker, but Danny was undaunted. The cattle were so tame after the first tiring day that he sent Doogoolook back at once. Dunn went across the Murrumbidgee, and then Danny pushed on alone to Bewuck. Hannon helped thence for a couple of days, when Danny dispensed with him also, intending to pick up the first helper available.

He could not dispose of his cattle at Goulburn, and was proceeding to Parramatta when he met a dealer who offered a decent price if Delacy would help him on the way to Bathurst. To this Danny agreed. He sold everything but the Nullah-Mundoey colt and his old pack mare, and with these steered at right angles to Major Mitchell's Murrumbidgee line on his way home after five weeks' absence.

He rode through rolling or hilly country on his strapping horse. The tall trees, the bright birds, the quaint animals filled him with wonder and delight. The spaciousness, the opportunity to pioneer was sufficient to his energy. "No man needs arms to protect himself from annything but jungle beasts," he was thinking, "and they don't exist in this paradise; and dayvil if anny one could expect people to be more civil than the natives."

The quiet pace of the fat cattle and the luscious kangaroo grass were as energizing to horse-flesh as boogongs to aborigines, and Lancelot Nullah-Mundoey was flash. When Danny stood in his stirrups and shouted "Arrah!" Lancelot was provoked into a tidy buck. A masterly prop landed his rider on the hard ground, stunned. Lancelot made off and devoted himself to getting rid of the slippery new saddle which had expedited Delacy's fall.

Sunstroke would have finished him on that blazing day but for the meat-eating ants. Pain partially brought him to. Subconsciously he crawled to the shade of a tree. There was no settler within leagues, but a few miles eastward, two bullock drays were snailing their way from the Port to one of the stations farther out, and were to cross Danny's track at sundown.

Mr Alwyn Evans, from Kilpoonta, two hundred miles farther along the overlanders' line, had gone down many weeks earlier to meet his bride, who had come out from England. On the previous day he had ridden forward because of rumours of hostile tribes on the Lachlan, and the fear that the home, which he had worked four years to establish in Major Mitchell's wake, might be in ashes to meet its mistress. The Rufus affray and other disgraceful incidents were only a year or two past. He had left his wife with the drays, and several assigned men, who had proved themselves trusty partners.

The dogs found Danny. The men unravelled the story from the horses' tracks. Injuries such as Delacy's were common in bravura days. With the help of her servants, Mrs Evans examined the man for wounds. His body was snowy where the sun had not touched it. The small shapely hands were work-roughened, but the delicate feet had always been booted. He was dressed in slops, the rough shirt none too clean, but in a pocket was a handkerchief of pure linen, unused. Danny was never a sniffler. The men were interested that his back was unscathed. It was evident he was a free man, and probably a gentleman. His papers had gone in Lancelot's saddle-bag.

Abrasions on the right leg had kept the ants from his eyes and ears. The flesh was eaten in spots half an inch deep and as large as a Spanish dollar. The bone was broken. Mrs Evans put her patient in her own sleeping accommodation and had a bunk prepared for herself in the second dray.

Danny remained unconscious. Mrs Evans and her men did their best, leaving cure to Nature. They swung the man on sacking fastened above the bed of the dray and went forward through a trying week. Then they were met by Evans who said that the danger had been averted. He brought a surgeon to look at Danny, a shepherd from a lonely outpost, a clever man driven to the Colony by drink, who in the lean 'forties could find no professional opening. He had his books and instruments and was playing a useful part in that pioneering which called the flawed, the outlawed and the surplus to nobler service than falls to many of the sheltered and redundant in crowded grooves.

There were dangerous symptoms. The leg was beyond setting. The surgeon hacked it off. There were no women at this station, so Mrs Evans would not leave Danny. Evans upheld her action though he was rampant to be at Kilpoonta ere rain should detain them. The swinging stretcher was improved. They moved forward before a week had ended.

The patient's state was beyond the surgeon, who attended him on the journey. His escape from death through mortification was a miracle attributed to healthy blood. Following the amputation he began to groan and then wandered into delirium. He sometimes called on his mother and sometimes on Johanna. His accents were Irish. An advertisement describing him was prepared to await a traveller as far as the nearest post office and thence to Sydney for insertion in the *Sydney Morning Herald*.

Weeks from the time that Danny had been injured he reached Kilpoonta on the Lachlan. In the joy of arrival the newly-married pair did not neglect the stranger. Who was he? Whence had he come? There was not much machinery for instituting inquiry. The mystery was of lively interest in the far solitudes.

The surgeon continued to marvel that life could be retained. He would be more surprised, he said, if the man ever regained his senses as the symptoms pointed to injuries to the skull. They were unaware of Danny's wiry constitution and vitality.

CHAPTER VI

EVANS's advertisement appeared when Delacy's family had no idea that he was missing. A lost man in days when convicts were for ever escaping did not attract much attention.

Moore shared a subscription to the *Sydney Morning Herald* with a friend in Sydney; when opportunity permitted he sent Delacy copies, but opportunity did not occur at the date. Mrs Urquhart did not read and Urquhart was busy. For one reason or another the news of Danny passed unnoticed.

The surgeon continued to marvel that life could be retained during the typhoid state which accompanied the gangrene lingering in the amputated leg. The sufferer showed dangerous irritation under light or noise, so the window was darkened and he was left in quiet for hours. He would take a sip of nourishment only from the hand of Mrs Evans. The probability that he was a person of importance was discounted by his Irish accent, and the fact that he had not been sought. His hosts had the idea that he was an escaping Irish rebel. They were conservative, but too kind to hand over to officialdom any creature so helpless and suffering, and the surgeon·was curious to see how long his patient would last.

Also at that time they had bigger worries than a helpless person to whom they had grown accustomed. Hostile blacks kept them in suspense. In that region there had been bitter encounters, with each side guilty of gruesome atrocities. There were floods, and scab in the flocks, and a struggle with an unscrupulous overlander, who tried to usurp Kilpoonta. Evans too met with an accident—broken arm and collarbone—which gave his wife and the surgeon a second patient. As Mr Evans convalesced, Mrs Evans had more time for her first patient and insisted that his improvement was so marked that he would recover. She and the surgeon watched with renewed interest. The poison slowly drained from the wound and at length youth and strength returned Delacy from death. No rontgen rays ever revealed to what extent his brain box had been injured. He regained his mind one morning following an easy night to find himself in a neat bed. A lady was sitting near fashioning tiny garments. That was all for the time. He fell into a long restoring sleep.

A day later he awakened to refinement and easy circumstances as compared with the primitive hut and fur rugs where he had left Johanna and the children. The gentlewoman—still sewing—reminded him of his mother in Ennis, so far away. Was it a dream? If he spoke would this angelic presence dissolve? He slept again.

When dawn once more reddened the levels, he recognized the guffawing birds. The lady was replaced by a rough, sunburned man. Neither heaven nor Ireland.

Another twenty-four hours and he had strength to demand, "Where am I? What has come to me?"

"You had an accident—nasty crack on the head."

His hand went to his shaven poll. "That dayvil of a Lancelot got rid of me; to some extint that I should be in bed with me hair off and not to know it."

His questions were cautiously answered.

"Is me leg broke?" he demanded, noting the hump in the bedding.

"It certainly is."

Danny was tractable. A broken leg was a mere inconvenience. The surgeon insisted upon sleep. Danny slept, too weak for anything else. At each awakening he was increasingly alert. He gave his name and history, but at intervals the surgeon shut off talk in the interests of Danny's head.

He was astonished to be so far out of his course, and startled when he found that the season vacated before Christmas was now into autumn. "Be the powers, me poor Johanna will be thinking I'm dead and eaten by the blacks all this time. How could it happen that I have been in darkness so long? . . . and a centipede could have recovered all his legs since then."

"Fever reduced you to death's door. Crutches are ready when you get a little strength."

By damn! he'd try his leg that very minute. Mrs Evans was summoned by his loud tones. She explained gently that the fracture had been compound, that to save his life, well, it had been necessary to remove a portion of the bone.

Danny's eyes blazed in blue flame with resistance. He flung the bedclothes back and saw that the mass of lint stopped short. He shouted. He tore the linen away and found an unpleasing stump. When he knew that he had but one leg he gave way, heroically unashamed. Such was his courage that he could afford to be. Implicit in his spiritual and mental fibre was a quality that excluded fear of conviction of cowardice, by himself or others.

Mrs Evans petted him like a child. When his paroxysm subsided he fell asleep and did not wake until the birds were laughing against the sinking sun. Had some long lost god endowed them with derision?

Danny sat up. Mrs Evans protested that he would bring on his death. "Not at all. 'Tis all in the moind, and my moind is set."

Evans could not send a messenger because the blacks were again hostile. Not a man could be spared. Danny was of opinion that the blacks had not been properly treated. He suggested that they should be conciliated with offers of sheep. "Why should ye not pay rint to the poor dayvils?"

This was dismissed as nonsense by the richer and more warlike squatters who had settled on the overland line. Delacy was a sentimental Irishman who had long been "out of his head". The alarums of encounters with aborigines served to detain him while he gained strength.

The tan had faded, leaving his cheeks white. Always spare, his flesh had wasted to show bones as slender as a girl's. He could have passed for a boy but for his beard. The pipe had been lost. He declared that he was the father of three children living, and two dead. His friends' hearts were moved by the hampering loss of a leg to one with such heavy domestic responsibilities plus the fate of wresting a livelihood from impenetrable wilds.

After the first outburst no word of repining was heard. "Sure, better min than meself have achieved greatness with wan leg." Delacy's cheerful pluck endeared him to all. At the end of a week he insisted upon mounting a horse, and would have departed but for the impending siege.

When the blacks retreated towards the Murray, the elder Evans returned from pursuit and agreed to accompany Delacy. He refused the escort of the younger brother because Mrs Evans was on the way to motherhood. She gave her patient her own mare. David Evans limited each day to Delacy's endurance and to prevent the re-opening of the wound. They cut distance by passing Keebah.

Danny could scarcely conquer the flesh during the last half-day. The mare trembled on the edge of the descents, but followed the more ruthlessly urged animals without falling, while Danny clenched his teeth and hung on. Evans suggested camping by the spring, now called Breakfast Lookout, but Danny would not leave his Johanna another night in solitude and doubt. He thought to find her there. What had she to do but superintend Dunn and Doogoolook? He accepted heroic passivity as Nature's design for women. When he was down on the level he asked for a nip of rum and his hand shook as he took the flask.

Onward, onward, the pain in his mutilated limb overlooked in the excitement of return! None but mild ridges remained. The horse track led where a salt shed was an obelisk of settlement; then the homestead with a timbered rise beyond. The sun had set behind a wild peak leaving the cultivation flat and house plot bathed in molten afterglow, and peopled with birds which had come down from the snow lands for the winter. Scrub wallabies and kangaroos scurried into the shadows at the approach of the horsemen.

Delacy raised his Irish halloa, and the shrill coo-coo-ee-coo that he had learned from his black friends. "Munny-munny-lumby-adjong-cooo!"*

No baying of dogs. No whuffing of Rover—part bloodhound—who guarded the children and their mother. Not a yelp from a cattle cur. Only the click of the disturbed plovers, and the vesper chortles of the master ironists tossed from point to point, taken up and repeated softly from afar, as in an orchestra—*crescendo-diminuendo-dacapo-coda*.

No smoke above the chimney. The nearing homestead looked strange and small. Delacy's senses had to accept the impossible. The main portion of his home had vanished as completely as the fences and lakes that melt upon approach from the vast levels of mirage land. No woman nor children, nor black retainer, nor cow; only the voice of the wild river which deepened a lornness ghostly and dismaying.

They reached the remains of a fire where a home had been. Desolation. It looked like the work of marauders. There was no message or sign of Johanna. The blow was too heavy for Danny in his weakness, his physical agony. He wept and called to high heaven for his wife and little ones, whom he never more would see.

Evans sat him down gently. He insisted upon camping. Night was falling and Delacy was unfit to go on. Exhaustion and rum brought him to sleep despite all.

* I am indebted to Mrs W. A. Lampe (née Wilkinson), for this lovely aboriginal call. She grew up on Yellowin Station, one of the early squattages situated in the fountain country of the boogongs and tea-tree and tree-ferns. The first Wilkinsons were gentle with the blacks, gave them bullocks for their annual feasts, and enjoyed friendship with them. The gins used to do the station washing, and Mrs Lampe relates that when they went to the creek for water they were often slow to return. One piccaninny used to wail when his mother thus left him. The other gins would try to pacify him without avail, and then resort to the call which meant *"Hurry-up, hurry-up with the water!"* The last word, *"coo"*, would be prolonged, and many notes higher—a clear, ringing top note.—M.F.

CHAPTER VII

WHEN DUNN, the ex-felon, turned back from his employer, he thought of a fellow lag who kept a sly grog shop in the ranges beyond Gounderu. He had stood to his trust when left in solitude, but a terrible craving, irresistible as sexual lust, suddenly began to torture him. For years he had been content with the station ration of rum, but an internal fire now sent him on a jag of weeks which dissolved his horses and gear. He returned to consciousness a pariah. Weeks had passed and Delacy would be home. Dunn felt himself a horse thief and worse. He was compelled to disappear.

Johanna waited valiantly. Dunn was to have returned at the end of four days. At the end of eight she concluded that Danny had needed him for longer, and composed herself for Danny's return, at the end of a month at latest.

She had neither messenger nor mail service, but the aborigines had. The cattle moved restlessly in the gullies of the wild runs. Doogoolook reported from smoke signals that his people were moving on Burrabinga. The lad was intelligent and of noble character. He could make himself understood by signs to Maeve, and she interpreted to Johanna.

She had an idea of making out to Keebah, but the army was approaching that way, and how was she to climb the mountain walls with a babe in arms and two little girls?

"Mary, Mother of God, help me," she prayed, dormant phrases coming to her lips.

The first wave of fear past, her courage and experience re-established her. These were Doogoolook and Maeve's people, so she sent the lad to inform them that she would give them some beasts.

The tribe was fat and hearty. Game was plentiful. The boogongs at Keebah had been more than they could consume. Even the gins were gorged. The whole family, including gins and piccaninnies, were making a detour to call on their patrons, out of curiosity, friendliness, and as part of the annual walkabout. Some of the gins, who wore a rag of clothes, were already known to Johanna since the Bewuck encampment, and when they called on her, her Irish warmth delighted them and cemented sisterhood. They talked to Maeve excitedly in their soft voices and filled the place with their laughter, in distant aeons captured and standardized by the big grey kingfishers. They were proud of Maeve's position among the whites. A miracle greater than reversal of a "boning" had established Danny as a chief of good magic. Here was Doogoolook, strong and happy, a member of a white tribe.

In warm weather he dressed in knee pants, and Johanna made him a gaily decorated shield for his scarred chest, which his people took to be the regalia of royalty.

"Minetinkit, that pfella budgery!" they guffawed.

In honour of the bullock they staged a feast and a play corroboree, in which women had the part of accompanists. Johanna was treated with honour and with her brood beheld a spectacle seen by few white women.

She gave her friends all that she could spare from her stores in the way of clothes, tobacco, flour, raisins and potatoes. They prized the potatoes, which the warriors carried away on their spears. They neither thieved nor destroyed otherwise and at the end of a few days moved on, working their way down the river before autumn, and looking for fight. They left the valley unspoiled. Not a tree was mutilated except to extract a possum. No bush fires followed in their wake. Graciously, peacefully they had ceded their territory to Delacy.

Enlivened by the *feis*, Johanna turned with fresh heart to her tasks, while looking hourly for Danny. He must have gone on to Parramatta, she concluded, as the weeks ran into the second month. Day followed day, but no horseman emerged from the mighty aisles of eurabbi and peppermint at the other side of the little flat where the curlews wailed so friendlily. There was only the ceaseless song of the river like a wild wind, and chortling birds, the warbling magpies and clouds of other songsters, or the "pheasants" mimicking her cock, to embellish the haunting stillness of the cathedral forests, and Doogoolook's shadow-like presence to accentuate the solitude. At night there were the unfailing boobooks and dingoes to augment the curlews' concert, and the native cats to make raids upon her precious hens.

Still no halloa or whip-crack announced Danny's return.

Rations were running low, and at the end of six weeks Doogoolook took a letter to Keebah. Doogoolook drew with a stick on the ground the fetching of Urquhart, but Johanna substituted his reading the letter, and Doogoolook returning next day. This was conveyed by one lie-down in sleep—head-on-hand with closed eyes— and quick jump-up.

Still a child in years by white standards, and mute, he went faithfully on his errand; Johanna watched him to the edge of the clearing, and, bereft of her protector, turned about in her internment camp and attacked a snake which had appeared as the boy departed.

She retired early, drawing her chicks about her, but doors cannot be barred against loneliness and fear. Bewuck, despite its bunyip and ghost, was by comparison, a centre of population. In those days she grew fond of Maeve, who was always cheerful, and unafraid of the great bush.

At the end of the fourth day the forest was still without Doogoolook, and Johanna grew uneasy lest the mare had lost her footing on a bad pinch, and hurtled into the gulf. However, Maeve was a good fisher, and the hens laid.

That afternoon Johanna and Maeve went seeking the cow that had escaped, Johanna carrying the baby. Kathleen Moyna and Della were left at home, and what happened, who can say? They had heard their mother speak of the need to keep the fire in because that morning there had been trouble to relight it from the ashes. From across the clearing Johanna saw smoke issuing from the roof. She deposited the baby and sped to the rescue. She reached the threshold in an agony of fear and found the children in flames. She extinguished the smaller in a tub of water, but Kathleen Moyna ran screeching into the breeze, with her mother in pursuit. She caught the child at length, and in beating out the flames was herself scorched on wrists and hands.

She screamed to Maeve to go after the baby lest ants or snakes should be endangering him, while she attended to Kathleen Moyna. The house was a bonfire.

As a fire precaution Danny had placed the kitchen at a ludicrous distance from the house. In this were the beef casks and other stores, and the distracted woman had this shelter when the fire in the main house subsided. Maeve had recaptured the cow, so the babies' principal diet was assured.

Kathleen Moyna's body was shockingly burned. Mercifully she had passed beyond consciousness and lay as if asleep. Johanna's hands were so painful that only despair and the demands upon her kept her from fainting time after time. The sole alleviation was in keeping her singed flesh in the cold water of the river. Maeve did the same for the other child, who was but slightly burned.

Morning came. Della was free from pain and slept safely. The fire had died out of Johanna's hands, but they were like bladders. She tore up her undergarments and bound her fingers in grease.

Kathleen Moyna still breathed though Johanna saw that she could not last long, that indeed it was better that she should not recover, though the mother's heart cried out against bereavement. The day was loud with jackasses, morn, noon and evening. The plovers clicked on the eerie flats with their tea-tree groves, beautiful as Asiatic art, and as alien to the early British settlers.

There was firewood to place against the loss of the fur robes at night. Only Doogoolook's remained. Johanna was doubtful of finding the track to Keebah and transporting three small children, one of them dying. Doogoolook had taken the quiet mare. It was unlikely that she could catch another horse. Even so, how could she carry sufficient provisions and tackle to camp during their slow and painful progress? Maeve was sure that she knew the way, and that she could carry the baby, with Della also walking, while Johanna nursed Kathleen Moyna on the horse. Johanna remembered the Burrabinga to be crossed three times. She had to abandon the project until her hands could heal. She would have welcomed a bushranger.

Meanwhile, Doogoolook had reached Keebah. Urquhart and most of his men, like Danny, were away with sheep to a boiling-down plant. Mrs Urquhart, with an immigrant woman and a ticket-of-leaver, was at the station, but they were all illiterate. There was no other neighbour within thirty miles. They could not understand Doogoolook's sign language, nor he make sense of theirs. He drew figures to indicate Mrs Delacy and the children. Those assembled understood that it was something about Mr Delacy. Had he tumbled down? No. It seemed to be some business between Danny and Sandy. Mrs Urquhart could only await a person who could read. At the end of four days Doogoolook grew so uneasy that he slipped away on foot in the dead of night.

Maeve discerned him reappearing one morning from the boles of the timber. He conveyed that Mr Urquhart was absent and that the others shook their heads over the letter. His return gave slight hope, but Kathleen Moyna ceased to breathe an hour later. Her mother determined to set out for Keebah with the body. Maeve and Doogoolook yarded the second quiet horse and it was packed with provisions and the rug. Johanna perched on top with the dead child, wrapped in a sack, in her arms. The boy took his turn with Maeve in carrying the baby. Della, clad in charred rags, toddled bravely at the beginning. Up the steep pinches Doogoolook held the horse's tail and put Della on his shoulder. In places he had to take his charges singly. Now and again Johanna struggled along on foot with her burden, while Maeve, with the baby in her arms, rode with Della behind her.

Kathleen Moyna had been named for the aunt who had sheltered Johanna, and also for the cousin who had aided her elopement. Johanna felt that old Cooley's curse had now reached even to her helpless child. Despair deadened her anguish and kept her calm. Progress was painful to her tortured hands in meagre binding, and to Della's scorched face and limbs.

They were settled for a third night when Urquhart found them. He was shocked by the tragedy and their present plight, and to learn that Mrs Delacy had been so long alone. He persuaded Johanna to let him take Kathleen Moyna and left the exhausted party settled with Doogoolook while he rode hard to Keebah for assistance.

He was back a little after daylight with helpers and comforts, and they all reached Keebah by ten o'clock that night.

Janet was awaiting them beyond the stables with hot soup and a capacious heart. Johanna was laid in a comfortable bed. Della screamed with pain and weariness and clung to Maeve until bread and honey tempted her. Doogoolook was commended as a budgery pfella in ear-splitting shouts. All waste of breath, but the gestures nourished his affections. Finally all were at rest.

Kathleen Moyna was buried at the foot of the flower garden beside an Urquhart infant who had succumbed to convulsions.

Delacy's horses had not returned and there had been no letter from him, though the mail had been collected from the nearest township. Janet kept Johanna in bed. To ease her mind Urquhart rode to Bewuck and thence to Mr Moore at Bandalong. He returned without news of Delacy. Mr Moore was much concerned. He started inquiries, but by now the Evanses were no longer on the alert for anything of the kind.

Johanna felt in her lonely nostalgic mind that Danny had deserted her for livelier adventures or the seductions of a fresher woman. This was unjust to her experience of Danny. Urquhart maintained that it was too early to regard Delacy as a deserter, that he was a pure merino who would not abscond from a fine young wife and children.

"Straight goers among men," said Johanna, "nevertheless don't care how crooked they are with a woman whin another takes their eye."

Mrs Urquhart nodded her head, and Sandy, remembering passages, steered from the subject.

Urquhart and Moore were of opinion that violence had ended Delacy. The disappearance of Dunn, transported for a criminal act, lent colour to this. Urquhart tried to rally Johanna, but she was haunted by sick fears and lacked inner sanctuary. She had repudiated her own creed and could not adopt Danny's personal brand of free thought. No dogma guilty of imposing mental shackles could have lasted with Delacy. Even in youth, tolerant and philosophical though he was, Johanna had found him adamant in Protestantism in so far as it meant freedom of thought. No womanly blandishments had ever affected him in this direction; as well have tried to cajole him to dishonesty. It was hard on Johanna. She accepted her trials as emanating from her father's curse, and retreated upon stoicism. The Uquharts were Presbyterians. With them she found hospitality, friendship and companionship after loneliness, but no religious solace.

Her future had to be considered as the weeks passed without news of Danny. Mr Moore wanted her back at Bandalong. Johanna desired to return to Bewuck. Danny or no Danny she had renounced Burrabinga for ever. Hitherto she had accepted the faithful Doogoolook as complacently as a dog, but now, despite his muteness, he had become something between an elder son and a younger brother.

Mrs Urquhart's welcome never waned. Her comfort in a companion was born of woman-scarcity and isolation, and the Delacy children mingling with the Urquhart's added zest to life.

So time sped and another day had broken at Burrabinga. Rain had obliterated tracks long since, but Evans found utensils that had been used after having been through the fire, and potatoes remained as evidence that there had been no robbery by blacks.

"Your family will be safe with the nearest neighbour," Evans remarked.

Danny's soul was renewed by hope. He set out for Keebah immediately, but his mind could not force his tortured flesh to the whole journey in one day.

It was a great moment when the travellers came within range of Mrs Urquhart's candles. Here was a Danny with one trouser leg pinned up, a Danny no longer as swift as a steel spring in recoil, an emaciated fragile Danny noisily clouting his way, but with authentic flame-blue eyes and booming voice, dismissing his pain in the excitement of finding wife and weans, with Doogoolook executing capers of welcome; a Danny without self-consciousness as to how a wife might regard a mutilated spouse, a crippled bread-winner; a Danny so overjoyed that speculations about his Johanna's attitude were crowded out.

Her resentment of imagined desertion was washed away in the reunion, but she was conspicuously pallid and unresponsive, the iron of tragedy fresh in her soul. The full extent of the catastrophe could not be withheld from Danny. He was already so near to collapse from pain and exhaustion that Evans enlisted Mrs Urquhart to prepare a bed and in it, with the aid of rum, his charge took this final blow lying down.

Delacy survived that journey as well as the shock of the calamity that met him, though he was compelled to lie up for several weeks at the Urquharts'.

He spoke of erecting another hut at Burrabinga, but Johanna vetoed this. "Me wits forsook me to go there in the first place to such a lost hole—collecting asses' loads of sorrow and heart-scald. Even ye should have more sinse than to think ye can scale those walls with wan leg. 'Tis a goat with four ye had better be, for ye'r owld Bunratty Castle."

"Arrah! Haven't I just been up and down with me wan leg, and me not yet restored to full fighting trim. Wan leg is as good as two if the moind is set."

"And what is more, Danny Delacy, while ye are capering about from wan place to the next, how am I to know if the leaks in the roof at Bewuck haven't dripped on me few best bits, and the weevils to have eaten the rest, if the place is not burned down entirely and somewan walked off with the unprotected remains?"

Danny's leg was still as sensitive as a boil, and his head had an unprecedented tendency to ache in the sun. He took to an outsize in straw wide-awakes that year and filled it with the cool leaves of the peppermint. When his head had recovered, the leaves had become a habit. They made his head look enormous, but his actions, motivated by utility, were unrestricted by what the timid might think. When the wags made him their butt, he was contemptuous, "With the wits of jackasses, and destitute of conversation, they should be thankful that I supply a subject."

The death of Kathleen Moyna, combined with Johanna's attitude and state, forced him to relinquish Burrabinga temporarily. He attributed his retreat to advancing winter and the need to procure an artificial limb. He was so proficient with his crutch that he sometimes resembled an escaping kangaroo. As soon as his strength returned, he departed with Doogoolook, leaving Johanna at Keebah.

CHAPTER VIII

THE voice of the aboriginal Dryopes held the welcome of old acquaintance for Johanna as she descended the gorge. The cause of their lamentation had retreated beyond the conjecture of mythology, but its melody was now consonant with Johanna's mood. Like Queen Pomare—lately dethroned—she would never permit one of her casuarinas to be cut down, and, in later years, when she rarely left home, she missed the lullaby of river and trees. Having survived searing ordeals, she was relieved by comparative peace, and revived among her prized household possessions, though there was now in her emotions a chamber sealed and silent, sacred to Kathleen Moyna. Contentment gradually grew out of acceptance. The exiled daughter of Erin graduated as a citizen of New South Wales.

She had renounced the mountains for ever.

Not so Danny. Unconquerable longing assailed him each time he came up from the chasm through which the Murrumbidgee elbows its way to the great plains. As he would rein-in to pick out the notch in the ramparts that led to Burrabinga, he would fall into worshipful contemplation of the ranges, thrown one upon another like storm waves petrified when the world had cooled. Their foreverness soothed and inspired. The dignity of permanence lay on a view superb as that from Edessa in Old Greece down the valley of the Vardar towards Olympus. But the view towards Salonika is bearded with legend reaching back to the dawn of human history. The spoliation and squalor, the desecration and degradation of which human history is compounded equally with glory, had been cleansed from Delacy's province since eras lost in time. There for the dreamers, the path-finders, the road-makers with the forcefulness to project their personality upon their environment, lay a world inviting light-hearted effort and glamorous deeds.

"Oh, moi, oh, moi!" Delacy would ejaculate out of that emotion which suffuses the receptive soul when refreshed at the well of beauty or nobility. He would flap his horse with his big hat, scattering the contents like moths about him, and go on his way with a tag from the classics or a verse from the song books, whose contents were deciphered by the light of camp or nut fire and put to a tune by the musical, or bellowed with tuneless satisfaction by the less gifted.

Bewitched anew by the ranges, Danny would be restless. "A man is a fool to leave that territory, after all the preliminaries, till it is jumped on him."

"Better it be jumped by another fool next time. You a cripple. Bunratty Castle, a prison of stone, crags fit only for the blacks to pick grubs, and the native dogs to howl in."

"When me artificial limb is attached, 'twill make a power of difference."

"Little difference! Ye'd better learn reason in time."

Danny was ambitious for an apparatus made by a renowned artisan in Sydney, who had learned his craft after the Napoleonic campaigns, but the tragedy of Kathleen Moyna was too fresh for him to disregard Johanna's views. He occupied himself by clearing more cow paddocks on the river banks. In the mortal combat with the trees—a combat waged by every settler—there was enough to engage his depleted energy and impeded activity for a year or two. He dreamed of having his holding as clear as the plains of County Clare, with mayhap a ladylike imported tree or two for ornament, and an orchard about the house.

Where Danny extirpated so ardently, the curious can find to-day a well-grown forest. A gnarled stick or two of quince trees withstand the sheep amid native shrubs just below the bunyip hole. Where Johanna set her garden, still live the flag lilies—royal emblems of republican France. Those educated to explore pioneer homestead sites may discern amid the lusty yellow-box and wattle trees the ridges of Danny's first cultivation. There are the "lands" where earth, purified by a thousand years, nay, aeons of fallowhood, first gave up its grannie grubs to the magpies who warbled liquid notes of thanksgiving, and to the kookaburras, who filled the valley with grotesque mirth, so disturbing to Johanna. A century has mellowed that laughter to enchantment for the children of Australia, has rendered her exiles nostalgic for the morning and evening fanfare of glee.

The indigenous standing army, which made and held the earth on the hillsides, has vanquished a thousand Dannies since then, and obliterated their works. Not yet is there understanding of this continent, so sensitive and gently fierce. Neither conquered nor despoiled, and only in parts defaced, it challenges the grandsons and great-grandsons and great-granddaughters of all the half-articulate Dannies to hold or to lose their incalculable heritage.

Johanna reared turkeys and set up a dairy. She had so much butter that she stored it in "kags".

Delacy hoped with butter, tallow, hides and other skins to obtain cash to renew squatting licences for Burrabinga, and to buy an artificial leg. He groaned to think of his stock being lost in the mountains.

"Ye'll never be able to get round there again," said Johanna.

"With a new leg, I'd lepp over the moon."

He commissioned the wheelwright at the township to build a dray, and when he announced that he was going to Sydney, Johanna said that she too would go. Her nerve had not recovered sufficiently to let him stray alone again. Danny welcomed her company. Hannon and his wife had a hut beyond the cultivation paddock, and with Maeve and Doogoolook could take care of the children. There were now five: Della and Robert; William and Honoria, the twins born at Keebah; Harry, the youngest, a few months of age. Three years had gone since Delacy lost his leg.

So the Delacys retraced their early journey along the Great Southern Road, convict-built from Port Jackson to Port Phillip, which they met at the Township. Two of Mr Moore's drays travelled with them for mutual protection. Her Majesty's mails had long run regularly to many points. Mails by private subscription went quite far out. The contingent of human beings advancing against the arboreal army of occupation was beginning to scrimshaw a history at the furthest extremity of the globe, where record of human achievements had been relegated to recesses of time beyond the research of ethnologists or archaeologists.

Mrs Delacy and the baby were perched among the malodorous merchandise. Mounted on Mrs Evans's mare, Danny drove or led his bullocks. The teams doubled in steep or boggy places. Danny was no bullocky, except thereby. Not his the patience to become a craftsman in any of his various activities. He triumphed by force of mind over body. With an "Arrah, by damn!" he dismissed obstacles. "The moind! The moind! It's all in the moind!" was the phrase by which his associates best remember him.

A journey of some weeks brought them to the turnpike at the end of George Street, and they wound downwards to the Quay, impressed by the progress made in the thirteen years since they had arrived. Many of the wooden skillings had been replaced by brick houses overlaid with cement to look like freestone. Some of them were as good as the houses in the better parts of Limerick. Even the lower orders had verandaed cottages and garden plots in Pitt Street that were more comfortable than Quebarra, Glenties or Bewuck. Hyde Park was being reformed from a racecourse.

They went again to the select boarding establishment on Church Hill, with its patrons of the first respectability. Johanna was captivated by the Markets, which were opened on Tuesdays and Fridays by ringing a bell at 7 a.m., and which were cleansed by water from a pump in the centre. Everybody was agreed that these premises were so elegant that they were an amphitheatre rather than a market.

Mrs Delacy loved Sydney and would that her lot had been there. This could never be with Danny. Neighbours within sight had a stifling effect on him. He thrilled to wide horizons. His spirit had been endowed by the seas that belaboured Erin's shores with an impetus unimpeded from the Pole, or rolled away to America without obstruction. His descent upon Sydney was a rare spree, an excrescence upon Life. Johanna had rather that Sydney were Life and the bush a removable excrescence. She was delighted by a play called *Blackeyed Susan*, preceded by "God Save the Queen", and followed by *Monsieur Tonson*, a farce.

Danny laughed and clapped with abandon, but more nourishing to him were the conversations with gentlemen at the boarding house, and anywhere he encountered them—in hotel bars, in banks and business houses and shops.

While Johanna was disrobing for the night he would serve up a résumé of the day's pabulum. The Colony was still in the throes of the 'forties, which had closed the Bank of Australia, and were driving mechanics to replace labourers at £12 and £15 per annum.

"Sure, the tonnage in the harbour is only fifty per cent of what it has been. 'Tis a mortal curious state of affairs in a new country when all we can do is bile down prime beef cattle for tallow, and suffer the stink of the plants from Yass on the Port Phillip Road to Bungarrabee on the Western Highway.

"The Colony is wallowing in a general financial stringency which is to be attributed to the premature and abrupt termination of transportation and assignment, and the extravagant over-speculation during several years. Sure, Johanna, I've been talking to a man at the hide store, and there is a great importation of grain and salted meats and other commodities, which has sucked the cash from us. I was talking to the manager of the bank about the high rate of interest on money, together with the monopoly of bank discounts. Says he, 'Mr Delacy, banks are not philanthropical institutions.' 'Bedad, no,' says I to that, 'they resimble more a bushranging gang.' "

"And now whoi would ye be so vulgar to a gintleman like a bank manager?"

"The depreciation of wool in the English market is resulting in the Colony being in such debt for English goods that the English merchants have refused further credit," continued Danny in unbroken flow.

Even as it was to be generations after Danny's day!

The wiseacres of his generation were assured that the Colony would prosper on stringent economy, especially if labour could be procured for the veriest subsistence wage.

" 'Tis a situation to give the old corruptionists a fit of the cholera. if the presint posture of affairs was permanint; but me moind remains undaunted as I look ahead. In a young and springing community with lashings of opportunity, there is no distress in a little stagnation. 'Tis but an opening skirmish to enterprises the extint of which cannot be dreamt—no, not even by a man who had enough drink to stiffen a tinker, and him not to be stiffened. . . . Though I can't help but be thinking they haven't much rayson who want us to be brought to the knees by economy. Doesn't it stand to rayson that what we want is more consumption of commodities, not less; and the way to further that would be to double all the workers' wages instead of halving them."

"It's well that ye came out of ye'r own accord, Danny Delacy, or I'm thinking, with some of ye'r notions, ye'd have been sint out as a seditionist."

"By damn! What I say is irrefutable! Couldn't wan with no more intellect than an eft observe throughout history that we always starve when commodities are cheap, and when we economize. We thrive when they are dear. Wouldn't you think, it's so obvious by now, that instid of economy to right things, they'd experiment on what extravagance and distributing things to the needy would do?"

"Och, there's no rayson at ye!" said Johanna. "Aren't all the wise ones at the head of things saying in the paper that it's the expensiveness of the Government, coupled together with private extravagance, that has brought us to this pitch of ruin. Didn't I hear that foine gintleman at dinner say that we have got ahead of German wool growers in the quality of merino wool, and that it is setting us on our feet again?"

"Sure, did you note he also said that there was ruin in Germany therefore? There is poor satisfaction to my moind in progress that is made at the expinse of trouble elsewhere. There can be no stability in cut-throat capers."

"Sure, I read in the paper with me own eyes that without cheap and abundant labour the community cannot expect to prosper."

"That's what I'm saying—at the expinse of slaves. I'm free meself and would wish every man-jack, black and white, to be the same—aquil before his Maker. If men are beaten down so that they work for rations and slops, who'll buy our commodities? Answer me that!"

"Och, Danny-boy, if what ye say was true, if it was ye who had the wisdom at ye, wouldn't they be putting ye at the head of things instead of to be ignoring ye among the native dogs and the precipices?"

"Wait till I get me new limb. As sure as there is a cross on the ass, there can't help being abundance for all. Think of the progress! The time between here and the old country has been cut in half since we came out. We can now get the Melbourne papers in a few days after they are printed. Me moind is on the grand future when all these little difficulties of disorganization will be dissolved."

It was beneath his vision that the human race—most inefficient of mammals—three or four generations ahead would still be unable to feed and clothe and care for its members with adequacy though in possession of a world teeming with every commodity raw and manufactured, and with inconceivable discoveries and inventions at its disposal.

Delacy attended some of the Usury Debates and met the representative of his territory in the Legislative Council. "To-morrow I must go see him again and give him some advice and information."

" 'Tis a pity ye couldn't moind ye'r own business and leave a man like that to his own. Too many can put their hand in ye'r bag. By ye'r tendency to be always helping others, and a scatteration in ye'r projects, ye will arroive nowhere in the ind. Let others look after themselves. They never consider ye."

"Sure, where would I be to-day if Mrs Evans had not made me her business, but had gone on moinding her own?"

"Och, ye'r waking the baby with ye'r blather."

"Put out the candle, me brave Johanna. I'll be as quiet as a mouse."

Danny disposed of his "kags", and hides and horsehair with fair profit, considering the financial stringency. In their place he procured axes and tomahawks, a saw, a tarpaulin, two-and-a-half and three-bushel bags, some suits of slops, a keg of hurdle and horse-shoe nails, a saddle and bridle bits, percussion caps; striped shirts with linen collars for township wear; a roll of China matting, and another "kag" of paint as a concession to Johanna's elegancies. He also purchased American flour and lemon syrup as delicacies; and Seidlitz powders and castor· oil, and bluestone and tobacco; and Day and Martin's blacking because he got a damaged case cheaply; and an inspiring pipe to replace the treasure lost these three years, as well as many another article indispensable to him.

Johanna found a companion at the select boarding establishment and had an enlivening holiday. Amusements, paved walks under her feet, to have vegetables, animal and other produce purchasable in the shops—this was life. It had been her ambition at Cooley Hall, but Danny had carried her off to a State where everything had to be grown or manufactured. She revelled as far as the capacity of purse and dray allowed.

She could not resist softest cashmeres and organdies. There were coloured handkerchiefs, and ·gimp and bugles for trimming. A pongee handkerchief and gay print were for Maeve, and a gaudy bundle handkerchief for Doogoolook. There were slippers and hose, and a leghorn bonnet ¸"richly trimmed"; and ribbons and perfume and lace; and a gingham umbrella for 4/-. There were green baize and steel busks, a worsted table cover, an Indian shawl, satin brocade; and a dainty pair of black lace gloves at 1/3. Johanna had an ineradicable joy in elegancies for their own sake. She had a longing for a set of horsehair furniture, but limitation in means and transportation postponed these. She compromised on currants and preserved ginger, a tea set of Staffordshire, and a little music box that played three tinkling tunes.

Delacy informed himself of the growth of the horse trade with India, and plumed himself upon the three mares that had travelled with their noses on the tail of the dray. Cornet of Parramatta, a blood horse of Arab strain, was to add his lineage to the walers of Burrabinga.

The return journey began as soon as the new leg was ready. When approaching the Gib they were stuck-up by one of the intermittent bands of bushrangers that had arisen to attack the mail coaches. All teams and other travellers were mustered in the hollow awaiting the mail from Goulburn. The contents of the drays were ransacked. Tea, currants and flour were emptied on the earth and the teamsters left to salvage what they could from flies, ants and grit.

Mrs Delacy had a triumph remembered by her descendants. She was still bright-eyed and handsome and plied a fearless tongue against the robbers. She was set to cook a meal while the men were bailed-up until disarmed and relieved of valuables. Danny was for chastising his jailer with his crutch, to which he still clung.

Johanna reassured him, "Sure, they'll do no harm to an old woman hurrying home to four childre as well as the wan that's crying for her now."

"The dam of five, and *that* for a sire! Were men so scarce?" guffawed the leader of the gang. "Does he put that forty gallon hat on to make him important?"

"No, to contain his brains," said Johanna.

"And he, the preposterous vaygabond," shouted Danny, "by the same token would need nothing but a paynut shell."

The man let Johanna keep her trinkets. "Begob, we can afford that to the only lady with us." Another had been ordered to halt but had whipped her horse into a gallop. She was a bride, and her husband was forced to gallop with her. "Let them burst," the man had decreed with a coarse imprecation concerning newly-weds.

Johanna tried to silence Danny. The leader set her at ease. "We'll not hurt your tom-tit, missus. He has a voice and a beard, and a pipe in the middle of it like a real man; and by cripes, what there is of him is worth a dozen of the pot bellies—swelled with importance and ordering the lash for their betters. He has no weapon with him but his crutch."

When the coach came and the mailbags were rifled, the travellers were released without further molestation, but Johanna's taste for journeys was ruined. After that she talked of trips to Sydney, but never took them. The growing city as well as the mountains dropped out of bounds for her.

CHAPTER IX

DELACY's grand artificial limb was a peg with a socket attached by straps to the waist. He became nimble with it on practice, and Doogoolook's wide laughter full of teeth, but empty of sound, conveyed that Danny and the brown horse were now both nullah-mundoeys.

The coolness of valleys and streams draped in ferns and shrubs, their fragrant aromatic purity, still enthralled him. The encircling ramparts guarded a kingdom, for which he would have forsaken the bread and butter of home and wife as for an enchantress. The beckoning fastnesses. should now guard twenty or thirty walers sufficiently mature for the Indian market.

"And how will ye handle them with but one leg?"

"Have I no ingenuity?"

Refreshed by her excursion into the outer world, Johanna now admitted that there was property in the mountains, but decreed that never again should Danny traipse off by himself. Therefore, in company with Hannon and Doogoolook, he set out once more when summer was bold in the land. Johanna had Maeve and Mrs Hannon, and an artisan, who knew something of farm work.

Delacy went by Keebah, and Urquhart accompanied him down the precipices. The mare had to carry him every yard of the way now. He detached the peg leg lest in the scrabbling and lurching it be smashed against tree or rock. Regardless of age or sex, Danny's mount was always a "mare". In this case it was the imported Irish lady of exquisite paces, given him by Mrs Evans, when her heart had been touched by his infirmity.

"Mules would be fine for this country," said Urquhart.

"Never wan of the unclean beasts would I run on me country. Nature repudiates such perversion and allows no further issue. That should teach a civilized man."

Danny uttered no word of repining about his leg, nor suffered any tremor that its loss made him less a man.

A nest of bulldog ants occupied the floor of the hut. Bats possessed the rafters. Wombats had burrowed under the wall plates. Kangaroo rats had snug homes in tussocks around the door step.

From one a black snake issued to his doom in the shape of Doogoolook.

Urquhart tarried to lend a hand and cast an eye on the country beyond Delacy's. His sons were growing up. "There's little sense to risk bones raising cattle in these wilds to make the land stink with rendering them down."

"But faith, a man who cannot look at the future is only a come-day-go-day contraption."

When those boys whom Johanna was rearing for him would throw their weight into the scale they would be bound to Burrabinga by firmer considerations that a paltry wage and rations of beef and flour, sugar, tea, rum and tobacco.

Nullah-Mundoey's headquarters were in the fields of kangaroo grass, as high as his withers, on the burned river bank. The cripple had kept the mob from dispersing and there was a fine display of mares, fillies and colts.

With a couple of stockmen Delacy began the trapping and branding of cleanskin cattle which had retreated beyond the domain of the horses. His brand and his earmarks were put on all cattle caught. Colts and fillies had their baptism. Horses with other brands were advertised.

Doogoolook was becoming a marvellous horseman and stockman, and yokels who came to Burrabinga had to follow his lead. That of Danny was hardly less daring. He rode the gorges at a furious pace, hallo-ing like a demon, depending on the "mare". Mind transformed horse and rider. Danny never fell from the horse nor the horse under him. He raged with industry from day-break and until long after night fell by the light of fires in the cavernous hearth. He struggled for money for extra labour, to put up adequate yards and huts, and above all to make a cutting around the worst pinches. It was almost more than could be expected of horses to traverse the precipices when laden. "But with the pinches reduced, sure an old woman in a donkey cart would have no distress in flipping back and forth."

Danny classified the live stock. Horses were taken to Bewuck, and Moore's breakers engaged to prepare them as cavalry chargers. Distraught heifers and steers went down the river to be tamed.

"Och, dragging the life out of ye'rself and no peace to anny one else," said Johanna.

"What else can a man do for an honest indipindence in a raw country with no capital but his hands?"

"There's plenty that don't drive themselves so extremely."

"Plenty of vaygabonds like the cattle spoilers of old." Danny waved his pipe towards squatters, men who had started with capital and whose fortunes were enlarging like snowballs. "Some of those who would have driven me off if they could."

" 'Tis not in ye to be rich. The rich have more hardfistedness. And ye bullock everything ye'rself, and wan man power can't extind. The great succeeders put other fellows to work for them while they reap the spoils."

Danny was a pioneer of Australian democracy in its levelling-aspects, which later socio-economists were to discredit as obstructing to intellectual progress.

The marriage had shaken down. Johanna now saw Danny and it for what they were. Danny, in the way of many spouses, had to take adventures of the spirit without his wife, but he valued her as a nest with eggs in it at the base of his fortune, while he experimented with the superstructure. The mountains were his *aisling*, his Dark Rosaleen. Not that this was a conscious indulgence, the physical campaign left no time for introspection nor even for sentiment, until he came to be accounted childish with age, but he faced the ranges with unabating zest. Arrived there he had the satisfaction of a bandit in retreat, only that Delacy had no strain of the outlaw in him. He was civilized.

The return of the blacks one summer, after two years' absence, was heralded by the unease of the cattle, which were driven away to safety. The aborigines' rights as ground landlords in the Burrabinga kingdom were respected by the payment of two beasts. No one connected with Delacy would have dared to "disrespect" a gin.

Two chiefs came to the hut and demanded Doogoolook. "I've often wondered that the wild taste has not come on him," said Delacy to Hannon.

Doogoolook went with his people. The alternative was death. Danny conveyed that his ward was entitled to a horse, blankets, etc., but this was disregarded. Danny could not be sure that Doogoolook was happy in departure, and in the days that followed sorely missed one whom he discovered to have been as useful as two newly-imported whites. "Sure, he's one of the whitest men I ever knew."

Two months later he saw a form emerge from the tall trees across the river, and welcomed the returning Doogoolook. He had attained his manhood; he pointed to tangible evidence. He was now entitled to marry, but the gins apportioned to him were the worse for wear, so he had been allowed to return, perhaps because of his muteness and Delacy's early rescue of him. The facts are not recorded. No aurist ever tried to decide whether Doogoolook's muteness was the result of destroyed vocal chords, or merely of shock.

Delacy's second decade of colonizing found him strenuously engaged with his two homes. New South Wales had settled down to a sedate tempo, when suddenly the composition of life in the new continent blew up over night.

CHAPTER X

GOLD! Gold!

Delirium set in and prevailed. From Van Diemen's Land to Moreton Bay the population skedaddled. Free workers set off as one man. Others absconded. Sailors deserted. Ships lay empty in port. Squatters, professional men, clerks, ploughmen, shepherds, stockmen—masters and men alike—forsook employment and family. The wise and the silly, the strong and the weak, the old and the young, the comfortably placed and the destitute, the good and the bad, the rough and the gentle scurried in the direction of Bathurst where it was rumoured that gold, man's most permanent god, his ablest and least changeable friend, was to be picked up from the surface of the earth.

From Sydney to Bathurst the camp fires blazed in a chain by night. The road was often a river of mud through which, by day, struggled a nondescript collection of humanity, burdened with nothing or anything from a garden fork to a compass. It was then that the Australian learned to roll a swag and pad the track hungry and cold, sweating or fly-tormented in a strange and lonely land.

Gold! Gold!

Richer discoveries in the new Colony of Victoria resulted in wilder and bigger rushes there.

Tales of gold went across the seas. Ships crowded south packed with diggers. Among them were heirs and cadets of lordly houses, desperadoes from many nations, skilled diggers from California, poets, callow professors from Germany, auctioneers, cheap Johns, impostors in rich release. People ran with greater alacrity than if St Gabriel had proclaimed an authentic heaven wide open.

Gold! Gold!

Gold trickled across counters from leather pouches and tinder boxes. It was carried in belts and small bottles and dusty tins.

On the sheep stations adjoining Bewuck the merinos were abandoned to scab and footrot and dingoes. Delacy himself, could no more resist such a call to adventure than the magpies the resurgence of spring. Johanna fought against the first rushes in New South Wales with barbed shafts.

"An old married man! Ye with wan leg already gone in ye'r

brave adventuring! Ye, that could have nearly been a grandfather had ye been a proper father, and not distressed me by ye'r capers."

It would have taken the Bull of Cocley to hold him from Bendigo and Ballarat. "Sure, I may as well go where there's promise. I can't be running the whole country with meself and Hannon alone. I might search the world with a small tooth comb for another chance of plucking up gold from the roots of the grass.'

"Ah, scatteration! When ye've dragged ye'rself to pieces to establish the horses and cattle at Burrabinga, and a depot and a home here, why leave everything to the native dogs? Ye'r stock unbranded for those who like to stick a mark on them."

"Och, every one will be running with me. The young stock will stay with their dams. And to think, me brave Johanna, if I brought you a fortune!"

"Ye'll more like be bringing me something worse than the wooden leg. How could ye work a claim on wan leg?"

"Couldn't I lepp over manny of them that has four, when I set me moind? Sure, it's all in the moind."

Urquhart, with ten children, and whom Johanna had thought a model of common sense, announced his intention of accompanying Delacy. Johanna was defeated, but luckily Hannon and Doogoolook stood by her. There was also a mild old poodle of an English gentleman as tutor. Johanna had to resign herself to observing the neglect of the substance for the chase of the shadow, but Danny was no longer a hero. She was seasoned to his sorties. His absences were a relief.

The hour came for him to mount the mare, a good animal in her prime. Attendant upon her were two able colts packed with digging and other gear, and merchandise, including tobacco. Johanna accompanied him as far as the sliprails beyond the household premises. From there she turned back to set her will on Bewuck.

She desired education for her children. Hitherto they had had only scrappy lessons by those ill-designed to impart their knowledge. Danny was accustomed to suspend lessons if tutor and pupils could forward the farm work.

Johanna prepared to send Della, now twelve, to Sydney to a boarding school nominated by Mr Moore. He was going down and took charge of the girl and paid her fare. Johanna held her breath about such a daring step, but if Danny was for ever to be capering about the country, leaving her no better situated than a widow, and in some ways worse, she must do something for her daughters. She was tempted to send them to a convent, but resisted because the Roman Catholic creed and the brogue would be detrimental socially, and they must acquire refinement and accomplishments to the end of securing husbands with civilized homes in Sydney. Her desire was to rescue her daughters from some of her own hardships and heartbreaks in "this blackfellow pioneering, with me life in me hand and me heart in me mouth from wan unholy terror after the other".

It was a year of floods. Every stream Delacy and Urquhart met was a banker. Several had to be swum at the risk of life. How Delacy swam the Yackandandah on the tail of the mare, and smashed his wooden leg in the passage, was one of his staple anecdotes when old, and swimming the Yackandandah was a by-word with his descendants.

Urquhart lost a horse in the Campaspe. They had to camp in their wet clothes several times, and without a fire, because their tinder was wet. They were also without food for forty-eight hours, on two stretches, until they reached some lonely shepherd's hut. At one they were offered £3 per hundred to shear sheep, as all the men had deserted for the gold fields. They refused this to haste to fortune and the livelier adventures which have but lately receded from Australia's pioneering scene, and which are recorded in the yellowing newspapers and in many a romance of the time, or in those since constructed with varying accuracy. They were arduous rough experiences, sometimes dangerous, and more coarsening than romantic, in aggressively democratic, not to say familiar association with bogus lords and parsons, soothsayers, table-rappers, medical quacks, harridans and strumpets, sleight-of-hand artists of exceptional daring and great diversity, audacious swindlers, bushrangers and other criminals—a hodge-podge savingly salted with men of grit and resource, and women of unconquerable endurance and respectability.

Delacy and Urquhart were robbed of their first £100 by a third mate, while asleep. Years later they learned that he was blown to pieces in a mine in Queensland. They were stuck-up by the notorious Black Douglas and his gang, and were triumphant that it was so soon following the first robbery that they had not an ounce of gold between them. Danny had one promising alluvial claim but was too slap-dash to win the good of it, and his leg hampered him in shaft sinking.

Homes and families at length became enticing to both men. Johanna's indifference concerning Danny's absence helped to draw his thoughts to the Murrumbidgee. Urquhart postulated that with the rise in stock, they were risking the loss of certain prosperity in

mere gambling. Live stock would not include so many "shicers"
if one were wary of "shysters". Neither had any affinity with the
lawless elements and were lucky in withdrawing before rebellion
culminated in the Eureka Stockade.

One evening at afterglow the dogs heard the jingle of hobble-chains
and quart-pot and gave tongue. The family ran out, saw the
silhouette on the dazzling skyline and answered Danny's hail. He
dismounted on a mended peg and shouted for each member of his
family. "Wait till I show you what I have brought."

"I can see the owld pipe ye haven't lost this time. Has it taken
root entirely? Maybe I should be thankful that it's wan leg ye
still have intact."

Danny went inside, for the moment he did not miss Della. He
was told that one of his colts sold on the diggings had reached
home ahead of him. He produced his nuggets. Johanna accepted
several as keepsakes, but maintained an aloof manner. Women
were compelled to be subservient, an attitude in which Johanna had
been racially bent from the days of Brehon law, but, psychologically,
the Danny who had lured her over the seas was dead. She was now
aware that she was wedded to an insignificant fellow, eccentric
because of his abnormal honesty, and incapable of providing the
refinement and elegancies she adored.

The moment came when Della's absence had to be explained.
Johanna made her plunge, her pulse not so confident as her mien.
Danny was astonished.

"Is it a school-mistress you are making of her? Aren't there
husbands enough in a country crying out for population?"

"What kind of husbands for those who know nothing but to run
after turkeys and chase crows? They'll be on the level of bare-
footed sluts from the bothies around Ennis, unless I contrive for
them to see something different. If it was not for Cooley Hall in
me own remimbrance, 'tis often I'd wonder was I annything but
wan of the savages that roam in a tribe."

"You should have consulted me."

"Consult the wind, and ye away with it!" Johanna threw up her
chin. "How did I know if ye'd ever return, or return with ye'r wits;
and me daughters running to seed."

"Maybe you did right," temporized Danny. "Sure, I'll have the
means hereafter to put things to right, and you'll be riding in
your carriage before long, me brave Johanna."

Having gained the ascendancy, she continued, "And me beautiful son, he must be a gentleman, with learning more than he can accumulate from a rouseabout."

"We'll consider all these things at the proper time."

Bewuck had prospered under Johanna. Wheat, also hay, hides and butter had soared to a fabulous price. There was a ready market for eggs·and poultry. Even feathers were saleable. Johanna had money to send her children to school. Danny was not so great a hero by comparison. Nevertheless he had yarns of the Yackandandah, of the new Colony of Victoria, of the bustling city of Melbourne, alive with rich diggers and their ladies, of men lighting their pipes with bank notes and shoeing their horses with gold. He had sufficient currency to renew leases at Burrabinga, to buy more acres around Bewuck, and make additions to the homestead.

Johanna did not allow her advantage to slip. Robert and Honoria must also go to school in Sydney. Danny gave his consent vaguely, and as a sop because he was wild to be away with stockmen to collect cattle, now worth as much as £20 per head, and all the world was demanding horses. He was also eager to retreat to Burrabinga because of another gift he had brought from the diggings, and which he wished to keep from Johanna as long as possible: a taste for rum. This had grown during long shifts of standing to the waist in cold water until dysentery became prevalent and rum the universal panacea, as well as a disinfectant for polluted drinking water. At Burrabinga he would be able to enjoy his grog, and would no longer refuse his employee's invitations to drink with them. However, he never tippled to the deterioration of his energy and industry.

Having his consent to the education of Robert and Honoria, Johanna cheerfully bade him go. He stipulated that the other two boys should be left to him to rear to pastoral pursuits. For the present they remained with the new London misfit in the school-house beside the bunyip hole.

The ridges of Delacy's territory, and for eighty or a hundred miles surrounding it, were alive with descendants of animals that had early been driven off by the blacks from the overlanders' route. In fenceless days many a beast sought a mate and founded a community in the wilds. In the withering droughts they migrated from the parched plains to the fountful hills; and from the head of the Murray to Monaro, to Bathurst and New England, they mightily increased, sometimes with the aid of well-bred runaways. During years when cattle had been unsaleable they remained on the runs until they died of old age.

Delacy erected trap yards and drafting crushes. Money flowed from effort. Urquhart, himself a straight man, deplored Danny's honesty as extreme, because he refused to confiscate the horses and cattle that drifted to Burrabinga. To Urquhart's remonstrance he would say, "Am I a horse and cattle thief? Sure, weren't min hanged in the old country for lifting a sheep, and am I to risk destroying me character? You can be a lifetime building a good character and lose it in twenty-four hours by a single act of foolishness."

His truthfulness was more than that demanded by common sense. Not another such horse-coper was known from the Murrumbidgee to the Lachlan. When vending he declared the blemishes of his stock before reciting their excellencies. This eccentricity had some reward. People in Sydney sent to him for horses. Novices in buying came to him because he could be trusted. He did not, however, grow as rich as some of his neighbours.

Wealth was not to be wrested from the land without more avarice than Delacy had. The earth has her lean seasons of droughts or plagues, or her times of surplus when demand hangs slack. There were dingoes and disease, and as live stock rose in value with the discovery of gold, bushranging and cattle- and horse-duffing became staple industries in the wilds of Monaro. Danny was a heavy loser to thieves who settled around him.

The family wanted more land at Bewuck, with the mountains as an outlet, but Danny still hoped to persuade Johanna to live at Burrabinga. He put up an abode to replace the burned hut, and made cuttings around the worst pinches. Notwithstanding, there was money to bank, and banks of re-established reputations to engulf Johanna's hoards. She hated to surrender her currency, and Danny failed to extend her partnership to his cheque book. Women's part in the struggle was accepted as their unpaid duty—by women as well as men.

The making a gentleman of Robert, as well as the polishing of Della and Honoria, was expensive, and Delacy was constantly in need of capital.

Robert was the pride of Johanna's heart, and it was her secret ambition that he might take to scholarship, and even return to Ireland and become a priest. He favoured his mother in features. He had her keen black eyes and her nose—the nose of an emperor. He needed it at college when he found himself in a class of select young gentlemen, much his junior in years, but so far in advance in their studies that they ridiculed him as a dunce and a country lout. He had neither wealth nor tony connections, nor was he fashioned to pound his way. Taller than his father, he had the willowy grace that distinguishes the Delacy descendants to this day, and the floss silk black hair, the delicate Delacy hands with the filbert nails.

No word of the agonizing humiliation of his first months escaped into his home letters, because the family were so sure that he was on a superior and enviable plane of existence. Nor would he admit defeat while Della could remain at her exclusive school. He had a weapon in his tongue and found his feet as soon as his prowess with horses earned him the protection of a leading boy whose father kept riding and carriage horses. His mother's generous response to his secret requests for money provided a wardrobe which also helped him to victory.

His brothers followed a different routine. On harvest days they were hullabalooed from bed before dawn, and Harry was so drowsy that he sometimes fell asleep in the wallaby hole in the log fence on his way to bind sheaves, and would not be found until the other workers were returning to dinner at noon. Danny had no mercy on these two children. He had none on himself. He took credit that he did not ask the meanest convict to do what he would not do himself, a procedure which with time has developed a national attitude of hostility toward special rewards for any outsize talent but that of money-making. It was not the procedure to make Delacy a wealthy overlord nor to hold the respect of the servile, who are refreshed by worship of a financial superior, and who can recognize no other. Delacy's superiority was of that quality which is derided, or at best tolerated as eccentricity in a private person, and which, in those dedicated to public service, is violently opposed until it succeeds, and which is posthumously acknowledged by the effigies which make disfiguring bird-roosts in public places.

The education of William and Harry was of the sketchiest, though Danny, son of a schoolmaster, considered tutors indispensable. There was always a sprig of sere leaf of the British upper middle class in the school-house in the orchard. Generally he would be the product of Public School or University, with classic knowledge useless to himself and unwanted by boys destined for the land, but which was pleasant to Delacy in conversation, to which he clung as a mental necessity as stubbornly as his wife clung to elegancies. Some of these tutors were victims of alcohol; all had some cardinal defect due to which they had been jettisoned by their families. Most had as little facility in imparting their superfluous knowledge as they had in enforcing discipline. School hours were relegated to

winter nights or wet days, when an hour or two would be set apart
for lessons by the light of a slush lamp. The walls had wide cracks
that let in the breeze; the boys were more concerned with the
possums that came in between the wall-plate and the bark roof,
than with the Wars of the Roses or Greek mythology, though
Henry VIII was of masculine interest. The hours were further
curtailed by slyly turning on the clock or by inveigling a nostalgic
exile to read national ballads.

The boys were tired and sleepy, whether the harvest were ripe
or only sprouting. Their evening meal—mostly of salt beef and
potatoes—was delayed until they shot a minimum of sixteen possums
each. The possums came at dusk from the pipy trees near by to
feast on the luscious imported wheat so conveniently set in their
habitat. The boys had to be quick or the marsupials scaled out of
gunshot. In the phrase of the day the eucalypts took two men and
a boy to see to the top of them.

The pelts had to be skinned and pegged out with hundreds of
fine nails on logs or walls, but Johanna would not let them
encroach on places adorned with the first "kag" of green paint,
or its successors. Then came the tanning and sewing of skins into
rugs on winter nights, by the light of big fires. Each sewer was
rewarded by the price of a rug. Some of the best brought £5—a big
sum when minors commonly worked for their fathers without wages.

Sometimes a tutor would do his duty during the quarter leading
up to pay-day, because in grotesque surroundings there was more
salt in occupation than in idleness. Thus, despite interruptions
and recreations, William and Harry had a little reading, writing
and "ciphering", and were literate for their day. Harry accumulated
stores of poetry to furnish his isolation and nourish his spirit. Old
expirees, casual labour, contributed tales that had descended from
the *seanachies* and bards of Tara's zenith, and earlier. Some were
familiar with stories of Cormac MacArt, the great king, grandson
of Conn of the Hundred Battles, and son of Art the Lonely, whose
reign was full of plenty and such honesty that there was no need
to guard flocks or to bolt doors. Stories from Gaelic legendry found
fresh voice to the song of the Murrumbidgee and disclosed a glint
of the glories of the Ard-Rights of Eirinn and of the grand *feis*.
The deeds of the Fianna and their immortal hounds, the high test
of learning which they had to reach, as well as those other wood-
craft tests, which young Harry could emulate, were especially
inspiring. The tales lost none of their spell in the garbling, tales
of Nial of the Nine Hostages; tales told originally by Oisin, son
of the chief bard of Fian, and which, though accounted pagan,

could charm the tired Patrick himself; tales which time could not extirpate and which in the language of would-be conquerors still spring fragrant and poetic from the soil of Ireland.

Harry, spellbound beside the roaring log fires, gave the honour anciently due to poets to their tales. Endowed with imagination, he translated dream people to his native forests. They existed for him in the voices of river, wind and rain, or stood in the shadows beyond the firelight—a company of friends that made him love the night. They were of his inner life which he hid from the profane. Oh, that he could be a *seanachie* and recite the deeds of noble men, and himself attain nobility!

The boys were fortunate in Maeve and Doogoolook, who educated them to their environment. Saved by Danny from superstition, they had no fear of the bunyip, and the area had no other terrors. Before he was eight Harry could swim like a binghi. A favourite sport with him and William was to dive towards the middle of the hole in the hope of routing the bunyip* on to the bank. The bunyip had a strong personality during his reign. William and Harry and another younger friend all but saw him one morning.

They had left the catch of their night lines on the table rocks of the fish hole while they sought grubs. On returning they found only the head of a cod which had weighed about ten pounds, and something, which they described as the size of a calf, slipping into the water. Cooees brought Danny and others, and they all saw the undecipherable tracks of an animal leading from the water to the fish head and back into the water.

* The oldest inhabitants of the district are agreed that a bunyip existed and that he was probably a large otter, shy and now extinct; or, that when the rivers remained undisturbed, except occasionally in summer by the blacks, a few seals may have worked their way all the thousands of miles inland from the Bight, to remain in exile until they died of old age.

CHAPTER XI

THE time came when Delacy could put William and Harry to the work of adults.

A large field of wheat that had escaped smut or rust, was saved by vigilance from cockatoos by day and marsupials by night. Much hung on the selling of this grain to a mill at Albury for 17/6, or possibly more, per bushel, and all was not going well with the harvesting. Hannon, who was in charge, was beset by cantakerous old lags whose intention was to pick a quarrel and put the onus of dismissal on the employer. Delacy increased the ration of grog but this did not pacify them. Hannon trembled lest a firestick should be put to the garnered stooks.

The climax came when Delacy was rushing the reapers to beat a thunderstorm. It was as hot as a furnace in the narrow gorge. Flies and sandy blight increased irritation. Usually the meal was served in two shifts in the kitchen, but on this day the men were squeezed at one table, and the reek of dirty sweating bodies, rank tobacco, cabbage and rum was nauseating to all but the inured. One man was given a seat at a side table. He tried to start a disturbance by flinging his plate on the floor and shouting, "I'll not submit to the outrage of being set apart because of what is past in my life."

Delacy seized the gigantic tin teapot and made towards the man. "Pick up your good victuals, you vaygabond haythen, or I'll baptize you to me own taste."

The malcontent, with one glance towards his adversary, who was about half his weight, six inches shorter, and hopping on a peg leg, fled the premises for ever, amid the laughter of his fellows.

Johanna was still without her carriage, though Danny now had two drays, in which the boys were to transport the wheat. They held back on a rising market until the frosts had come, then Danny escorted them up from the homestead to the plateau commanding a view of the ranges southward, and left them to make a daylight start towards that part of the road to Port Phillip which served the upper reaches of the Riverina.

William Delacy, now nearly seventeen, was of staid dependable character, and his shoulder had long been pressed to the wheel of responsibility. He was already clever at training steers, horses and dogs. He worked with more patience than his father, but with equal noise, and could be heard admonishing his creatures a mile distant. He had his father's honesty but was more prosaic, "more practical" said his acquaintances, though Danny was ultra practical in acting as he preached. William's actions contained less of the flights of the wild geese of adventure. He thought more of the immediate return for his enterprises, less of their ultimate concern with destiny.

Harry, nearly two years younger, was an eager laddie, slender as a wand, with delicately chiselled features and Danny's blue eyes, with a drop of Johanna's to deepen them. Never were loins so slim nor backs more flat than the Delacys', but whereas Johanna and Danny were a doll-like pair, the men that sprang from them were all tall.

William was conscientious, and Harry squandered himself in the trust committed to him. William had the best leaders and polers with frisky characters between. Harry's team was steady throughout. Four or five mature spares, tame servitors, walked free, and disloyally (to their own race) horned any youngsters into keeping the pole-chain straight when timidity or rebellion slewed them from the line. William had been on a similar trip with Hannon two years earlier and would have been accounted wanting had he forgotten any turn of the way.

The boys woke to an icy dawn with a wind that would shave a gooseberry—Harry's words—sweeping full across the plateau from the high peaks down Monaro way. When they unrolled from their possum rugs beneath the dray, Harry saw a man taking the bell from his riding horse. A second man was trying to catch William's. These fillies were the reward of heroic labour. Danny abhorred the vice of "horsiness" and sold all his prime geldings, but youth will have its swagger, and these fillies were the apple of the boys' eyes.

Harry rushed towards the robber yelling language that his mother would have asserted was unknown to him. He kicked the man's shins wildly despite a couple of holsters in his belt. With similar recklessness, William ran to rescue his idol. Both lads had Danny's fearlessness.

"You fine young pup! You —— fool! I might have put a bullet in you." Harry was small for his years, he looked childish. The robber remained good-humoured because his Wellingtons had protected his shins.

"You can't have my filly," screeched Harry, who had not been taught to modulate his voice.

"How are you going to stop me?"

"I'll soon show you!" The lad seized his bridle and flung the reins over the filly's ears in such a pelter that the sudden up-jerk of her head sent him sprawling in the swamps. Whack! He was a comical spectacle, feet in air, the rearing filly above him. The bushranger guffawed. The boy was unarmed, his work-marred hands as delicate as a girl's. A kick would have thrown him into the middle of the coming week. He sprang up dripping, frozen, and foolish, but undaunted.

"Hold on," said the man. "If you had your paddy under control, you'd be gamer still, but you'll never make a pug."

Harry's sensitive features betrayed a struggle to hold back tears. William had reached his horse ahead of the other thief, and now cantered up to see what was happening to Harry.

"Are you unarmed, too?"

"Why should I be armed in a free country?" countered William. He recognized the men from descriptions, and was prepared for the loss of both horses.

"This —— young pup is as fresh as a gander," remarked the leader. "Are you going to enter the fillies for the gents' races at Bong Bong? Nullah-Mundoeys, ain't they?"

"Yes," replied Harry, to whom hope suddenly returned. "They're out of Cornet mares by Knobkerrie, and he was by Shillelagh out of Miss Nullah-Mundoey, and she was by Whipstick, and then came the original Nullah-Mundoey."

"Good iron! I don't rob little boys, not when they've been flung by old fearless Danny of the mountains. He parades about unarmed. Tell your old man he's flung a couple of pups as game as himself, and that it was Clark said it. You can keep your mokes. I'll pick up a couple of the same breed from them who don't deserve them."

The boys were elated by this encounter. It lent adventure to their passage as they camped in frost or rain and lived on damper and salt junk, cooked by themselves at night. They had no warm clothing. A poncho of sailcloth protected them from water or wind, as, unconscious of hardship, they thrashed their way in mud or dust, with bullocks that grew tender around the necks and sore-footed as they endured their share of the bovine torture which advanced Australian colonization. Harry survived whooping cough, his vocal convulsions having given more amusement than concern to his fellow travellers.

While the boys were toiling with the drays, Danny went to the Township to take a pack load of skins and to call at the post office. During Robert's stay in Sydney, his mother insisted upon letters being collected at least once a month. A tutor was to be selected from Hennessy's hotel, where there were generally remittance men open for such a post. The clergyman who examined the boys' educational progress, reported that Harry was backward, so he was to renew his studies during the winter nights when he returned with the teams.

Danny chose a soft young fellow in the hotel yard, where he also became enamoured of a carriage. A queer shingle of military aristocracy who had come to inspect the country, had been vanquished by his cardinal enemy, and liquidated his carriage and four horses. The publican offered the vehicle to Danny, half in jest.

Here was the carriage which had been promised to Johanna in the coomb near her old home. She had given up riding, and complained of being a prisoner at Bewuck. Danny decided to take the vehicle home that day. All the talent of the Township, from masters to tag-rag and bobtail, collected to grin at the odd team which was yoked to it, two heavyish pack-horses on the pole and two blood saddle mares as leaders.

The pub groom put the horses in with unholy glee, and the new owner took charge. He was neither whip nor horse-trainer, but through inability to recognize impossibilities, frequently overrode them. The two ladies Nullah-Mundoey never before had been yoked to anything.

"Be careful! They may go mad when you start," warned a more kindly onlooker.

"Arrah! Why should they? Child's play to what those mares have achieved and never showed the whites of their eyes."

"Wait till the collars begin to nip them."

"Fearless Danny only needed a carriage to be king of the Murrumbidgee."

There was admiration as well as baiting in the rude sallies.

"Sure he's as big a swell as the best, and honester than all the others put together, only he's never concerned with howldin' on to schnobbery," said the publican, one Hennessy, a big fat man of Danny's age. He owned the grand hotel and had lately risen to it from a sly grog shop, which, before hotels were licensed, he had kept under cover of the little general store, from which the Township had been hatched as from an egg.

The chorus increased. As the yapping of curs Delacy regarded it, to be dispersed by his horses' heels in the clatter of his enterprises

Never was being more indifferent to criticism, and he was as far above scandal-mongering as a lark's song above a snail's track.

Flowers of originality in eminent men are cherished by the mob as signs of greatness. Originality in the obscure makes him a butt for lesser wits. Danny in his loose slops, clumping on his peg, was a leprechaun figure. He settled his hat full of leaves, with the chin strap jostling his pipe.

"Taking any passengers?" someone called out.

"Too many jackasses for me to accommodate you all, and I never make invidious distinctions among me fellow men, but you can draw lots for the honour of riding with me, and be damned to you."

He called for a chair, which Hennessy himself brought with goodwill. From this Delacy climbed over the wheel and took the reins. He looked around and saw the tutor. "Sure, make yourself a place among the saddles inside."

The young man obeyed, reddening like a cherry.

"Lead out the mares till they see what to do," Danny ordered a native lout, who grinned and remained where he was. He would not align himself with a butt. Danny caught him a flick with his stockwhip, and cackles against the lout brought volunteers. The mares, inured to much, found this too much. They reared into the collars with hysterical desire to leap over the traces. The men at the bit-rings had sufficient neighbourliness to act as a brake on Danny's recklessness. A hardy pair assumed the positions of postillions.

"Leave go now. A sound skelping is the way to dispose a horse to harness."

A second young man dived into the carriage on top of the tutor.

"Sure, iver since the owld man's daughter came home from boarding school the young feller has been squinting at her," observed Hennessy.

"You owld spalpeens, with your experience to balk at a ladylike carriage," exclaimed Danny, who had his own way with bolting horses, proved by experience. With a yell to be heard for a mile in the clear autumn air, he laid the whip about the leaders. They sprang ahead from the flaying thong, but the polers' speed was not dangerous. All the loafers ran to the crest of an eminence. Those with horses rode farther; not every day was there such a lively clown.

Familiar and deafening advice soon assured Delacy's four-in-hand that nothing untoward was happening. The polers were winded through being dragged by the Nullah-Mundoeys. They bowed to domination and hung into the breeching. Danny's disregard of anything but his purpose had added another story to the records.

"It won't be a week till he uses the carriage to cart possum skins out of the mountains," remarked Hennessy.

"I've never seen the beat of him."

"Where did ye iver see his aquil? Whoi, Danny Delacy could tame a woild elephant, and him naught but a nullah-mundoey himself. Not a fear at all, anny more than if he was made of injy rubber."

Not at all timid was the young man pulled into the carriage by the tutor, and who had called to a mate, "Bring my horse when you come."

Gerald Butler, young native squatter, and Walter Dillingham, imported, had a rough passage among the gear until the mares were encrusted with sweat and dust and their shoulders were growing tender. One jibbed. Young Butler revealed himself.

"Wait a moment, Mr Delacy, I'll lead her."

"Did you spring conveniently out of a bush?"

"Out of the carriage. I was one of the jackasses who accepted your invitation."

"Not so much a jackass, I'm thinking, as the right man in the right place."

The gratified young man took the mare's bit-ring.

"He's in a more manly situation than his feyther was behind the trees waiting to see me cattle driven off," thought Delacy, and did not allow the father's character to prejudice him against the son. "Where's me other brave warrior?" he shouted. "Jump out, unless you're glued to the seat, and put a boulder to the wheel."

The man put a stone in front of the back wheel, on to which, however, the carriage backed and saved him from ridicule as a new chum.

The mare continued to jib. She had been trained to tow people up hills, so they tied her tail to the swingle-bar and she pulled thus with spirit to the end of the day, when they descended to the homestead. Danny hacked down a tree and lashed it to the back axle. With stirrup leathers, Butler and the pop-eyed tutor held on to the upper side to prevent capsize. The dogs brought out the family.

"A carriage," cried Jane Hannon.

"Father is driving," said Maeve.

"He's got himself killed again in some new way," moaned Johanna.

"How could he be killed and driving too?" demanded Della.

"Gerry Butler and a strange young man," announced Maeve.

Della withdrew to re-arrange herself. Gerald Butler was the most comely of the Murrumbidgee callers.

"Where are you, me brave Johanna?" shouted Danny. "Come, see the carriage. Now you can drive around in comfort when you have the moind." He was at the foot of the descent across the cultivation paddock. Young Butler was detaching the drag, while the tutor was investigating the damage done to his hands.

"Wan of these days 'tis a circus in full cry ye'll be bringing me, and ye the clown all complete in it," Johanna called with mixed emotions. A real carriage was exciting when her circle had not yet achieved spring carts, but some little trap would have been more manageable. Danny had surpassed himself this time, so he took his pipe from its fastnesses to kiss his wife.

"Sure, ye're getting to smell like a hogshead as well as a tobacco kag," she complained.

"I've had no more than a taggeen, and it a day past. I've brought a young man—sure, I forgot to inquire your name. He can bring Harry on and lend a hand when necessary."

"The carriage certainly makes you the first lady in the district, Mrs Delacy," said Butler, giving her good evening.

The vehicle was placed behind the hen house and protected by a tarpaulin until a house of its own could be built.

Six weeks later Harry and William returned from the wheat expedition, William unkempt and aged for his years, Harry looking like an· ill-treated orphan, but swaggering manfully and unaware that the task had been above his years and strength. Their exploit was soon dimmed by the home-coming of Robert, his education completed. Johanna's idea that her darling could ever be a student would have convulsed his teachers. Nevertheless, he had imbibed from his Sydney sojourn sufficient to gain the ascendancy in his family. Harry basked in his brother's glory.

Harry had his father's tendencies, and, according to William, was "the damnedest fool that ever drew breath". Notwithstanding this plain speech, Harry was fond of William for his underlying kindliness, and because they both had inherited Danny's principle, and lacked respect for any but honest men.

Robert's qualities were not defeated by gauche self-consciousness. At bottom he was perhaps the least generous of the brothers, the least affectionate, but he was a better politician than either, and there were perquisites in cultivating the affections of others—even brothers. He thought Harry a greater fool than did William, but instead of mentioning it so bluntly made capital of Harry's romantic attitude towards him and life. Robert was eighteen, the age at which his father had married. Only a suggestion of beard smutted his lip, but he shaved with ostentation. He could swagger with style, an art denied to William. He was lithe and a light-weight despite his seventy-two inches and well-squared shoulders. The Delacys were race horses rather than cobs, of lean and wiry staying powers through Danny's transmitted lung capacity and hardy rearing.

There Robert's resemblance to his father and brothers ended. He had more qualities than they for rising to eminence. He could enlist others. He had plausible reasons for riding the best horses and undertaking the pleasantest jobs. He remained the darling of his mother's heart. His manners were pleasing after what she had endured from rough employees and the casual Danny. She considered Robert fit to mate with the Governor's daughter.

The wheat money and Robert's homecoming helped Danny's determination to settle in the mountains. The deciding factor rankled. During the winter he had come home from the Township the worse for liquor. His babble had wearied Johanna. He was now forty-six and she forty-seven years old. Her urge for man-flesh had dulled. She craved peace. Years since, she had had to relinquish her day-dream of returning in affluence to the people of her girl-hood. She saw Danny as an insignificant, ineffectual old man, hopping on one leg. His once gallant daring now seemed foolhardiness. Tippling made him insupportable. She had outgrown or out-worn him and was as careless of his feelings as though oblivious to them.

"Ye'r a black-jack and tobacco kag combined, and I have no taste for sleeping with such. I'll make ye a bed in the ind room," she said.

For a moment Danny felt old and defeated. He became aware that he was a cripple. He looked in the glass for the first time in years and was not reassured by the unclassical features ambushed in beard, from which a pipe protruded like an obelisk. The pipe was rank, he decided, and threw it from him. He picked it up again helplessly. It had become part of him.

"I am an old tobacco kag and a rum jar," he murmured in the smallest voice he had ever employed, facing truth as was his wont. He could have reduced Johanna to obedience. The community was behind him, including the Church, and women themselves, but Daniel Brian Robert M. Delacy was gallant. He had been too active for introspection, but he thought now in swift impressionistic style. He decided that Johanna was a trifle "touched". She had been overstrained by what she had undergone at the time of the fire and the death of Kathleen Moyna. She would recover.

No parallel case was known to him. There were women who had cut the painter because they were "loose", or because the husbands were recognizedly unbearable. In either case the odium was crushing. There were milder cases in which the woman's health was a factor, but Danny could not cover his situation by muttering about Johanna's health while she was announcing that she had never been better in her life. She remained casual and assured in a practical piece of feminism, which, as pioneering, eclipsed her achievements in other fields.

Her dumbfounding attitude drove Danny to the Township to a tailor—an emancipist settled there. He ordered a suit "fit for a modest gentleman". He bought also a gentleman's hat, and had a boot made for his delicate foot. When the outfit was ready he rode home in it. The result was reducing. His head seemed to have shrunk in a hat of normal size without the gum leaves.

Johanna was convulsed. "Sure, ye've shrunk back to childhood ahead of time. What has come to ye? Ye look like Harry in a false beard."

Danny murmured concerning the need of a suit when he sat on the jury. A big brooch remained forgotten in the pocket of the waistcoat. He bawled an order to put the horses in over night in readiness for big doings, and bustled in and out of store and harness room until a late hour. A civilizable being in a race largely composed of anthropoids—that was his only demonstration.

Sophistry supervened to comfort him. Johanna herself would lose socially by her untoward conduct. His absence at Burrabinga would defeat the curious.

CHAPTER XII

IF the withdrawal of land grants in 'thirty-one was manipulated by those with capital and influence, the Robertson and Duffy Acts redressed the grievance thirty years later in New South Wales and Victoria. The small man was given his chance. The free selectors closer-settled the vast empty squattages and penetrated even to Delacy's province. The inexperienced were often to lose their all and abandon their nests in the wilderness; some were to be squeezed out by the big squatters; others were to harry the flanks of the squatters and drive profitable bargains; more were to establish desirable estates.

Delacy applied for blocks at strategic points for himself and sons. To fulfil the regulations he engaged a man to build huts. To employ substitutes was against the Delacy principle, but "dummying" became an avocation, and through this Delacy added to his retainers.

One day a forbidding looking man of fifty appeared at Bewuck and called Delacy down below the pigsty. This was the man whom the Fullwoods and Butlers had set to the work of eating Delacy out in the beginning. He averred now that Delacy was the only white man he had ever met, and offered himself as a dummy to secure part of Burrabinga run.

"You would be more congenially suited at that with wan of your owld friends, Butler or Fullwood," said Delacy.

O'Neill then threw himself on Delacy's mercy. It was difficult for him to find employment because of his bad name as an old lag who also had been colonially convicted. His early patrons dared not employ him; they had to be more careful of their respectability. O'Neill had been sent from Ireland for some act of just rebellion, but had done fifteen years in New South Wales for "bad work wid a horse". To one who had gibed at him as a horse thief, he replied scornfully, "Never in me loife had I anny timptation to another man's goods. Moind ye'r own step."

Rumour fitted to him the case of a man of violent temper at Liverpool, enamoured of a girl who played with him. In days when horses were rare, and he a ticket-of-leaver, O'Neill rode as a gentle-man's trainer. Pretty Kitty Magee led him on shamelessly, and like

Young Lochinvar, he one day invited her to his croupe. Kitty dissolved in giggles.

"Since last I was talking with ye, I've been promised a carriage and pair."

At that O'Neill spurred his horse on to her. She was crippled.

Delacy saw in the Free Selection Act an opportunity for the outcast to re-establish himself on a horse camp south from Burrabinga. Delacy was nobly forgiving of human mistakes, and no intimation of his ever confirmed the facts which he had from O'Neill.

"Has he committed anny fresh crime that ye exile him anew?" was Johanna's question. "The loneliness there would send a man mad."

"Och, he'll come down for rations once a fortnight," said Danny, who feared not even loneliness, though of all men he was the most sociable. "Am I not helping him to honest indipindince, opening up fine country for the generations that come after?"

"The generations won't be much concern of poor old Larry O'Neill, and there are some not over-joyed by what happens to them in dingo country."

O'Neill set out with the sawyer-carpenter, the three Delacys, and the tutor. Doogoolook was to put the finishing touches to his foster brothers' education as unexcelled bushmen. As an afflicted boy in a strange civilization, Johanna had depended on him as she could not have done on a whole white youth. As many another of his race he did not fail in his trust, and has gone without medal or monument to add to the rich aura of his incalculable country.

Robert remained at Bewuck to assist Hannon, and Johanna was content that Danny should take his goslings to the hills, where an arduous life awaited them. Not only were there encroaching selectors, but bands of fossickers treated Delacy to a gold-rush at Bullock Gap. Gunyahs and tents met him on the edge of Burrabinga north when the spring mustering took him that way. Before many months, however, their occupants disappeared to a bigger rush on the Eucumbene.

The snow was deep that year on the highlands as early as June, and one night Delacy was camped in a stringy-bark hut on the deserted goldfield preparatory to meeting the boys next morning at trap yards fifteen miles distant. He was snug in his possum rug when aroused by a voice too human for a dingo. It came nearer. It reached the door of the hut. Delacy arose and stood on the door log, clearly outlined by the firelight.

"Anny wan there? Is it murder, or what? Speak up!" he bawled.

A foreign voice squeaked, "By Cli, Boss, give 'em lelp?"

A tall form fell at Delacy's feet. He dragged it in as well as he could. "By damn! Wait till I get me leg."

The firelight revealed a Chinese, whom Delacy drew to the warmth. The man's extremities were chilblained so Delacy applied neat's-foot, and tendered damper sopped in hot tea. The stranger then slept from exhaustion in his host's rug while the host himself lay almost in the ashes. Delacy had acquired another picturesque associate.

Wong Foo could not be taken to the trap yards next morning. Mongols were not horsemen. A suffering one on a packsaddle was not practicable. A man's health was more to Delacy than the capture of a mob of cleanskins. Explanations were impossible. Delacy lacked savvy in broken language. With any foreigner he roared ever louder and louder until he was winded and the victim bewildered. The stranger trusted his rescuer sublimely as he was put on the mare.

Arrived at the homestead, after a journey difficult for both, Danny administered the general panacea and bandaged the nipped feet and fingers. He placed Wong in his own berth, and laid himself on the floor.

"What else would a man do, and calling himself a Christian? No man has the rights of neighbourliness if he balks at colour, class, or even character."

The notice on the hut door aroused the curiosity of the other musterers, and their laughter crackled when later Wong Foo's face looked from their father's bunk. They had not seen a Chinese so magnificent of pigtail. At first sight he was as ugly, as non-human as a joss, but Danny insisted, "He's a whoite man, I predict. He has a foine expression."

"What are you going to do with him?" inquired William.

"He'll make a mate for Doogoolook," piped Harry.

"I turn him over to you. Shall you tie a firestick to his pigtail? Use your moinds—if you have anny?"

"Oh, hell, I don't know," said William.

"By damn! None of that bad language or I'll take a waddy to you."

During this colloquy Wong Foo beamed upon his hosts.

"At any rate he's a cheerful old cove. He'll be good company," chirped Harry.

"I reckon he'll be worth his tucker for that," conceded William. "If he's kept lying around handy, he might come in useful."

Company, entertainment, was almost as prized in solitary days as a good horse.

"A pity he's not more intelligible," said Danny. "Maybe he's full of enlightening conversation if we could tap it."

The Oriental mind remained unknown to the Delacys, but legends indicate that Foo felt himself born again as a blood brother of the family, consecrated to that best-wearing fabric of the emotions—friendship. The question of inequality did not occur to him. How could it in light of Danny's reception of him? The unique alliance was never spoiled, rooted as it was in the goodwill, the sterling character of both parties, and protected by the inability of each to use too searchingly the other's tongue.

"Missa Delacy belly good man!" Wong would explain. His breeding was so good that he deferred to his patron as he walked around with him. Doogoolook, at first suspecting a usurper, walked on the other side of his foster father, but soon grew friendly, and the inimitable trio was long a decoration to the district.

"I know," shouted Harry one night, "Wong Foo can drive the carriage you brought Ma, and Doogoolook can sit beside him to open the gates."

"Small moinds delight in small jokes," said Danny, "but you must be above catering to them. Get out your bocks now and the tutor can exercise your mental capacity."

The stranger's feet and fingers quickly healed, and then he did wonderful things to the unfinished house. He also started a garden. He tried to explain his need to return to Bullock Gap, but Danny boomed and boomed that he would be lost again, and Wong was forced to desist for a time.

A stockman opportunely arrived who had had three years on the diggings with Chinese, and in pidgin interpreted that Wong was twenty-six years of age and had come from Canton, the City of Lambs.

"I thought he was a hundred, by Cli!" interposed Harry.

"He reckons he's a chemist in his own city," said Aldon, the stockman.

"By damn! He's a man of education, I knew it!" cried Danny.

Having tastes above the coolies who came to the goldfields, Foo desired to fossick alone on Burrabinga run. Danny suggested other fields as more lucrative, but the matter was determined for Foo by the nearness of the Delacys. Foo had left his gear in one of the deserted huts and was sure he could find it if taken back to Delacy's camp. Danny ordered a second mare, the most sluggish salt lumper available.

"I never saw a Chow riding," remarked William.

"You can see this wan," said Danny.

Wong Foo would ten thousand times rather have walked, but was too surely a gentleman to say so. The Delacys rode. He too must ride. There for ever he renounced peasant pottering with a bamboo pole. With the yokels from Europe this Asiatic was transformed willy-nilly into a horseman, if not of one sort, then of another. With much vociferation Danny got his pupil from a fallen log to the back of the horse.

"He's going pale, by Cli, under the yaller," giggled the boys. Even Danny was not above laughing, so ridiculous were equestrian ineptitude and timidity. The rouseabouts and the birds all around chortled deliriously. Menura across the river mimicked them all impartially. There was merriment in the taming of a continent where even the birds laughed. The Oriental conformed by raising a sickly grimace.

Doogoolook rode ahead, turning now and again to show his noiseless grin. Foo held on to the pommel and lay as flat as he could. His legs dangled useless as those of a wooden doll. Each time the horse lurched from Danny's larrups, Wong thought his hour had come, but he was stoically silent.

Wong selected one of the deserted huts. Delacy had a squatting licence for that part, and Wong had a miner's right, and thus he was doubly established.

With the boom in live stock, two young men named Angus came and took up the station between Keebah and Burrabinga. It was called Birrabee by the blacks because the sand of the creek was infested with fleas.

"Hasn't it been my ambition to lead the way for population?" observed Delacy. "And sure, covetousness bursts the bag."

If on the wrong side of matrimony, Delacy was on the top side of the horse trade. He had been improving his stud for years, and at the time of Johanna's disturbing action had a champion sire, Bewuck Nullah-Mundoey. A strain of Arab was evident in his head and the clean muscular barrel, and in his strength and speed, but the horse was sixteen hands. On the flats of Burrabinga was a crowd of fillies and colts ripening into walers of reputation. There was respect for the Nullah-Mundoey blood among spielers and stockmen.

The last of the tutors went, leaving Harry in possession of his library. The huts were up on the selections, the new house at the main homestead—a mansion of four rooms—was completed. Despite hard work, Danny's mind had been riveted on the provoking frowardness of Johanna in the hope that during two years her tantrums would have subsided. Bewuck called. He drafted out the biggest bullocks and maturest walers for market, and set out to be at home for Christmas.

William and Harry were left at Burrabinga. Doogoolook always attached himself to Delacy with the surety of the best heeler. " 'Twill be easier to tell the story with Wong as illustration," he explained, and rode out to Bullock Gap to collect his second gentleman-in-waiting. By this time Wong could at least mount on a horse, and Delacy had supplied him with suitable beasts at equitable prices.

Bewuck was to wear a new air to meet him.

He had scarcely been out of sight when Robert assumed charge of his mother and Hannon. He laughed at the carriage beside the hen house, but recognized its social possibilities, and began his career as a whip by training a pair of saddle mares to run in traces. He further set men to grade the dray track so that the carriage could ascend to the plateau without overturning. When he was ready, he put Hannon on the box beside him and drove his mother to the Township.

Then began for Mrs Delacy the nearest approach to happiness she had known since the illusions of her teens. For nearly thirty years she had been dragged after Danny's rough-riding kite, she whose ambition was a conventional city existence. Her soul was sick of colonizing rigours. Squatting, pioneering, grazing, bush-whacking—settling by any of its classifications—to her taste was little above bushranging in quality or status. Danny's democracy was full of trials to her. Coming from the educated classes in the old country, Delacy was entitled to the best society the Colony afforded, but he was destitute of social ambition. To Johanna's irritation he allowed emancipists to climb past him while he was a brother to any man who cared to use his hospitality. Danny was a separate soul and too engrossed in the struggle of home-building to cultivate any society as society *per se*. The haughtiest and humblest welcomed him on his sorties in his district, and he called upon all grades impartially.

Few came to Bewuck, leagues off the main highway. "The raggle-taggle can't injure me," Johanna used to think, "but 'twill be different when the girls are ripe to marry."

With Danny risking the necks of his two sons in a wild region, she felt she had earned the right to Robert and her daughters. Robert was up to her dearest expectations. His years of schooling in Sydney had made him as dashing a young man as the ranks of the corn-stalks—or native born—could show. The business of Bewuck, as distinct from its labour, fell to him because of his address; he arrogated to himself all transactions that took him to the Township on horseback instead of with the pack-horses and bullock drays, and was credited with "having a head on him".

All the Delacy boys had wit, but Robert had a tip on his tongue to prick dumber persons to his purpose through fear of ridicule. His gallant swagger took the eyes of women, and he had enough for all. He did not discredit the bunyip nor the ghosts in the crossing; he was not himself free from fear of such things. His mother could now admit her tremors.

The Township had grown with the discovery of gold. There were attractions for Robert in its hotel parlours, and also in the bedrooms, before he left his teens. He differed from the others of his name by an embracive taste in wenches. Those who disliked him—and he had more enemies than the others put together—said he was a flash fellow, lascivious with women. Flash was a man's word never used by ladies nor of ladies, though they might be doubtful, but it fitted Robert in his adolescence. Sly and uninstructed, he was indebted to servant girls for the most vital education of his youth, and he shrewdly left others to fight his battles. His staunchest champion was young Harry.

Robert cultivated his mother. He warmed her lonely heart adrift from family moorings, and which had never found sanctuary in Danny's impersonality and selflessness. Handsome and smartly dressed, Robert renewed her life. His indifference to higher education was forgotten in the joy of his companionship and protection. It was unthinkable to her that he should be squandered on some hussy. In the absence of worthy mates, she cultivated the least unworthy at Glenties and Heulong. She encouraged Gerald Butler for Della. Old Butler was unequivocally among the gentry, and his ruthless financial tactics made him prosperous. Della was rising in the twenties unwed, which surprised her mother, because she was good-looking and sprightly. Admirers were plentiful, but Della was inhibited by a love dream dating from her term at school, where she had become infatuated with a cornet in the —th. He never saw Della except *en masse* as the school crocodiled abroad with its instructresses, so he could not respond, but the image of a smart uniform was a fixation in the heart of the girl from Murrumbidgee solitudes.

Danny and his companions dismounted by the new stables one December day when the jubilation of birds arose in the orchard, and the voice of the river and its hamadryads made silvery music in an aromatic world.

"I've come to invite you to the new home, sure, me country seat at Burrabinga," he said in greeting.

"The Saints preserve us! Ye have a new clown in your circus," exclaimed Johanna.

Wong Foo bowed and beamed. He had gold in his pockets to be made into jewellery for the ladies. His hair had been cut in colonial fashion to mark his adoption by Delacy. Johanna was in high spirits. Some of her youthful vivacity had revived, but Danny was not sure that she was welcoming him with open arms.

"Sure, we can't treat Wong as a serf. He will have to sit with us for meals. He can sleep in the ind room. He's an educated man and a Christian haythen, if ever there was wan."

There! That would dispose of the end room!

He was astonished by the improvements. Paint brightened doors and gates. The house had additions. Johanna had a parlour with a carpet and a suite of the horsehair furniture she had coveted years before. The earthen floors had all disappeared. Danny generously admired everything.

When the evening meal was served, Maeve was cooking, while a girl brought in the dishes. To these had been added a cruet with a dozen bottles and a set of dish-covers. There was a chiffonier as a substitute for the sideboard with the foxes' heads at Cooley Hall, and on it were displayed a toast rack, glasses, and an epergne.

The girl was a shepherd's daughter. Johanna was a disciplinarian in turning a gurrl into a surrvant. Robert was at the head of the table, carving in assured style, and at the end of the meal he toyed with a pencil-case in a topside manner. Danny was proud of the way Della queened it among the tea cups. He repeated his invitation to Burrabinga.

Johanna laughed. "I'll go up when me carriage can bowl along a proper road. I've had enough of scrambling into that backward place."

"A couple of accomplished navvies would soon grade the road."

"I'd need evidence, me vehicle not to be bounding like a corruk in a torrent, with men hanging on to it trying to rescue it from the rocks, and me rattled about inside like a pea in a pannikin till I had a skin full of sore bones, if not shattered entirely."

Danny went to Johanna's room at bedtime and remarked conversationally, "Aren't you a little severe on the girl?"

"A surrvant is better for being kept in her place."

"But what is a servant's place? What is anny wan's place but what he can make it?"

"I'm furrm that a surrvant shan't have my place, and me to be waiting on her." Presently she said. "Ye'r bed is ready for ye in the ind room."

Danny was checkmated. "Wong Foo was to go there."

"Sure, ye insisted that I should accept him as a gintleman and an aquil at me table. Ye would surprise me if ye would object to his sleeping across the room from ye."

Daniel Brian Robert M. Delacy could face a charging bull without a tremor, but Johanna Cooley had the upper hand of him. He could not raise a clamour in the hearing of Wong Foo, who beamed and beamed. He retired with his protégé to the end room. He was unable to explain that his wife was—well, by all the pipers, what was there to explain? His business was his own, but, as he snuffed out the light, he hoped that Wong Foo would think separate apartments the fashion for husbands of the best carat on the Murrumbidgee.

To disguise Johanna's attitude from himself he was impelled to extra energy, if that were possible. He quickly discerned that too much time had been given to elegancies and amenities at the expense of fundamentals to be profitable, but excused Robert on account of inexperience. Besides, he was so perfect in his mother's eyes, and so confident, that Danny hardly knew how to cope with him. He pointed out the top-heaviness of the youth's management. Robert plausibly agreed, and expressed his intention of tackling various things immediately. He had done what he could to arouse his mother. She had been melancholy but now she had an interest in her house and garden, and visited the neighbours. The novelty of this bemused Danny for the moment.

"Moi, oh, moi," he murmured, as Johanna's side of the case now came to him. He felt let-down that she had not confided in him, but, without rancour, looked inward and blamed himself. His disposition was pure wool throughout. His brave Johanna must have her desires in the homestead and in the housekeeping. He would support them. Johanna would by and by return to normal.

He ordered a holiday to the Township. Johanna, Maeve and Della were to go inside the carriage. Robert was to drive with Wong beside him. The trip out of Burrabinga had so wounded Foo that stoicism could not hide his state. Robert was not brave enough to confess that he had been employing Hannan as coachman, and Danny's training made him endure the Chinese.

"They'll think he is my footman," he chuckled to his mother.

"He can't talk enough to explain." Robert's Sydney years had partially liberated him from local opinion. He would go his own way and be damned to the criticism of the tag-rag—while he did not come to grief.

Danny and Doogoolook capered ahead and democratized the carriage. Danny could have turned a hearse into a family coach without embarrassment. The pack-horses and miscellaneous collection of dogs careered ahead into the backyard of Hennessy's hotel, their advent enlivening the Township.

Robert escorted his mother on his arm across the yard to the entrance door and thence to the ladies' parlour, winking as he went at the barmaid and the house girl. Danny had rarely been situated to take Johanna on his arm. Geography had defeated him. Since the loss of his leg he was no figure for a pageant of ladies in crinolines, but here was Robert doing the stylish thing. He was waiting to do it again on the straggling street as Johanna went to the general store. How happily she bowed and condescended to the Fullwoods and the Butlers, who also happened to be in town.

Gerald Butler seemed to spring out of nowhere as he had sprung out of the carriage on the day of its *début*, and offered his arm to Della in imitation of Robert. Wong curvetted near to Robert as well as his infirmities permitted. He recognized the leader of the family.

Doogoolook and Maeve were for Danny to escort. "Oh, moi, oh, moi!" he murmured, wistfulness invading him, but only momentary. He boomed at Doogoolook. He had a repertory of signs, but in moments of stress could not contain his voice. He handed sovereigns to all the women. He bought every one material for an outfit from the store, and ordered an extra keg of rum for rations.

He and Robert had entertainment in taking Wong to the tailor and the saddler. Danny gave copious advice, which bewildered Wong, who pointed to Robert and insisted upon being a copy. What was the good of a flash turn-out to regale the dingoes at Bullock Gap, Danny boomed, but it was lost on Wong. He was still young and was having amazing experiences. He was nearly Robert's height, and was excited by Robert's swagger. He would have assumed one like it but for the effect of the hard journey. He chose a showy saddle and Robert was flattered by this imitation.

"They'll think he's my illegitimate brother or uncle when he's fully rigged," he observed.

"Humph!" said Danny.

Wong's deference to age kept Danny well in the picture too, and

Danny was proud of Robert's style and "the head he had on him", only, when he was about to project himself upon the stage, Robert would be acting a leading part so that his father's energy returned upon himself like the wuff from a slackening sail. He took a number of nobblers that evening and was excited and loud in political and poetical dissertation.

The hotel room had a large double bed, but Johanna objected to tobacco and rum as perfumes, and rested on an ottoman and let Danny snore by himself. He did not snore as a matter of fact. Johanna's contempt sobered him and he lay awake and planned immediate return to Burrabinga. He had meant to spend the summer at Bewuck, but now decided that Hannon and Robert could be left to carry on as before.

At breakfast next morning he said to Della, "Can you be ready to come to Burrabinga with me and housekeep?"

Gerald Butler looked at Della, so for the effect on him, she said she would love to go.

"Are you going to drive up, Mr Delacy?" he inquired. "You will need me to hang on to the vehicle again."

"There's always need for a good man annywhere," said Danny. "Why don't you take up a run on the other side of me? There's a crowd bound that way now, and I'd sooner the dayvil I know."

"I shall take a look at it, at any rate," said Gerald.

Johanna believed that marriage was the natural end of women, but was not disturbed by Della's indifference to her suitors. All the district could see that she had numerous chances. Johanna defended her with many a quip when people rallied her on remaining unwed, and had a dream about her ultimate disposal, which had been transferred from Robert. A handsome daughter, who could have married well, would be a more desirable bride of the Church than a disappointed failure.

A week's restraint from riding was necessary for Wong Foo, and when he was ready to take the track his horse was fitted with the new saddle and bridle and a gaudy saddle-cloth. Wong had boots and spurs and a town hat, like Robert's, in which he looked quaint indeed. Johanna had accepted him. He had done wonders for her garden, and presented her with a set of earrings and a massive brooch with dangles, which had a cavity for hair at the back and a frame for a photo before. " 'Twill hold Robert's photo nicely," said she.

"Better have Wong's hair at the back," suggested Robert, which shocked and delighted his mother.

Della was relieved to be going to Burrabinga. Inquiries as to whether she intended Honoria to outstrip her were not enough to drive her into marriage without love, but she would be glad to escape them. Her mother was acquiescent. Della would mature safely at Burrabinga, and Honoria would be home from Sydney at Easter. Johanna insisted that Bella Rafferty, the girl she had trained, should go with Della.

"She must have wan of her own sex, not to be imprisoned in that lost hole with only a black and a haythen, and ye'r feyther lacking the circumspection of an eft."

Bella was avid for adventure with Miss Della, and rode gaily by her side, with Doogoolook and Wong as equerries. Gerry Butler suffered Danny's conversation.

The Urquharts held them for two days for company. Danny had much talk with Urquhart. Agnes and Janet, Jessie and Donald were eager for the second generation of Delacys. The young men showed Gerry that he could not have the accomplished Della to himself. Also present were Tom and Ned Angus. Tom was the smart young man from the Victorian side of Monaro, who had taken Birrabee, between Urquhart and Delacy. Ned was fourteen, but already with a noticeable moustache. He became page to Della, who used the sunny good-natured boy to keep her adult admirers at a distance.

Doogoolook took Danny away behind the stables and staged a pantomime of a man with a revolver, using the signs for bad man. Danny grasped that neither Tom nor Ned were bad, but had a bad man behind them. He put the charitable construction on it. "It's wan of those things that will have to develop or die out," he said. It was in the maturing pattern of his life, which, so far, had been as uncomplicated as a windlass.

Burrabinga was no longer inaccessible and did not remain remote with two pretty young women singing about a house with girly curtains on glass windows, "crockery" on shelves, a white tablecloth for meals, and boards on the main floors.

Gerald stayed a week watching Della and doting on her house-keeping. "Surely," he mused, "she must take me soon now for fear of being an old maid."

CHAPTER XIII

In his transition from parent of nestlings to middle-aged man maintaining his manhood among maturing sons, Delacy ran parallel with the progress of the Colony.

Rebellion had early thrown out the "Rum Corps" and burst the shell of the garde-major regime. Land grants to the favoured had ended twenty years later. The financial doldrums of the 'forties, the momentum of the golden 'fifties, more recently weathered, advanced a spirit of robust democracy.

No section of society can maintain aristocratic amenities and elegancies without a submerged race, whether slaves of another breed or the unprivileged of its own, to do the hard and menial labour. Australia began with manacled slaves, mostly misdemeanants, many of whom were bedevilled into irreclaimable outlaws by archaic officialdom and its right to prescribe the lash, but many factors operated against the continuance of this ancient social composition. Wentworth and his colleagues were early leaders in its disruption. Distance from old-world authority and traditions of serfdom, and the scarcity of population of any kind from which to draft menials, coupled with inebriating opportunities for virile humanity loosed into an unspoiled continent, were defeating to class demarcation. Due to a dearth of well-bred females, the difference between freemen and emancipists was sunk in unions among the native born. Landed gentry and budding plutocracy were invigorated by marriages with the progeny of outlaws, in whose veins was some of the hardiest and most adventurous blood in the human race. Freedom and space, which in a virgin continent demanded courageous resourcefulness, sharpened wits and ingrained self-reliance in the people, and their isolation had, at its inception, an expansive influence.

Wentworth's demand for autonomy, and later the surging equality inevitable among the diversified congregations of freemen under the compulsion of gold-rush condition, smashed the aristocratic assumption in Australia and left an indelible stamp on Australian behaviour. With the passing of the earliest "old hands" the national idiom had been democratically fixed, its spirit a fresh attempt at egalitarianism, the brothers of the Utopia to be at least as equal as blood brothers under primogeniture. Distinctive national characteristics, some of them paradoxical, were being ingrained by the force of environment.

Conditions, generally, were against the squattocracy entrenching itself as a squirearchy. The squattocracy it had to remain, with the difference between the Australian Bush and the English County so firmly marked that the Australian squatter and his missus—save in lamentable examples—have always been noted for a physical independence, a dignified ability to fend for themselves, resembling that of the higher animal world.

Thus in attacking, with single-handed hardihood, the wilderness beyond the fringe of the transplanted squirearchy, Delacy was a symbol and a portent of an Australia which still pecks at its shell a hundred years after his arrival. His practice of equality with all men was part of a continent-wide experiment, which, when Delacy was in his grave was to flower in measures of political freedom and protection for the ordinary man which raised the personnel of the Australian working class to an unprecedented level and then left it shoaled for lack of continuing inspired leadership.

Absence of backward breeds diminished the flunkey class; the transformation of the peasant element was in part the contribution of the horse. No man can remain a peasant and go a-horse. Willy-nilly the blood saddle-horse will limber him out of his peasant characteristics. This four-footed brother cannot supply what Nature omitted, and change dunces into intellectuals, but he can lighten their bovine peculiarities.

Horses! Horses!

The whole population took to horse. Wishes were horses from the 'forties onward.

Those congenitally unsuited to excel in horsemanship nevertheless climbed on to nags and were forbearingly carried out. Even Delacy's Chinaman used an aristocratic Nullah-Mundoey. The stodginess of the yokels from Europe was swiftly massaged into something more flexible. The bumpkin was exercised towards a swagger. The galoot, for good or ill, was transformed into a stockrider, a jockey, a spieler, a drover, a horse-breaker, a horse-coper, a horse-breeder—a caballero of one kind or another. He plodded no more on foot. Only derelicts walked.

The man at one with light horses may be a brave dashing gentleman at large, a cavalry officer at heel, a soulless undersized simian or any of the intermediate grades, but he ceases to be a peasant. Australia has remained a peasantless Commonwealth, a peonless community.

Cavalier qualities were heightened in the Australian by the class of horses available. He rode no mustangs with strawberry hides like those of their horned brothers, but animals with a dash of good blood. The brumby of Australian beginnings was an escaped blood on one side of his family tree. Nevertheless, the dearth of menials, which forced pioneer tasks upon the squatter, likewise saved the yokel from developing into a full-blown caballero. The Australian horseman lacked the leisure and the arena furnished with peons and flunkeys in which to develop picturesque flourish in manners and to pursue *amour* as a fine art. Complementary to his responsibilities as wood-and-water joey and general rouseabout, all the pioneer women, who pulled their weight on the frontier, had to cope with toil which in Great Britain was relegated to "general slaveys".

The rough rider had little time for serenades and genuflexions, his lady less to accept them. That perhaps is why the Australian has been described as the world's worst lover, though he developed his own commendable qualities and habits. Australian women, though inured to hardship and deprivation, had true mateship and the large measure of marital faithfulness attendant upon monogamy enforced by conditions; the dignity of equal citizenship was early theirs.

Delacy, freeman by the accident of parentage as well as by the richer endowment of mental and spiritual independence, reared his family when the Colonies were expanding towards Commonwealth—not, however, to be consummated until fifty years later—and he reared them on horseback.

The Delacys were woven into the great days of the horse, when he was transporter in two senses, when all release, romance, adventure, travel, hung on his withers. His usage demanded ability and daring and included all the exhilarating swagger invested in furnishing the superbest of creatures in hogskin and silver. His was a high destiny which remained unchallenged for half a century.

Johanna's forbears gave their male children a horse at seven, and a sword and spear. Regardless of sex, the Australian bush child had a horse long before he was seven. Children went a-horse in the parents' arms before they could sit up. At an earlier age they rode with their undefeatable mothers to be born, for though property rights for women on the Murrumbidgee had not then advanced far beyond Brehon law, the exigencies of pioneering put women on horseback. A lop-sided saddle and long robes were indispensable to constrain female limbs to spurious femininity, but were not entirely discommoding.

The Australian Alps came near to being populated in the decades succeeding the gold-rushes. Not only were there squatters, selectors and fossickers. Horse shooters were present to do away with thousands of horses. (Horsehair furniture was fashionable, to tickle the bare legs of children.) There were kangaroo shooters and those who slaughtered the lyre-bird. The mountains were alive with these fairy creatures. American gold-seekers of the 'fifties remained to fossick through the 'sixties, and saw the trade in their tails.

No one thought of conserving anything. Men worked to the limit, grunting with effort. Women bore children without restraint and thought it God's will. When jellied, fly-blown human backs had the sanction of society, there was no tenderness towards animals, no artistic and scientific realization that in Australia's living unique flora, fauna and avifauna were masterpieces beyond anything she can ever contribute to museums and galleries. Here was a wonder continent, a vast garden of Eden free from sin and disease, left intact by the aborigines. The aim was to rifle it, exploit it in greedy haste. People unable to project themselves beyond the ancient soul-case wrought for them by the inspired members of their race through a hundred generations in Europe were driven by their immediate needs to uproot Australia, to tame it into a semblance of familiar fields and towns. And there was abundance for all. Fire the forests, destroy them, man was merely as an ant against them. Millions of square miles of the stateliest trees in creation remained. Exterminate Menura for his tail regardless of his magic powers of mimicry. Snare and trap the possums, the kangaroos and all the marsupial tribes, droves of them still appeared. Nemesis was not in that generation, nor the next.

That generation earned by sweat, endurance and deprivation the right to a harvest of some kind, salted with a little swagger. It lies forgotten now, while a less-inspired host of exploiteers, without hard toil, reaps where the old hands blazed the track in sturdy if ignorant hardihood.

Kiandra and Adelong, the leading goldfields of Delacy's area, provided a market for beef, for working bullocks, for every kind of horse. The Delacys profited, so did the Anguses of Birrabee and the Urquharts of Keebah, and many another. That region appealed to the native born. It was rather beyond immigrants unskilled in bushcraft.

The influence of the Urquhart girls, and Della and her hand-maiden Bella Rafferty, was to transform the hobbledehoys of their runs into blades who gave time to boots and horse gear, and naïve and sometimes obscene speculation upon the mysteriousness of women. Tom Angus was a model. He had travelled and knew the Victorian side and Port Phillip as well as Port Jackson. Down about Rose Hill and Liverpool he had learned the niceties of pacing horses, the social graces of addressing ladies without utter confusion, and he set the fashion in all that swagger, beyond the Murrumbidgee.

CHAPTER XIV

"ONE door never shuts but another opens," observed Johanna.

The shut door was that of her friend Mr Moore, who had died during Robert's final term at College. Johanna's youthful annoyance had sold Bandalong Station and departed for Dublin to rejoin his brother, who had refused to return to Australia years before on completing his education at Trinity College.

The new door opened by grace of Robert, whose career at Bewuck revived his mother's spirit. She ascended from her gorges to take her place in the pastoral society of the country that stretched away to Goulburn on one side and Monaro on the other. It had chafed her to be held back to take the dust of expirees. Danny's notion that a man should be judged by character regardless of financial or social success, was to Johanna rankly foolish. Who was Danny to judge men? He had no special rights in divination. It had been lively enough for him, leathering about the country, but she had been restricted to uncouth loneliness beside the waterhole of evil reputation in the sombre river with its lorn casuarinas.

Robert took her to call on the Butlers of Glenties and on the new and stylish owners at Quebarra and at Bandalong. She had the satisfaction of refusing her acquaintance to Mrs Wells, farther up the river, because her father had been a convict. When the river permitted, Robert set her on a gentle horse and visited the Fullwoods of Heulong.

The Fullwoods displayed the portrait of an ancestor in an Elizabethan ruff, as well as a sword, and a few pieces of table silver bearing a crest, and were authentically from the flanges of the squirearchy, whereas Johanna's parent was Irish and somewhat of a squireen through being the younger son of a younger son too many times in succession in a subject country.

In the Heulong family were two daughters of suitable age for Robert, who was not at first aware of his mother's hopes, though the association pleased him because he too found his father's democratic eccentricities distasteful. He was, and felt himself the equal of the crackest young men in the district, and in a position to make intimates among them as he willed. He could resist few women unless they were grandmothers or as ugly as a mormops. He did not

relish remarks about himself as coachie, but when Grace Fullwood
came to stay at Bewuck and sat on the box beside him, he was
compensated. His gallant manner was taken for serious attention
by Grace Fullwood, but little Mollie McCathie at Hennessy's pub
was more seductive. She was generous, and Robert was a taker of
all gifts from women. The tall insipid Grace, with a nose like his
own, only sharper, and weak blue eyes and sandy hair, was out-
classed by the plump and ticklesome Molly of the button nose and
darting wit. She was merely the orphaned niece of the publican,
but that gentleman had orthodox Irish ideas for her behaviour
and kept a shrewd eye on her admirers. Maidens were in demand,
and Hennessy had ambitions.

Johanna enjoyed making purchases in the Township as much as
Robert enjoyed other entertainment to be found there. Her turkeys
throve like the rabbits of later years on the grass and grass-hoppers
of the river flats. There were no enemies but native cats and crows,
and Robert perfected his marksmanship on the crows. His mother
was glad to give him the latest swagger in firearms. She would have
felt safer in the beginning had the blacks been kept in their place
(or out of it, as Danny would have maintained), by lethal weapons
instead of conciliation, though Danny's policy had been vindicated
by results.

Mrs Delacy was not any longer afraid of the blacks, though they
visited Bewuck in force the year that Della went to Burrabinga, and
Maeve interpreted their demand for a beast. Cattle were now a
high price and Robert was against paying this rent until his vanity
was prickled by the leader, who said, "Him plurry flash, minetinkit.
Him no budgery old pfella Nullah-Mundoey."

The old gins—very witch-like towards the end—crept in as softly
as shadows and sat in the kitchen fireplace, and emitted wild
guffaws when they startled Johanna. That was the last season that
she heard against the soughing of her casuarinas their piercing cry:

Munny munny lumby adjong cooo!

They moved on to fight with rival tribes on the tableland towards
Monaro, where the fray was ended by the settlers, and it was in
that decade that the aborigines began to dwindle from the district.

Robert was developing a thriving business in harness horses, whose
subjugation was furthered by a turn in the plough, on which
occasions Robert's daring furrows would not have earned him a
place in the ploughing matches of The Plains. He coveted a gig
and tandem with which to eclipse a bullet-headed young man from

one of the big stations down the Murrumbidgee beyond Wagga
Wagga. Once having seen such a turn-out he wearied of the carriage,
and at that date the horses bolted with it and broke a window and
sprained an axle. Many turkeys would be needed to pay for a gig,
but chance aided Robert. A messenger from Burrabinga brought
instructions to sell the surplus horned cattle and leave Bewuck
for topping-up beasts that were coming down. Robert kept the
money from a steer he sold to a teamster and told his mother that
Hennessy had found a gig for the sum of her turkey money.

Robert trained a likely pair for the gig, and his handling of them
up and down the street, and curving in and out of the pub's back
yard, was so capable that Hennessy consented when Robert invited
Molly to drive with him.

"Git up to no foolery, and stay widin soight of me," said
Hennessy. This was concession to propriety so that Molly's matrimonial stock should not be lowered.

Molly put on her new leghorn bonnet, her shawl and mittens,
mounted a chair and into the gig with ostentatious modesty in
handling her skirts. Her heart fluttered. Robert was the most
striking young man in the district, with his aquiline profile and
Johanna's eyes—grown blacker and more piercing. He could not
ride as well as his brothers, but chose the most showy of the Nullah-
Mundoeys, and had the finest tackle and boots and breeches, and
with his willowy grace was the perfect figure of a horseman, like
the Magyars of old.

Hennessy saw him as a profitable catch, if nothing better came
within reach. Old Delacy was too white a man to grow rich, like
some of the squatters, but Bewuck would fall to the eldest son,
already in possession. The profits to be made from fools by pubbing
could add to it. Also, Hennessy's was the general store, which
retailed everything from marbles to hairpins, a pennyworth of pack
thread to a ship's cable, jaconet to moleskin, as the broadsheet—
forerunner of a Township newspaper—announced to Hennessy's
"distinguished patrons". Farmers were surrounding the Township,
and Hennessy had a tract of the Moore station where he depastured
the horses of his patrons. Many animals thus melted through alcohol
into his permanent possession. The township had grown as a centre
for fossickers beyond the Murrumbidgee, and the Great Southern
Road was crawling with teams carrying goods from Sydney and
needing accommodation for man and beast.

Hennessy was growing rich, and he craved position. He remained
unmarried because the women available would not advance him
socially. He longed for Molly to marry into one of those families

which had snubbed him as a lag, a terrier from the bogs of Ireland, and a publican. Delacy had been neither familiar nor superior, but had treated Hennessy as he did all men. Hennessy was therefore well-disposed towards the Delacy breed. Delacy was a "black Prodestan'", but Mrs Delacy had been born in the "wan thrue Church", and Hennessy would not permit creed to stand in the way of social ascent. The Church had not been so ready with comfort when he had been a lag as it was with requests for support now that he was behind an auriferous bar. So he allowed Molly to christen the gig and got Robert on his books with an advance for it.

Honoria, shortened to Norah, had also been some time at home, her education completed, her life begun, and Stewart Butler, brother of Gerald, was among the most frequent callers at Bewuck.

Gerald went to Burrabinga, but Della remained unmoved by his pleas. She enjoyed her position in charge of a house of her own, with no husband to dictate to her. Bella Rafferty found life with Miss Della a holiday, and queened it in a kitchen full of admirers. Bella was more popular than her mistress, and had nearly as good a chance as Molly McCathie at the pub, of marrying into the squattocracy. Della was of unbroachable maidenliness. Bella was full of fun and more approachable. There were large crumbs from her table of maidenhood as well as the probability of a real helping.

There was facetious "teasing" when James Fullwood appeared every Saturday night. He was the bachelor and younger brother of Charles at Heulong, and held a rough run near Wong Foo. He was attributed to Della and Bella in turn. Della repudiated the imputation with scorn. Bella tried to ape her, but furious blushes defeated her.

Danny discouraged that kind of raillery. "Arrah! 'Twould be better to occupy your moinds with something essential. What James Fullwood likes is a good dinner cooked and laid out by a woman after a week of beef and damper on a log. A few soft words in anny direction is little to pay for it, and comes natural to bachelors, old or young—more to the old than the young, I'm thinking. They're more brazen in the horn."

Bella resented this. Her pate harboured an apophthegm concerning an old man's darling. Mrs Wells (on whom Mrs Delacy refused to call) had married old Wells who had a better place than Bewuck and Burrabinga together. The father of Mrs Wells had worked in irons and made no secret of it. Mrs Wells had shepherded the Wells sheep barefooted, and had been called Polly by every one until she was sixteen. Now she wore a silk dress and a lot of rings and brooches, and sat inside with old Wells, and ate his mutton openly instead of that secretly obtained by her dad from the same source, while any one who dared to address her as Polly was caustically set right by old Wells and sent to the hut or kitchen to eat.

Bella resented having to eat in the kitchen, when all the men were agreed that she was much prettier than Della. It looked as if Della might be an old maid—a failure and a disgrace.

Nor did Danny approve of Bella eating in the kitchen. It increased his burden as chaperon, as in his day virginity was guarded by eternal vigilance. The girls shared one bedroom for safety, but Johanna decreed that Bella should be kept in her place for meals, otherwise both girls would be recalled. Johanna said that while there was breath in her body, she would not submit to her daughters being ruffians as well as "haythens". Danny yielded more to Johanna in her recalcitrance than he had done since the larks sang loud and high to them at Cooley Hall.

Della's early fixation remained. Her ideal was an urban life with a sleek city man. The bush had not quickened her imagination; she absorbed nothing from its differences to add to her natal endowment. She liked the Anguses best of the circle. Tom's flowery manners appeased her romantic idea of what a gentleman should be. Young Ned, now advanced to a full moustache, remained her devoted page.

Tom and Ned were rich, with girls on both sides of them. There was room for them all, and plenty of live stock to be captured by the resourceful. Danny stuck to walers. The Anguses had a rare beast named the Bedouin, advertised as pure Arab, with a perfect head and a crest as lordly as the English thoroughbreds. He had no flaw except a too-feminine head. The grace of the muzzle and clean-cut jaw, with the full bright eyes in the mane that hung to his knees, suggested a houri in her tresses, but such was his prepotence as a sire that no brand was necessary to distinguish his progeny.

The two breeders did not tread on each other's skirts. The Anguses worked up a reputation for polo ponies, and they and the Delacys once chartered a ship to take their horses direct to Calcutta. Tom Angus and Robert fell into fervent friendship, with their love of showy horses as a bond. Robert saw the possibilities of the Bedouins as harness horses for small vehicles and coveted a tandem for his gig, but there would be trouble with father, who had a mania for big horses, like his notion of an over-roomy hat filled with leaves, and a large boot padded with cloth—the Prince Alberts of the derelicts.

"With wan leg wouldn't ye find a smaller horse easier to climb on?" Johanna would demand.

"Och, I like to be where I can look around, not crawling about with the efts and ants."

Robert and Tom called on the Butlers and Fullwoods and did the Township in company. Tom was charmed by Molly, and she seemed to favour him more than Robert, but Hennessy did not encourage Tom. He knew just what the Delacys were, and were not. In Tom he saw a young man as astute as himself, and who, like himself, never mentioned his antecedents.

At this time Mrs Fullwood's sister came to Heulong, Mrs Euphemia Fitzhugh, widow of a Major of Crimean fame, a topside lady in her own estimation, who gave a social fillip to her relatives. Her crinolines and ringlets, her bracelets and shawls were the twitter of the district.

Mrs Delacy and Mrs Fitzhugh met in the parlour of Hennessy's hotel, which ascended socially with the widow's arrival. It was regarded as a palace since a recent addition of a wing of two stories. "Sure," said Danny, "There is a man who sees ahead. Hennessy is going to be the biggest man in the district."

"He will be able to show himself in a circus," said Johanna.

"Och, woman, there's no sense at you."

"His brogue would carry a horse," said Johanna contemptuously.

Danny chortled. "You think yourself has less brogue than Hennessy, and I think I have less than you, but outsiders would lump us all together."

"Only those who don't know a grape from a gooseberry would be so ignorant," maintained Johanna.

Johanna was over-impressed by Euphemia Fitzhugh, so long had she been exiled from gentility, and so eager was she to offset Danny's oddity in practice of equality. Mrs Fitzhugh was recruiting an army of satellites and was condescendingly gracious. Hennessy had long been looking for a widow suitable to his secret ambition, and eyed this one as he might a likely blood mare. He ambled up on all occasions and was excessively ingratiating. The lady encouraged him. She was of the old country school, and felt that she conferred favour and happiness on any members of the lower orders by accepting their service or substance.

Mrs Fullwood, her sister, a much quieter bird, murmured of the trouble in crossing the Murrumbidgee, which separated them from the Township and the best of the seignorials.

"We need," said Mrs Fitzhugh, "two vehicles. We could then come to the river, cross in the boat, and take up our travels again on this side."

Mrs Fullwood had but recently acquired her only vehicle, a small cart.

" 'Tis a pity," said Mrs Delacy, "that my carriage is out of order. I could lind it to ye without anny inconvenience at all, as I have a gig now. Me son is a great whip."

"Oh, yes, your son, that young gentleman I observed this morning. He was educated in Sydney, I hear."

Johanna glowed. "And Norah, too, and also her sister Della, in the mountains."

"I understand that your husband has his main seat in the mountains."

"I'm thinking his main seat up there is a-horseback," responded Johanna with humour. "There's not much other in those regions. 'Tis not like the old country."

This conversation was taking place at dinner. "That is very handsome of ye, Mrs Delacy," interposed Hennessy, in reference to the carriage. He was carving a mighty roast. Since he had enlarged the hotel, he sat at table and carved for his select guests. There was a tag-rag table downstairs, and people could also be exclusive by dining in a sitting-room. Hennessy was real host, no vassal. He turned with a flourish to the widow. "Sure, 'twould be noice if a lady who has come to ornamint our disthrict could move about at her aise. Would ye'r carriage be nading much repairing, Mrs Delacy?"

"More than I want to spind on it, me having no use for such a caravan."

"If ye'll be so gracious as to lind it, Oi'll kape moi ind up by having it repaired in me own shop."

Johanna was uneasy, thinking of Danny. Hennessy beamed broadly. Mrs Fitzhugh languished and gushed. She would not be out of pocket by the undertaking: it was the privilege of inferiors to pay. Robert, in debt to Hennessy, offered to bring in the carriage.

When the job was tackled the carriage had to be put on the dray, and took more than a week of Hannon's time with Robert's help, when they should have been mending the fences, and always, when no other tasks pressed, have been grubbing ring-barking and cultivating if Bewuck was to prosper. Robert did not drive the bullocks. He delegated labour.

Mrs Fitzhugh was amiable to those who might be useful, and

Robert was up to Colonial standards. She liked personable men to curvet around her crinoline.

Hennessy played for attention by talking of his orphaned niece. "God hilp me, Oi nade the advoice of a lady such as ye'rself, if ye'll pardon the presumption in bothering ye. Ye would be a motthel for anny young faymale that had the distinguished opporchunity of observing ye."

Hennessy's manner had none of the brusque independence which made the native born so odious. She would be enchanted to influence the unfortunate Molly, and jumped to the conclusion that "these persons" would supply her with a free personal maid as well as a carriage.

Molly astutely perceived the lady's condescension. Their meeting bristled into an encounter. Molly did not curtsy. She did not smile. She stood as uncompromisingly as a corner post. Mrs Fitzhugh assumed hauteur. Molly made such an unabashed inspection of the widow's person, district by district, that the proprietor grew conscious of defects. Mrs Fitzhugh felt that Molly was too odiously a hussy for anything but salutary reform. Molly meant to copy Mrs Fitzhugh's tricks of adornment. She left the widow to make all the advances. Euphemia lost her way and covered her defeat by languishing. "I declare I feel so overdone that my head aches."

"Maybe," said Molly, "if you cut your stay-laces you'd feel better. I'm always afraid of apoplexy when old people are so stout."

Mrs Fitzhugh looked in danger of a seizure and felt too like one to retort.

"An odious hussy, the real malapert," she remarked to her sister later. What would have been her state of mind could she have seen into Hennessy's where she reposed as a possible aunt for that hussy, because of successful marriages in the squattocracy between persons equally incongruous?

He insisted upon Molly sitting at table with the guests, and would not permit her to do any menial tasks. He measured his money-making powers with those of his contemporaries and knew he had few equals, and that money was the most powerful key to any society, even that of the angels—with their harps and pavements of gold.

Overhearing Molly's blague with the young men, when their women were not by, Euphemia warned her sister, "You had better watch that creature unless you want her in the family."

Mrs Fullwood replied that both her sons of suitable age were pursuing Della and Honoria Delacy.

"Dear me, is that desirable? Mrs Delacy is a well-meaning little person; she knows her place better than the McCathie minx, but she is so Irish. I suppose Mr Delacy married beneath him. Have they money?"

"No, they are comparatively poor."

"Then why do you acknowledge them?"

"Every one thinks highly of Mr Delacy's character."

"I should not encourage them. Much more than honesty is necessary to make a good match."

"They are going to provide you with a carriage."

"I wish I had known before we accepted it. We must not let such people presume upon our condescension. The young man will take it as an encouragement for Grace, I fear. We must use the carriage to take her away from his attention. That would be a just rebuke for his presumption."

Mrs Fullwood sighed. Euphemia had a great deal to learn in the Colonies. Mrs Fullwood had been reared in the same snobbery, but there had been much of loneliness, hardship and childbearing to counteract it. "I don't think Robert Delacy thinks so much of Grace as she does of him."

"She must be cured of such foolishness. It would be helpful to let Molly Mc. have her way with the Delacy boy."

"If we could be sure that she would have it with him and not with my Aubrey."

"Hennessy should be spoken to. Surely he knows his place!"

Euphemia had surprising things to learn of Hennessy's place. Mrs Fullwood sighed again, uneasily, remembering her account at Hennessy's store. Charles Fullwood, Esq., always had more classy—upper-classy—work for the money made at Heulong than payment of Hennessy's bills. Charles, like his sister-in-law, felt that it was the lower orders' privilege to run big bills for their betters.

"Sure, there's a foine thriving lady for ye—a hoigh sthepper if iver there was wan," observed Hennessy to his niece, Molly McCathie.

"Fat old thing! Thinks she's Lady Muck, and we are the dirt beneath her feet," said Molly to her uncle Hennessy, the Township publican.

"Ye from the convent, and have ye no genteeler language for a lady who could bring ye on?"

"Bring me on!" snorted Molly. "She'd rather put me down."

"She's maybe a little hard to howld," conceded Hennessy. "But loike a blood mare, when ye git used to her stroide, a great goer."

Molly tossed her head—like a blood filly. There were others she did not much care for either. Mrs Fullwood was a rag, but old mother Delacy had started to be top-lofty, and that was worse than Mrs Fitzhugh. Johanna had seen alarming passages between Molly and Robert, and the other hotels were no more than shanties for bullockies; besides, she quaked lest Danny might consider Molly a fine girl, fit for any man.

When the carriage was repaired she suggested that Mrs Fullwood, her sister, and Grace should visit Bewuck. Mrs Fitzhugh consented to one night there on her tour of the district's (would-be) manorial families. This would reward the Delacys for the carriage.

Mrs Delacy prepared a turkey feast and used all her elegancies, from the Irish linen to the plated toast rack. Jane Hannon cooked. Maeve was free to hand the dishes, and entered into the spirit of the occasion as she always did into everything that her family staged. Mrs Fullwood thought how comfortable the place was, how swimming in plenty; and Robert was so charming to his mother, so gallant to the guests. It was a treat to see him managing.

Euphemia was more critical. "She's a kind little woman, but so *dreadfully* Irish." Her tone implied that to be Irish was socially as bad as convictism.

"The Duke of Wellington himself was Irish," said Mrs Fullwood in defence of her helpful neighbour.

"Yes, but not Mrs Delacy's kind. She has a brogue that you could cut with a knife."

Mrs Fullwood—very foolishly, Euphemia thought—asked Mrs Delacy to accompany them on the tour. She rather timorously accepted, expressing the fear that she might be crushing the others.

"Couldn't Grace stay and keep me company till you come back," suggested Honoria.

Mrs Fitzhugh instantly vetoed this.

Robert interposed. "Go with Mrs Fullwood, Ma, as far as Glenties, and I'll bring you back in the gig. If Grace will drive with me going it will leave room in the carriage."

"I should adore a spin behind your tandem," promptly said Mrs Fitzhugh.

"Even better," said the adroit Robert. "I should have to plead with Grace, but you offer kindly to keep me company."

Horses and driver were supplied by the accommodating Hennessy. Mrs Fitzhugh was relieved to drop the Delacys at Butlers' and proceed from there as though the carriage were her own. "The carriage is totally above the poor little person," she observed to Grace. "She means well, but she is so *dreadfully* Irish."

Mrs Fitzhugh had her own hunting to attend to. The Major had been so gay a buck that she was comparatively destitute. She was now chary of the army and navy, but had heard tales of prizes among pastoralists. Well, here was a carriage placed at her disposal, without apparent reason but the right attitude of inferiors towards betters. An auspicious beginning.

Robert's business increased. Fancy prices were obtainable in Sydney and Melbourne for well-matched pairs. Tom Angus picked the animals and sent them to Robert to educate. Robert felt himself flowing in money, so that he postponed paying Hennessy. Hennessy let the debt increase without remark. Robert became independent of his mother's turkey bank. Money that came so easily seemed his own, without the recognition that it was made at the expense of Bewuck.

When she had canvassed the élite for eligibles, Mrs Fitzhugh did not bother to thank the owner of the carriage, nor return it. She left it at Hennessy's hotel, where it was speedily referred to as Mrs Fitz's by the menials who had to tend it. She had to travel from Heulong on horseback, and bluntly deplored the station being on the wrong side of "that absurdly named river".

Charles Fullwood was with James in the mountains mustering the cattle near Wong Foo's claim. Euphemia was waiting to see James. She could not consider him while he remained in the impenetrable wilds, but in a new country everything was open to a man of family, if he had the sense to insist upon his rights.

Grace wrote to Robert in care of Hennessy's hotel, if his visits to Heulong were too widely spaced

CHAPTER XV

ROBERT's father maintained his hardihood at Burrabinga. Johanna had called it a lost region in days when none wanted it, and up to the time of her great-grandchildren its caves and gorges, streams and mountain crests, were to remain but little-known to any save wombats and eagles or those who would ride the Federal Capital Territory. In the beginning hundreds of thousands of acres were held in Crown Leases at less than £50 per annum. At that, the lessees paid high in endurance, hard sweat, loneliness and physical danger, and if ever a holding was earned it was Burrabinga by the Delacys, despite the racial or legal rights of any other man's posterity.

The distances round about were estimated from Burrabinga. Old Nullah-Mundoey made it a landmark and it was called sixty miles from everywhere, because it was sixty miles from Gool Gool as well as the Township. It was thirty miles from the corroboree grounds, twenty from Wong Foo, also twenty from O'Neill's out-post to the south. He was jealous of intruders at his end, and Wong Foo was an acute inspector at his. Delacy had won their loyalty.

On their frontiers the Delacys had trap yards baited with salt and supported by drafting plants. These were built like stockades with logs drawn into place by bullocks, labour which entailed sweating among swarms of flies from dawn until dark on a diet of damper and salt junk and tea without milk. Foxhunting squires might have balked at the ordinary performances of the Delacys' days.

On a morning in January when the century was in its sixties, and Danny in his fifties, he was to be seen at the top of his form at Dead Horse Plain. Scrub bulls were deteriorating the wild mobs and could be shot, or emasculated for working bullocks. Shooting at large made too much packing of hides, the cutting-out process was impossible in that country, and drafting in the yards was dangerous.

"We'll take out the visitors first," was the order.

Honest Delacy was punctilious about other people's stock, even in careless fenceless days. He would weary horse-flesh to send home strays, and man-flesh was squandered by all the Delacys, even by

Robert, as compared with other men. The strays dealt with, Danny proceeded to test a theory. He said that if he stood still he would be safe from a charging bull, though not from a cow. In the big yard were posts to duck behind, but a man who took to the rails too often was howled out of composure as a new chum or yellow.

"You can't prove that without being gored to smithereens," protested William.

"Am I an eft not to learn from experience—with the beasts a lifetime!" However, he compromised.

He would test his theory with an effigy made of tussocks and his coat and worked with a rope. With a yapping of dogs and a whirlwind of dust a few of the luniest scrubbers went into the big yard. They charged with a mad bellow to within a breath of the figure, then swerved and walloped up to the high fence. Catching sight of the scarecrow from a fresh angle they rushed again, and again halted without touching it. Half a dozen more bulls were run in maddened by the chase, but it was always the same.

They were put through again while Danny pulled the string. One old fellow pawed the earth and threatened with angry roar, and when he saw it move rushed to gore it.

"Didn't I tell you to keep still and you're safe."

"Who in thunder could keep still?" demanded Harry.

"Sure, I'll take no chances with the ladies, but drive in that Bullock Gap mob and I'll pick out the stags without anny confusion whatever."

Doogoolook, stockmen, O'Neill, Anguses, William and Harry were all helping. Tom Angus had his revolver quietly ready. Danny took a position in the big yard, plunking his hat on his head and planting his peg stoutly in the ground. His beard was now long but without a grey hair.

William and Harry were at the drafting gates armed with heavy roping poles. Others were at the flood gate. In rushed the cattle. There was not a move in Delacy. The beasts charged on and away leaving him so at ease that when one rushed back instead of to the split, Danny, full of enjoyment, wheeled with a "Whist me boy!" and met him again.

"By Jove! I take off my hat to you, Mr Delacy," cried Tom. "The most fearless man I ever saw, bar none."

A thunderstorm soaked the dust at noon. Later Danny took the fairway to open the gate. A cow charged him and he tripped and fell. The cow bounded over him and on to that freedom, more enticing that revenge. In her wake dashed the mob. Danny lay still in the mud. The spectators were as helpless to arrest the rush as if the bottom had opened in a sack of onions. They leapt towards the mound left in its track, Harry with a screech of horror, William an oath. Danny, hearing their exclamations above him, sat up, a weird figure, clad in mud—safe.

"Aren't you hurt at all?" demanded William, as they helped him up.

"Hurt, by damn! Sure, I'm smothered and murdered in mud with all the wild cattle in the kingdom lepping over me! Be all the poipers, there's intelligence in brute creation—not wan so much as flicked me in passing. 'Twould be incredible if you heard it as a yarn. I'll go clean meself at the creek."

His pipe was in place so that the onlookers were taken with uncontrollable laughter—hysterical relief.

"Moi, oh, moi!" he observed, "It takes little to amuse those not too capacious in the top story."

All the men rode home to Burrabinga that night. Now that the girls were there they returned as often as possible for the bright company and the good cooking. There were vegetables in the garden started by Wong Foo. Slips or pips brought during Johanna's day were in full bearing. Quince suckers took root if merely stuck in the rich dark loam. There was adventure in seedling apples, and they grew in great glory at Burrabinga. In autumn their branches bent to the earth in a harvest as free from disease as the first garden ere the sins and weeds of man intruded.

The salt of necessity and the sugar of hearty admiration urged Della and Bella to lively housewifery. There were ever volunteers to help them with storing the quinces, apples, pumpkins, and pie melons, which remained until fruit ripened again. If the girls' supplies ran low, Wong Foo, by some telepathy, would arrive with vegetables or exotic luxuries.

He was awaiting the men on their return from the drafting. A member of the family by right of being swaddled in Danny's rug, he was sitting in the principal room on a prized chair carved by a stockman. Wong was wearing his grand suit. Like his saddle and gear it was still in perfect order.

"Such a pity those things are wasted on a Chow," said Bella.

Family business had brought Wong. He noted that Burrabinga cattle were disappearing from his end of the run while the Delacys were elsewhere occupied. Cattle could migrate, but when they left a hide behind them Wong saw that it was always of the Delacy mobs. He was too astute to blurt out his suspicions until he had prospected.

"You sellum muchee clattle Missa James Flullwood?" he inquired. Danny said no. "You sellum any lulla man?"

A list of sales was given. Wong proceeded.

"Whaffor hide off you clattle lie in sclub out by me alla samee sclub longa gladen lulla side liver?"

Wong pointed to the tea-tree groves of the swampy flats in the direction of Birrabee.

"Some fossicker has helped himself to free beef," remarked William.

Wong resorted to diagrams on the ground behind the cow-yard, safe from the ears of women and "hands". It appeared to be bigger than beef for a few men. "Any strange men there lately?"

"No. Alla samee ol' fliends, Missa James Flullwood."

"Wong has got hold of a bull's nest," said William. "We must ask old Jimmy if he has missed any stock."

Wong was too cautious to mention names again, or all that he had noted. He urged Delacy to muster the Bullock Gap runs and to stay the night. "Blinga lun ladies. Makee big fleast. Ladies one hut, men lulla."

The girls seized upon this.

Wong went off in the morning at full gallop, his hat on the back of his head, his coat flapping, his body swaying from side to side as if he were drunk. He was eager to begin on one of the biggest occasions of his Burrabinga career.

"Enough to give the horse a sore back through to the girth," remarked Harry.

"Golly, yes! A Nullah-Mundoey wasted," said William.

"I'd rather see Wong on a good horse than manny of the scoundrels that ride about the country," said Danny. "Often the best riders are the worst men." The young men asserted that there never was a Chinese horseman. "Arrah! You can't swim without water, and Wong was a townie in any case."

"But town men here can ride," observed Harry.

"They sit on horses to save walking," corrected William.

Wong rode in again during the week with a pack-horse and two hides, which he spread behind the cowshed in triumph.

"Me chasen honey bloke, and see ol' fella clows, and findem."

The Delacy boys decided to investigate. They were inviting the Urquhart's to Wong's party. Danny sent a note asking Urquhart to chaperon the girls.

James Fullwood rode in to Burrabinga the day following Wong's arrival. He paid his respects to the girls impartially, but Della was indifferent, and Bella effusive. As soon as possible he took Delacy behind the shed, that spot where secrets were told.

"I know you keep that Chink prospector as a pet, but do you let him do what he likes with your cattle?"

"I let him have a beast when he needs it."

"He wouldn't need two in a week."

"Och, he's preparing a great feast for us all and maybe has exaggerated notions."

"But I'm speaking of two weeks past. I found a hide pegged out above his claim. When I found another it looked pretty rum. The tracks all round were Wong's."

Delacy led Fullwood to the hides. "Those are off my spotted steers that ran at Bullock Gap—would it be those you saw?"

"You found them yourself?"

"Wong brought them. He thought someone had duffed them."

"I'd keep an eye on Wong, if I were you. There's a lot more in that old Chink head than comes out."

"That's because we are too ignorant to understand him."

"What's yours seems to be his, but if I catch him meddling with my beasts, I'll make it hot for him."

"Ah, sure, Wong Foo is a foine man."

"I thought it my duty to warn you."

"Sure, you've done what you thought right to a neebur. Turn your horse out for the night."

O'Neill came down for rations that Saturday after a month's absence, and Delacy instructed him to keep his eyes open for evidence of any cattle or horse duffers in his direction.

CHAPTER XVI

Wong Foo had two prospectors' huts set in cultivated plots. In one he kept utensils and table implements, which he used in imitation of Bewuck. In this he had berths prepared for the girls. His feast included one duck per person cooked in Chinese fashion, with a great array of vegetables, followed by Oriental comfits.

The Delacys were proud of Wong Foo and justified in their fosterage. Wong's gallantry jacked-up that of the others, and the girls had pretty presents and more attention than they could absorb.

There were practical jokes and games—old games designed to aid *amour* while preserving convention. James Fullwood most frequently chose Bella Rafferty for partner. Della contented herself with her young cavalier, Ned, who had remained deep in calf-love with her. She found him useful as a buffer between her and men better matched to her years. William Delacy fancied Janet Urquhart, but was so gauche that she did not become aware of it. Harry, eager, impressionable, and starved for the humanities, monopolized her. Any young woman untarnished by familiarity could be placed in the role of a princess, and Janet, shapely of form and pleasing of face, served well.

Urquhart approved of William Delacy; other suitors were none so desirable. Keebah was shut away from many families by the Murrumbidgee during half the year, and his two eldest daughters, Sarah and Agnes, had not married well.

Wong took the gentlemen to his own hut where Delacy and Urquhart revived memories of Bendigo and Ballarat over a jug of Jamaica for another hour. Wong reserved his couch for them, and the other men rolled in their own blankets. The boys awakened at daylight to find Wong already stirring, while the red Scottish and black Irish beards intermingled as the old mates slept it off.

When later the two told the tale, they proclaimed, "Ghost it was laughable to see a Chinaman so tight!" But the young men gave their version, and comments from Johanna were so puncturing that Danny relinquished the story. Mrs Janet Urquhart suffered it with a cold steady glare that was attributed by Sandy to feminine kill-joyism and lack of sense of humour.

James Fullwood himself had been "three sheets in the wind", but the fall of Danny and Sandy was the subject of his facetiousness with Bella. She giggled flatteringly and contributed spirited accounts of what happened when her father (nominal) was drunk. She had a robust sense of humour free from kill-joyism.

"I like to see a man a little on top of hisself," said she. "But Ma is always joring."

Della was contemptuous of Fullwood's familiarity with her servant and turned her smiles towards young Urquhart.

The day was spent in visiting caves, and the second night at Fullwood's station. There was no such feast as at Wong's, but the baching was improved by rice and potatoes boiled in the one billy-can with the salt junk. On the third day Urquhart Senior escorted the women back to Burrabinga homestead, while Danny, with a whoop, assembled dogs and men and started after the mobs of the region. The Urquhart sons joined in to see if any of their own cattle were in that direction.

They were all surprised by the few beasts sighted. Doogoolook confirmed the theory of duffing with evidence of a mixed mob being driven towards the Great Southern Road. He pointed to the tracks of two horses. One belonged to the Anguses. His pupils, William and Harry, were equally acute, and verified the Angus tracks as those of a mare that had disappeared a month before. The young Delacys and Anguses turned into troopers instanter and left the mustering to Fullwood and the Urquharts.

"I expected this," remarked Fullwood to Delacy.

"There's been a power of cattle lifted down Monaro way, and it's a curse for it to start here," he responded.

"I mean the horse tracks. You might owe Wong a beast or two for all the feasts he provides, but the Anguses are close about their past. Never any brag about *their* family."

"What the dayvil good is a man's family? Descent gave an unfair pull in the old country, but out here a man has to be a man and make his ascent himself."

"You'd think twice though before giving your daughter to a man of no family?"

"Are you proposing for me daughter, James Fullwood?"

"There are too many younger blades in the running."

"She takes her time. There is no telling where her fancy will evintually settle."

"Are you proposing to me for a son-in-law, Mr Delacy?"

This point fell in jocularity. Fullwood persisted with the other. "Jokes aside, it was about the Anguses' reputation."

"Have ye annything definite? If so, let's put it to them, and they can defind themselves. A hint without evidence is a snake in the grass, like that boomer you dispatched to-day at the lickhole, and moi, oh, moi!" Danny took a meditative pull at the pipe, "I'm thinking that the poor snake was moinding his own business, and we intruding. If you begin to contimplate the injustices of the universe they are beyond disentangling."

Fullwood headed Danny out of a philosophic gully. "Most interesting, Mr Delacy, and I'm one to live and let live, but the tracks of that Angus horse following a mob of your cattle off the run are rather more interesting to me."

"It looks as if the Anguses had lost their mare."

Doogoolook returned a day later with the Bedouin mare, leg-weary and galled. He deposed, by signs, that he had found her among wild horses between Birrabee and Keebah. Delacy pointed to the saddle galls and asked if Wong had made them. Doogoolook intimated otherwise.

"It would be easy to make a mistake on his evidence," remarked Fullwood. "I wouldn't convict a proved criminal on it."

"Let's ask if William made the galls," chortled Harry, but William snorted that he could not make such a mess of a horse if he lived on it.

Fullwood promised to report any further evidence immediately. Danny remained a night behind the others and enjoyed a talk with Wong.

"Who you tinkem bad man, steal um cattle?" demanded Wong.

"Some fellow up the Bland, maybe."

"You likee young Angus—tinkum good fellow mally glels; or you likee betta Missa Fullwood, tinkum betta gentleman?"

"Sure, a man could be a king and I would not consider him a gentleman unless he was an honest man first. One man is as good as another if he is as good—do you understand? But, of course, it has to be proved first."

"Which you likee good best, Tom Angus or Missa Fullwood?" This question of relative merit plagued Wong.

"Be the poipers, if put to it I could not say. Wan is young and the other is getting on for forty-five, but you are a better man than ayther."

"Which you tinkum blest—bad once good now, this time once, or bad once, good once, bad again?"

"Sure, Wong, 'twould take a Philadelphia lawyer to unravel your meanings. But do you mean that if a man was bad for half his life, is it better to be the first half or the latter ind? That is a quischun for the bishops, and they know as much as an eft, when all is said and done. It will be aquil when we carry our hides to the tanyard, but," and Danny puffed loudly, "if 'tis your own morals that are involved, sure, as me neebur, 'twould be more convenient to me if you gave me the reformed ind of your career."

The sons wanted the troopers. Danny said, "What troopers but ourselves would have anny chance against min in these ravines? We'll keep our eyes open."

Cattle stealing did not cease. Two weeks after the picnic James Fullwood rode in to say that a mob of his were missing and their tracks pointed toward Dead Horse Plain.

"Your cattle are safe with O'Neill," said Danny. "I shall spind a night with him this week, the man maybe is lonely."

"He might find it profitable to shut his eyes. I'd watch an old lag like that."

"He let himself be employed once to do a dirty trick, but I'd trust a lot of the old lags beyond those that employed them."

Fullwood ignored the imputation in this. He thought Delacy a fool, who would trust any scoundrel, and went at once on the tracks of his own cattle.

Before Delacy set out, O'Neill appeared to report the tracks of a mob not ten miles from his hut—mixed cattle driven in the direction of Gool Gool by two horsemen—as plain as a Government notice. Harry, William and Doogoolook set off, but their efforts were defeated by a thunderstorm. To catch the cattle lifters in the act now became the great endeavour at Burrabinga.

Fullwood returned days later and said that most of the cattle were his. He had tracked them to within ten miles of O'Neill's hut, and thence towards the Snowy, but lost them because of a thunderstorm.

"This doesn't look like stopping till we are stripped," he said to Danny. "It has been pulled off too easily. I'll inform the troopers, and I'll make no bones of my suspicions of both Wong and O'Neill, not to mention others."

"Then I'll postpone my suspicions. Too manny names maybe would moider the troopers."

The trooper came with his tracker from Queanbeyan, but he had to depend on the Delacys to lead him about. Doogoolook was better than the police tracker. This inspired Harry, who was rampant for romantic adventure.

He and William took no one into their confidence, not even their bosom friends the Anguses. They were not so bosom to William as to Robert, because Tom had a more taking style with the girls. William was shy and had a fear of making himself

ridiculous. Thus while he looked longingly on Janet Urquhart,
her eyes were cast on Tom Angus, who could make her laugh.
With William she could find nothing to say. He, therefore, could
pick many faults in both the Anguses, and objected to young Ned
hanging around Della. He was alarmed that she was becoming an
old maid, and the boy's presence held grown men at a distance.

No cattle were removed during the ensuing weeks. No unaccounted
person either as fossicker or lyre-bird hunter was to be seen. William
and Harry unearthed families of wild horses from remote places
and thought that the cattle duffers must have gone elsewhere, when
suddenly crows led them to a tea-tree clump five miles from Wong's
hut. Tracks ran to Wong's claim and also in the direction of James
Fullwood's hut. The hide could not be mistaken, it was black on
the sides and white on the back and belly. Hoofs and head were
not about, but could have been dragged away by dingoes. The boys
agreed to say nothing of their find, but cut out the brand and took
it home with them. They were beginners. Later in the day James
Fullwood missed the branded portion of the hide. His detective
efforts were being spoiled, so he rode in to ascertain what the
Delacy boys knew.

On the following morning William and Harry found that their
evidence had disappeared. They had not reckoned on the feats of
a kangaroo dog when they stuck the hide in the wall-plate of the
veranda.

Fullwood put another spoke in their wheel through Bella. While
she was washing-up in the evening, he went to the kitchen on the
excuse of a feed for his dog. "Say, Bella," he began, tickling her
and attempting a kiss, "I want you to help me in a little bit of
work—a woman's wits, you know."

"Go orn! You'll make me squeak so Deller will hear, and she'll
be out. She's as jealous as a bear."

"What of?"

"Ole maids is always jealous. Lor' I wouldn't be an ole maid
for anything. I'd sooner take that gawky William."

"He wouldn't take you."

"Oh, wouldn't he, if I cocked half an eye at him."

"I'd rather take you myself that let you be wasted like that."

"Go orn! Ole coves always talk loving and mean nothink . . .
Wot was you going to arsk me?"

"See here, you've heard of cattle being duffed about here?"

"The dust about it has died down. Who done it?"

"That's what I'm trying to discover, but these oafs blundered in and blew the gaff. I found another of my beasts skinned, and was setting to watch when they hacked the brand out."

"That was the piece of hide I found larst night. Stinking thing, was stuck nearly in me face. I threw it in the fire. I larfed till me sides ached to see them looking for it, and thinking the kangaroo dogs ate it."

"You're a hard case," said Fullwood with admiration. "Next time they bring home bits of hide I want you to save them for me. I suspect Wong Foo and O'Neill, but these —— mugs want to keep them as pets."

"What do I get for keeping the hide?"

"Don't you love me a little?"

"How much do you love me?"

"As much as you let me." Woman hungry, he swept the juicy Bella on to his knee. Bella lacked experience but she made up in daring.

Some weeks later the Delacys put two pieces of hide high in the kitchen rafters. Bella had to put a stool on the table to reach them. Though she could not read, she knew the Delacy brands. She cunningly evolved the pieces of the puzzle and threw the hide into the fire. Della came out to inquire the cause of the odious smell. Bella was highly indignant at the stuff being put in the rafters to fall on her head. "It hurted me, and it stank." Forthwith she washed her head, and every one had to keep out of the kitchen while she dried it before the fire. Only a hussy would allow a man to see her with her hair flowing. Bella published her maidenly modesty for the benefit of the virtuous William who had rebuked her advances. Harry inquired through the door about the hide.

"Er course I burned the stinking stuff. It pilluted the kitchen. Miss Deller was singing out about the smell. Full wop on me head! I might have been stunned and have fell into the fire. And having to wash me head at this time er night; might ketch me death er cold!" Bella hugged her glee.

Della could not put Bella in her place. She had not Johanna's confidence. William and Harry had to begin all over again. It was not difficult, for the cattle-duffer, like the dog in Proverbs, returned to his waywardness, and there was high riding about the bush on the part of the amateur troopers.

This time they felt so sure of their quarry that they arranged witnesses, and whispered in the shed at night, or in their skillion bedroom adjoining the girls'. Bella's ears were bush trained; she could hear like a dog and listened with virtuosity. There was no wool over her eyes. Instinctively she was against authority and resented the Delacy honesty and irreproachable respectability. She was her mother's daughter, and old mother Rafferty was notorious.

The young Delacys were all for the police, but Danny said, "Wanst you begin law, it never ends, and law helps the wrong man much more than the right one. To boot, it stirs up dangerous enemies."

The Anguses were not going to allow their cattle to be taken without saying boo. Next their polo ponies would go, and they might as well retreat from the district.

Two young men were to go for the police and two remain on watch. This time the brands were put in a billy on the dining-room shelf for safety. Bella chuckled as she hid the bundle in the ridge pole in the dark of the stable, where one smell more would not be betraying. In case of accident, she wore Della's boots on this errand.

At piccaninny dawn, the billy with the lid off was found rolling on the floor, the dining-room door open and the hide gone. There was recrimination for whoever had been careless. Della had gone out first and confessed to leaving the door unlatched. The combined tracking ability of the place could find no remnant of the parcel, nor any slot of dog in the house precincts. The young men retreated to the shed for confabulation.

"You'd think it was a plot against the Roosians," said Danny, breaking in on them. The confabulators stated their suspicions of a plot. There could not have been three accidents to the pieces of hide.

"It looks pretty black against that Bella. She's been getting very bold lately," said William.

"If she is in it, she would be acting cat's-paw for one of the min," said Danny.

"And he's acting cat's-paw for the duffer."

"Whoever that is," said Danny.

"There is no doubt who that is," said Tom Angus, supported by William and Harry.

"We must pay attintion to common sinse," said Danny. "You want to be double-sure before you can be half-sure enough to lay a charge."

The many dogs, visiting and resident, bayed a loud announcement, and James Fullwood approached out of the timber on the Keebah track. The disturbed plovers ran stiltedly away and rose with protesting tut-tut-tut-tuts from the tea-tree swamps. The men dispersed to their horses.

Disgruntled by the loss of the hide, the Anguses said they were on their way home. William, in his township suit, which Bella despised, felt foolish. Noting the signs, Fullwood was a mass of curiosity.

Bella came to the back gate, ostensibly to give some meat to the dogs, and made signs to Fullwood. "Oh, what a nice horse," she exclaimed.

Fullwood stepped toward the animal, which was hitched to the grindstone. "Be careful, he is savage."

"I don't want him to know what fools we've been made," said William. The others nodded.

Bella was patting the harmless horse's neck and muttering to Fullwood, "I got them all safe, right from under their noses, when they was all off to the police to play old Harry."

"Got what?"

"You know—the pieces of hide you wanted."

"They're the softest louts I know. A cat could hocus them with dingo pups for kittens. The Anguses must be splitting their sides with laughter, but all the same, very relieved that you have saved them."

"Go orn!" said Bella, shrewdly narrowing her eyes and enlarging her suspicions. In suspicions she rarely went astray, except with the Delacys, who antagonized her. She suspected their honesty as hypocrisy, while the hypocrisy of those practised in dissimulation of misdoing had her ready applause.

"Get me the brands as soon as you can."

"I'd have to be terrible careful that they were all away on the run."

Fullwood rejoined the men. The meal was now ready, to which no invitation was necessary.

"Better turn your horse out and stay the night," said Danny.

After the meal Tom Angus departed for Birrabee. To explain the town suit, William said he was going with him to bring the mail from Keebah. It was six weeks since Burrabinga had had any, also, William was famished for a sight of Janet. Harry and Ned rode aimlessly out towards Bullock Gap with their spoiled plan. Danny gave the stockmen a start for Dead Horse Plain with a mob of horses that had come down from the highlands too early. Fullwood lingered talking to Della and awaiting opportunity with Bella. This came when she went to pen the calves for the night. They dawdled in the cow bail.

"Now is your chance to get me those brands."

Women were scarce, and Bella was a tantalizing morsel to an ageing man. She drove her terms and was fertile in stratagems.

When preparing the evening meal she said that Fullwood had been down to Heulong and had a letter from her mother.

"It was like his cheek to forget it and not give it to me the minute he come," she declared as she handed it to Della to read.

"If Mr Fullwood has been down without giving us a chance to send a letter, I do think he's mean."

Bella's family was illiterate. Someone had acted as scribe. Bella was informed that her mother was poorly, as an addition to the family was due in about a month. Bella must come home at once to take care of the smaller children.

"I'm going," said Bella, affecting to be perturbed. "Poor ole Mar is forty-five; it might finish her this time."

Danny returned shortly afterwards. Fullwood explained that the letter had been brought by a stray prospector, and that he also had received word which made it imperative to go to Heulong. He could take Bella with him.

Delacy said he would take Bella. She demanded a pack-horse for her belongings. "Arrah, you'll be back before you know it."

One swag-bellied old mare was given to Bella's packs and another to her person. Danny said Della could have a holiday at Keebah. The four set out. Bella refused to cheer up, and in the manner of the sullen, garnered propitiation. The first night they scrambled up to Birrabee and surprised the Anguses, who gave them camp welcome. The following day they reached Keebah. Delacy felt it his duty to go on with Bella, but Fullwood asserted that the girl would be equally safe with him. They would make on to the next settler—twenty-five miles distant—and early the following day reach Bella's parents on the left bank of the river.

Delacy was seduced by the rum and the talk at Keebah to let them go. "The lass will be all right," said Urquhart. "If Fullwood, who is one of us, can't take care of himself, he's a fule who deserves what he gets. And it's a cold wet day with no comfort for canoodling. He! He! Ha! Ha!"

The old mates had a spree, not quite so free as that nurtured by the sympathetic Wong Foo. Mrs Jane's glare acted as a slight brake. Intoxication brought no poison to the surface in Danny. He merely babbled philosophical speculation, recited ballads and enjoyed a spate of hyperbole, but alcohol in its lees had an inflammatory effect on Sandy.

CHAPTER XVII

THE desolation of a camp that is empty all day, enfolded Burrabinga homestead with the loss of the two young women. Winter had come. The mountain tops were white with snow, the gullies slippery with unmelted frost. The icicles rose nightly like stubble on ungrassed spaces and crunched underfoot. Callers ceased. The Delacy men were not driven by table greed or other spurs to comfort. Their meals fell back to primitive consistency. They shut up the house, awaiting the girls' return, and pigged in the kitchen.

O'Neill sometimes lingered half a week when he beat his way down for rations. In the glow of the big log fires scores of muzzles were whittled from the light but tough woolly-butts, and thrown aside to dry for the next weaning. Harry knew by heart the few books left by his final tutor; Danny had read every line, including the advertisements, in newspapers of London and Sydney, months old when packed up from Keebah. Ned Callahan, a stockman, had a greasy song-book, dearly prized, from which Harry read him the songs and to which Ned put tunes he had heard. He had an ear and played hop-jigs and song-tunes on the mouth organ and jew's harp. He was also a Grinling Gibbons with a pen knife. The Delacys had no accomplishments. They had been reared only to bushcraft. William had no other interest, but Harry was famishing for intellectual contacts. A few great novels would have released him into another world.

Danny wearied of the winter routine and longed for Bewuck and Johanna, so uttered his intention of going down the river. "Sure, you are big and ugly enough to run the place till spring. You can make a trip to Keebah to see Della, but don't ride the tails off all the horses."

Keebah would see them as soon as his back was turned for there lay their magnets.

"None of this police business, no matter if the house is lifted off you by the roots. I'm in a firmer position with the knowledge of the duffer in me hand than if it is exploded. Is that clear beyond misunderstanding?"

It was. Danny continued, "Sure, there's nothing to be done here

now but to keep dingoes down for their depredations among foals
or calves that will be dropped out of season, and the snaring of
possums and wallaroos. In your spare time you can make that new
horse paddock, no more than eighty acres. Keep it small so that
horses can be handy for use overnight. Pile up the logs so that it
can't be jumped out of. You'll be clearing the ground at the same
time. *Absolvi meam animam,* so now I'll be gone."

He chose two pack-mares to carry fine skins for Johanna. He had
little else to take her this time excepting a few nuggets exchanged
by prospectors for beef or horses, and a dozen prime specimens of
lyre-birds' tails. Doogoolook prepared himself. He had become a
habit with Delacy.

The whisky flask at Keebah was low; what remained was firmly
held by Mrs Janet for emergencies, so Delacy was saved from delay
and surprised his family one wintry dusk at the hour when the
back log for the morning fire was being taken into the kitchen by
all the man power available armed with crowbars. The sun had
set without a fleck of clouds. The sky was a frosty arch of electric
pallor deepened on the eastern rim by rose tinged with blue, and
lightened along the western ranges by the gleam of nacreous tur-
quoise. He descended with whip-crack and halloa, his dogs loping
ahead to make trouble with the Bewuck pack and dispersing the
jackasses sitting on low snags awaiting a belated grub.

"Here's your father," exclaimed Johanna, and ran in her old
eager way to meet him.

"Me brave Johanna, are you all well?" Danny dismounted and
removed the pipe.

"That can't mean much to ye," said Johanna with spirit. "It's a
widow I've been off and on for years."

"That's more so with me than you, I'm thinking," he said with
a self-conscious grin.

"It's lucky I am to have a fine son."

Robert, Maeve and Norah came forward and dispersed uneasiness. Danny observed how striking a man Robert had grown.

Danny changed his clothes, brushed his hair, and felt subdued
to a mere guest at his own table, where Robert presided with
flourish.

Talk loosened during the evening, though Robert was not a
talker. He rarely explained. He went across to Hannon's on pretext
of business, leaving his father with the women. Johanna liked to
gossip, or read the new paper that had started in the Township.

"Make ye'r father a bed in the ind room, he will be tired from
riding all day," she said to Norah.

Danny was chilled and disappointed. Time had emancipated Johanna from the urge for a husband, but Danny was not yet released from sex.

Johanna had much to tell, so she began, "I don't know that I should bother to tell ye. I've been deserted in the eyes of the country for half me life."

"You could have paid me a visit; and you never sent me a letter."

"That cuts the other way round, I'm thinking."

"Sure, what had I to report but tigrinizing about the scrub with horses and cattle. It was you that had all the news; and sure, didn't we sind a letter by Bella when she came down; and did James Fullwood sind on the two old mares?"

"What's this about Bella coming down? And in that case what have ye done with me daughter—left her to be the prey of dingoes and stray min in ye'r owld Bunratty Castle?"

"Have you heard if Old Mother Rafferty has had another child?"

"Sure, what is that but a regular occurrence this twenty-five years or more. It's nearly as common as old Rafferty going on the spree, and more regular, surely it's come to an ind at last, and ye'r concern is rather late."

"But James Fullwood brought Bella down more than a month ago to be with her mother for the purpose designated."

"The river has been high, and 'twould not occur to such tag-rag to inform their betters about what they should know."

"I'll find out to-morrow."

"And where is Della?"

"With Mrs Urquhart till Bella comes back."

"Are ye marrying her on wan of the Urquharts?"

" 'Twill take more than me to marry Della to anny one. She has a distant way with her to all men."

Johanna heard this with satisfaction, and divulged that the second Butler boy, Stewart, wanted to marry Norah, and that she and Mrs Butler were both satisfied. It only remained for the fathers to come to terms.

In the morning Danny saw that Robert's management still furthered elegancies at the expense of fundamentals. The cutting was accepted as necessary for Johanna's carriage, also the pointed palings around her garden, but there was stable and carriage accommodation, for which clearing and cultivation had been neglected.

"It is not necessary to be pampering horses, like in the old country. If they can thrive in the open at Burrabinga, this would be like the tropics by comparison." He was confronted by the showy gig. "Whoi? What : . ." He looked towards the carriage house. The door was open upon vacancy. "Where's your mother's conveyance?"

"She lent it to Mrs Fitzhugh."

"And why should Mrs Fitzhugh be provided with a carriage by your mother?"

"She's Mrs Fullwood's sister."

"Och, I remimber now. Sure, 'tis your mother's business what she does with her own carriage, but I must find the rights of it. Is this vehicle Mrs Fitzhugh's?"

"No. I got it for a mere song to take Ma out a little. Her health was suffering from the years of confinement."

Danny muttered, "Oh, moi, oh, moi," to himself, and saddled a mare for inspection farther afield. He was astonished by the number of milch cows and the flocks of turkeys.

"Do you do the milking?"

"I haven't time. Maeve and Hannon and his old woman do that. I reckon it pays better to see that others don't loaf than to do everything by one-man power."

Danny was further surprised by so many Bedouins. "Did the Anguses come out and me not to be told?"

"No. These came when you sent the draft together."

"And why are they devouring winter grass here?"

"Huh! They pay better than cows. Norah has kept books. There's a chap I knew at school, his father runs the bazaar in Sydney and has the right connection."

"Moi, oh, moi!" repeated Danny, overwhelmed, but not convinced that the business was sound. He spent the day outside. A virile man did not remain indoors unless there were women guests or it was Sunday or there was a deluge or he had a broken leg. He had to confess, though with private reservations, that Robert "had a head on him".

That evening Stewart Butler came to see Danny, whose tracks through Glenties had been reported. After supper Norah and he were permitted the sedate occupancy of the "parlour"—Johanna's prized elegancy—while the parents had the dining-room fire. Robert went over to Hannon's hut to talk horses. He could not talk to his father. Maeve, looking old and worn, had Doogoolook in the kitchen, where she showed him pictures in a London periodical. Convention did not permit Norah and her affianced to be hermetically sealed in their own society. Norah emerged at intervals on some maidenly pretext, or Danny or Johanna intruded to make specific inquiry, or to mend the fire.

One of these interruptions was to ask Butler if he had heard of James Fullwood being home a month before to bring Bella Rafferty.

Mrs Butler employed one of the girls younger than Bella, but Stewart had not heard of Bella or Fullwood being down. Charles Fullwood had been away, some said, dealing in cattle and taking them to Victoria. So prized was news that the whole region would speedily know that Delacy was down from the mountains. It was puzzling that James Fullwood's visit and Bella's homecoming had escaped attention.

"Sure, the punt is washed away, and it puts people in prison," remarked Johanna.

"I had forgotten the mournful crying of the wind in the oaks."

"Didn't it nearly kill me getting used to them, and now the night is empty away from them? I had to take banshees for me familiars and become the aquil of black haythens for want of better company."

"But think of the cramped life in Ireland—and here the width and freedom."

"The width and freedom with native dogs is such that it defeats civilization in the loneliness."

Danny felt that it was time to be mending the fire in the parlour. On returning he asked Johanna why Mrs Fitzhugh should be wearing out the carriage.

Johanna advanced her hopes for Robert and Grace Fullwood.

"Surely you'd never help things on with that sawny bean-pole?"

"My Robert has looks enough for two."

"And too manny for himself, I'm thinking," grunted Danny, depositing his dottle in the fire and beginning on a fresh plug.

"It is the family. Beauties don't always make the best wives."

"It's the family I'm against."

"Now what could anny sane man have against the Fullwoods? They visit at Cobbramorragong as well as at Camerons of The Plains, and *they* have never come here."

"That's because we are not rich enough. Whin it comes to breed, me family is better than anny of them for education and principle."

"Och, if I didn't keep ye up a little ye'd soon slip back to the emancipists."

"There's manny an ex-ticket-of-leaver I'd rather be allied with than the Fullwoods, though they might be of the nobility and visit on royalty."

"Ye'd maybe prefer Hennessy of the public house?"

"Hennessy, when all is said, never hired a felon to beat me up and oust me cattle from their run. Hennessy is as foine a man as can be met in the Colony, a rale man, not like these whining down-looking Fullwoods, who can only honk and hah through their noses. They never look you in the face."

"I despise bold glaring men like Walter Moore. I had to fight to preserve meself from him."

"Well, now, Johanna, 'tis no use of getting at cross-purposes over a bottle of smoke. What is behind these veiled observations about Hennessy as a substitute for Fullwood in the matrimonial sense?"

"I saw passages between Robert and Molly McCathie that showed he had better see something higher. Boys are romantic at that age, and 'tis time he was settled."

"Of the two evils I prefer Molly, and of the two prospective fathers-in-law Hennessy is the best man."

"A lag."

"He was lagged for struggling for freedom. When I see the way some of these jumped-up squireens look down their noses and say a man is Irish, I'm counting it an honour to a man who had the pride and indipindince to want Ireland cleared of the English, a milk-and-water, conceited breed, with great proclivities for grasping the globe and pretinding that it is for the good of those they dispossess."

"Wan might as well try to rayson with the wind as with ye, Daniel Delacy."

"It's yourself cannot reason. After all, what is the use of us bickering here? The young people might be settling their affairs in the way we did. Has Robert shown anny predilection for Grace?"

" 'Tis Grace that is eating her heart for him."

Johanna would think that all the country wanted her precious son. Danny was more interested for the moment in ascertaining if Bella had been landed at home sound in limb and virtue. She was his particular responsibility. "To-morrow I go to the Township to straighten me business. Will you go with me, Johanna?"

" 'Tis too cold across those plains these short days."

Danny invited Robert to ride with him, but Robert said he could not spare the time just then. "How often do you go in?"

"I can't remember when I was in last—a couple or three months ago."

Danny was pleased that Robert did not waste his time around town. Doogoolook prepared himself to accompany his master, but was sent instead to discover if Bella were safe. This had to depend on signs as the Raffertys were illiterate.

Danny found Mrs Fitzhugh established at Hennessy's. She refused

to be marooned on the other side of the Murrumbidgee in winter.
La, she was used to lively society, not that of dingoes and possums
interspersed with blackfellows. The censorious sneered at her
husband-hunting, illogically, when any woman evading marriage
was considered abnormal or a failure.

Mrs Fitzhugh had her own sitting-room to which she retreated
when smitten with an attack of de Vere. Otherwise she dined at
the public table to inspect the squatters who blew in on the way
from Riverina. Her sister deplored the money spent in hotel
residence, but Euphemia said that the bogtrotter Hennessy was
delighted to make nominal terms for one who gave distinction to
his wretched backblocks shanty. Hennessy was pleased with her
mounting bill. Their designs upon each other, though obvious to
onlookers, were ludicrously veiled from both schemers.

Euphemia was interested to meet Delacy of Bewuck and Burrabinga, of whom there were many diverting tales, and whom
Hennessy advertised as the most honest and fearless man on the
Murrumbidgee. Oh, that she had had someone in whom to confide
her first impressions of that shrimp of a being thumping along on
one leg; with a long black beard; and slop clothes some sizes too
large for him! La, what a country! And this spectacle aspired to
be father-in-law to her niece! So deplorably Irish! He made her
hilarious. She anticipated no difficulty in retaining her carriage.
Such an object would be hat-in-hand to court her favour. She
impressed him by her gaiety and dashingly crinolined swagger,
while she regretted a loutish society which provided none to
appreciate her expression behind her fan. Had Johanna been more
cordial to Danny he would have had more effulgence to loose on
Mrs Fitzhugh. As it was, he treated her to political dissertations,
demanding of her, as a comparatively recent arrival, information
and response which she was too hare-brained to give. He was not
obtuse to her sense of her own superiority, and she was sobered
before the end of the meal. "Me wife has lent you her carriage, I
understand," he remarked before withdrawing.

"It was quite obliging of her."

"I'm thinking it might have been better to lend it to some poor
woman who needed it and not to you who has so many fine friends
waiting on you."

Mrs Fitzhugh did not know how this was intended. She was too
little a lady, too much a self-seeking snob to return the carriage
with gracious thanks.

"How lately have you been at Heulong?" Danny inquired.

"Not for months. I got away before the river rose."

"Then you did not see James Fullwood when he was down?"

"He has not been down or my sister would have mentioned it. We get the post and parcels across quite often in the boat."

"It's dayvilish mysterious," thought Danny, and stumped away to find Hennessy, who was waiting for him in his private room behind the bar. He could give no information about James Fullwood, but had other business which soon put Bella out of Danny's head.

"If Oi could hev got away, Oi'd hev taken a thrip up to see ye, not wantin' to commit impoortant matter to a letter."

Danny removed the pipe to receive a communication with such a prelude. The trouble was concerning Robert and Hennessy's niece, Molly McCathie.

"In the name of God!" ejaculated Delacy, thoroughly upset, as Hennessy presented the shameful details of such cases. Robert had been found in Molly's room at an ungodly hour; she had been sent to the Sisters at the Convent in Goulburn; matters could be mended by marriage. "Sure, I had other ideas and thim a little betther," he continued, gaining confidence as he perceived the consternation of Delacy. "But seeing phwat has happened, I can do no other. That young divvil of yours has so much swagger that the girls is bloinded on behowlding him. Sure, he's so flash in full feather that it would take coloured specs to protect the ois."

Hennessy was called away to quell a disturbance in the bar. Danny pondered the evidence. Johanna had spoken of Molly, and Robert had kept away from town for some months. With his gig and plated harness and tandem Bedouins!

Hennessy returned.

"I must have time to inquire into the rights of this. I'll condemn no man unheard, not even me own son; but me own son, if it is proven against him, shall do justice to anny woman—black, whoite or green," said Delacy. He did not take his noggins that evening nor become loud in poetical recitation and political discussion.

Hennessy counted upon the Delacy integrity. 'It could be a very good match," he said. "Oi'll treat her as me own daughter. Oi'll be open-handed because it is your son. Afther all, 'tis a vaynial sin for the gossoons and colleens to be fond of wan another. We've been young ourselves, Danny Delacy."

"I was never young to that extent, *Mister* Hennessy."

Hennessy took the hint in the emphasis on the *mister* as he replied, "But in this new counthry, Mr Delacy, things have broadened considerably. Shure, Molly is fit to wed wid anny wan in these jumped-up Colonies. She's been eddicated as well as your son, and that's betther than anny wan else in the disthrict."

"I'll sleep on it," said Delacy.

He lay awake for an hour or two—an unusual state for him. Hennessy's declarations and demands were a blow. He could not be sure of Robert, and Johanna had to be faced. Also, despite his theories, he had his pride—pride in honesty of breed, and he did not welcome as a daughter-in-law the niece of a convict. Molly's parents were unknown, at least to any one but Hennessy. She might be a by-blow of Hennessy's, or worse, and she was a Roman Catholic. Delacy was so honest that he would have preferred the daughter of a humble man of principle to that of a scoundrel grandee, and he was all for helping the erring to re-establish themselves, but he did not enjoy the prospect of alliance with the disreputable.

CHAPTER XVIII

DANNY returned to Bewuck so early on the following day that Johanna inquired what was the matter.

"Me business was finished. There was nothing to hang around for. And I am curious that nothing has been heard of Fullwood and Bella Rafferty."

Doogoolook came home at evening. He had crossed in the Quebarra boat, nine miles down, and let the horse swim. He had no news. Bella was nowhere to be seen, nor the two mares who should by now have been morganatically awaiting young Nullah-Mundoeys at Bewuck.

Robert, sick with uneasiness, awaited his father's return. Shrinking from the inevitable reckoning, he had ridden home with Stewart Butler to look at a colt. Danny was relieved to hear this. He, too, shrank from the encounter. In a way he was glad of the lesser problem of Bella, and announced his intention of swimming the river on the morrow and riding to Heulong and Rafferty's to settle the matter.

"Ye'll get your death of cramp in the river. There's no need to be in a flurry over that streel. She'll be setting herself up somewhere on the strength of my training, and telling a cock and bull story about her escape from Bunratty Castle."

Danny was not to be deterred. In the morning he saddled the river-crosser—a tall old grey—and tying-up a head bundle went down to the dark swirling waters, a man in the fifties with but one leg, but who retained his nerve.

"Mother of God! Will ye never gather a little common sense? An eft would be an elephant to ye in common sense. What ever has come to that Rafferty streel, another day or two wouldn't worsen it."

Danny had his bundle on his head, the string held in his teeth. With a muffled arrah he drove the hunched and protesting grey forward to the girth, the veteran feeling his way and keeping his feet nearly to the farther bank, where he swam bravely and completed a safe crossing. Doogoolook exposed his teeth in a silent laugh of admiration. His chief was invincible.

Neither of the Fullwood men was at home, so Danny was for

holding all parley on horseback and departing. Mrs Fullwood was too kindly and hospitable for that. She brought out a crutch that had been used by James when he cut his foot with an adze. Grace was also desirous of being helpful. They were eager for news of Bewuck.

"Are Della and Bella Rafferty still in the mountains?" Mrs Fullwood inquired.

Danny saw that nothing would be gained by telling of Bella's disappearance. He let her slide for the moment. He found that Mrs Fullwood had not seen James for months and that Charles had been up in the mountains for nearly all the past summer Delacy was surprised by this news. Charles was away now. It was a disappointing visit to Grace, as Danny never mentioned Robert.

Leaving Heulong, Delacy turned the grey towards Learmont, a settler between Heulong and Keebah, where he arrived about nine o'clock, and, while being fed, learned that the Learmonts knew nothing of Bella or Fullwood. Danny remarked that he had expected Fullwood to leave two old mares there, and said nothing of Bella. He loathed scandal as the plague, and was careful not to start any.

All that day Johanna watched the crossing until it was dark. and Norah persuaded her that Danny had remained at Heulong. Robert returned at dusk, much relieved to find that his father was not at home, and to estimate that Danny had not divulged anything. The evil hour was postponed. He had already been arraigned by Hennessy, and had taken a defiant stand.

Johanna's vigil was rewarded next afternoon. Danny had pressed himself and the grey to outstrip additional waters on the way from farther up. Robert wished that his father would catch pneumonia and be too ill to bring him to judgment. Danny arrived with his teeth chattering and blue with cold, but a change of clothes and a nip of rum before the fire soon made him ready for a hearty meal, while he told the latest instalment of the Bella Rafferty serial

"She must have eloped with old Jimmy," said Robert. "They could not both have fallen down a precipice."

Danny wrote to William and dispatched Doogoolook. The boys were bidden to go out to James Fullwood's and do everything to find out where Bella had been taken.

Danny was now ready to address Robert. He waited until after supper and took possession of the kitchen.

"Well, Robert, Hennessy has laid a charge against you that I never thought would be laid against son of me own. Have you anything to say for yourself?"

"If you are going to believe what an old lag . . ."

"It's when a man has no case that he resorts to abusing the other side. I asked, have you anything to say for yourself?"

"What is Hennessy saying?"

"Had you no words of your own with Hennessy?"

"He's been trying to rope someone in for that bitch of a Molly, and I'm one that's been attacked, if that is what you mean. He hasn't a leg to stand on; she's the town harlot."

"Now, look here," said Danny, removing his pipe, the better to emphasize his words, "another low thing is to blayguard a young woman as a way out of your own sins, if you have had anny gifts from her."

For all his brazen air, Robert's heart was thumping against his chest. He could hear the river and the oak fronds weeping in the night, and wished that he was a little boy again plunging in the bunyip hole with Doogoolook, and never a thought of girls, blast them! "Every one knows what that Molly is."

"What I am concerned with is your own behaviour. Have I ever taught you to make others the keeper of your actions as a decent citizen? Have you, or have you not, had certain relations with Molly McCathie?"

"Aw, we had a lark or two with her. She let us go too far, but there were half a dozen in it."

"It's true then, that you have had relations with Molly McCathie in accordance with Hennessy's allegations?"

"He just picked on me."

"What others do you accuse?"

"Gerald Butler and Tom Angus and Branston and Aubrey Fullwood to name a few. Athol Macallister was the one who started it."

"How came this?"

"After a bit of a dance one night in the Hall beside the store, we might have been a little on, not being used to liquor. Molly only put me to bed in her room to save waking the old man, and he got toothache or something in the night and came in. I never did her any harm. Old Hennessy is mad to get up in the social stirrups and he picks on me because he knows you will be the softest to handle."

Danny put him through a searching cross-examination, and so hammered home the enormity of "tampering with anny girl—black, whoite or green", that Robert's bravado was plucked and he was left in the undergarments of shame.

"I've heard you and Hennessy separately," concluded Danny. "The next is to bring you face to face and see how you stand up then. 'Twill be the girl's turn next. No accusations will ever be laid involving me family's character but I'll clear them up. If you have incurred anny responsibility, by the Lord Harry, me boy, you'll discharge it. You'll ride in to Hennessy with me to-morrow."

"I won't," said Robert flatly. "Why should I lick-spittle after a — old lag because he is acting as a criminal to me?"

"I'll concede your point. Hennessy shall come here."

"If he comes here Ma will wonder why, and it will upset her."

"It's too late to think of your mother's health now."

Robert's experience at college in Sydney made him contemptuous of his father's narrow standards, though none so desirous of esteem as he, and he crumpled at the prospect of being the oaf to hold the parcel in a company affair. Unconvicted of sin he feared only ridicule, and would have sold his soul to keep the matter secret.

Molly was equally unabashed spiritually or socially, though such generous behaviour as hers to lovers was not made safe by science for unmarried women until a later generation. A lady of pleasure was in a plight but trusted to extricate herself by marriage. Robert really was in danger. Her favourite was Athol, son of old Bandy Macallister of Curragoobill, and half a dozen other stations from the Murray to the Darling. Bandy was cynical and vulgar, and able to drive a bargain. His only legitimized son was the wildest blackguard unlicked, and the bullet-headed whip who drove tandem with such dash that the dazzled Robert had taken him as a model.

In time Robert had been able to drive a tandem of Bedouins through the Township when Athol was there to behold, and be conquered. He made an offer. Robert refused. Athol must have those dun beasts with the silver manes and tails, no matter what the cost or conditions. Robert pursued his advantage. Athol made him a familiar, but such was Robert's up-bringing that he would not take Athol home to Norah.

He brought Gerry Butler to Athol, and both lads imitated Athol's gracelessness. Athol led in appreciation of Molly's satisfying charms. All her paramours remembered her as long as they lived, and grinned with glee when they met her. Molly adored Athol, but drunk or sober, she could not noose him into marriage. He was the kind of rapscallion to hold all women lightly unless proved under test. He would kiss a servant girl as soon as look at her, and seduce her as a sporting incident. Casualties in virtue were entirely a feminine responsibility in his philosophy.

He was the supreme example of all the masculine insolence of the bloods of his decade. He jeered at Gerald and Robert for being old maids, and led them after him on thoroughbreds, jumping in and out of the flower gardens fronting the straggling main street of the Township and of Queanbeyan and of Cooma. They likewise followed his lead in the lark of breaking the crockery in one or two shanties, when Robert, due to fear of his father's principles, had to pay. In Athol's company the two young men first became drunk—taking lessons in how to carry liquor like a swell. Blood horses, kangaroo dogs and greyhounds, guns, plated harness, top boots and cabbage tree hats at £7/10/- or £15 each, all the squatter swagger, which embellished drinking, swearing and wenching, came natural to Athol. He was protected by the conventions in virility of the times, and by old Bandy's wealth. He was wild where his imitators could not ascend above flashness. There were plenty to say: "There's no harm in young Mac at bottom," though he was but a simian in human shape, graceless and uncivilizable.

When a scapegoat was needed, he cunningly had one. Robert was left in Molly's arms after a certain debauch. The best fun had been in leading Hennessy to find him there. Athol had blundered up and down the passage to awaken the old terrier, and when he emerged blinking with his candle, he saw Athol near Molly's door. Hennessy demanded admittance to Molly's room and found Robert.

"Too dead to the world to be dangerous, but that, by hell! makes it funnier." Athol cackled as he told his crew in Sydney.

"Christ! But it must have been rich," they agreed.

Athol ran gaily away with his Bedouin tandem, for which he had paid £250 in cash; but ah, he had his revenge for that. Robert would need more than £250 before he was done. Molly pleaded and pleaded. Athol showed her letters around with inflated swagger, and told her he wanted no wife who was found asleep with dirty young Irish dogs like Bob Delacy.

Hennessy had the measure of Athol, and was relieved that Robert was so fully compromised. Molly, made desperate and revengeful by Athol's repudiation, let her uncle have his head. If he could make Robert marry her, she was willing. Too uncertain of consequences to claim innocence, she was obstinately silent. Hennessy sent her to Goulburn for safety, and started on Robert.

The interview with Robert, Hennessy and Danny was disastrous to Robert's case. The facts were incontrovertible as stated by Hennessy, with the housekeeper's corroboration.

"You must bring the girl out to my place, and me wife and I will interrogate her," said Delacy, "first by herself and then with you and Robert present . . . I'll be thankful to have me wife's carriage brought home. Hospitality can go too far for them that's not worth it—not meaning you, Hennessy."

He marched away with dignity, notwithstanding his sloppy clothes and peg-leg. It was Robert, in the panoply of unmarred youth and smart gear, who was shorn of swagger. Hennessy was satisfied with his progress. The Delacys would kick for a while, but he would set the young folks up and then use the connection for every ounce that it would yield, Mrs Fitzhugh his next objective. He regretted the youthful rebellion that had put ostracizing wales on his back. There was now no cause for rebellion in Australia. The Irish famine in the 'forties had exterminated those members of his family who had not escaped to Canada or the United States. Poor old Ireland was in a hopeless mess, but in the Colonies a man had outlet for ambition and energy. Hennessy meant to go up and up, all obstacles but a spur to endeavour.

"Your mother will have to know. Will you tell her or shall I?"

"I'll tell her myself," said Robert sulkily.

"And I'll be present."

Robert was thus cornered to divulge the fact of discovery in Molly's bed at 3 a.m. "I was drunk, was the reason. Gerry Butler, Athol Macallister, Aubrey Fullwood, Tom Angus and I all went in together, but I was not used to drink, and it made me dizzy. There was no harm, really. The others went out when I went to sleep. Molly does nothing but throw herself at men. She is playing her cards now to land me."

Danny's comment was a loud "Humph!"

"Mother of God, have mercy, that such a thing could befall me son!" shrieked Johanna, in such grief and excitement as Danny had not previously seen from her. He was dazed.

Robert thought he had driven his mother mad and was scared to hysteria. He put his arms about her and tried to quieten her, "I swear, Ma, I am innocent. We were just daring each other to get drunk to see what it was like."

"I know that hussy!" Johanna screamed between paroxysms. "I've seen her at work to capture me innocent son, and him trapped in a net. God help me, that I should have come to this! It is a just punishment . . . And what are ye doing, Daniel Delacy, to save ye'r son from the clutches of that foul harpy, and that criminal, Hennessy?"

Danny's statement that he had investigated so as to have justice in hand and had discovered Robert's culpability, brought a fresh outburst. It did not move Danny fundamentally. He considered it on a par with Johanna's marital aberration, and thought that if he had met that firmly she might not now have been so wild. Justice he would have and was so reasonable that he knew all the virtue would not be on one side, even with his son.

"Peace, woman!" he said at last. "Nothing more can be done till we hear what the girl has to say."

"What she says! She should never be let open her mouth again to her betters. If such a slut ever comes near me, I'll tear her eyes out by the roots."

"Come now, Johanna, if the case was your own daughter led astray by the love of some young man, and she motherless and fatherless, wouldn't your heart break if there was no justice for her?"

"Ye to name wan like that with ye'r own daughter—shame on ye!"

"Your daughters had you to look after them."

" 'Tis plain they would never have had ye in anny trouble. And where is me daughter now? And where is that surrvant I trained for her among the dingoes?"

Danny was tempted to interject that Bella had been put in charge of one of the aristocratic Fullwoods, but felt it more than his position as a husband would carry.

"And ye to be tigrinizing about after Hennessy's by-blow—no father and mother! None that can be mentioned at all events."

When Robert recovered from his alarm, his mother's attitude was an immense satisfaction to him. Danny shut his long stained teeth hard and stumped away on other business. Johanna's outburst had unmanned him, but did not deflect him from procedure necessary to the upholding of character. The next move was Hennessy's. The girl had to be brought from Goulburn.

"Ye'r father increases in oddity till sometimes I don't know what to think of him," Johanna observed to Norah, in making a report in which Robert's liability was unscrupulously minimized.

"That Molly was always an odious, forward creature, who tried to put herself on a level with every one," observed Norah, fearful lest her precious Stewart might also have been contaminated.

Men's indulgence with certain women beneath respect was known to take place, but when it happened with a member of any circle, the accommodating female was known for an enemy and could be given no quarter by self-respecting ladies.

CHAPTER XIX

Danny tried to offset his uneasiness by furious action, but found that Bewuck was Robert's. Every one looked to Robert as the boss, even the dogs. Danny's special servitors forsook him to run after Robert, in spite of the wars this entailed. The canine fraternity are psychologists, and in selecting Robert, dogs knew that only against their master could lese-majesty be committed. The other Delacys imposed humiliating discipline on their dogs, but Robert's personality, as it ripened, compelled other people to guard against his servitors' depredations or to suffer them as quietly as possible.

Deprived of more urgent business, Danny crossed the Murrumbidgee again on the Bella business. Johanna raised no protest this time. She hid in her bedroom and waited anxiously until Maeve announced that Danny was safely across. She laughed grimly at the worry about Bella. "Another streel who can take care of herself to the injury of others, or she wouldn't be true to her breed. Your father deserves the pair of treasures he has on his hands now."

Robert was disquieted by the impending private meeting with his mother, which could no longer be evaded when she had the fire lighted in the drawing-room that evening and summoned him. "And now, my son, tell me how ye came to be trapped. Ye will never be so innocent among wolves hereafter."

Robert, affecting candour, told little, but made a plausible defence. He had already admitted the intoxication. He considered that Gerry Butler, Athol Macallister and the others had gone too far with Molly, and when they were in danger of old Hennessy, had rigged the evidence on him.

"That wily old wretch will stop at nothing to crawl into a good family. God help us, and your father no more use than a broken umbrella in a thunderstorm to withstand him."

"I'll clear out to Queensland where they can't get hold of me."

"If Grace should hear of it, 'twill distress the poor girl; but if she's worthy of ye, 'twill be a nice little test."

Robert was indifferent to Grace's attitude for or against him, but was too diplomatic to say so. "In any case, I'll go away to Queensland for a spell. I'm full-up of Bewuck. It's a tin-pot hole. Out on the Darling Downs . . ."

"Have I not endured enough in the furthest wilds from civilization without me heart to be torn from me by me eldest son going where it is like an oven all the time, and with the cannibal blacks eating ye, and the fever at ye."

Robert would almost as soon have married Molly as fulfil his threat, but young men in New South Wales were making it as their fathers had cited the Antipodes.

"Would ye be running with ye'r tail between ye'r legs, like wan of the curs out there, and leaving the field to the lags and their bastards? Shame on ye, Robert! That would be to admit ye were guilty, and that I never would do, even if ye were—not to sweepings like that, or they would soon be in the stirrups, and their betters in the gutter."

Delacy had no pleasant prospect as he approached the Raffertys. They were of objectionable quality. The mother's easy virtue was a byword, therefore they would make a noise about their daughter, and by damn! where were Bella and Fullwood?

The Raffertys came streaming to meet Mr Delacy, and held his stirrup and hampered him in alighting, noisomely servile and genuinely hospitable and eager for news. Their hut was squalid. They were shepherds for Wells, a squatter adjoining Old Gienties, and under the Act had selected a few acres around their abode. They treated dogs, pigs and fowls as equals. Mrs Rafferty's hair was matted and verminous, her dress filthy and tattered.

"Begob, and 'tis ye'rself, Mr Delacy, that is the kind gintleman to come all this way around to inform me of me darlint Beila. And how is the darlint gurrl? And it's blissed she was to be trained by ye'r dear woile—a dear koind lady if iver there was wan. 'God bless her!' sez Oi to Mrs Rafferty at the toime, Oi did, ' 'tis the chance of a loife-time.' "

The woman was less effusive but equally servile. It was difficult for Delacy to open, but he was justly known as Danny the brave. The deterring factor was the likelihood of the woman's false grief. For what might he not be blamed to disturb an expectant mother, though she was a notorious polyandrist? He withdrew Rafferty, "To talk about a bull, Rafferty, and that no lady's subject."

Mrs Rafferty retreated in a "refined" manner taking some of the smaller youngsters with her. At a hint from Delacy, Rafferty threatened with a kick the bigger ones.

"Did ye send a letter to Bella by James Fullwood about three weeks past?"

"Divvil a wan of the Fullwoods have we seen for months."

"I do not wish to disturb your wife with something that maybe can be cleared up," Delacy continued, and related the circumstances of Bella's disappearance.

"Begob!" said Rafferty. He suspected that he had no responsibility for Bella's being, and had been glad to be free from her tongue, but he had a property claim on her. "Ye did wrong, Mr Delacy, not to bring her on ye'rself, ye having promised the mother to guard her as wan of ye'r own."

"But Fullwood—a man of years—and coming straight down."

"Min of years are none too safe—but he shall be made to pay—he must be follered and made to pay."

"I've sent me black boy with instructions to me sons. I went meself as far as Learmont's."

"I thrimble at the thought of telling me poor wife. Her sowl is wrapped up in that darlint gurrl. If she is rooned, 'twill be a bad day for all concerned. They'll be made to pay, and to the limit. Ye'll come to tell me owld woman."

Danny did not balk, though he nearly gasped as he endured the unrestrained and fetid blasts of Mother Rafferty's tongue.

"Shure, iviry wan concerned will be made to pay," was Rafferty's monotonous reiteration.

"I'll do me best to clear it up," said Delacy.

The female Rafferty continued to vituperate in fluent Cockney about the ruination of her child. The male Rafferty kept on and on that every one should be made to pay.

Delacy rode away followed by execrations, and murmuring to himself, "There's a cask of maggotty meat for you!"

At nine o'clock the Bewuck household heard his halloas above the Murrumbidgee. "Save us!" exclaimed Johanna. "Is that your father, and the river up, and as cold as ice, and him for ever thinking he's as young as he was in 'fifty-two, swimming the Yackandandah, and it the dark of the moon? Sure, he's stark mad."

"He'll be all right," said Robert. "You couldn't kill him with an axe. The grey could do the crossing in hobbles."

The crisp stars faintly showed the rushing water in the deep gorge. A small wind cancelled frost and sighed in the casuarinas' mermaid tresses. The curlews retreated wailing. The plovers protested noisily. All the dogs howled or yelped. Danny loved their welcoming commotion. Johanna was nervous.

Robert was not alarmed for his father's safety. His sudden disappearance would have been a relief. Danny had never demanded affection from his sons, and at present he was in the position of a judge. Robert and Maeve went out with lanterns and soon the traveller was casting extra logs on his roaring fire, while the drenched horse shivered without reward or care under the frosty sky.

Danny was not communicative about the Rafferty episode. He remarked that the letter had been a ruse. The Raffertys had not heard from Bella.

"Most likely she's run off with somewan as soon as ye'r back was turned," observed Johanna.

"It's for the police now. If annything has happened to her and it not reported, 'twould look queer on my part."

He took so much rum on going to bed that he awakened late next morning, and his stump of a leg was paining as though nails were being driven into it. Two immersions in icy waters during a long day without food had been too much.

"There's a wind sweeping down from Monaro all laden with gusts of sleet," Johanna reported.

"Sure, I have a cold as long as a wet week. Wan day more won't hurt Bella either way." He made a noise about his rare indisposition, and doctored himself with one remedy more drastic than the other in such quick succession that only an invincible stomach could have escaped disturbance.

In the evening a messenger arrived with a letter from Hennessy stating that he had brought Molly from Goulburn, and that she was ready to meet Delacy and Robert. The messenger was put up for the night.

"Shall I send word for Hennessy to bring the girl out here?"

"Ye'll sind word that she'll never place her foot in this house only over me dead body. Neither me daughter nor meself will contaminate the place with such trash."

"Then, Johanna, will you go with me to face the girl and sift her story?"

"Me, to go to the beck of her! I've sifted her story. Shame on ye, Daniel Delacy, ye have less gumption than an eft and ye knowing me, to suggest such an indignity."

"Well, Robert, you can ride to the Township with me to-morrow."

"I won't." Robert swaggered rebelliously.

"Arrah! 'Tis as I thought. You're too guilty to face the girl. There's no man, woman or child on this earth that I am not game to face about anything."

"I'm not guilty at all. She's a liar and a ——. I'll go to Queensland before I'll say a word to her."

"You are mortal uneasy about her accusations if it will take Queensland to pull you up—running from a girl no more than five feet high. I've seen you smirking after her often enough. While you are on Bewuck, you'll observe what I say. I'm ashamed that wan of me breed hasn't the pluck to face a bull's nest and explode it, if it's false. You should have heard the bally-ragging I faced from the Raffertys, male and female."

Put this way, Robert said he would go. Danny barred the gig as flash, and they set off on horseback, Robert considerably subdued.

The encounter was in Hennessy's private den. Molly was dressed with girlish simplicity and a manner to match. She hardly raised her eyes to Danny and hovered touchingly on the verge of tears. She was so pretty and healthy that she charmed Danny, who had always liked her cheerful friendliness. Whatever she was, he thought her worth a whole boiling of Fullwoods.

Robert, braced for belligerence, was nonplussed by Molly's chaste, shy mien. Could such hypocrisy be! He had thought his mother rather soft as to his own virtues, but he marvelled at her acumen regarding the perfidious Molly.

"Now, Molly, bear up," said Hennessy. "Though ye've done foolishly, ye and Robert were both vaynial young folks. Things can be minded, as Mr Delacy has shown."

Danny removed his pipe to address seductive girlishness. Robert felt as many another man—and woman—has felt on seeing a jury of males bowled over by the attractively presented sexiness of some designing hussy.

"Now, Molly McCathie, you've brought wan of the most serious accusations in life against me son, and what have you to say for yourself?"

Molly fluttered and choked and took refuge in a handkerchief. "I didn't want to, but Robert kept on and on, and I was frightened, but he swore by everything holy to marry me."

"What a boomer!" burst from Robert. "I could never make you have me because you were so mashed on Athol Macallister. He was always in your bedroom as if he was married to you."

"Phwat do ye know of anny young gurrl's bedroom? Ye are admitting that ye bothered her with advances?" bawled Hennessy.

Robert saw his mistake. Hennessy continued. "Ye cannot denoi that Mrs Rooney and meself found ye in me niece's room on the noight of the dance?"

"I don't remember anything about it. I took a nobbler of your poisoned grog, and Gerry Butler and Athol Macallister and Tom Angus played a practical joke by landing me there. I never harmed Molly, I'm sure of that."

"Sure there's no harrum at all, if ye'll shoulder ye'r raysponsibilities loike a gintleman. Molly's heart is scalded for ye, and if ye'r feyther will put up a little caboose for ye, Oi'll set ye up rint free, with as handsome a prospect as anny one."

"It's not my responsibility. I was too dead drunk."

"It wasn't that time but all the others," whimpered Molly, "and every one is talking about you and me, and I'm ruined. I wish I was dead."

"As to being ruined," said Danny judicially, "scandalmongering japers are like the magpies chattering on the fence posts; but are you really ruined to the extent of prospects of motherhood?"

Molly bent her head and fostered wild sobs, satisfactory to Hennessy, touching to Danny, but dismaying to Robert.

"I'll have to kill myself," she wailed, with shattering sobs.

"I'm not the only one."

"Ye're the only wan Molly has ever encouraged," said the good-tempered tones of Hennessy. "Oi was not anxious for ye, as Molly has betther chances, but there is no evidence from here to Goulburn of Molly being out with anny one but ye. Whoi, didn't ye come straight here and get her to christen ye'r gig? The divvil mind ye, if Oi had known that ye were not honourably intintioned to me motherless orphan! I tawt, being the son of a gintleman, the sowl of honour himself, that Oi was safe wid ye. There were plinty others—Macallister for wan, but the crows could see that he is dangerous, and niver did me gurrl go out of soight wid him."

Asseverations and denials were powerless in face of such mendacity. When Robert got out of that room he would steer for the Queensland border without waiting for fine weather.

At the end of a hacking session, Hennessy observed that his poor child was fainting, and, dramatically picking her up, carried her from the room. He threw her on her bed none too tenderly, "Don't ye move out till I give ye lave. Begor, 'tis safest to put the key in me pocket."

He returned to Delacy. Robert was contemptuously silent, his scorn suiting his eagle features.

"You can go to bed, Robert. I want a word with Hennessy."

Robert removed himself with open contempt, but it made no dint in Hennessy's purpose. Robert was damned if ever he'd allow the old man to tell him to go to bed again. He'd sooner tell him to go to hell than obey. If those two old fools thought they were going to settle his affairs, they'd find out their mistake, but uneasiness arose through his debts to Hennessy. As many a one with a "fine head for business", finding money easy, Robert had squandered it. Was Hennessy reserving mention of the debts for a knock-out blow?

He picked his overcoat and hat from the rack, went to the stable for his horse, and galloped into the sharp night, reaching home at two o'clock. His mother called out to him and he told her of Molly's hypocrisy and the attitude of his father and Hennessy. His mother's support was comforting. "No matter what they do, I'll never marry her," he maintained.

" 'Twill never come to that. If ye'r father is such a newt to be put upon to that extint, we'll have a plan as simple as shelling peas that will leave them looking like a pair of plucked geese in a thunderstorm."

Under seal of secrecy he confessed to debts. His mother took this the right way too. "Me poor foolish boy. He has prepared a trap for ye, the unholy scoundrel. We can make it up out of the egg money."

Robert confessed to about half. Even that staggered his mother, but did not daunt her.

"Are you convinced that Molly is to become a mother?" Danny inquired of Hennessy.

"We can be sure wid a doctor," said Hennessy smoothly. "Shure, 'twould be a raylief to know otherwise. Oi'm no advocate of forced marriages."

"I propose Dr Britton in Goulburn. A certificate from him would convince me."

"Oi'll take Molly to-morrow and Dr Britton can sind worrud in his own hand."

Molly washed her puffed face and reviewed her position. She was incensed by Athol Macallister's indifference to her last plea, his cruelty when her hunger for him was unendurable. She was forced to do something to offset it, and Robert was an instrument. His superior attitude filled her with a desire for revenge, and the hardihood to go through with her uncle's plan. He was only a puppy, a lout, whining after her like a little boy, crying even for kisses, and now to blacken her and throw the blame on others!

She could have picked on Athol, but he would have laughed at any threat of being sued for maintenance. He had never babbled of marriage as Robert had. Her attempt to force Robert into marriage had in it more of revenge on Athol than desire to save her name. Such infatuation and delight as hers in Athol could not be quite unreturned. She sought to arouse his jealousy.

Danny was not surprised to find that Robert had gone. It left him free to return by Butler's and confront Gerald. His honesty and candour unsuited him for such investigation. Gerry had enjoyed Molly's generosity. He had been a floater for years because he could make no headway with Della who nevertheless did not accept any one else and thus end his uncertainty. Gerry's only concern was to clear himself, though it might put Molly in the family into which his brother was about to marry and where he too had not given up hope. He was cautious, but admitted that Robert had been fond of Molly.

Danny reached Bewuck before Johanna had retired. Robert kept out of the way. Johanna extracted what had passed in Hennessy's room, and put her own construction on it.

"Robert must shoulder his responsibilities. It doesn't matter to me if the girl is Molly McCathie or the Governor's daughter." Argument was useless when he closed his mouth that way. Johanna had not prevailed over him religiously when he was young and amorous. She compressed her lips upon her own purpose. Her beautiful son was not to be sacrificed to a faggot, let Dr Britton's verdict be what it might.

Robert found the atmosphere unbearable. It was against the training of horses. Danny had Hannon in tow and Robert could not give orders in view of his own doubtful status. He was relieved when his mother asked for help in her garden. Matters were not advanced for him by the arrival of a big working bullock who attempted to get into the cow-paddock where he had been born. "Sure, that's old Daisy's calf," observed Danny. "I thought Robert gave him to the blacks with the hipped cow for a feast a year ago." Hannon was silent. He never made trouble with his tongue.

Danny pursued the subject at dinner. "'Tis plain he's a worker; someone must have got him from the blacks."

It was the beast that Robert had sold to pay for the gig. Robert longed for his father to go away that day so he could manage the cursed affair, but Danny turned the bullock into the cow-paddock and pottered about the premises all the afternoon.

At dusk the owner appeared, a teamster named Bell. He was carrying stores from the Township to The Plains and the bullock had bolted for home. "And how did you come by him, I'd be interested to know?" inquired Danny.

"Bought him from the young cove here. I got a receipt."

"Sure, that was the lot me son told me about when I was in the mountains. You'll stay the night?"

The man said he must push on, but he first had a good meal in the kitchen.

Danny went into Robert. "Did you sell the yellow bullock to Bell separate?"

Robert was caught.

"This will need explanation," said Danny, returning to talk with Bell, who later departed with his beast. The disappointed creature had to be heeled all the way up the cutting by a dog and striped by a whip till he bled. Danny called his son out behind the stables in the frosty night and gave him such a dressing-down that Robert trembled. Danny was at a loss to account for such a lack of principle in a son of his loins. "And what did you do with the money?"

"Bought the gig to drive Ma about," said Robert sullenly.

"I bought a carriage more comfortable to your mother."

"It's as big as a circus."

"I thought at the time you were wanting in judgment to give a young bullock to the blacks, but I would rather that you lacked judgment than principle," said Danny, showing his own lack of business values.

Robert could have been cutting, as he grew to be with years, but was subdued by the fear of his greater debt to Hennessy coming to light.

"It looks as if you lacked principle right through. Molly McCathie is too good for you." Danny stumped back to his fire. Christianly lenient to others, he set an inexorably high standard for himself and his own.

Robert's vanity, of which he had an inordinate share, was painfully wounded, a stinging experience, following upon the other. In his passionate humiliation he actually contemplated flight to Queensland, and that was desperation. He was a homer, not a roamer by nature.

That evening Danny retired early, and to his bed proper, the big double bed of marital years. "Bring me nightshirt," he requested Norah. "I'm free from me cold now." Robert's debacle was not all distress to his father. Obliquely it gave him conjugal courage.

Johanna remained up unusually late, but she found Danny awake waiting for her, a candle set on his chest to read the paper. "Ye'll set the place a-fire wan of these nights," she said, but omitted to complain of the ripe odour of the pipe.

"I came to bed early to have a private talk with you."

"And I stayed up late to balk ye," thought Johanna, taking as long as the frosty air permitted to prepare herself for bed.

A sore and sorry Robert lay awake wondering what his father was saying as the murmur of voices continued for some time.

"If the blacks demanded two and he satisfied them with wan, sure, he was entoitled to the money,' was Johanna's argument.

"He wasn't entitled to tell a lie and deceive me."

"A little whoite loi!"

"A lie is a lie."

"And a fool is a fool," thought Johanna. "Sure, ye can't expect a foine young man of Robert's address and education, and a head for business on him, to manage and improve everything and be contint with the position of an assigned man."

Danny thought with satisfaction that Robert would be relieved of management.

"Ye cannot educate a foine boy to be a gentleman and expect him to drag around like a peat cutter," persisted Johanna.

"An honest man is more to me than the shiniest gentleman. Be the poipers, no man can be a gentleman at all unless he is honest first."

Johanna might have approved of the misappropriation of the bullock, thought Danny. He was shocked by her attitude, and, in the way of parents, inclined to attribute the bad streak in Robert to her side. He laid her unreasoning partisanship to the maniacal qualities of mother love, the protection of the offspring by the female, to be seen even in the magpie.

"If his own father can't protect him whin he makes a little youthful slip, it's a poor chance for me boy in a world full of lags and harpies." Johanna sounded like tears.

"Och, woman, there's no rayson at you," said Danny, turning over, and half wishing that he had kept to the end room. "By damn! she's just like a magpie with a nest," he thought as he drifted to sleep, comforted that it was a natural rather than an evil phenomenon.

A cold sweat would break over Robert when he thought of Dr Britton's report being affirmative. The days hung like a blight. He was thankful to retreat to the barn and husk maize, a task formerly beneath him.

CHAPTER XX

WILLIAM'S arrival was a welcome break in the strain.

As soon as Doogoolook had reached Burrabinga with Danny's letter, Harry investigated as far as Learmont's while William went to Wong Foo and to James Fullwood's hut. Bella had been at the hut, as a garment testified. Wong had further information about Delacy cattle going to market with the Fullwoods, and this time there was nothing to cloud the issue.

"That streel must have gone off with James Fullwood," said Harry to William in solemn consultation.

"She even made up to me, but I threatened to throw a dish of water on her," responded the unconscious Joseph.

"And we'll get the blame of it and all the disgrace. Will she have a baby?" Harry sank to a hollow whisper.

Billy Aldon, the stockman baching with O'Neill, came for rations, and as the matter was no longer secret, the Delacys talked with him. He was enamoured of Bella. It was for safety that Danny had latterly banished him to Dead Horse Plain. Jealousy loosened his tongue. He was ready any time that a witness was needed as to who lifted so many Delacy cattle during the past year. The boys left that in abeyance until they could reinstate their respectability regarding the abduction or absconding of Bella. Billy was eager to follow Fullwood to Hell or Hay in order "to belt the stuffin' outer the —— ole morepork".

"There's not much stuffing in old skinny Jimmy, but we'll let Billy rip," chuckled William.

Fullwood must have left Bella somewhere, if he had gone on to Melbourne with cattle, as reported. The three young men set out to find her, leaving Ned Callahan to patrol Burrabinga, a great deal of which was then under snow. From the ranges across the river for twenty miles to Bullock Gap and beyond was girth deep in dry snow as if coarse salt had been scattered, and every denizen of the bush had left his track, whether Menura or wombat, dingo or bandicoot.

William rode to Gool Gool, Harry to Queanbeyan, and Billy Aldon to Gundagai on the Great Southern Road. He had no difficulty in tracking Bella. Women riding that way were an event in winter. He followed to Cootamundra, where Bella was established at the best hotel, and calling herself Mrs Wood. When Aldon said he had a letter for her she ordered him to be sent in. She was in gay mood, which incensed her discarded lover.

"Is this what you've come to! Too flash for an honest man's offer to make a decent wife of you, but that —— of a rotten cattle-duffing swell can have his own way."

Bella stuck her tongue out and giggled until she was breathless.

"You may be all right for a bit in yer fine feathers, but wait till people know what you are—Mrs Wood! Think yer very smart, ain't you. At any rate I'll foller ole Jimmy and belt the stuffin' outer his ole hide."

"Cripes, that would be funny! He could have you took up by the police."

"He can be took up for abduction if you ain't of age."

"Took up for abducting his own missus! You are a hard case!"

"So that's what he promised, and you are green enough to swaller it."

"Seein's believin'. I'll show me marriage lines, and me ring."

She brought her left hand into view and took from the bosom of her dress a document which elated her every time she beheld it. Billy could not read, but was duly impressed.

"Crikey, Beller, is this true, or only gammon?"

Bella swore glibly that she was Mrs James Fullwood, and calling herself Wood modestly until James could take her to his family. "Golly, I'm splittin' me sides to think how that Annie and Grace will look w'en they have to call me Aunty."

The disappointed lover was cheered. Bella was a merry wight. "They mightn't have nothink to do with yer."

Bella tossed her head. "Just let them try any larks!"

"Oh, well," said Billy with resignation, "Seein' you have done so well by yourself, I wish yous luck. I reckon I had better not welt the stuffin' outer ole Jimmy."

They waxed familiar and Bella commissioned Billy to take the news to "pore ole Mar". "This is sure to git out wrong end fust as soon as she misses me, an' the ole cove will be runnin' round roarin' as if he could do somethink. Tell them to keep it quiet till James comes home, as he wants to take me to his family hisself."

"Cripes, I'd like to take the news to Heulong meself," grinned Billy. It was impossible to be depressed with Bella.

Billy was pleased to be messenger. One was necessary seeing that none of the parties could write a letter. "You really are married by a priest or parson, not just hocussing me?"

"I was married by the ole parson here in town. Go an' arsk him. Tell him ye'r me brother."

Billy did this and was assured that the marriage had been duly solemnized. The clergyman congratulated the young man that his sister had done so well for herself.

Billy returned to Burrabinga with his blithe news. William put Harry and Callahan to winter tasks and rode with Billy on his errand. William went on to set his father's mind at rest. His report was a triumph for Danny, but a blow to Johanna to have that streel in a family she so much admired and into which her heir apparent was to wed.

"Have I been rearing a shepherd's slut to enter the quality," she remarked.

Dr Britton's report confirmed Molly's statement. Hennessy had ensured that. He took Peggy Bell—daughter of the teamster who owned the yellow bullock—with him for the purpose. She had been employed in the hotel, had come to grief, and had just been found out by Mrs Rooney, the housekeeper. Her swain, a young bullocky, was eager to make an honest man of himself. Hennessy offered to take her to Goulburn with him and Molly, to meet and marry her man, on his way with loading, and thus save her from reproach. It was she whom Dr Britton certified as Molly McCathie. She was so terrified that she merely wept and submitted to examination as part of her fall. Mr Hennessy was so good to her. He gave her ten pounds as a wedding present and had her cared for at the convent until her man came through.

Dr Britton's report, made in good faith, filled Robert with fresh dismay.

"He'll marry the girl," said Danny, setting his jaw. He went riding about the place, shifting stock and inspecting fences, followed by what dogs he could command.

Norah said coldly, "We'll be dragged down to that level."

Robert sought his mother, startled by the prospect of exile to Queensland with not so much as a horse except by permission of his father. To be cooped at Bewuck as Molly's husband was hardly less terrifying, and he could not remain on his old terms and refuse to marry her.

"There's wan very simple way to ind the trouble and be safe," said Johanna.

"Too good to be true, but tell me."

"Silly choild! Off this night and ask Grace to elope with ye. Ye could take her in the gig."

The carriage had been borrowed by Hennessy, without asking, to take the erring females to Goulburn.

"That!" said Robert without enthusiasm. "That is not possible."

"She would run this very night if ye asked her. Whin I was years younger than she is, didn't I run to the ind of the globe with ye'r father!" Johanna's gurgle of laughter meant that if Danny could succeed, Robert could not fail. "If ye were safely married to Grace, it's certain ye could not be married to that other drab, not by all the bishops, nor the blessed Pope himself, for even ye'r father does not hold with polygamy or anny loose ideas, I will say that for him. Go you this afternoon, ye are sure of a welcome."

Robert was too sure. He loathed Grace's clammy kisses. If he could go where he'd never be seen again, he was bothered if he wouldn't prefer Molly.

"Saddle-up and off ye go, boy."

"The river is high."

"Och, me son is not going to balk, whin his poor old father with wan leg goes back and forth. Besides, me rheumatism is troubling me. I need some of Mrs Fullwood's liniment. I've forgotten the recipe. Go, bring me some, like a good son."

The errand would bring escape from his father. When Danny was out of sight during the afternoon, Robert caught the tall grey and followed the routine, but when safely across galloped on without changing, regardless of chill. Danny inquired where he was, uneasy lest he might have flown to Queensland.

"I'm kept awake at night with the rheumatism and I sent him for some liniment."

"Arrah! Johanna, there's no use in throwing him with Grace. I won't countenance sons of mine planting nameless children about the Colony—black, whoite or green. He marries the girl, or he leaves the place for ever."

"No other man would take such a hard stand against his own flesh and blood."

" 'Tis for, not against me own flesh . . . I want no bastard grandchildren."

"What ye'r doing is groping for the bastards of others."

Robert had a month's grace to marry Molly or go from the Bewuck roof. He hoped against hope for reprieve. Molly McCathie remained with the Sisters. They had been informed of the state of affairs and instructed to guard Molly and allow none but young Delacy to see her. She was demure and tractable and the good souls were eager to see her made respectable.

Hennessy knew of Delacy's edict.

The river grey had a desperately hard life that winter, turned out drenched night after night to freeze in the frost. His ribs could be counted in his pinched hide, though it was not a droughty season.

Grace had a happy fortnight following Dr Britton's report. Robert seemed to be in love with her at last, yet there was a canker of uncertainty. He put a hypothetical proposition rather than a direct proposal of marriage.

"My mother and father eloped, what would you think of eloping?"

"When a young lady really loves she thinks only of her intended's happiness."

"What would you do if someone arrived to take you at your word?"

"If it was the onliest one . . ."

"It would be better in the summer time."

"All times of the year are the same to real love."

Still he hung off, clinging to freedom, turning over plans to save himself from exile. He sent a statement to Tom Angus suggesting that he should send down harness horses in which they would be partners. Robert would train the animals somewhere near Sydney where buyers could come for trial. If this was too ambitious Robert was sure that Tom would lend him a couple of horses to go to Queensland. There was no need to submit to either Grace or Molly.

He waited feverishly for Tom's response, embracing every opportunity of getting the post. When a letter came Robert went down to the bunyip hole to read it. His letter to Tom fell out of the wrapping, accompanied by one from Ned, who wrote that Tom had departed for Calcutta in charge of a shipment of horses. Doings had been slack at Birrabee and Tom was glad of the adventure.

Danny and William were astonished by Tom's "clearing out as if he had a firestick behind him" without saying good-bye or asking Burrabinga if they had any horses to ship.

Robert later had a letter from Tom in Sydney explaining that he had had to rush to catch the chance. The real reason for his sudden departure was rumours of the Molly embroglio. He was, however, safe, because Hennessy would suppress his name for Molly's sake. This was Robert's first example of how boon companions consider their own safety in a jam. It was bitter in his soul and left him without a prop.

"All the Bedouins must go back to Birrabee," announced Danny to William, pleased with this further opportunity to re-establish his mastership of Bewuck.

Johanna tried to enlist William in marrying Robert and Grace, but William was as firmly against the Fullwoods as Danny, and for the same reason, plus being of the age to feel Grace's lack of charm.

William had Robert's story first from Danny, and William's principle in such issues was as straight as his father's. He thought it a low business and shared Norah's point of view that Robert was dragging the family down. Remembering Bella's advances and knowing Molly, he was fair enough to say, "She must have snared Robert."

"Snared be damned! There are always snares. Principle will keep a man out of snares."

William was young. How could his father, old and one-legged, and an "oddity" understand the lures cast for such dash as Robert's. William then had his mother's presentation. He atttributed her attitude to motherly devotion and to the ease with which a weak female's vision could be clouded. Then the brothers got away behind the stables and Robert gave his version. William accepted this with reserve.

Robert could not raise much swagger for all his obscenity and his allegations that the other lads were equally guilty. He could not minimize the plight he was in, nor feel anything but humiliation under William's searching questions. The hearty guffaws from one side of William did not hide his disapproval on the other. It was William's opportunity to swagger a little in relating how Bella had tried similar tactics with him, and how he had threatened her with a dish of water. Robert felt William's respectability sitting in judgment. William determined that Della should be informed of Gerry's participation, but a letter from Norah had already done its work.

The Delacys did not announce Bella's romance, but such news speedily leaked out: only from the Fullwood women at Heulong was it kept, as at that date the river separated them from the Township and other centres of gossip. The Rafferty joy was great— a Cophetua fairy story. "And, by cripes, on one side, if not both, she's a bigger swell than the Fullwoods," grinned her mother.

Charles Fullwood returned from the droving expedition and slipped quietly home on the left bank of the river. His wife reported Robert's frequent visits.

"Encourage him all you can," said Charles with an urgency that surprised her. "It won't be easy to get rid of Grace."

"Why? I like Mrs Delacy, but she is *dreadfully* Irish."

"It is a matter of business." Mrs Fullwood was never enlightened about business. "Encourage Robert. Get them married."

"He has no prospects."

"Let them set up here to begin. He'll soon make his way."

"There are stories about his familiarity with Molly McCathie."

"Young men will have their fun. Molly might have been trying to trap him. Grace had better nobble him; her chances won't last."

Charles postponed the news of Bella as a sister-in-law. Robert had never mentioned it.

Mrs Fullwood sighed. However, as a meek wife, she spoke tactfully to Grace. On Robert's next visit he was flattered by Fullwood's cordiality and the way he was consulted about horses.

"Papa would like you as a young partner," Grace beamed at him, her heart in her eyes, such as they were. The quality of her eyes made that of her heart negligible to young men. Surely Robert would hang off no longer.

The Fullwood attitude was balm to his deflated self-esteem, but still—*Grace!* No. Exile would not be so unendurable as Grace's sickly sentimental gush and inept embrace. He dwelt on Molly's delights—Molly before whom he was hauled as an enemy. If Molly loved him best of all—that was a softening thought. And the girl was in a dreadful fix. It was, he supposed, a serious matter for a girl—but then all those other fellows. Life could be complex.

He awoke each morning with a shudder to realize that another day was gone from those wherein to decide between Grace, Queensland and Molly. The most harrowing prospect was in being sued for maintenance by Molly so that all his cronies would whoop from Riverina to Goulburn, and his fall be known even in Sydney. Grace seemed the better way out. He would be reinstated all round. He could make his way with horses. The Fullwoods were so welcoming that it was like coming from frost to sunshine to escape from his father to Heulong. It weakened his dislike for marriage with Grace. He rode down the river nearly every evening and crossed in a boat from Quebarra. His father did not ask where he went, but waited for the month to run.

Johanna swung between fear of Robert being drowned of cramp in the river, and the hope of hearing that he and Grace had eloped. Danny kept watch so that Robert could not abstract the gig. Hennessy retained the carriage. He sent Robert a private letter hinting that his debts could be cleared up as a wedding gift; but those other men turned Robert against Molly. He made up his mind to marry Grace.

He laid hesitation to his father's disapproval. When Charles Fullwood heard of this he knew the reason. "Let them run away," he said. "Robert has a taking way with the opposite sex and old Danny is looking for money with him. Grace will be lucky to hook him."

Hennessy wrote that he would bring his niece and a priest as soon as the month was up.

"He'll need an armed guard to take me," said Robert defiantly to his mother. "You warn me of his approach and I'll be off to Grace, but I don't want to throw in my hand until the last round."

"That way you might lose Grace."

This prospect was not without comfort to Robert.

Molly was equally distraught. She passed her days in feverish longing for Athol Macallister, smuggling letters to him and begging him to rescue her from Robert. No answer came, so one day as the month was ending, such are the fluctuations of *amour*, that she wrote one more letter in a style absorbed from the sentimental romances she favoured:

I don't want you to come now. I find that the diktates of my heart are no longer for you. Your immage is being thrust out by that of a manlyer figure. A week ago I loved you to *distrackion*, but you *trampled* on my love and did not care that you had left me in trouble. I find that I have been spared the punishment of my reckless love. You have no power over me now. I could pass you by *without interest*. My pulses would not flutter at beholding you. I am now happy in my love for Robert and will make him a good wife. He has been nobel and generous. He is a better man than you in every way. He is taller and *handsomer*, and a *better whip*. I don't care if I never see you again but I wish you well. I am longing for my wedding day—only six days more now. Robert and I will drive to Sydney.

CHAPTER XXI

THE day came. Robert, worn by the strain of the past month, worked with his mother in her garden, and she kept watch. Danny stumped about, elaborately casual, ordering and consulting with Hannon and William.

The short, cold afternoon waned without the dogs announcing any thing or person coming down the cutting. The sun, attended by a few clouds, sank in winter brilliance as though a universe of gold had exploded beyond the rim and scattered islands and mountains in seas of molten glory around the globe. Robert was unresponsive to its grand beauty. His mother urged him away to Grace.

"I'll wait till daylight—safer for the river," he said, and went to bed early.

Danny sat up late. Johanna sat with him. "No sign of Hennessy," she said triumphantly, when they retired. The dogs curled against the cold, had not announced so much as a possum.

"He has been delayed," said Danny.

The household was tense for an arrival during the following day, but it too ran away undisturbed, its full sunlit silence palpitating on the clearings like a spirit that had escaped from the sombre brooding scrub. Robert was acutely nervous. All felt the drama. Danny was tormented by curiosity and the desire to go to the Township to broach the situation, but dignity forbade.

On the third day the ballyhoo of the dogs portended something special, and Mrs Delacy's carriage and Hennessy's pair were outlined on the skyline preparatory to descent.

"Away to Grace," counselled Johanna, but Robert felt suddenly that he preferred Molly as a woman *per se*. If old Hennessy would set him up near Sydney, where he would escape local pother, and if it were not for doubts of the paternity of that coming child, he would be willing. Molly, after all, was a first love, and deliciously in her teens, while Grace was leanly his senior by two years.

"Are you staying to meet the bride, or will you swim the Yackandandah to Grace?" William asked him.

"If he has dared to bring that slut, she shall not enter this house," said Johanna, embattled.

Danny went out. William stood in the background. Norah and Maeve peeped unseen. Robert hid.

"Good day, sir," said Hennessy's groom, reining-in near the stables.

Danny gave good day and went forward.

"Where shall I leave the vehicle?" inquired the man. The horses lowered their heads to relieve their shoulders from the collars, and mouthed the bits. The man descended. No one came from the body of the carriage. "Mr Hennessy sent the carriage back with his compliments."

"Have you a letter?"

"No, sir. He only told me to return the carriage."

Danny opened the door. There was nothing inside but a saddle and bridle for the man's return journey. Danny was mystified, but hospitality was imperative. "Turn the horses out and stay the night."

William passed the information to his mother. Robert overheard and his spirits leapt up like a flame at the unexpected reprieve from both Molly and Grace.

Danny would not make direct inquiries from Hennessy's employee. He talked to him in the kitchen and supplied him with grog, but could learn nothing clarifying. Hennessy's move was cryptic. Danny would stay on his own preserves and await another. His and Robert's tactics had become one.

Several days earlier Hennessy had pounded off to Goulburn because the Sisters had written that all was now well with his niece. The young gentleman, unable to wait any longer, had whisked her away, they said, though Hennessy knew through his informants that Robert was still at Bewuck.

There was a flutter among the Sisters when Hennessy arrived. They showed Molly's letter thanking them and stating that she was off to be married to the man she loved. They were satisfied because the young man had come in a dogcart with horses of queer colour with white manes and tails. When he had Molly safely in his trap he came and left the letter, because Molly, bless her kind heart, in spite of her venial sins, did not want them to be worried.

"What loike was the young man?' demanded Hennessy, a grim certainty settling on him. He knew those liver-coloured horses.

"He was smallish and thin with hair as red as the fox."

Hennessy said no more. He paid his debts and withdrew to prepare for a shotgun marriage, not the first nor the last of its kind among the nobility, and their parody the squattocracy. He rushed to the train to Sydney, sending back instructions about the Delacy carriage. He was in a humiliating position with Delacy, whom he respected. Hennessy was somewhat honest, though sensitiveness had been killed by the lash. Society must pay for that. Arrivism was his creed.

The momentary sincerity of Molly's indifference, reflected in her letter, had worked upon Athol's vanity, and he bowled along to reassert his sway. Molly's wounds still smarted and she was clever enough to work upon him about Robert's jealousy until he believed her. "Mr Delacy is as mad for me to marry Robert as Robert is himself because Uncle Kevin has promised to set us up and make me his heiress. I'd be afraid to go with you. Robert is a dead shot."

Athol knew the truth of the last.

"Uncle would shoot you like a wallaby too, or get the blacks down there to put a spear into both of us, and end the disgrace."

The blacks around Macallister's holdings had not been conciliated.

Athol, remembering Robert's infatuation for Molly, was brought to promise marriage, whereupon Molly consented to go with him to Sydney. He put her up at Petty's and was surprised to find that no marriage, no favours. Molly had become silent and pale, and even more seductive to the hardy male animal. The hotel was above reproach, so Athol put up around the corner and enjoyed Molly in the correctest fashion.

The liver-coloured Bedouins were as easily traced as a comet, and Hennessy caught up with them before Molly's resistance had buckled, fortunately for her career. Athol was indignant that Hennessy should mention firearms, such was his temperature at the moment.

So it was a romantic marriage and Hennessy welcomed Molly and Athol effusively until old Bandy should come to reason. Marriage was final and Athol was a bigger prize financially than the Delacys and Fullwoods combined. Socially, therefore, he could lord it where he willed, and Hennessy was strengthened in his ambitions for Euphemia Fitzhugh.

"Shure, were ye just playing ye'r cards to bring him up to scratch?" chuckled Hennessy. "Ye're the deep wan, Molly asthore."

"For two pins I'd have had neither of them," said Molly, recovering her spirit with safety.

Her career as Mrs Macallister did not become part of Delacy's epic, though she made him look foolish before Robert, now victorious. Johanna did not let Danny off lightly.

"The poor lamb," she crooned. "Wouldn't anny parent with a

speck of natural instinct in the heart of him know that the boy had been led to take a drop of grog—and him not being set a good example by his own father—and it to go to his head, and the rest to be put upon him as a felonious practical joke."

"He did tamper with the girl, whatever."

"A drab, and she and her scoundrelly so-called uncle with two min bailed-up till she saw which was the weakest under blackmailing, no less."

Robert's right to swagger offensively was tamed by uneasiness lest the debt to Hennessy should come to light; nor was the thought of Grace reassuring. He shuddered to think that he might now have been tied to Grace's fishy kisses for life! Never again would he let himself be scared into anything by a woman. Still, he wished he could disappear until the matter cooled with Grace.

Fullwood had a picturesque version of the affair. He recognized that Robert had contemplated safety through Grace, and, now that danger had passed, would discard her like an icicle.

Instead of stiffening her pride, Grace nearly wept her eyes away, and courted a decline by exaggerating a common cold.

Fullwood came around by the Township and made a formal call upon Delacy. He opened mildly while smoking a pipe in the sun after dinner. He sketched a pathetic picture of his daughter, and stressed Robert's responsibility. Danny allowed him to talk himself out and then repeat while he drew deep gurgles from his hippo of a pipe. Then he knocked out the ashes on his wooden leg.

"Sure, Fullwood, I have the advantage of you in this leg to empty me pipe. There's philosophy in that now, to make some use out of everything when it's turned against you. 'Tis aisier in theory than in practice, but if it would be followed 'twould make a man invincible."

Fullwood regarded this as an evasion and waited until Delacy loaded up again. It was like asking a man to go into battle unarmed to deprive Delacy of his pipe. "Whin I swam the Yackandandah in 'fifty-two, sure, I broke me wooden leg, but me pipe remained in place."

"I wonder that it is still detachable."

" 'Tis a lamentable weakness, whin a man ponders on it."

Fullwood was far from wishing to ponder on it. He noticed Maeve taking a couple of drums of swill to the pigs, and suggested inspection to get away from household ears.

"Sure," said Delacy when they were at the sty. "I've heard that Robert has paid a few visits to Heulong. 'Tis lamentable when young women take these things over seriously."

"A few visits!" rasped Fullwood. "He has been at my house constantly, and made himself inseparable from my daughter. I should not have permitted it if I had been at home, but my wife is easily imposed upon."

" 'Tis true you've been away this past year on a great deal of business," dryly remarked Delacy. This time he was to stand by his own, because of principle fundamentally, and inclination humanly. Grace was no motherless maiden, nor dimpled darling.

"Yes, I was unavoidably absent, and your son took advantage of that," said Fullwood tartly.

"I'm sorry, Fullwood, if what you say is true, but there are anny number of gossoons running about the district looking for wives, and your daughter can have her pick."

"But I have to remember that I am a Fullwood of Fullwood Manor, County Sussex, and my daughter cannot . . ."

" 'Tis so. And I have to remember that I am an honest man—or try to be—and like Denny Blake, I'm from County Clare. That's all there is at it Fullwood, except that we'll have to carry our hides to the tanyard ourselves in the finish—and under our own brands, Fullwood—under our own brands."

Fullwood cursed him for a rambling old Irish fool, and attempted to bring him to the point. "Well, Delacy, what are you going to do about it?"

"About bringing me hide to the tanyard eventually under me own brand?"

"Philosophy may be well enough for educated philosophers, but I am speaking of my daughter."

"And she having no education in philosophy, you imply."

"You are evading the point."

"That's no lie, neither. Sure, I'll return to it. *Auribus teneo lupum.* I advise your daughter to look for another beau who will be proud to marry on a Fullwood from the dayvil knows where."

"Damme! Is your son to go about the country breaking a refined young female's heart and wrecking her health? Her very life may be at stake."

"Sure, hasn't she been able to find a second string for her bow? I wish her every success in the world. I don't hold it against anny girl who her father is, or in what County he was born. 'Tis a dispensation beyond her entirely. . . . That's a fine sow, Fullwood. . . . She's likely to farrow a dozen piglets. What more could you expect of a lady?"

"Your flippancy shows a lack of sensibility. I'm willing to pass it over as the Irish idea of a joke, but I shan't let the matter rest there."

"What do you expect of me, Fullwood. There can be nothing more likely of disaster than a young man to marry where he has no love."

"Then he should not court in that direction."

"He should not. If me son has done that he shall be reprimanded, I promise you."

With this, Fullwood was so discontented that he went for his horse. "You'll turn your horse out and stay the night? 'Tis a long stretch back to the Township, and the days not much longer yet." Fullwood declined. He did not return to the house to say good-bye to the ladies. He muttered when in the saddle, "I hope Delacy that this matter will be settled in a gentlemanly way."

"I hope so too, I'm sure, Fullwood, ab imo pectore, and definitely. I have no policy of ungentlemanliness to anny man of anny nationality—English or Irish, black, whoite or green. 'Tis that your idea of a gentleman and mine might differ. No man without principle is a gentleman to me no matter what County or palace he may come from. Good day!"

The dogs rushed out and heeled the departing gentleman up the cutting, Fullwood lashing furiously at them with his whip. "Sool him, boys! Sool him!" Danny chuckled under his breath. Aloud he bayed above the dogs, "Come behind! Come behind, you mongrels! Lie down!"

"And whoi did Mr Fullwood go off without a good afternoon, and he a gentleman?" inquired Johanna.

"His title to gentleman was not aquil to the sudden strain put on it. Matters are a little awkward by reason of his accusations that Robert has been philandering with Grace. He as much as threatened proceedings, if Robert doesn't marry her."

"God help us! I hope ye told him that we will welcome Grace. The best thing for Robert is to settle down with her. He has been put off romance a little by that impudent drab's attack. A shock to a sensitive boy."

"Humph!" said Danny. "Get all foolishness out of your head about the Fullwood piece and Robert. Though Robert was reprehensible to court her, I shall not expect him to marry in this case where there is no suggestion of a nameless offspring. I would not countenance wan of me own marrying with a Fullwood if she was hung with the wealth of the whole County of Sussex."

"No, ye'd rather force him to marry with a by-blow of a lag."

"You talk against the facts. You accuse me of not caring for family, and I hope I never shall in the low snob sense, but I'm sound on breed, and never will wan of mine marry with so low a breed as Fullwood's, I don't care if they have an orchard of family trees all hung with titles instead of fruit. The Fullwoods talk in a whine and look sly. I have plenty more in hand, but let that content you. *Auribus teneo lupum.* There is no use in bidding the dayvil good day unless he is about to enter."

CHAPTER XXII

MOLLY and Athol were at the hotel until old Macallister should show his hand. Hennessy was working the connection for all he could socially. Molly had her own suite in glory equal to that of Euphemia Fitzhugh, now shorn of a carriage. Euphemia, hearing of the half-dozen stations and endless flocks and herds of old Bandy—a widower—was looking forward to meeting him She was, therefore, less hoity-toity to Molly, and Molly victorious, was not so touchy. Hennessy was beamingly hopeful. His unmentionable days having shown him the fibre of those in the stirrups, he was determined to be among them, and believed in and depended upon push, though one sound thing in him was his appreciation of character. Delacy was a favourite with him. He was desirous of healing any lacerations, so wrote to Robert begging the favour of a few private words.

Hennessy was none of your illiterate terriers. He had been a bright scholar at one of the little Hedge Schools born of the Penal Laws, where he had learned to read out of a Catholic prayer book lent to him by a soft-eyed, bare-footed maid with a shawl over her curls, and a dream in her eyes, which she had shared with young Kevin. She was to have been his, but his ability to read and write had later made him prominent in the Anti-Union agitation and resulted in his transportation. An untamable dislike to conform had earned him those shameful wales on his back, though he did not forget Brigid. When he had earned his ticket-of-leave, he wrote home, but an unknown parish priest replied that the family in question had perished during the famine. There had been another woman then, generous in concupiscence to the handsome young lag, and she had later dumped Molly on him. He had done his best for Molly, not so much because of her mother's generosity as for the memory of the little Brigid, who had died of hunger waiting for him, whose dream died with her. In its place came a hardy desire for power and consequence. Euphemia Fitzhugh was a possible stepping-stone in his ambition, which would not be helped by enmity with Robert Delacy, whom Fullwood, brother-in-law of Euphemia, was pursuing for his daughter.

Hennessy's letter was extremely tactful and Robert appeared without delay, driving his gig again. His father was under-dog for the moment.

"Well, young Robert Delacy, it was about that money ye owe me, Oi don't suppose ye can pay it all off in wan gulp?"

"Not just at the moment." Robert's business head came to his aid. "You owe me more than I owe you for what you tried to put upon me and the old man."

Hennessy loosed a genial guffaw. "Ye've a great head on ye! It was moi intintion to tell ye not to throuble about the interest. I had no ill feelings to ye at the toime, and hope ye howld none now."

"None at all, but business is business, Hennessy. I have a sound case for an action, but the worry is not good for my mother. We'll call it square if you like to give me a note of discharge. I don't want to hurt Molly. The mud would dirty her. It doesn't matter to a man," Robert concluded with daring swagger.

"Ye flash pup, ye never came from the owld man's soide. It will soon take double dark glasses to protect the ois whin behowlding ye," thought Hennessy, but he liberated another spurious chortle and clapped Robert on the shoulder. "Ye're a bright fellow, Robert Delacy. No wonder Molly didn't catch ye, though she pulled the wool over her owld uncle's ois to hilp her, she wanted ye that bad."

Robert's vanity began to recover from some of its wounds. He could say, "Looks like it, when she leathers off with another."

"Be japers, ye hurrt her proide, and ye know how we'll clutch at the second bist to save our proide."

This put Robert in an amenable mood. "If you give me a note of full discharge, properly attested, we'll wipe the slate clean on both sides and let bygones be bygones."

"Shure, we will. Come and have a dhrink on the house."

The snob in Robert prevailed, also recollections of the consequences of Hennessy's grog. "Thanks, but your grog was the cause of my trouble." He said it haughtily without a twinkle. Already he could be as uncompromisingly aristocratic as his mother.

"It's the last toime ye'll iver rayfuse a dhrink wid me," thought Hennessy, but he said, "Ye've a head on ye, Robert, to learn by experience, and Oi applaud ye, but come and call on Molly McCathie, _alias_ Mrs Athol Macallister."

Robert condescended to this. Molly was eager to second her uncle in her social reinstatement. Robert was a ladies' man. He could be cutting to women, but not insensible to their allure, if it existed. Molly was acting a shy ladylike part reminiscent of her convent training. Robert must make the first move. Hennessy left them together. Molly languished in the best style, fluttering a lace handkerchief above her flounces, displaying an embroidered sandal on a footstool.

"I have called to congratulate you. I suppose I must call you Mrs Macallister?"

"No, I am Molly to old friends—in private. In public maybe it would be better to stick on the Mrs seeing that I have shocked the fogies." The old roguish Molly peeped out. Robert became himself.

"What the hell did you mean, getting the two old men after me that way, and then running off with that Athol?"

"Why did you break my heart? I was desperate. You had ruined my reputation, and poor dear Athol is so desperately in love with me, I was sorry for him." Molly sighed.

Robert knew the rights of her pose about reputation, but it was so gratifying to learn that he had broken her heart and that she had to turn to Athol in despair, that he overlooked it.

"Well, Molly, I wish you well. I must depart. I am not good for ladies' reputations." He turned at the door with bravado, "Are you going to call it Robert?"

Molly tossed a cushion after him. He heard her gay laughter as he descended. She came running down the passage and called over the bannister, "Stay to-night and we can go over some names. Athol is in Goulburn."

Robert, elated, said to Hennessy with a tone of authority, "You won't forget that note of discharge.'

"Shure!" grunted Hennessy. "And ye can sind in the gig."

"Tell you what," compromised Robert then, "we might both, as well as not, let the tail go with the hide. Let me have what I paid on the trap, and it is yours; and I'll train a pair for you for good measure."

"Roight ye are, on wan condition."

"What is that?"

"That ye'r women folk don't look down on Molly."

"I'm afraid I do not control the ladies of my family."

"Ye can say a word. It won't do to hurt Molly's feelings." Dealing with these jumped-up Colonials, one needed a sledge-hammer style, and Hennessy's determination was to jump-up himself without bashfulness.

"If ye'r women folk were kind-hearted enough to call on Molly," he continued without a qualm, "well, ye could kape the gig, and Oi'd give ye what ye laid on it as well. It is betther to run ye'r mother about than the owld circus van. Now, if ye'r mother was to call on Molly it would be aquil to the Quane's condescinsion to clear up the little misunderstanding on all soides, and choke the gossip out of the tongues of the sweepings that abount in this district—a bargain on it—ye've a head for business on ye."

"I'll see what can be done," said Robert, hesitantly.

"Be japers, it is done thin already, me bhoy, for no lady could resist ye, not wan so condescinsious, and of the rare gentility of ye'r own mother. Shure, here is the cash, and Oi'll have the note of discharge ready whin ye'r mother comes to call on Molly, no less. . . . Norah too, would complete it."

Hennessy retained a trump, but Robert came to the Bewuck supper table on the following night with more self-assurance than he had enjoyed for months. He could hold up his head again, and a fine head it was. Tall, haughty, slender, he was the hidalgo to perfection, and gave body to Johanna's legend that far back on her mother's side was a grandee of Spain; that one of the women of the family having found on the beach, unconscious, a man from the fleeing Armada had been so taken with his beauty that she had him carried home and hidden in a garret while others were being murdered and rifled for loot; that she married him and that he turned out to be the son of a nobleman.

" 'Twas all written down in an old book that me grandmother had from her great-grandmother, as sure as the Book of Ballymote," she would muse. When Della and Norah would ask her to write home for a copy of the entries, Johanna would change the subject. That she would never write home was painful to her. "Maybe ye'll go home ye'rself wan day," she would say, "and find out if anny of them escaped the famine."

The girls, as they grew, found slights put upon the Irish by those prejudiced against the breed and its creed. They heard people mimicking their parents' brogue, which is a sore shame to adolescents, and so they were not ambitious to trace themselves to a dago— some sort of half-black in addition to being Irish—and Johanna's story was but faintly remembered.

Robert took his father aside during the evening and brought the sovereigns from his pocket. "There's the money for the yellow steer. I only sort of borrowed it."

"It's a good thing never to borrow in that way. As often as not there's an accident and such borrowing is embezzlement in a court of law. Whatever, you've had your lesson."

"I'll never be so green again," said Robert, but with a different connotation from his father's.

"And now, how did you come by the money?"

"I had it paid on the gig, but in consideration of the way Hennessy treated me, I am to have the gig and the money, and let bygones be bygones."

" 'Tis quite decent of Hennessy."

"Decent of me to let the old bushranger off for bailing me up, you mean. I could pull him for defamation of character only it would upset Ma, and show up what a fool you were."

Danny did not prolong the interview. He let the Fullwood case go for the time being.

Robert recounted the denouement to William that evening by the dying kitchen fire. "The old hide caved-in; was glad to let all the money go and give me the gig, or I'd have pulled him for blackmail. Asked me to have a drink. 'Drink your —— poisoned grog yourself!' I said. Thought he had me cornered, but he found out his mistake."

Hennessy was a shrewd bargainer, William duly admired Robert's business ability. "But all the same," he giggled, "you had better be careful next time. You don't want to be swimming the Yackandandah for fun."

The next move was from Fullwood. He informed Delacy two days later in the Township, that he would begin an action for a breach of promise. "Your son made a convenience of my daughter's affections because he was caught in another direction. He gets free, and leaves my daughter in such a state of suffering that her health is permanently injured."

"And would you injure her health further by exposing her misplaced affections for the tag-rag to delight in?" Danny was not to be stampeded a second time.

"Robert shall marry or pay."

"*Ad Kalendas Graecas*, Fullwood—at the Greek Kalends."

"He shall marry or pay."

"Let sleeping dogs lie, is sound advice. I'll bid you good day."

"This is not the last of this," called Fullwood.

"Please yourself, Fullwood. Please yourself."

Fullwood did.

A few days later Robert was stunned to receive a legal document, which he read behind the stable, his hands trembling. Just when he had been cleared, to have this dam burst, and no likelihood of a fresh miracle to extricate him! He could not face the old man again. He would go to Queensland this time. For the moment he went to his mother.

He had been saved from the disreputable Molly, but Grace, of

unbroken chastity, was equally formidable. Women were the deuce.
It would be a wily one who would get the better of him again,
unless he meant to give way to matrimony.

Johanna was Grace's advocate. The threat of Queensland made
her urgent. If Robert married Grace he would be set up near by,
and Bewuck must be his, he, the eldest son. Robert was afraid of
the writ of summons. His mother showed it to Danny and advocated
marriage to scotch the trouble.

"Fullwood has no case against Robert or me. Sure, Fullwood is
a fool—hink-honk-ha-ing through that nose of his."

"And how could he be honking through annybody else's nose?"

"He's so smart with his law. Sure, I'll sit tight. It may be all cry
and no wool, as the dayvil said when he was shearing the pig."

Robert was thankful those days to work with William, who was
putting up a split-rail fence on the outer boundary to replace a
cockatoo erection. At night they shot possums off the crops or
mended harness. They improved the hen house and enlarged the
orchard, and re-painted doors and gates for their mother. It was
Robert's first experience of hard work. During these winter weeks
when there was a lull at Burrabinga, Danny was glad to remain at
Bewuck for the outcome of the Fullwood complications.

No one was concerned about the lack of amusements for Harry,
at Burrabinga with no company but a deaf mute, and two stockmen, one of them discarded by Bella Rafferty. Harry did not notice
it himself. He never expected to reap from others. His eager
desire was to give what he could with two-handed generosity. He
brightened wet days and the evenings by the vocal fires in telling
stories. Aldon and Callahan listened entranced. O'Neill struggled
horse-deep through the drifts, risking his life and suffering the
belligerence of the station dogs against his own pets, for the sake
of such rare entertainment. When Harry came to the end of stories
he had read, he recited his own, now that William, the literal, was
not present to blight imagination. Right down to the present day
a remaining old hand or two can remember Harry's thrilling stories,
some of which were rooted in Celtic legend, while others welled
from the lad's own virginal depths to echo in the poignant silence
of a land bewitched.

Fullwood shortly reappeared at Bewuck demanding a conference
with Robert. He said he had no wish to wash dirty linen in public
and was desirous of settling the case out of court. This visit was
due to his wife's assurance that Johanna was eager for the match,
but Danny forbade Johanna to talk, and she retreated to her own
sitting-room like an offended hen and brooded on the elegance of

her china dogs and wool mats, the Waterford lustres and the cedar workbox, which she had maintained in the tradition of a manorial hall despite all "oddities" of democracy or difficulties of pioneering.

The men went to the old school-house and lighted a fire there. Delacy smoked with loud smacking of his lips and an occasional "Moi, oh, moi!" as if he were absently philosophizing, while Fullwood restated his case.

"What have you to say for yourself?" Fullwood suddenly demanded of Robert.

"I—er—it wouldn't be fair to marry Grace when I don't care for her that way."

"Do you refuse to fulfil your obligations to my daughter?"

"I never undertook any obligations."

"Oh, yes, you did, and I can prove it."

"No, I didn't. She was so dam' friendly—like all the girls, and I couldn't be rude to her in return."

Danny continued his loud smacking and ejaculation as Fullwood rose to whining rage. Suddenly Danny bluntly demanded of Robert if he had had any wrongful relations with Grace. Robert was able to deny.

Fullwood ranted his astonishment that any one claiming to be a free man and a gentleman should act as Robert was acting toward Grace, and that Delacy should countenance him

"You're not half so astonished as I am, and that is a lie, because I am not astonished at all—having made me judgment whin I found out who duffed all me cattle this last year. That's the reason, Fullwood, that no son or daughter of me own will marry with wan of yours with me consent. You compel me to let go the ears of me wolf. I'll not mention your gentlemanly action nearly thirty years ago to set a lag to beat me up. I have not proceeded against you out of mercy, and because of the neeborliness of your wife. I could afford to lose me cattle better than you could afford to lose your character, not your character, for you haven't anny—but your reputation."

"By Christ, what do you insinuate?"

Joy spread through Robert. He nearly crowed aloud to be rescued by the old man.

"Bluster won't help you with me, Fullwood. . . 'Tis never used except in weak cases—false feathers that floi off in the wind. You don't think I'm an eft to be fooled by you—me with me invincible blackboy and two sons the best trackers in the world, not to name Wong Foo with his eyes open, and O'Neill trained by yourself. I give warning that the next tracking will be done by the troopers.

If me son has attracted your daughter and has nothing to give in return, I regret it, Fullwood, and to make matters square, though I have the evidence and the witnesses, I'll lay no charge against you—this time."

"By God! you'll pay for this. I was willing to come to terms, but nothing will hold me back from demanding my pound of flesh now. If you think I shall tolerate this from a social inferior . . ."

Danny emitted a disconcerting grunt of amusement. "Bedad, every man thinks himself the social superior of every other—'tis a matter of the moind. The truth is that wan man is as good as another, if he *is* as good; and none of us anny better than we should be. You can have as many social pretensions as you can afford, but not at the expinse of duffing me cattle hereafter, Fullwood."

Fullwood grabbed his hat. "I'll open proceedings next week."

"Go home to your daughter; tell her the truth of the fix you are in, and she'll be willing to recover from her broken heart to save your social pretensions."

"You, you young blackguard! I'll see you lagged yet."

Robert spluttered vulgar glee in Fullwood's face.

Daniel Brian Robert M. Delacy, who had been so genially conversational, put down his pipe and stood up on his wooden leg, his hackle well up at last.

"Fullwood," he thundered, and could have been heard half a mile away, but only the Murrumbidgee was listening. "You've gone too far! Social boasting wan above the other is waste of breath whin there is nothing for anny of us but to carry our hides to the tanyard in the ind. Manny a man was in the chain-gangs wrongfully, and manny who were there by rights were better than them who sent them there; but there's limits, Fullwood, and you've gone outside them. I know you for what you are, wan of those that should have been in the chain-gangs, you and your flash owld scrag of a brother that's ran off and married on Bella Rafferty, whose mother has the social pretensions of meeting the gentry on the wrong side of the blanket. And bedad, while I remember it, I'll be obleeged for the immediate return of me two owld mares. Wan is branded BB under the mane, off-side, and the other GM under the saddle flap, near side, and wan has a switch tail, and both will throw Nullah-Mundoey foals that are not to be sneezed at.

"I know plenty to get you and James a long sentence of hard labour, and if you don't reform you shall not be let off hereafter. And when you cast social aspersions at me, it's time for an honest man to assert his principles. I'll have you know, Fullwood, that me family have been honest min as long as they are remembered, at home in the old country as well as here. Me and me wife came here free and dragged with honest sweat, cultivating here, and opening up the mountains, where no wan wanted to go. I was none of those pretentious big capitalists that by the aid of their tools, the Government officials, grabbed all the easy land and grew rich by driving the convicts like slaves. I've worked for annything I have, and have never touched a farthing of another man's rights. If I didn't make this testimony of me breed and me principles I'd be failing as a decent citizen. As for the social inferior business, sure, I hope me family will never be connected with you, for I know you as a cattle and horse thief, and not anny more of a gentleman than old Rafferty. Rafferty has the better blood—more upstanding manhood in it."

Fullwood muttered scurrilous insults. Robert for the first time was delighted with his father.

"Keep your ill-nature and bad manners for someone else, Fullwood. I've never been in a position where I've had to throw dung at another man because of me own case being contimptible. Maybe I'd be a poisonous crawler too in such exulcerated circumstances." This habit of philosophical disquisition was more exasperating to his opponent than normal vituperation.

"I'm giving you more than you'd ever get by breach of promise. Reform your evil performances and receive your new sister-in-law. Me wife will be pleased to know that her training has such rich results on black, whoite and green. Me brave Johanna is all for the aristocracy, coming from a fox-hunting squire, who is a great swell indeed, though why is not to be seen under intelligent consideration."

Fullwood whined more insults.

"You'd better control yourself and stay to a meal," said Delacy at length, too neighbourly to order Fullwood away. With the pluck of Conn of the Hundred Battles, he was never belligerent.

Fullwood departed with renewed threats, and insults as copious as his poverty of vocabulary permitted. "This is infamous—infamous! I'll have it handled by the right authorities."

"It is so infamous that I'll leave it to Sergeant O'Gorman hereafter. 'Tis O'Gorman has the authority, and I the evidence. Remimber, I've warned you."

When his father's back was turned, Robert thumbed his nose and swelled his cheeks and made vulgar explosive sounds incongruous with his grandee physique. He thoroughly earned Fullwood's enraged, "Flash lout!"

"Arrah, Fullwood, don't make a noise over sour grapes, it draws attintion to your disappointment," said Danny, whose temper had returned to normal.

Johanna was startled to learn of the Fullwood thievishness. "Father was immense," chortled Robert, as he told the tale with embroidery and mimicry. "I didn't know he had it in him."

Johanna bridled. "Would I be wan to pick a nullity?"

"But he's so fond of making us take other people's dust."

"He's an oddity about democracy, and carries honesty to foolish extremes, but sure, don't I remember him in County Clare when he was younger than ye are."

Honoria was equally tonicked that her father should have defined his social status. William cackled, "Robert won't have to go to the Darling Downs till another darling chases him."

Robert differed from the other men of the family by his disposition to gallantry, but they, measuring him by themselves, always rallied to vindicate him. Freed from entanglements, he was his old self with intensification, and, without reference to his father, invited his mother to go to town in the gig. Danny's vanquishment of Fullwood had not brought father and son nearer together, because Robert recognized that the "old man", as he now began to call him, would not champion his son any more than black, white or green, unless principle supported the case.

Robert itched to show himself abroad with his tandem, but Hennessy's clearance was dependent upon the Delacy women's attitude to Molly Macallister, and there was embarrassment in the confession involved. Johanna had rehearsed to be haughty with Molly, but she hid her disappointment and bowed to the necessity of completing Robert's success.

"Let this be a warning to ye, once and for all, me son."

"It's all that," agreed Robert, genial through gaining his point. "And you can take it out on the Fullwoods. They are for everlasting trying to put on airs, and they are in such a mess that they can't do anything."

"Poor Grace's only sin was to want ye, me boy; and her mother has been a kind friend since I settled here. It's not in me to bite the hand that stroked me." Johanna was silent a moment and then brightened, "But I'll not allow that Fitzhugh faymale to condescind to me in future."

"'Tis mad weather to be going to town," said Danny, "With a wind that would perish the Danes." But Robert wrapped his mother in wallaroo fur and put a hot brick at her feet.

Hennessy's effusive reception had an emollient effect. Johanna's refusal to encounter him during the embroglio had spared them both humiliation. She extended her hand as an ancient Cooley might have done to a liege.

"Ye've come to see little Molly," said he, beaming broadly, and continuing torrentially, "Shure, 'tis Herself, sez Oi, that is the rale quality from the owld place itself, and none of this arrogance of Johnny-come-lately-jumped-up Colonials. Oi've had me thrubbles r'arin' Molly, I don't moind confessing, since ever me poor sister died sudden and destitute. She now to have put upon me such a mistake that Oi seemed harsh in me demands to Mr Delacy and that foine son of ye'rs, but they carried it off as only rale gintlemen can. Whin Molly was off laughing at us all, me chief disappointment was that she had picked wan that was not such a gintleman as anny son r'ared by ye'rself would be, but Oi'm thinking *ye're* the betther pleased for that, and I hope by that you'll let bygones be bygones. If ye could see ye'r way to show a word of friendliness to Molly, 'twould be the bist illustration in the worruld of how the quality can act, and be the turning inflooence of her loife."

Johanna was willing to be a patroness of virtue. Macallister, Senior, had arrived, and she was curious to see how he was bearing up as a father-in-law. There was the glamour of wickedness as well as wealth about that braw pioneer. Molly was now independent of her old acquaintances' favour, and Johanna thought it showed good feeling in Hennessy to value it.

"Shure, Mr Macallister, saynior, is here this very day. He would deem it a great honour entirely to meet ye at dinner in his private soot. Oi shall be as proud as if the Queen herself came to dine with me this day."

Johanna was relieved that the matter was thus arranged for her. She had only to be a lady, just a little stiff, and all would be well for Robert.

Bandy Macallister had come down hot-foot from his gins on his farthest-out station, away at Yambooca where the Darling meets the Murray, where men had laws of their own, and Cockenzie men surfed out to sea over the Murray bars in tublike craft with reckless disregard of consequences.

Bandy approved of marriage for others. For himself he preferred mistresses. "As soon as you marry," he would declaim, "the besom begins to dictate to you, but you can get rid of a mistress if she doesn't suit, and she knows it, and that makes for peace and pleasant service."

Rumours of how Molly had trapped Athol so pleased him that he laughed until he creaked at her demure airs, and thought that with her health and prettiness she might be just the keeper to tame his son and carry on the name. He desired a legally begotten grandson but had no parental illusions concerning Athol.

Molly was expensively dressed and excessively "refined". Johanna was kept at a distance. She was amazed by the cynical ribaldries of Bandy, and glad to fall back on a genteel bearing and accept Hennessy's solicitous attentions for her comfort. Athol was not present. Robert, likewise, had the *nous* to absent himself.

Euphemia spread herself effulgently before Bandy, who would not risk familiarity with her, but she put him in such coarse good-humour that she fancied she was advancing. She was gushing to Molly and contemptuous of Johanna and her brogue. She had not been across the Murrumbidgee since the autumn rains, and Charles Fullwood had forbidden his wife to mention the acquisition of Bella, or Robert Delacy's and Grace's misunderstanding until he should have brought off his *coup*.

"When my husband was stationed at Dublin I had a personal maid with your amusing brogue," she condescended to Johanna.

"And ye liked it?"

"When I could understand it."

"And does it remoind ye of happy days?"

"Yes, when I was a girl bride."

"Then 'twill be pleasant for ye to be with ye'r new sister-in-law, me surrvant gurrl, Bella Rafferty that was. Sure, I had a struggle to civilize her from a rough bare-footed shepherd's brat. Belike she has picked up some of me brogue as well as some civilized habits, if she doesn't fall back into her streelishness."

Mrs Fitzhugh was thunderstruck.

" 'Tis true, thin?" inquired Hennessy.

"Yes. An elopement. Molly, ye're in the fashion. Sure, didn't I elope meself, all the way from Ireland to New South Wales."

"I've heard of another in the air," said Molly, who loathed the widow naturally from the beginning, and now because she suspected her uncle's ambition and feared he might succeed, and disinherit his niece. "The lady was your niece Grace."

"And who was the young man?" inquired Bandy of Mrs Fitzhugh.

"There was some lunkhead trying to pay her attentions, but his family were socially inferior."

Noting the lightning in Johanna's eyes, Hennessy hastened to avert friction. "If that is off, we'll have to foind another. Mr Macallister or meself moight obloige, if we could foind the ladies."

"That would be easy with our bawbees," cackled Macallister.

Here Hennessy was called from the room by a groom who had

difficulty in restraining an English aristocrat—a victim of delirium tremens—from burning down the stables where he was lodged, in an attempt to get rid of the reptiles in his straw. 'Can I have your word to rope him?" demanded the man before he was out of hearing.

Johanna, inflamed by Euphemia's last insult, could scarcely bridle herself to inquire, "Are ye not going to elope ye'rself? 'Twould stop the high talk and be a ripe romance."

Euphemia's mind, running on the senior Macallister, was prepared to be indulgent about badinage. "Dear me, do people talk?"

"Sure, gags wouldn't stop them. Some say ye must even be secretly married."

"Monstrous! I've not known Mr Macallister a week."

The ladies had risen and were on the way to the parlour.

"Och, 'tis not Mr Macallister at all, but Mr Hennessy himself, and ye living here so continted and comfortable.'

"My goodness, woman," she said, completely outraged, "He was a convict. An ignorant bog-trotting Irishman—an innkeeper! A servant who is helped by my patronage!"

"I've been longer exiled at the furthest extremity of the globe than ye have, and to be sure, society is topsy-turvy out here. I never thought I was training Bella Rafferty to be wan of me equals. . . . There's a deal of speculation anny way."

"Among vile scum of servants, I presume."

"I see no surrvants but me own, and I never encourage them to be vulgar at the expense of their betters. Sure, ye've been settled here a long time now, and 'tis to be seen that Hennessy is powerfully set up with ye. Bella Rafferty, as ye'r sister-in-law, wanst removed, and Molly as Mrs Macallister, must be a great encouragement to him."

"But a woman of my family—a married woman—surely no one would dare?"

"Sure, widows are said to be more comprehensive than shy young girls in all their modesty. After love's young dream is dispersed, it becomes a matter of business, and Hennessy is a powerful man. He owns the Township."

The Fitzhugh gave Johanna a curdling look and swept from her presence to her own apartments. This evil Irish fishwife could not be concocting her slanders without foundation. Euphemia recalled passages with Hennessy which she attributed to Irish exuberance. The odious presumptuous monster! She thought with alarm of her bill. And the Bella elopement, when she had been awaiting James as a possibility! Her means would not run to Sydney. She must return to Heulong. The Colonies were a racking nightmare; but a colder, more cramped prospect was the life open to her in England, in shabby lodgings with a chasm between her and desirable men—and the competition!

Macallister followed Johanna to the parlour—a tremendous compliment—and overheard part of the brush between the women. "You've disposed of the big besom in one shot," he grinned, placing a chair for her. "She desairved it . . . my certes, Mrs Delacy, I wish my Athol had married one of your daughters, if you have any like yourself. I hear there is no certainty but that your son has fathered me a grandchild. I would approve of the breed."

"Mr Macallister, for shame! Ye shock me. Me son . . ."

"No offence, little lady, no offence!" The twinkle in his eye was so disturbing that they both laughed.

Johanna preened her draperies and in victory was amiable to Molly. She was extra virtuous of deportment before the rakish Bandy, but invited him to bring his daughter-in-law to Bewuck, "Sure, me husband dearly loves a little political conversation with anny wan from the old country."

Hennessy was so excited by this invitation that he made Johanna a present of stuffed humming birds under a gloss globe, an elegant and fashionable ornament which he dearly prized. Johanna carried it home in front of her like a monument.

"By damn!" exclaimed Danny, when all was explained. " 'Tis you that has got the wedding present on account of Molly, instead of having to provide wan, me brave Johanna. Dayvil if ever I heard of such another propitious advinture." He laughed until tears ran down his cheeks.

"Whin was I ever a nullity?" cried Johanna.

"Ma got a prize for swimming the Yackandandah without getting wet," chortled William.

While the novelty lasted, one or other would slip in to dote on the new ornament as it sat on a wool mat on Johanna's round table of walnut with claw and ball feet.

Robert had Hennessy's note, so worded that he had quittance of his debts to date in consideration of the misunderstanding about the Molly McCathie elopement, but only on the further understanding that Robert's women folk were not to slight Molly Macallister. Before Robert could show it about or tell Hennessy to go to hell, he would have to pay his debts in full.

CHAPTER XXIII

DURING the absence of Johanna and Robert, Danny arranged his "moind". Robert's returning swagger had determined him. There had been more good luck than triumph of principle in Robert's exoneration, and, in addition, Danny was not sufficiently tanistic to enjoy the election of his successor thus early in his career.

"I've been thinking," he said that night. "Robert is getting too soft and ladified around town here. He has never done his share on the axe, or in camping out, and fencing, and running wild horses and cattle. Burrabinga would be the making of him, and remove him from the wrong women—that Molly Macallister piece—who I'm thinking marriage won't settle for long—and the poor Fullwood flourbag on a pole, with a lip that you could trip on."

"I'd like to see me boy safely married, which he can't be if he's strewed up there among the dingoes "

"Arrah, he needs straightening-up. The Urquhart girls are as fine a lot of young people as ever walked."

"And Janet designed for William?"

"Och, he walks around her and doesn't know how to come to a head. There is a drove of others. It maybe will bring Della up to the mark to see Norah ahead of her. '

Both families were agreeable to the marriage of Norah and Stewart Butler, which was to take place five weeks hence.

Robert was relieved to go to Burrabinga, out of reach of Grace. He and William set off accompanied by a lusty brigade of dogs. Danny had to tie up his to keep them at Bewuck. Even so, two broke their chains and departed. William was to send Della home as soon as the river fell. Johanna said that she would provide no more wives for the unconvicted gentry by strewing her daughters and their "surrvants" about the furthest extremities of the wilderness.

Sandy Urquhart escorted Della home and spent some days with Danny in yarning, in visiting the neighbours, and the two old mates got drunk together in the Township. Through this fall, Danny lost the ground he had been regaining as public consort if not private spouse of Johanna. She relegated him to the "ind room" again on the excuse that her head suffered from the perfume of rum and tobacco combined.

Danny felt this banishment to be a social disgrace out of all proportion to its actuality, especially as he had no sensuality to harry him, but his honest idea of the sanctity, the inviolability of the marriage-bed demanded that it should be double. To propitiate Johanna he permitted his grog to be entirely regulated by her, thus emulating Sandy Urquhart, who had to submit to Janet's dispensing. Johanna never had to endure any bullying or malicious onslaughts from Danny comparable with those suffered by Janet. Danny's disposition contained the innocence of a pure heart mixed with considerable wisdom, as all thorough-going decency demands, and in the rationing of grog, his taste for alcohol bitted him more firmly in the fall of his life than ever his sexual appetite had done in his prime.

Bella Rafferty came home to Heulong at the time that Della returned to the other bank of the river. James had a fleshly craving for her—personable young women were scarce—and he and Charles had finally been held to ransom. Married, she would be their accessory, otherwise she threatened to expose them. She and Aldon, the Delacys' stockman, had the evidence. Charles had resisted at first, fearing his wife's attitude. She was a meek woman, but honourable, and the sister of that formidable brigadiere Euphemi Fitzhugh. Bella threatened boldly. James coveted her, and loss of social caste would have crumbled Charles. Bella drove her bargain to the hilt. She must be openly accepted by the family, like a certain Mrs Wells, and "made a lady of". Her idea of this was fine clothes, idleness and the right to order servants to do her bidding.

The advocacy of Bella devolved upon Charles. He drew attention to her good looks and pointed out that Mrs Delacy had partly civilized her. The marriage was no worse than that of Athol Macallister to Molly McCathie, and many others contracted by squatters because of the scarcity of well-bred women.

Mrs Fullwood said that Molly was free from family except an uncle, who could leave her much property, and that she had been educated in a convent, whereas Bella did not know her letters. But Mrs Fullwood had to resign herself to one more cross and consent to train Bella. Bella was to forswear her family: she and the family agreed to this.

There were times when Bella was not all a cross. Euphemia, disturbed to find that there was truth in Mrs Delacy's riposting, had returned to Heulong, despite the river Murrumbidgee. She was enraged by such a family accretion as Bella, but Bella, shameless, and sure of her men, was not squelchable by a dozen Euphemias, and the encounters were studded with comedy.

Charles felt like hanging himself to have given-in when he found that Delacy had long known the facts of the cattle-lifting, and was not going to prosecute. He threatened to throw Bella out, and told her it was he who had the whip-hand of Delacy through the fear of an action for breach of promise, but Bella bared her teeth and told Charles that she knew of a certain widow in a pub on the way to Riverina to whom had gone as hush money large sums gained from other men's cattle.

The elopement was the subject of gossip from Goulburn to Gool Gool, having superseded the Molly McCathie scandal-romance. Then it was displaced by the Bewuck wedding.

The Fullwoods presented a problem. Danny said that he had no wish to maintain enmity with "anny" man—black, white or green— so long as he did not duff Burrabinga cattle. Johanna said she had nothing but goodwill for Grace and her mother, but could not risk sending an invitation and being set down.

" 'Tis a good policy to let the other fellow do the setting down. Whin you come off top it rankles, but if he snubs you, it pleases his vanity and doesn't hurt you."

"Likely I'd put meself in an invidious position!"

"Invidious! By damn! All this tongue-lashing is chaff in the wind. Invite them all, and if they rayfuse, 'tis their own dispensation. The boys have not reported any cattle missing lately."

"What about Bella Rafferty?"

"Sure, Bella, whoi, Bella will be the flower of that flock! Have ye forgotten the widow Fitzhugh?"

"It's the sunflower she'll be—a great big red wan with bunions, if such iver was seen. I'd better invite Hennessy to dance with her," giggled Johanna, who had her sense of the humorous. People could make an "omnium gatherum" of a wedding; she remembered her girlhood, when all attended as their right. Hennessy, if honoured, would not be angry with Robert.

At the festivities, Mrs Janet had sometimes to confront Sandy and concentrate until her stare grew glassy. She could not risk his breaking loose to chop up the furniture or smash the globe of the humming birds—so much admired. Great was her relief when he retired to the "ind room" from whence his snores accompanied the dancing. What mattered the giggles they evoked when compared with his usual threats to kill her with an axe or to burn down the house? Mrs Urquhart was free to enjoy Bella and to wonder why she had thrown herself away on bob-tailed old James. She invited her to make an extended visit to Keebah. Bella's laugh was the heartiest, her manner the most friendly and boisterous of any present. She had no shame about her past, no airs about her present, nor fears for her future. She slapped the old men on the back, and rallied the young ones like a popular mid-wife having a night out with her clientele.

Euphemia Fitzhugh was present. She could not afford to neglect opportunity. "Ye are welcome," said Johanna in receiving her, "and I've invited Mr Hennessy specially for ye, his first time in me house. He's still on the market, and the richest bachelor in the district."

This early put Euphemia in her place. Fight died in her before the spanking self-assurance of Mrs James, former servant to her hostess, and "adulterated" daughter of old Rafferty, as the wags put it, whose wife had been a passenger on a "girl ship", and boasted that she had been the toy of the officers on a warship when becalmed in the doldrums. Such a mess! Euphemia raised a smile by main force for Hennessy, remembering her bill.

Hennessy was effulgent and mellow. He had always liked Delacy and respected Johanna. There had been years when Danny's fearless straight-going had had its effect in reclaiming him.

Doogoolook and Maeve were paid every attention. Wong Foo was resplendent and had brought a pack load of presents for the bride. The story was retold of how Delacy had saved the life of Foo, and also of the two blacks, and made them members of the family.

Young Harry was excited by the company. He had much of solitude and had grown so shy that he would hide behind a tree at the approach of a stranger, but Bella "brought him out". He worshipped all the girls as divinities. His hero was Robert, who had such a fine swagger before maids and matrons, who danced even with the terrifying Mrs Fitzhugh, and was such a "ladies' man" that Danny, for safety, acted as patrol. Harry's eyes dilated to note what would happen when Robert and Grace met, but they managed to keep apart with skill. The two senior Fullwoods had had business to take them to Goulburn. Gerald Butler, who found Della difficult of access, was seen to dance with Grace and saved her from being a wallflower. Della danced more often with Hennessy than with Gerald, which delighted Hennessy.

The carriage took the young people to their new home, fifteen miles distant, on a run called New Glenties, in honour of the parent station, which was named from old Butler's place of origin.

Robert drove four horses with ribbons in the manes and Harry sat beside him.

The vehicle was disabled on its return journey down the cutting, so it was propped up in its house and sank to decrepitude. The poultry in the end had more use of it than ever Johanna. Nettles grew about it in summer. Hens brought forth new life in its shelter as it drowsed in the ceaseless lullaby of the river and its sighing trees—the pioneer carriage on the Murrumbidgee.

Much of the attention given to Della at the wedding, by reason of her residence in the mountains and as mistress of the new Mrs Fullwood, took the form of jokes about her being an old maid. Gerald Butler was as assiduous as ever when the wedding pother subsided but Della would having nothing to do with "Molly McCathie's leavings". Gerald retorted that if she wanted a sissy who was not somebody's leavings she would have to clutch him straight from the cradle as she was now old enough to be the grandmother of all the bachelors excepting a few shepherds and Hennessy.

The lively girl grew silent and thin and did not enjoy circumscription by her mother after her liberty and consequence at Burrabinga.

Danny was concerned about her old-maidism, though she was not yet thirty. Johanna watched with satisfaction. "What can ye expect after strewing her among the dingoes? It's meself that is thankful that she has not taken up with some cattle duffer."

The responsibility for his daughter's spinsterhood, thus thrust upon him, impelled Danny to action. As soon as Christmas was past he decided to visit "me dear old frinds the Evanses, who saved me life in the first place, but for which we wouldn't be here at all. Maybe the great frindship will act as incentive for Della to pick up with wan of the young men. . . . Sure to think it has been all this life-time and us never to have seen each other!"

The carriage demanded four horses and Robert, the whip, and Danny was bent on keeping Robert Chanticleer in his place. He harnessed three horses abreast to the gig. Della rode her pleasant-mannered Nullah-Mundoey and wore a habit that swept the grass and had to be gathered up from snags. Victorian draperies called for prestidigitation in handling but the need produced the virtuosi. Doogoolook rode too and opened the gates or sliprails. Some parts of the country were now fenced between Bewuck on the Murrumbidgee and Kilpoonta on the Lachlan. Doogoolook led a lovely Nullah-Mundoey, broken by Harry and paced by Robert, for

N

Mrs Evans in memory of the mare she had given Danny in his need. Packed in the gig, or as excrescences on the horses, were other presents, including rose cuttings and a China peach tree, two guinea hens, a specially cured ham, a "kag" of dried fruit, a china teapot, and some yards of silk brocade. Nothing could be too good for the Evanses.

There was joy, and effusive demonstration of it in the reunion of Danny with Mr and Mrs Evans, but as sometimes happens with all but the rarely understanding of wives on coming in contact with a husband's life-saving friends for the first time, Johanna did not quite thaw.

Della was a disappointment to her father and the Evanses. They were sure she must have favoured her mother's family. The eldest Evans, four years her junior, was the nearest to her age, but he told his mother that she was as dismal as a motherless foal—a real old maid, and easy to see why. Della, in her turn, said she had never seen such a stupid boor as Penhryn Evans; that he never opened his mouth except to put food in it, and that it was big enough for him to put his foot there too.

"Moi, oh, moi! What can be coming over the young people, at all? Whoi, the very breed of the Evanses would attract me. Do you see anything at all the matter with young Evans?" he demanded of Johanna.

"Sure, after a view of him, I can see whoi all the girls are woild for my Robert."

"Arrah, but thirty years in the future is what tests a marriage."

"Och, if marriages were gone into knowing what thirty years would bring, most women, I'm thinking, would be nuns in preference."

There was nothing further after a visit of some weeks but to return all the way from Kilpoonta on the Lachlan to Bewuck on the Murrumbidgee, where the latest gossip was that Gerald Butler was going to Heulong regularly. Della was now without a suitor. Danny interrogated her, "What is wrong with the young men? Are you hankering after someone you can't get?"

Della said she cared for no one, and unless she cared she preferred to remain unmarried.

"Leave Della be," advised her mother. "She will be a pleasant companion to me—and ye too whin we grow older. Ye won't always be able to cover the country like a wallaby."

Johanna cuddled her idea of Della being a bride of the Church, thus should she win glory and sanctuary for herself and atone for her mother.

Della conveniently turned religious at that date. Johanna let her alone in the Church of England for the time, but was bent on turning her thoughts the right way later. She visited Father O'Brien, when he toured the district, and gained comfort and some holy books lost to her for years. When the Reverend Father went back to Sydney he sent her a print of the Blue Madonna elegantly framed, which Johanna made the centre of a shrine in her bedroom. Danny was inclined to oppose, but philosophy restrained him. "Sure, 'tis meself would be the slave to superstition to think there could be harm in a pretty picture. 'Tis only when it is worshipped as an idol that the mischief enters, and I'll have no idols in my house. I'll have no man tell me how to think, or stand between me and God."

"Ye have ye'r own clergyman come here," said Johanna, "and he tells you how to think."

"I reserve me own opinion."

"Sure, 'tis ye that has all the wisdom."

"No wan has anny wisdom when it comes to an altercation, but if the parson tried to dictate to me about the mysteries that are hid from us all—black, whoite or green, Protestant, Catholic, Jew or Pagan, sure I'd tell him to go to hell at wanst. That's the privilege of Protestantism, that if ye have a moind ye can use it; but if ye had a moind, Johanna, and it went contrary to Father O'Brien or Father Shannon, there would be the dayvil to pay, and talk of damning, and look askance. I'll never submit to the like of that, and me a free man."

"Ye'll submit though to a poipe and a kag of rum," sniffed Johanna.

CHAPTER XXIV

DANNY had banished the second planet from his personal sky. Johanna was dependent upon him once more. He sank into the comforts of Bewuck varied by visits to Norah and Stewart Butler at New Glenties. There was the expectation of grandchildren. There were cures for rust in wheat, and new varieties of potatoes, but with the slackening of effort he suffered from dullness, and went often to the Township for the alleviation of conversation. He had a lively interest in the progress of the Overland Telegraph to Darwin, and the explorations of Forrest. He was conversant with Polynesian affairs, had opinions upon the annexation of the Fiji Islands, and the proposal for a Customs Union with a levy on trade along the Murray. He threw himself with gusto into the fine points of the Parkes-Robertson Parliamentary wrangle, and elections were high points of existence to him. His voice, and that of other settlers could be heard literally for miles when loosened by grog and opinionatedness regarding public issues towards which Johanna maintained an indifference which was accepted as typical of women.

Burrabinga remained a camp stripped of table and bed linen; crockery when broken was replaced by tin ware. Danny said there was no "sinse" in wasting elegancies on "min". Saplings sprang up in the orchard, holes were worked in the fence of the garden, and marsupials destroyed everything. The possums were always first to harvest the fruit. The presence of women was necessary to drive the Delacys to home comforts. They never used any but packing needles, nor learned to cook beyond salt junk and damper and tea without milk.

Robert missed human association after his reign at Bewuck, but quickly arranged the work so that others took the brunt of running wild cattle and horses by Bullock Gap or Dead Horse Plain while the business down Keebah way fell to him. For this he took the best saddle-horses. There was a difference between the saddle- and stock-horse as wide as that maintained by Johanna between herself and the "gurrls" she trained as "surrvants". The saddle-horses were bent to paces as young ladies and gentlemen were taught deportment and dancing.

Robert's taste in horses was infallible, but his aristocrats were sometimes second-rate for following mobs up and down their native precipices, and he was out-classed in rough riding. Nevertheless Harry worshipped him and took hard labour off his shoulders as much as possible. Harry had his father's fearlessness. He craved a hero, to die for if necessary, and Robert, with his plumes freshly upon him, fitted the conception, accepted the homage and brought a new element into the Keebah circle. He wore top boots, stylish breeches and showy spurs, had a marvel of the whip-maker's art, and was following by all the dogs. Harry's whip was roughly plaited by himself, had a hickory handle, and his raiment was in keeping, but the contrast he presented only added to his pride in Robert as a dandy. Robert had glamour, with the tales of girls doing scandalous things to trap his love, and glamour is as necessary as salt to youths of a certain temperament.

William was more judicial and critical, and his attitude grew censorious after Janet Urquhart fell desperately in love with Robert. He had never believed Robert guiltless in the Grace and Molly cases. No charmer ever is, Janet, Elspeth, and Jeanie, all three, could see no other sun when Robert's shone. William contemptuously attributed this to Robert's breeches and boots. He secured a good turn-out for himself but nevertheless remained an honest frump. He had no long mirror in which to appraise the difference in deportment between himself and his brother, but saw it in the indifference of the girls.

The community received another woman. The Charles Fullwoods had had enough of Bella, and she was weary of the restrictions of Heulong. She had acquired a set of manners that could be put on and off like a dolman, she could write a letter and read the news-paper, and so was literate for the times. She insisted upon James making a home near Bullock Gap, at Cherry Tree Hill, and the Delacy men did not stand aloof. Fullwood had not been caught stealing their cattle for over two years, and there was no with-standing Bella. She gave them good meals. She rode to Burrabinga with a pack-horse and possessed herself of flowers and shrubs from Della's garden. The Urquharts and Anguses liked her. She was a woman free from complainings, ready and able to bring forth a brood in solitude and hardship. If her husband took a nobbler or a beast here and there, no one held her responsible.

Tom Angus had married in India and meant to make his home there. George Angus arrived to support the precocious Ned, who had been carrying on alone at Birrabee with a stockman. Robert very nearly had to take second place. George had more address than all the Delacys together, and handled harness horses in a way to turn Robert pale with envy, especially as he was jailed in the valley behind Delacy's mountain to be scaled only by horses as surefooted as goats.

The Keebah girls thus had two glories, with William as a fall-back and young Harry and Ned as reserves. Janet adored Robert, but he was no longer very young, had had two disastrous entanglements, and could find pleasure in more than one woman at a time. Little Jeanie was the joy of Ned and Harry, to whom a divinity was necessary. Ned missed Della, who had so long been his tutoress.

Saturday nights now found the young men gathered at Keebah instead of Burrabinga. There was a deal of horseplay and practical jokes. William saw what he saw and thought what he thought. Having been buried in solitude, he was too shy and nervous to push to the front, he resigned himself to talk with old Urquhart of the relation of fencing and dingoes to woolgrowing.

One evening a stupendous racket denoted a race in progress. All the hardwood forms from the school-house and kitchen were in line, each with a jockey—males astride, females crumpled sideways. The male winner was to bestow a kiss upon a maiden of his own choosing. The lady winner was to name a gentleman to embrace her. The proprieties, independent of science, held that male *amour* was a Niagara that must be stemmed, and that women's resistance, armoured in distaste, had to be stormed.

William longed to be a contestant, but would have bolted from the prize as dangerous immorality. The men romped away with limb-endangering determination to be first. The girls all ended level as a concession to self-conscious modesty. Robert proclaimed that every girl had won. Much giggling and blushing ensued.

George Angus won and claimed Janet, the handsome and inarticulate, whose unselfish appreciation of the social contributions of others made her a favourite with exhibitionists. Harry said that George had not won fairly. He resented George's aspiring to any young woman favoured by Robert, but this George ignored as jealousy. The girls were all compelled to choose. Baby Jeanie picked both Harry and Ned, and hilarity relieved the tension. The Keebah boys were dependent on Ellen Learmont from farther down the river. No one challenged their interest in the girl, who was of the Grace Fullwood type, material for drudging wife and uncomplaining mother, but unalluring.

In the second race Robert chose Janet, who exclaimed, "Oh, I couldn't be kissing with every one looking on!"

Laughter and bucolic ribaldry greeted this, but Robert was equal to the occasion. "Come into the garden among the roses; anything to please a lady."

A dangerous precedent was established. William concluded that all the girls were as bold as Bella, and took to his role of Joseph. He neither desired to sin nor to be subjected to shopworn goods. Thereafter he was regarded as being "cut out for an old bachelor".

The Anguses brought their sister Susan to Birrabee, a bright girl who could ride as well as her brothers, and was popular with all. Three of the young Urquharts fell prone in love with her, and Mrs Urquhart took her word on household arrangements as inspired. George hoped that Robert would be attracted by her and leave Janet alone, but Robert and Susan played the same game and did not progress beyond the preliminary moves.

Soon the friendliness between the Delacys and Anguses was endangered. Robert could do no wrong in Harry's eyes, and so when the Anguses clashed with Robert they could do no right. It fell out one Monday morning as the young men rode from Keebah that Harry was hopping off his horse every mile or so and shaping-up to George on Robert's behalf.

Robert accepted all homage without embarrassment, but this demonstration distressed George. He liked young Harry, and both Anguses were bent on keeping out of trouble. George wished to marry Susan to a Delacy or an Urquhart and himself marry Janet.

One Saturday night the school-house was used by Robert and Janet when reaping prizes, and they were unaware of the old tutor in the corner away from the firelight. He reported what he saw. Mrs Urquhart was always for peace and did not suspect evil until its fruits were ripe, but she could not calm Sandy even by laxity in grog rationing.

On the following Saturday the gathering was at Birrabee, where the Urquharts did not appear. Their absence was attributed to a thunderstorm.

During the week Harry went to Keebah with an important letter for the post. For once Robert had left this pleasant task to his brother while he packed salt out towards Bullock Gap and had a feast with Wong Foo. Harry returned at midnight on the same day, having pushed his brave brumby there and back without calling at Birrabee.

No sooner had the dogs announced him at the stable gates, a quarter of a mile from the house, than Urquhart had put out to meet him. "He must have been looking out for me with his old spy glasses. Holy Ghost! he had a gun, and I thought he was going to fire it off. Acted as if I was a bushranger!"

"Was he drunk?"

"Hanged if I know. He didn't let me get near enough to smell him. He sat straight enough on the old moke."

"Didn't he make any explanation?"

"I was so taken back, I didn't know which way to look for Sunday."

"But he must have said something."

"He said a whole thunderstorm. If one of us comes inside his boundaries again he is going to put a bullet in us. He said he treated us like his own family, and this is the low-down way we've treated him in return. I said I never did anything. He said if I didn't, it was only because I was not old enough. He said William was all right."

"Robert up to his tricks again."

"He said Robert and George, but I bet it's that Chow of a George, and he's putting it on Robert."

"You have the faith of a mother in Robert, but the Yackandandah can't always be swum dry."

"You mean that old Urquhart is trying to trap him now for his females like Fullwood and old Hennessy did? Golly, it must be exciting to be Robert."

"It will be so exciting some day that he'll be facing a jury, and they won't be so damn' partial as you and Ma."

"How can Robert help it when the women are just mad after him? Gosh, old Sandy was crying like an old woman."

"Aw, the D.Ts often takes them crying. Did you see the old woman or any of the boys?"

"Not a sign of any one else. He was sitting in wait."

"How could he be sitting in wait in the middle of the week?"

"Find out for yourself. I'm not going to have a gun at me again, and be called names that would blister an anvil."

Now justified in his policy of total abstinence from any association with the girls, William could afford to laugh. "I reckon the old man caught you slobbering over Jeanie."

He suggested that they should say nothing and await developments. Harry accepted this with regard to the Anguses, but warned Robert, who swaggered, though he was startled, and went in fear of old Urquhart appearing to haul him away to marry Janet. A week's uneasiness brought him to say that he had heard of some blood horses up by Wild Horse Plain and would join O'Neill and try to trap them. In view of the fondness and softness of Janet it would be safer to be out of the way for a while. He made jokes about going into the wombat wilds to take the hard going, but William inquired, "When old Sandy comes looking for you, shall we say which way you went?"

Robert departed two mornings later on a prime Nullah-Mundoey, with the two best pack-horses and a contentious retinue of dogs. William and Harry were left to the boundary fence they were erecting between Birrabee and Burrabinga—hard, heavy work, felling trees and rolling them into line in rough country. They toiled all day long in the vast solitude where never a man appeared, and in the evening had salt beef and damper washed down by tea, and then rolled in a rug before a fire and slept to the lullaby of dingoes, curlews, and other night creatures, and the bullocks' bells against the delicate song of some rivulet. They had put up fifteen miles single-handed and the Anguses were working their way towards them.

In due time they met, and Harry, blaming George for the departure of Robert, hurled insinuations of his being at the root of the trouble with Urquhart. George tried to keep the peace, but Harry was not to be quieted and grandiloquently challenged George to a duel.

George laughed in his face. "What about?"

"You know well enough. Others have suffered from being mixed up with you."

A cloud passed across George's pleasant face. "If that's it, how shall we fight? Fists—I'd be guilty of cruelty to animals."

"Revolvers."

"No thanks. I'm not a murderer."

William tried to bring Harry to sense. At length a riding duel was decided upon, but the logical William wanted to know what it would prove.

"Which is best rider, I suppose," said George, still in charge of his temper.

Ned strove for peace, almost to tears, as a warm affection had always existed between him and Harry. However, rough riding was in the day's work. Little harm could come of such a contest but waste of time, and the Delacys had all the time of the year at their disposal. Each was to bring in an outlaw, five or six years of age and never yarded, over precipitous country. They tossed for places and Harry got a roan brumby that ran beyond Bullock Gap, George a chestnut colt towards Dead Horse Plain.

The stock-horses were saddled before dawn. Harry had picked a quiet, low, long, goose-rumped animal as ugly as sin. She was flat-sided, had a big head and always a long tail, which ill-suited her, but she went raving mad if it was reduced.

George laughed at her appearance. She had been out at grass for twelve months following a staking and he had not yet seen her feats in descending impossible grades strewn with every kind of obstruction, from fallen giants to wombat holes. George's nag was a piebald colt, phenomenally active, a bit pig-mouthed but acquainted with rough country.

They started at sunrise, reviled by William and Ned as fools. These two agreed to follow, Ned on Harry's trail, William on George's in case of accident.

A few miles along his way Harry found the tracks of George's mob leading towards Bullock Gap, and presently saw that the two colonies had combined so both men started after them together. William and Ned came up at a strategic point, and in the excitement of finding the colts in company turned it into a special day's muster.

An escaped blood mare fell early and hipped herself. Ned's filly put her fetlock out and was also dropped from the chase. He had to make to Wong's and borrow a horse to return to camp. William, a fearless rider, kept up with the others. The wild horses frequently disappeared with a crash of hoofs and the dislodged boulders cannoning down the gorges, and reached some distant crest, only to be out-manoeuvred by one or other of the pursuers. A young stallion fell on a slippery sideling near Cherry Tree Hill and broke his neck. A handsome grey mare snapped her leg in a tough vine; never were there so many casualties in a day. George and Harry rode as if on winged steeds that lifted them past obstacles on ways that the young men in cold blood could scarcely have trodden on foot—the fastest mob in the region followed by the most reckless riders. In the afternoon William was left behind by the laming of his horse.

The duellists remained, joined to yard the two remaining colts, which they did at sundown, having run all day without food or drink. Even the wild things were weary, and after one mad rush at the rails, which they struck with their forefeet, settled down defeated, with wide nostrils and heaving flanks.

George had been so careful, as well as skilled, in avoiding jostling that Harry was warmed to admiration and a realization that there might be two sides to the question of George and Robert as stars in one firmament.

He flung off his suffering, but far from foundered beast, held her from more than sip of water and came forward to congratulate

George, but George spoke first, "I take off my hat to you, Harry. You're a rider for fair! If you could get a saddle on hell you'd ride it to a standstill; and that mare is a wonder. Any time you want to sell her, let me have first offer."

Harry was equally cordial. The enmity engendered by his unreasoning partisanship was healthfully tempered and reflection was later to incline him to judgments in line with his father's.

CHAPTER XXV

Old Sandy did not come to Birrabee or Burrabinga, nor go to Bewuck. The young men kept to their own lairs and ceased to visit. To William, Robert's disappearance was evidence of guilt. When O'Neill came for rations he reported that Robert had stayed only two days with him. William set out to ascertain if there had been more than alcoholic distemper in old Urquhart.

If the Anguses had been chased from Keebah they were keeping it to themselves. "We've been imprisoned for ages," said Susan, with her usual manner. "Every Saturday we waited for you till it was too late to set out. I've had a scalded hand, too." She still had a rag on it.

William rode on to Keebah. When the dogs barked, Donald hastened to meet him, red with embarrassment. "I'm awfully sorry, Bill, but it would be better not to go to the house till things blow over."

"I'm not a horse or cattle thief. I'll certainly keep away but I must know the reason of the insult to my character."

"There's nothing against you, Bill . . . only . . . well . . . you see Robert is too much of a ladies' man for the dad's taste. The tutor has reported more than happened between Robert and Janet in the school-house, I reckon."

"I don't like this."

"No more do I, but what can I do? The dad has forbidden any communication. I thought we could meet at Birrabee, but that has gone smash, too."

"And how are you going to see Susan?"

"This can't last," Donald reddened and turned to other topics. "Ma has been in bed with an accident. It keeps Elspeth busy, with Janet away."

"Where is Janet?"

"Gone to Sarah's for a spell . . . There has been the devil to pay, I can tell you . . . If you are hungry I'll sneak you some grub."

William disclaimed hunger. He lacked the address to go past Donald to ventilate the matter with Sandy. It was a blow to an inexperienced young man of his probity in every relation, including women—especially including women. The unfairness of being

declassed because of the behaviour of Robert or George rankled
in his breast. It was imperative that his father should be informed.
Harry's concern was to find Robert and reinstate him, but William
insisted that he should stick to Burrabinga. A day later William
rode down by way of Learmont's, passing Keebah.

"Be the poipers!" exclaimed Danny. 'Robert is a light scoundrel
with women, and I shan't have him ruining the daughters of me
best friend. Who took me family in when I was lost? This viper
in the grass to be me own son! Janet, the foinest girl in the Colony!"

"Och! Janet!" snapped Johanna, "a great soft bag of flour that
could no more take care of herself than a pumpkin."

"The more disgrace then to Robert that she should not be safe.
Get in the brown mare for the morning. I'll follow Robert to—
to . . . sure, I'll follow till I catch him, if 'tis off the ind of the
continent. This time he'll fulfil his duty. He's escaped too lightly
hitherto."

"Ye'll find another bull's nest," said Johanna. 'Robert cannot be
responsible for the sinful capers of drabs that should be shut up
and whipped and be made to leave him alone.'

"Och, woman, there is no consistency at you at all. Was it you
or me that was trying to rise among the gentry by collaring Grace?
Answer me, yes or no."

It was liberation to ascend to the plateau and turn again towards
the beckoning hills, blue and still, wreathing on and on to Victoria.
Bewuck irked him but he would not relinquish it to Robert again
because he was weary of hearing of his son's perfection in management. He would have been back in his fastness long since only
that Robert reigned there. Now this!

To be in the saddle all day again, with a Nullah-Mundoey under,
and the dogs and Doogoolook capering fore and aft, with the
eternal splendour spread before him as a banquet on the table of
the universe, generated a spiritual exaltation beyond the miniature
condenser of human articulation.

They rested at noon to boil the quart-pot in surroundings
aromatic and primeval; they crossed the Murrumbidgee by Keebah
punt at sundown and reached the homestead at dusk. They were
met by Donald at the stables. There was no ready turning-out of
horses. Donald compromised by putting them in the stables, and
was nervous as he went to the house. Danny was unhappy to be
approaching the hospital door with the possibility of enmity
meeting him. He halted at the garden gate.

"Go tell your father I'm here."

Urquhart was some time appearing. As Danny waited, his ire rose against Robert.

"Good evening, Mr Delacy," said Urquhart, and did not extend his hand.

"Good evening, Sandy Urquhart. I never thought to see the day when you would not shake hands. Sure, if wan of mine has done you wrong, I'm here to face the facts, and prove or disprove them, and do all in me power to make amends."

Urquhart led the way to the office where he kept his accounts. "Sit down," he said, as if to a stranger, and left Delacy to open.

"What is this I hear, Sandy?"

"What have you heard?"

"That you have ordered me sons away with a gun."

"Your bairns were as welcome as my ain, till I foond disgraceful proceedings in my ain hoose. I had to take steps to pluck my daughter from ruin."

"Which of me sons was it, Sandy?"

"William I believe to be a decent mon, but that other one must never come near this hoose again."

"This is a dreadful business."

"How he came to be son of yours and your guid wife I dinna ken. No young woman would be safe wi' him."

"I'll be honest with you, Sandy, as I would with black, whoite or green. If Robert has left annything behind, he shall marry her, or I'll take the gun to him meself. But I must be fair to him too, though he is my own son. You may have heard of me forcing him to marry on the niece of Hennessy, the publican. You never saw anything so plausible, and sure, while I had the boy bailed up, by damn, if the girl did not exonerate him by running off with the son of old Bandy Macallister, the millionaire. It made me pause, Sandy, when the next wan accused Robert; and that was Fullwood with his daughter . . ."

"That cattle duffer!"

"Have you his quality, too? Sure, I squashed that, and now the Fullwood piece is trying to marry young Butler, and me not wanting the connection. Moind, I don't say that Robert is guiltless, but the girls do throw themselves before him. It's this dash with his spurs and all that swagger that does it."

"It appears that Robert is beyond you. Some of the ugly tattle may have been leasing, but Robert has a way of escaping. Could you lay your hand on him now? Most likely he has another lassie all ready to marry in case I should bring him to book. There are plenty better lads than that swaggering birkie o' yours. It is my will that he shall come here no more till he has a wife to keep him frae being a menace to other women."

Urquhart had never seen his old mate look so dashed, and it went hard with him, but Robert's offence had been deep. However, his cellarer partly retrieved the occasion by extra rations. After a nobbler or two Urquhart softened to call his visitor "Danny", and to tell him precisely what damage Robert had wreaked. The old mates wept together as they grew maudlin, and re-pledged the fealty of the Yackandandah, but Urquhart did not relax towards Robert. He was too proud to expose his trouble to the community, and preferred his own way of settling it. He said that his friendship with Johanna and Danny stood, but when Danny sobered there was a constraint upon the old open-heartedness.

Danny rode on to Burrabinga where he helped William and Harry to chase wild bullocks from Bullock Gap. He thundered through the scrub down impossible declivities, holding his wooden leg in his hand, as he had done in his youth, and his mare never so much as stumbled under him. The mind still held dominion over the flesh. He held his own against his sons, but Robert had jarred his dream of opening up territory for posterity. He had spoiled the human association so precious and so sparsely rationed in the lonely pioneering days. Danny hardly knew what to do. Robert was mature and had long since been promised partnership.

He spent a night with Wong Foo and was comforted that no moth deteriorated the fabric of that friendship. He called upon Bella and was cheered and amused by her jovial camaraderie. He had little against Bella. She had eloped, and Danny had done that himself. It was not the custom to visit a husband's lack of character on his wife unnecessarily. Bella asked Mr Delacy to carry a letter and parcel to her mother and to say nothing to James. The union remained morganatic: the Fullwoods had not relaxed towards the Rafferty collection.

Danny returned to make his difficult report to Johanna, who was waiting in a fury of nerves.

"And you, Daniel Delacy, not to see it's those Anguses making mischief and putting the blame on me beautiful boy. That sour old fox-coloured Presbyterian to talk of taking a gun; and that ignorant old trollop of a Mrs Janet, the shape of two flour bags set wan upon the other—she'd do annything out of hell or in it too—and that's where she should be for such wickedness—annything to trap me beautiful boy. And ye with no more circumspection than an eft in controversy with them. If ye had a proper proide, Robert could have been married with wan of the Camerons of The Plains by now."

"Nonsense, woman, there's no eligible Cameron above ten years old."

"And what did ye say whin he ordered Robert to keep his distance? If ye had anny backbone, but ye wouldn't have; ye'd be crying around a kag of rum, and taking ivery side but ye'r own, and blathering like the *feis* of Tara, and nothing in it but wind."

"There's this, Johanna, you're over-excited now. That is all that can excuse you for talking of Janet Urquhart, who took you in whin I lay with me limb gone and me moind astray."

"I'm thinking it's still astray. And whoi were ye capering around an impty continent, and laying on an ant bed till ye'r limb was ate off . . ."

"Och, woman, there's no sense at you at all." There was no appeal but justice to Danny's impersonality and large magnanimity; and justice was coldly repellent to the over-wrought mother.

"What has come to Robert, wandering the wilds alone? He might fall in with the bushrangers and lose his life," she wailed.

"By damn! I'm thinking he would be at home with them. He can shoot and strut and swagger about while honest men do the hard work."

"Me poor scandalized boy!"

"You're wrong in the evidence, me brave Johanna. We've weathered manny a storm, and we'll weather this wan, but Robert cleared out when there was no breath of scandal, so he must have had raysons known to himself."

Della refused to be goaded into an opinion for or against Janet or Robert. She had settled down to all the odd tasks as well as the major management of Bewuck homestead. The stitches dropped by others were picked up by her. Her mother was satisfied with this as progress towards religious retreat. Della had put aside a number of things as ungodly, among them the bustles, panniers and flounces of the 'seventies, and looked so skinny and unnatural that her brothers found it a trial to take her to town. Johanna devoted herself to her garden and pot plants and the dairy, which she superintended with Maeve and Hannon. She still delighted in her turkeys and other poultry. For the remainder, she loved to gossip. Not an item of news but percolated to her in the end if not sooner. A frequent complaint was that Robert was not there to relieve her imprisonment with his gig and tandem.

Danny, on the contrary, was no gossip. He condemned scandal. If any one brought him a foul story he would say, "If it is as bad as that, leave it to Sergeant O'Gorman. It is beyond you, and the Sergeant is there for the purpose of enforcing decency."

No sooner had Danny and Doogoolook dropped out of sight on their way home than Harry took a pack-horse with provisions and camp gear and set off to O'Neill to seek Robert. When O'Neill saw Harry's earnest spirit he said he was sure that Robert was on the next occupied squattage, no more than forty miles beyond Wild Horse Plain on the watershed between the Murrumbidgee and the Snowy.

Here were the Lillingstons, in that generation somewhat taboo socially, but who went in succeeding families to the top on Monaro, so that the representatives of the name to-day swagger under as big a mortgage as any other polo players and merino riders in the Mother State. Their hunting ground in Daniel Delacy's day lay in the Crown Lands between Burrabinga and their own holding, Bunbilliko. Tales were that they trapped every hoof within reach, regardless of brand, and drove it by way of Jacob's Ladder to Melbourne. Rumour may not have been excessive, as they rose to be soundly rich in two generations.

Robert was heartily welcomed to Bunbilliko. Boots and breeches, spurs, whips, plated gear, blood horses and rough riding had notorious exponents in the Lillingstons. Delacy, Senior, had kept away from them, disapproving of their lack of probity, but as he never slandered any one he had not impressed this upon his sons.

There was a family of four sons and three daughters. The men were dashing fellows and Robert was known to them for his ability with harness horses. When he stated the reason of his visit they were ready to assist him. They were unfailingly plausible and said that their own cleanskins were running where Robert proposed to muster so they would make it a partnership.

The open downs of Bunbilliko were suited to the training of harness horses, so Robert put his business head to work and escaped the bone-racking operations of sliding down precipices or buck-jumping. He began by yoking horses to a log, and quickly had them fit for the spring cart. The Lillingstons ordered a dogcart and soon they were all flashing in and out of Cooma, but Robert remained excessively business-like. He was uneasy concerning his absence and determined to reinstate himself by a fine catch of horned cleanskins as well as horses.

Old Lillingston had done five years for horse-stealing on the northern rivers, and his marriage was one of the variety common where the couples went ahead and awaited the benefit of clergy when bishop or priest visited remote places. He and Mrs Lillingston were delighted with young Delacy's advent. Connection with a family so renowned for respectability would lay the foundation stone of their social ascent, and they did everything to woo Robert for one of the girls, but he was careful to show no more favour to one than the other and to be as circumspect as if he were married elsewhere and strictly monogamous. They were of the type of Susan Angus, lively and able to take care of themselves, and to put forward any side that suited. Robert was beginning to consider himself a sultan to choose as he willed, and his maturing ambition was for a maiden conventionally unspotted, clean as crystal, staunch as hemp.

CHAPTER XXVI

ROBERT wrote to his father a glowing account of the numbers of cattle and horses he had reclaimed in partnership with the Lillingstons, and urged the need to take advantage of a rising market.

Johanna was jubilant. "Me beautiful boy, what a head on him! And there were those to disbelieve him and throw scandal on him!"

"It would be like him to take up with the fastest lot in creation. People of questionable antecedents, and flasher even than Robert. Sure, I've seen the Lillingstons in Queanbeyan, swaggering like dukes. Fellows with small heads and long legs and smooth tongues."

While Robert's letter had been travelling to Bewuck, Harry had reached Bunbilliko, and was effusively welcomed. He was like Robert in tall willowy physique, soft black hair and chiselled features, but his eyes were blue. He had no fine gear, and his small delicate hands were scarred and calloused, with nails broken to the quick from the incredible miles of fencing he had put up with them naked to sun, rain and frost. His horses too were suitable for wild riding in impossible country as Robert's for showy appearance. Robert's were almost clean bred; Harry's were brumbies, tireless and surefooted as goats.

Harry reported the Keebah commotion as he knew it. "Blinded old jackass!" said Robert.

With a showy collection of oaths he placed the blame on other shoulders, mainly George's. Harry was stirred to ride away to settle scores anew with George, but Robert persuaded him to be quiet. "A decent man always holds his tongue and stands the gaff if a woman is concerned," said Robert nobly, lighting a pipe as large as his father's, and more striking. To save a woman at his own expense was the swagger for gentlemen in the printed romances that came Harry's way, and there was zest for the spiritually hungry young man in living up to even a spurious ideal.

Harry's eager selfless disposition made him a favourite with the Lillingstons. The girls adopted him. He remembered them as sweet women for ever, nor ever suffered any deterioration by the association, because of Danny in him as well as freshly componded depths of his own. Mike Lillingston and he became bosom friends. It was

Harry's first taste of the delight of a mate who could match him in bushcraft and poetic imagination.

Harry was enthralled by this country of tussocks and daisies, bluebells and snow gums and little plains, where the Murrumbidgee begins as a crystal and vocal sylph and roams about the forehead of Monaro gathering volume and experience. In the numerous limestone caves within ride, the young men found a world which they furnished with imaginary peoples and cities. Fantastic metropolises buried beyond archaeological recall arose at their bidding. Even the scrimshawing of the insects on the trunks of the eucalypts was weft into fiction which held a younger generation spell-bound when Mike's beard was grey. A few of their tales linger half-remembered, but more have escaped to the faery of some outer circle of time from people too engrossed in the arduous mechanics of pioneering to keep a log of imaginings.

Horse buyers were due from Melbourne, so Robert decided to extend his absence. With Harry, unexcelled buck-jump rider, to rack his frame, Robert would prepare a draft of trained saddle as well as harness horses. Harry was childishly proud of what Robert had accomplished, and he and Mike were engaged day in day out. Their rewards were a girl's smile or a word of commendation from a colleague. The companionship of girls, whose kindness could relieve him of the painful shyness grown in solitude, was a heaven of reward to Harry.

Also employed was old Peg-leg from the Gulph, a free selector, a hang-over from Kiandra diggings, a lag who had lost his limb in trying to escape from the chain-gang, and never denying it, nor excusing his misdeeds. He had been a stable boy in England, and though old and crippled was a mountain of help in training horses.

Robert's leadership was accepted by the Lillingstons, who never slackened their flattery of him. He paced a filly for each of the girls and for the old man, and for this they gave him the best colt of the muster.

Harry got nothing but the chance to wreck his bones, but he had an imagination to illuminate a province ere it was raped by the axe or knew the desecration of sheep, the intrusion of roads, the confinement of fences. Wide days of dazzling light, and nights massed with stars or white with inebriating moonlight brewed the spirit of romance.

Two dealers came. Long Tom Bradford was known for his projecting teeth and a glass eye, which was the wonder of his decade. It was not polite to mention it, especially before the ladies, but Tom sometimes took it out as a private treat for men and boys.

His crony was Yorkie Driffield, a short broad man with an out-sized laugh, and they were as powerful a pair of horse-copers as could be matched in South West Ireland.

A big week ensued. Robert and Rodney were masters of the harness pairs; Mike and Harry were jockeys. Robert presided at the bargaining and whacking of the horses, and all concerned were satisfied with the results. Long Tom and Yorkie perceived a bonanza. Trained horses "free from vice" were in demand. They paid a wad of some hundreds and undertook to bring the balance six months hence. Their word was their bond; they had been trading throughout Monaro for years, and never a penny had they diddled any man.

As a finale to the summer's business, Robert and Harry appeared at a ball in Cooma with the Lillingstons. All Cooma and neighbour-hood were in attendance, some of the men in evening dress. Robert could not achieve that at short notice. Harry looked on in a second-best suit of one of the Lillingstons because his own clothes were worn out. He laughed until he was exhausted, and behind the scenes made friends with Meg Syme, a tall young woman of serious mood, who generously gave a hand where there were gaps in the service. Her younger sisters and a brother disported them-selves in the dance, which was by public subscription.

Robert and Rodney found the ball dull, but would not leave without supper. Robert went to the table in the tent in the back yard and began to help himself and companion. This brought one of the junior stewards, who happened to be Douglas Syme, brother of Meg. "Go away, you lout and carry guts to a bear," said Rodney.

"He's not fit to carry guts to a bear," added Robert.

The chief panjandrum was fetched, old Major Rawson, whose station joined the Lillingstons'. He was panoplied in full evening uniform and his status as top sawyer of the district's swells. When the Lillingstons had business near his homestead and appeared at meal times, Rawson offered them a feed in the kitchen. This mis-take had been repeated recently during a call by Rodney and Robert to see about some colts. Rodney had hoped that the presence of a Delacy would make a difference, but Rawson discerned and resisted these tactics of a social climber.

"I'm sorry we've finished dinner, but the cook may be able to find something for you," he had said.

Robert refused haughtily before the sentence was finished.

When Rawson was called in by young Syme, he was flustered to find Robert and Rodney. He suspected the Lillingstons in the matter of his cleanskins. As the Lillingstons knew, Rawson was an adept in popping a brand on a Bunbilliko steer or colt himself, and was, through his influence with the Commissioner, trying to squeeze out the Lillingstons.

"This won't do," he said to Rodney, who was slicing the breast of a turkey cock, reared by Meg Syme, as it lay on a platter in its own juices.

Rodney ignored this. Rawson said he would throw him out, and put his hand on Rodney's collar. Robert thereupon seized the bird and wiped gravy and grease down Major Rawson's white shirt front, thus relieving his envy of the Major's sartorial superiority, as well as having revenge for the intended social insult at their former meeting. "Sorry, my hand slipped," said Robert with assumed regret. "The cook very likely can find a tea-towel or something in the kitchen."

All ears were strained, many with delight in the incident. Rawson had an overbearing manner; all but his intimates had suffered from it. He felt he was defeated for the moment. Meg Syme came to the rescue by pinning a handkerchief across the irate bosom. To raise a froth on their swagger the two worthies returned to the ball-room for one more dance before departure. Robert's fancy was taken by a pretty little outsider, who refused him because of the Rawson incident. "Go to hell," whispered Robert, swaggering off to another girl, who, to his consternation, also turned from him.

"You insulted my brother!"

"Never intentionally would I insult the brother of such a pretty girl," said Robert grandly, "and if I insulted him accidentally I'd apologize."

"You ought to, if you are a gentleman."

Harry came to explain that the young man who had first tried to turn Rodney from the supper table was Douglas Syme, brother of his new friend Meg, who had cooked the turkey, and that the girl Robert had asked to dance was Nessie Syme. Robert was not abashed. "If I apologize will you dance with me?"

The girl agreed, confused and afraid of a commotion. "Bring your brother," said Robert.

"Douglas wouldn't come," said Nessie.

"Then I must go to him. I was in the wrong," said Robert.

Harry beamed on his hero.

Robert strutted down the room. "You come with me," he said, tucking the girl's arm under his, *nolens volens*.

"I've come to apologize," he said loudly. "I was wrong, Mr Syme.

I said you weren't fit to carry offal to a bear, but you are, you *are!* . . . And now for our dance."

The dance past, Robert was confronted by young Syme with his hackle now raised on two counts.

"You told my sister to go to hell," he said angrily, "And you can just come outside until I take it out of your hide."

"Your sister?" said Robert, a little taken back.

"My other sister."

Robert caught sight of the third Syme girl at the far side of the room. "I don't want to hit you, my lad, for my fault," he said to the youth. "I'll apologize publicly and abjectly." His mordant wit was stimulated by champagne, and he went across the room to Jeanie Syme with mock humility, "Say, Miss Syme, I advised you to go to a warmer place than this freezing hole, but your brother has seen me about it, and now you needn't go; you are to dance with me instead." Before the shy girl could parry this she too was being whirled around the dancing floor. All eyes were upon her partner in the hope that he might further enliven the meeting, but he prepared to leave at the end of the polka.

Harry reported from behind the scenes, "Ghost! Every one is pleased you did that to old Rawson. He's always trying to show his authority. I'll introduce you to the eldest Miss Syme. You'll have to be civil to her if you want to do a line with Jeanie and Nessie."

Meg was distant and dignified and nearly as tall as Robert, but there was a twinkle of amusement in her eyes. She had observed this celebrated bachelor several times previously displaying his horses around Cooma. She inspired him to genuine apology. "You see, old Rawson tries to come the nabob. Every one was so paralysed before him that perhaps I went a little too far."

"Quite a long way too far," said Meg, but her eyes smiled.

Harry was excited that Robert had brought ridicule on the would-be baron of the district. The following morning he showed Robert the bundle of goodies that Meg had given him for the road. Robert was so expanded by his own triumphs of wit and adulation that he went to a celebrated saddler's in the town to procure Harry a new saddle. He asked for pig-skin of a man too full of his own conceit to appreciate the celebrity before him.

"We keep only hog-skin," said he in a corrective tone.

"What a pity; I wanted pig-skin."

"But," said the man, seeing a customer for an expensive saddle, "they are the same article."

"Oh, no," said Robert. "You only had hog-skin when I asked for pig-skin, so I'll go elsewhere." He strode away with a fine flourish of his heels to show the fine length of his spurs.

The home-going was full of pleasure to Harry. A crisp April sunset reddened the valley, the garnered hay paddocks and naked orchard were grey under the nightly frost which already tingled in the air, and the voice of the Murrumbidgee came loudly from the crossing as they descended the cutting and were announced by the dogs. Robert's contingent rushed forward, some to engage in plunder while others disputed with the home pack. The hens were safely on their roost and Johanna free to run across the cultivation paddock to meet the travellers. Danny followed as far as the wood-heap, shouting orders about the dogs, and Della and Maeve came out to the stables.

In the evening when Della settled to the mending and Maeve went to bed, Robert brought out his gains and told of the partner-ship with the Lillingstons. It was hard to tell who was the more moved during the recital, Johanna or Harry.

"Can ye trust the dealers, me boy?" asked Johanna.

"They have a good name," interposed Danny. "You mean the long man with the glass eye, and the broad man with the guffaw. Sure, the short fellow's guffaw is heard all over Monaro."

But it was never heard there again. Never.

"In any case, see what we have and all because of Robert," eagerly interposed Harry.

"A few clothes would improve you," said Johanna.

"He must have a new suit," said Robert. He did not press his own rights, waiting for what Danny had up his sleeve about Janet Urquhart.

That came up next morning when they were inspecting the colts which Robert had selected as saddle-horses.

"I never thought Urquhart would warn wan of mine off with a gun. Forty years in the Colony and such a thing has never happened to me, yet wherever you go there is trouble. What is your side of it?"

"Looks like the same old play to get a husband for his trollop of a girl."

"The mention of you as a husband made him talk of a gun."

"Long Tom could see through that with his glass eye. Two guns wouldn't run me into being a husband for any of them."

Danny was gagged by his oath of secrecy. "At anny rate you've ruined me best friendship. If you don't want Grace; and Molly ran off from you; and you speak like a low-down scut of Janet—wan of the finest young women to be seen, who is fit to make a home and rear a family—in the name of reason, who do you want? Have you taken up with a Lillingston?"

"I have no more thought of them than of Molly or Grace."

"I hope they have none of you. The safest thing would be to marry a steady woman and cease to be a candidate for mischief with all the faymales from Goulburn to Cooma—rags or silk."

"I'm in a fine position to marry, with never a penny of my own."

"I'll set you up if you choose the right woman."

Robert asked for a share in the cattle and horses reclaimed from Bunbilliko, and Danny agreed to consider the question of partnership with his sons, so often deferred. For the present Robert was allowed to set off for the cattle, and to take Harry. Doogoolook was also contributed to the expedition.

William was left to slog at Burrabinga with two stockmen through a long snowy winter. Cut off from Keebah, his one social outlet, he grew more shy and awkward. He would not go to Birrabee. He feared Susan as dangerously attractive, and also he was too proud to go where he would have to refer to his proscription by old Urquhart. Bella and Wong Foo were his only relief in isolation.

CHAPTER XXVII

ROBERT and Harry came out of the cattle enterprise with profit sufficient to advance Robert's prestige. Harry had none to bother any one. The months ran away after that without any word from the horse buyers. Winter lingered with snow and sleet throughout September and October. Robert went through to Bunbilliko and took Harry with him. By the end of November the new tussocks were strong and green, the plains aglow with bluebells and daisies, other horses were finishing their education, but Long Tom and Yorkie did not appear.

Rodney and Robert continued their career in Cooma. Robert had his eyes open for Meg Syme, whose dignity had impressed him at the time of the ball. He saw her one day in the leading store and asked her would she give him a shakedown for the night as his horse was suffering a stone bruise. He winked warningly at Rodney. Meg naturally consented, hospitality being obligatory. Rodney was glad to flirt with Nessie and Jeanie. Old Syme had a small place not far out of town and since the death of his wife, Meg had kept house for him and the younger children.

Harry and Mike roamed the far recesses of their region, where only a shadow people, who had neither despoiled beauty nor left any monuments, intervened between creation and the young men's reign in an emptiness awe-inspiring and splendid. Thousands of magpies showered mellow notes into the aromatic silence; butcher birds practised their rich phrases; the crashing mockery of jackasses echoed far and near; a feathered host threw their smaller harmonies into the interstices of a spring orchestra, with the alien rhythm of hoof-beats as its drums. Crystal water rilled hill and plain. Flowers were everywhere—a carpet of blue and gold underfoot, an arras on the lower scrub, a canopy overhead exuding honeyed incense which the tempered winds swept pure and free from eternity to eternity.

A human intrusion was the death in the ranges of a lone fossicker known as Taffy. Rumour was that he left a hidden can of nuggets. Old Peg-leg, mad to find the treasure, dug everywhere like a wombat.

Mike and Harry's intention of teasing Peg-leg by reporting the finding of the nuggets was forestalled one day by the ferocity of the old man. His wife, Brandy Mary, tottered to meet them, clothes awry, waving her arms and weeping and shrieking that she must tell them something, but was afraid that the old man would murder her. Peg-leg rushed from the hut and dragged her inside by her matted locks. The boys, horrified, rode away, leaving Peg-leg to exercise his marital authority. The vast solitudes were often a jail where a conjugal prisoner had no redress from a warder, brutal as any that operated in officialdom. The screams and terror of many a tragedy evaporated into the palpitant and pregnant silence.

The year drew to a close without news of the horse dealers. The three Delacy men with Doogoolook and Wong homed to Bewuck for Christmas, while O'Neill took charge of Burrabinga.

The women were full of bustle and importance preparing the old-world feast in baking weather. The men were still able to enjoy the Bunyip Hole. Honoria Butler came home for Christmas Day but took all her family and guests to Old Glenties for the picnic races which the elder Butlers always organized for Boxing Day. The Fullwoods appeared there in force and Charles said good day to Delacy again. The Fullwoods had been the greater losers by the long avoidance. Gerald, Della's one-time flame, was now pursuing Grace, and Grace met Robert with equanimity.

During the dance in the evening Gerald and Grace decided to marry. Della did not dance since she had turned religious. It devolved upon her to find sleeping places for the infants of the self-satisfied matrons—the conventional role for one who was such an "oddity" that she had thrown away her chances. She met with pale wit the crude humorosities about her spinsterhood, while her mother was secretly satisfied as to her final disposal.

Danny at intervals broke into song, for which he was fitted with one of the most resonant voices in the world and not a thread of ear. His masterpiece was:

> I'm Denny Blake from County Clare,
>   And ready at command,
> To sing a song in praise
>   Of my own dear native land.
>
> etc. etc.
>
> I love my native country,
>   I'm loyal to my Queen
> But I can't forget old Ireland,
>   Where the grass grows green.

Old Butler, who had a true tenor, brought tears to the eyes of the elders with:

I'm sitting on the stile, Mary, where we sat side by side,
On a bright May morning long ago, when first you were my bride.
The corn was springing fresh and green and the lark sang loud and high,
And the red was on your lip, Mary, and the lovelight in your eye.

Then he repeated an old favourite:

Those evening bells! those evening bells!
How many a tale their music tells,
Of youth, and home, and that sweet time,
When last I heard their soothing chime!

And so 'twill be when I am gone;
That tuneful peal will still ring on,
While other bards shall walk these dells,
And sing your praise, sweet evening bells!

Danny called for the other song again and again. He bellowed it with Butler, ruining the effect, but was so saturated with the sentiment that he grew maudlin.

"Moi, oh, moi, but doesn't it fit like a glove, me brave Johanna? . . . 'The lark sang loud and high, and the red was on your lip, Mary, and the lovelight in your eye.'"

"Ye'r getting sintimintal in ye'r old days, which ye never were in ye'r young," said Johanna. "A sign of childishness, I'm thinking. Ye've had too manny taggeens. Get away before ye make a bigger fool of ye'rself. Ye'll wake all the babies, roaring like the Bull of Cooley, and destroying the chances of those who can sing without pulling the rafters down."

Danny went without protest to a bed reserved for him by Della. "Moi, oh, moi!" he murmured, as he unstrapped his stump. "'I'm sitting on the stile, Mary, where we sat side by side, on a bright May morning long ago, when first you were my bride.' The moind! The moind! 'Tis all in the moind, Johanna. In me moind I'm sitting there with you, as we did long ago in old County Clare, and yet here we are on the Murrumbidgee."

Too active to dwell in the past or to realize he was getting on in years, this song suddenly struck a deep chord in his being, and filled him with wistfulness. He was startled to find that the glow of life, in which he had walked as in dawn-light, had stealthily slipped behind him, and that he had to look over his shoulder to behold it as he went on into the night—a lonely shadow reflected against the afterglow.

The Delacy brothers were back at Burrabinga. January passed. Still no tidings of the horse dealers.

"They've come and gone and the Lillingstons collared the swag, most likely," said William.

Harry repudiated this on behalf of his friend Mike.

There was other news to flutter the Delacys. George Angus had married Janet Urquhart. William heard it when he went to Birrabee for the post. "George makes no secret of it. He grins from ear to ear like a dingo scenting a calf."

Harry rushed in, "That proves that Robert never even looked at fat old Janet."

Robert left Harry to do the talking for him while he threw his legs about in transcendant swagger and went to yard his colt, presented by the ingratiating Lillingstons. Smiles played across his features during the afternoon. In the evening he announced that he was off to Bewuck in the morning on business with the old man. Attended by his canine court, he called at Birrabee and George accepted congratulations. Robert generously offered Harry to cut shingles and adze posts for additions to the house. He reached Keebah a few hours later. *He* had never been ordered away, and was bold in the knowledge of Urquhart's absence and Janet's marriage. He entered and asked Mrs Urquhart, who had no skill in enmity, if he could do anything for her in the Township and was affable while his champions disabled a milder animal or two and killed a few hens. He refused the invitation to spend the night in favour of riding on to Learmont's. He would discipline Keebah by a little hauteur.

George Angus was whole-heartedly in love with Janet, and in the determination to improve his social position by marriage into the Urquhart family, had used the rumpus with Robert to further his suit. Old Urquhart would be glad to dispose of Janet—blown upon by scandal—so George had said that he had had Janet nearly won when Robert cut-in, and believed he could make her care again. He had been permitted to write to her.

Janet was overwhelmed by his ardour and the command of her father to marry him. She was ill of homesickness in banishment as a blight upon the prospects of her younger sisters. Robert was out of the picture. By marrying George she could make amends and return to her circle. It seemed a small price to pay. Whether her reinstatement made her as jubilant as his exoneration rendered Robert, Janet was too lymphatic and unawakened to know or show.

On arrival at Bewuck, Robert ill concealed his elation. When

appetites slackened towards second helping, Danny enquired,
"Have you anny news?"

"Only Janet Urquhart's wedding, but that is stale, I suppose?"

"Janet! Ye don't meant it! And who did she marry?" demanded
Johanna.

"George, of course! Who else do you think would have her
after their carryings-on?"

It took the wind out of Danny's sails surely enough, and filled
Johanna's. "Just what I knew. There goes another scandalous plot
of some designing slut to capture me son."

"Is this wedding fact or rumour?" was Danny's question.

"Had it from George himself. They confirmed it at Keebah.
Janet is coming to Birrabee as soon as George has the house ready."

"Ye were at Keebah, and did they receive ye?" Johanna fluttered
with excitement.

"Fell over me, but I came on to Learmont's. They deserve a little
of the cold shoulder for what the old dingo tried to pull off with
his talk of guns. A man has no chance against a woman's lies but
if you let 'em alone they bowl themselves out. The old man had
D.T's and saw snakes."

Danny felt that Sandy had somehow let him down, but Sandy's
secret remained and Danny kept it courageously against all provocation, kept it so well that it came to Danny's grandchildren only
from the last remaining member of Danny's brood, when there
was no longer any one living for scandal to wound. George
had cleared up the field for Robert, whose triumph Danny had
to suffer, a common ordeal to persons of spiritual integrity when
in conflict with those of less or none. Again Robert by a fluke
had emerged as a hero. Luck was his evidently, and a fine business
head, but he had not his father's respect. Neither had Danny
Robert's. He was inclined to dismiss his father as a silly old man.
The most trying result to Danny was Johanna's harping upon
Urquhart iniquity regarding her splendid son.

"Surely ye could see Urquhart was at his drinking! It shows
how drink takes the brain from a man entirely and leaves him
like an impty kag with an offensive smell."

Danny would have welcomed the peace of the "ind room" but
for the marital demotion involved.

The horse dealers never reappeared. Other men took their place.
Horses were saleable property. Robert and Harry went regularly
to Bunbilliko. The Burrabinga stock followed the river to its source
on the austere plains that exalt Monaro, a province with Kosciusko

as its king, a king not permanently crowned with snow, but garlanded each year with daisies.

The Lillingston girls abandoned hopes of Robert. Their brothers found that Robert took them to Burrabinga but never to Bewuck. The connection simmered down to the friendship between Harry and Mike. The reclaiming of stock from that area was finally delegated to Harry. It was he who brought the news that Brandy Mary had died drunk and that Peg-leg lived on alone. He had given up work; a son who lived fifty miles away brought him provisions. Gossip was that the son extracted heavy payment for this, which Peg-leg produced from a hoard about the place. He threatened to shoot intruders at sight and his temper was so evil that even the clergyman gave him a wide berth.

"Poor old devil," observed Lillingston. "He's mad with loneliness. A useful old cove with horses. He's got a mania against trespassers. Transported for poaching and it takes him that way now."

CHAPTER XXVIII

MEG SYME tutored her younger sisters and brothers, made all the clothing for the family, masculine and feminine, and was a splendid figure on a horse. Some said he would be a lucky man who won her; but men made little progress with her. She was too sedate, and only six years younger than Robert, who was now thirty-seven. She had no glances or blushes for Robert, who found her an enigma. At first he was regarded as Nessie's conquest, but Nessie discovered that Meg was the attraction. This created a sensation. Meg began to blossom. The neighbours said it was a shame that Robert Delacy should make a fool of her, and tried to warn her with gossip, but like Johanna, Meg was Robert's partisan for ever.

He measured Meg by his own instabilities and forays and felt that he had what he desired, and that to her nothing but full dignities could be suggested. He confided to his father that he wanted to marry.

"Have you chosen the girl or is it wan of them chasing you again?"

Robert said that he had chosen, and left his father to break the news. In this case he knew Danny would be more of an ally than Johanna.

"Mother of God! Some streel has got hold of him again!"

Danny knew nothing of the Symes and bade her hold her whist until he made inquiries. Della was overlooked. Norah was consulted, being married and of the pure merino squattocracy. Her mother-in-law wrote to a friend near Cooma, old Mrs Rawson. The reply came from Major Rawson of shirt-bosom fame!

The Symes as far as I know, are respectable people, who derive from the farmer class in the North of Ireland. I do not, however, know them personally, and would not think of inviting them into my house on an equality with my family.

"I knew," wailed Johanna.

"I don't want to be dragged down to people of that class," said Norah.

Della was silent.

"If she is an upstanding faymale and her people have good principlies, I'd as soon have her as the Queen's daughter. Robert is lucky to get such after his miscarriages."

"It's a wife for me son, I'm considering, not a horse."

"There would be more sinse in considering a wife on the principles of a noble horse, seeing what she is put to, r'aring children and dragging about amid arduous conditions. Sure, 'tis not a canary bird to put in a cage that Robert's needing. If you were choosing a horse would you pick the weakest of the mob because it was a pretty little thing that would fall down at all critical moments because of its refinement?"

"Ye have no more sinse at ye than the snipe in the bog at home in Ireland."

" 'Tis yourself that lacks the rayson. Sure, when we consider a horse, 'tis breed that gives him stamina and makes him able to do more and do it with a spring, while the common slug would rack your bones and wind himself and not accomplish half the distance; and whoi should it be breed in a woman, or a man, to be weak and helpless? There is food for thought there."

" 'Tis a wonder in picking ye'r own wife, ye did not choose wan of those big bony fishwives from . . ."

"Arrah, me brave Johanna, 'tis the example of the polo pony we have; and 'tis the most striking in the whole boiling. 'Tis a polo pony you were, me brave Johanna." He shouted this after her as she ran away to hide her smiles. There were moments when her choice of Danny was justified.

> I'm Denny Blake from County Clare,
>   And ready at command,
> To sing a song in praises
>   Of my own dear native land.

he chanted in the resonant voice that was sometimes husky, perhaps through constant smoking of stale twist.

He took a Nullah-Mundoey mare and packed his valise preparatory to inspecting the Syme family.

Della suggested that Danny should go by gig and let her mother accompany him.

"Me," snorted Johanna, "to be running about after her! She should bring herself here for me to see, but if she did, I'd slap the door in her face."

"What sense could there be in that? In moi moind there's a good chance of her being too good for Robert."

He stayed one night at The Plains with Cameron. The next he quartered himself at a shepherd's hut without interest in social gradations and equally careless of the difference in quality of bed and food. The sublime panorama spread before him as he journeyed by tracks all night with flowers and birds, and quaint shy marsupials

P

assured him of an unending force harmonious and indestructible of which he was a part, and he approached the Symes in a mind to estimate the proposed marriage on its merits.

The Symes knew many anecdotes of Nullah-Mundoey, whose heroic performances were already a legend and had earned him more titles than an earl, in days when "jarl" meant strong man. He had started as Danny Delacy of the Murrumbidgee and now was Nullah-Mundoey, Fearless Danny, and Honest Delacy.

It was a shock to Meg Syme when a strange little man with a long straight black beard, wearing sloppy clothes and a copataine hat—kept from sliding over his eyes by a stuffing of gum leaves— boomed a flowery greeting at her, and then broke into a guffaw. "Sure, you're as tall as Robert himself—a pair of bean poles. You'd be good for spreading a hop vine."

When Meg accepted his queerness, she liked him, he was so homely, so good and wise, so free from acidity and malice. She read everything procurable and was educated to enjoy the philosophic epigrams that poured from Mr Delacy. He and Syme had fundamental congeniality in principle, but Syme was the more thrifty and likely to die the richer, as Delacy recognized.

Danny's report was that Robert had done well for himself. Here was a fine powerful woman old enough to have shown her quality. "She looks sound and sensible, but sure, a wife is only to be proved after hard trials and constant companionship. But I never expected annything so promising of common sense from Robert. Now if it had been William."

"Hasn't Robert always had more head on him than all the rest of the family slapped together?"

Inconsistently with this, Johanna's back was up against what Danny reported of Meg, and she insisted upon regarding her as a designing woman who was sniggling the prize by sharp practice.

"Sure, I'll be thankful to the woman to take possession of him so I can settle without expecting to hear of me best friend turned into an enemy, or other members of the community coming at me because they think he has meddled with their women. She's a brave woman, and good luck to her, I say."

"But she is so old—over thirty."

"Och, isn't Robert an old rake himself?"

"But has she anny beauty?" Johanna demanded beauty in her daughter-in-law as an elegancy due to her own refinement.

"I thought Robert had enough beauty for the family. Enough is better than a feast, even of baits for the dingoes."

"I judge that she is plain as old Eally, but ye're a nullity when it comes to judging all such things."

"Sure wasn't I a judge of beauty, or how could I have chosen the prettiest girl in County Clare and got her to run over the seas with me? 'And the red was on your lip, Mary, and the lovelight in your eye!' Moi, oh, moi! me brave Johanna!"

"I'm reduced often to thinking it was an accident."

Danny smoked with loud smacks and pensive emissions of, "The moind! The moind!"

Della questioned her father quietly, "Is she dark or fair; has she curly hair or a long nose, and is she good-tempered?"

"Would she let me know her bad timper at this stage of the game? That has to be risked. Wives can't be had on trial."

"But surely, Father, you can describe her features?"

"She has a nose in the middle of her face and a mouth below that, and an eye on either side of it farther up. Her face must have been all right, or I'd have noticed it."

"Sure, it was only by good luck I wasn't a two-headed monster," observed Johanna.

The coming wedding called for a family conclave. The partnership of the men Delacys, so long delayed, was at last to be put on a business footing. Danny had Bewuck. Burrabinga homestead was to be improved for Robert. William and Harry were to live there with Robert, or with Danny at Bewuck, as the work demanded, until they should marry, when a home each was to be erected for them out of the general budget. It was the loose and generous arrangement of Danny, of whom Johanna said, "He has too much scatteration on him and not enough grasping ever to make a fortune, no matter how great the opportunity."

Neither Johanna nor Della was mentioned in the new understanding. The work they had put into making both homes was not officially acknowledged by so much as a new bonnet. Johanna was in a better position than Della. The butter money was hers, except when Danny happened to be pushed for cash, and remembered it; even then, if Johanna said she needed it, Danny would not question her statement. There were also the turkeys. The rearing of these fell to Della now, also the dairy and the care of Maeve, who was frail, and needed help, and sat much in the chimney corner, and when left to herself, crouched in the ashes.

Della had slipped into drudgery without any one being aware of it. She was growing scraggy and her thin little hands were as rough as Harry's. She dressed in drab winseys or something equally cheap and depressing, was firmly embedded in spinsterhood, seldom mentioned, never discussed, unnoticed by any one but her mother, who had designs upon her. Johanna was hoarding every penny now towards Della's *dot* as a *religieuse*. But this Della did not know.

When she was left out of the new partnership she retired and sobbed herself sick. Very little recognition would have saved her this hurt—a small sum yearly to hoard against old age. She envisaged her end, and did not like it. Even the gawky Grace Fullwood had married Della's old flame, Gerald Butler, and was settled with home and children and good social position.

A new home of slabs and shingles was pushed forward. All strove in the cause of Robert. Danny came up to lay out gardens, and his friend Wong Foo came in to help. These two with a stray rouseabout and the bullocks went across the river and enclosed five acres of rich loam where it would be safe from the poultry. The inconvenience of crossing the Burrabinga on horseback bothered no one. There was a power of mares to be mounted. Some old prad was always dozing at the back gate or in the stable awaiting a chore; picked horses were in the horse paddock—forerunners of the telegraphs and telephones. Everywhere were mares with foals at heel; none escaped. Fecundity was prized in man and beast.

Wong brought vegetable seeds. Danny took his mares and packed flower plants and shrubs from Birrabee. The gentle Janet met him with her usual friendliness, unaware that her father had confided in his old mate.

Robert was glowing, his swagger moderated by affection for a good woman and approaching responsibility. Harry was indefatigable and ecstatic. William kept judicial watch. Danny was released in enterprise as he had not been of late. Bewuck had not scope enough for him; he often looked wistfully towards the mountains which he had opened up, but which Robert was taking from him.

Danny was becoming a worn-out pioneer. Empires rise on the unrewarded efforts of such indomitable individualists. Only a few of the many emerge to the ken of recorders to give new lease to tales of daring and fortitude. They pour out their strength and courage in taming new territory. They are givers. They provide lashings and leavings of raw material, or father the exploitable rank and file for the shrewder investors—the takers.

Danny, the ineffectual old pioneer, was to have his reward—if any—in a zest in life which did not stale until he was past seventy, and which sheltered him from all the ghosts and devils that invade the pillow of the complex and introspective. And he rarely had an ear-ache or stomach-ache; when a tooth ached he prised it out with a pen-knife. Rheumatism passed him without toll, indigestion was

a stranger to him, though his most constant food was a cut from a
salt round enlivened by mustard applied like treacle, a diet which
had become a habit while he bached. The fiends of physical torture,
finding his courage invincible under their first attack, were won
henceforth to clemency.

Johanna refused to go to the wedding, and Danny would not go
without her. No one thought to invite Della, another uninten-
tional slight, which showed her her position. Norah Butler declined
because she was not proud of the match. Meg, therefore, tactfully
decided that she would have only her own family, and William
and Harry to support Robert.

"Shall I bring Meg here to see you?" inquired Robert.

"Time enough when a child is coming. Ye can't leave her up
among the dingoes for that event. Della will then wait on her."

Della stiffened her back. "Indeed, that is keeping my new sister
too long waiting for a welcome from the women of the family. I'm
becoming a nullity in prison by the river, year after year, with no
companion but the bunyip, and the oaks for ever mourning. I'll
go up and prepare the house for Margaret."

Robert was delighted and clinched this support before his mother
could demur.

"And what am I to do alone, with Maeve not fit to do a slap
of work?"

"Jane Hannon can sleep in the house. Della needs a change."

"I need some new clothes. It would be small recommendation for
me to appear before my new sister looking like a workhouse inmate."

Robert agreed grandly as a partner of the firm.

CHAPTER XXIX

DELLA sang around the new house as she papered its walls, made curtains for its little windows or stuffed mattresses with straw, or painted the shelves that Harry put up. She was reinvigorated by the release from her mother's exactions and looked ten years younger in the fussy new dresses which Robert had sanctioned.

A house! A house! A home of one's own.

She saw now, when nearing forty, and all chances gone, that she had been foolish to demand a dream man. The home and the business standing afforded by marriage were the more important. Any not too impossible man would have served.

Harry had helped with the Angus nuptial building. Ned was returning the obligation at Burrabinga. "Ned used to be your puppy lover," remarked Harry, tactlessly facetious.

Ned braved the accusation. "Not so much of a puppy!"

Della enjoyed his kindness, his gaiety, also his carpentering ability, in which the Delacys were conspicuously deficient. They had a happy time in making the house comfortable for Meg, or Margaret, as her new family called her, following Della's lead. As they progressed, Ned remarked, "I wish I was getting a house of my own ready. Now that Janet is not well, I'm afraid to tread inside."

"I was wishing I had a house myself," confessed Della.

"Holy sailors! You're a wonderful housekeeper: you've had so much practice. Why didn't you marry Gerry Butler?"

"I did not like him enough, and he was fast."

Ned smiled in his brown beard, which had never known the razor and was round and furry as a possum.

Masculinity leant heavily on beards. All the bushmen had beards. Some of the older imported men had theirs trimmed in hedges around the chin, or lawns under the ears. Others cleared a putting space around one or both lips, or the chin appeared as a bald hill in a jungle—diverting patterns to modify the affliction of a frowsy mane on the face.

Ned's beard gave him several years among men who did not know his youth. He had grown it much earlier than any of the Delacys, who were a smooth-skinned race. He laughed a deep bass laugh into his hairy maturity because he was not "fast". The urge

was on him for a wife, and he wanted Della. On the strength of
his beard he quickly essayed a lover-like statement.

Della was resistant, but she remembered Ned's early partiality,
and as his advances gained firmness, she hardened in the determination necessary to marry a man so many years her junior. Ned
would give her a home of her own. No matter how humble or
remote, it would provide escape from the constant unease of a
mother's dictation, sapping of harmony and hope. Anything to
escape from her mother, though she could scarcely admit this, even
to herself, without a sense of blasphemy.

She too had satisfaction in the volume of Ned's beard.

It must be confessed that the splendiferous Robert had a similarly
Biblical beard, long enough to blow about in the wind. Incredible
that he could have appealed as a lover! But the girls of his day did
not expect the impossible in husbands: they had it. They did not
quail before the impossible in life: they unconsciously achieved it.

Ned continued to smile in his beard, Della to regard it contemplatively while the family failed to note anything significant because
attention was focused on preparations for Robert's bride.

Robert's policy towards Keebah had had the desired effect. Now
that Janet's slip was safely submerged in marriage, Mr and Mrs
Urquhart wished to avoid any action that would inform the curious,
and formally invited Robert to bring his bride to Keebah for a
visit on the way from Cooma. Robert graciously accepted.

After enclosing the garden Danny went home and reappeared
with one pack-horse laden with fancy fowls and another with
turkeys and geese. The gobbler and the goose raised a clamour that
brought out the dogs in full cry from all the settlers *en route*. The
turkey-hen bore her passage with her meek whine, the gander said
"shush-shush!" all the way; a bantam crowed perkily; the pack-
mares endured heroically. The pride of Danny's argosy was a third
horse with a nanny and two kids, one of them unrelated, from
which to begin a Burrabinga dynasty. Mrs Rafferty had been loath
to part with her old Nanny but Mr Delacy was the patron of the
socially-ascended Bella. Johanna remarked that the idea of goats
was as sensible as if it had been generated by the snipe in the bogs
at home in Ireland, "When ye have more cows than Brian Boru
himself."

Danny roped the recalcitrant matron's horns and a Nullah-
Mundoey had to tow her. When the she-kid wailed in front Nanny
rushed forward and butted the pack-horse. "The dayvil such a
botheration was never encountered," Danny remarked to his dumb
beasts, including Doogoolook.

All this cargo had to be unloaded at Learmont's, Keebah and Birrabee, where Danny made halts and had his animals fed and watered.

"Golly, the old cove is a hard case—gets rummier every day," remarked George Angus, but the kindly Janet tended the fowls, and Ned helped with the goats because of Della.

Transit down the precipices bred legend. Doogoolook took the horses singly while Danny held the others, and when both were occupied with the goat horse, the others broke away and bolted for the homestead. The cages were not completely smashed. The mares knew where to step lest a bump against a tree hurt them more than their load. The geese and turkeys kept their heads in and so were not brained.

At the homestead the tortured beasts were unloaded by Della. The bantam cock had his leg crushed but crew so gamely that Della's heart was touched and she kept him in a box to mend. The turkey-hen was dead. One of the mares was injured by a shaft of the pack-saddle penetrating her withers and she lay down for days, but Della would not give her up to a bullet.

Wong Foo appeared with pack loads for the great Robert's wife. O'Neill came down in mid-week bringing the hide of a piebald brumby, tail and all, tanned as a carpet He too, was invited to remain until Mrs Robert's arrival.

She and her suite came home in detachments. She rode on a beautiful saddle and a Nullah-Mundoey—the gifts of Robert. He rode the Lillingston gelding.

William drove Mrs Robert's horses and heifers, with satisfaction in this accretion to the Burrabinga property. Robert had the best spending sense, William the squarest idea of the power of property, but Harry finally, when the dross of the flesh was purged with years, though a beggar financially, had a spiritual kingdom that none could take away.

Harry left for home with the bride's handmaiden on a safe brumby of such rough paces that the child was like to be jellied. Old Syme insisted upon providing his daughter with a serving-maid, no matter how incipient. Meg must be supported in her new squatter status. There was such a demand for women that they were prematurely plucked from childhood, and to have Fannie Monson, aged eight, fed and trained was a relief to the packed shepherd's hut that was her home. She was so shy that she hid under the bed in sick terror on hearing the proposal, but she was hauled to light, and a rig-out—it could not be called a wardrobe—gathered for her. One of her brothers, for some reason, had once had a pair of boots, and, because of ineradicable self-respect, these were put on the little creature.

Convention was so rigid that Fannie must not straddle a horse. Harry improvised a horn on a man's saddle and the rider clung on as best she could, the gullet of the saddle bruising her thigh. She was inarticulate, and all her sobs were worn away. She looked back with dry gasps, while the hut was visible, and when it sank from view she tried to get off the horse and run back. Her attitude was touching to Harry. He put her astride for her safety and started the brumby to his bone-racking jog. A mile or two on the way Harry had to retrace for the boots, which he then tied on with horsehair. The child grew so weary and sore that she had to stay in bed for a day where they first halted. The kind settler's wife gave Harry a pillow for his pommel and he let the child sit there when they set out again. Fannie had given Harry her trust. He was so absent while he dreamed his own dreams, that she came out of her shell. Then he sang her a song which brought a smile:

> Sally had a magpie that was very fond of talking,
> She plucked a feather from his tail,
> Every time she went out walking,
> Soon poor Mag's tail hadn't a feather upon it,
> But you had the pleasure of seeing them stuck,
> All round Sally's bonnet.

He was ashamed of the naked pipe-stems, with the livid ring around the ankles chafed by the rough boots, so he enlisted a Queanbeyan barmaid to buy small boots and stockings. He also bought the child some "lollies" and a mouth-organ, and a hat to replace the tattered rag that blinkered her. He hurried to be home to welcome the bride, who was paying visits as she came, and it devolved upon Della to clean and clothe Fannie.

Mrs Robert's live stock were depastured in the house paddock, and her poultry made the place homely as she rode across the flats in her stylish habit. She was a fine sensible woman in her prime, heartily in love with Robert, and of a mind and experience to accept whatever the bargain brought. Her little serving-maid was so over-awed that she peeped at the newcomers from Harry's coat-tail. Wong Foo and Doogoolook added to the originality of the Delacy collection.

Danny and Wong grew merry and fuddled, but no one was disturbed by that. Wong had taken to grog as part of his Europeanization. The man who did not drink was as rare as the one without whiskers. Not sobriety so much as whether a man could carry liquor was the standard, and no vices came to light in Danny or Wong when wine cast out wit.

Danny had to return to Johanna at the end of a week, but Della extended her visit indefinitely. Margaret was pleased to have her. They made dresses for themselves and rearranged their tresses in the prevailing mode. Fannie's curls came off in the interests of hygiene. The women not only reared and trained maids, but made their clothes until they could do this for themselves. The best mistresses also taught them to read and write. Fannie thus recovered from loneliness, for when she was not learning housewifery, she had books to con.

The prevailing mentality attributed long hair on women to the will of God: interference with it was approaching hermaphroditism, so when Fannie's mother heard of the cropped head, her shrill execrations drove Monson to leave his sheep and rescue his child from "that jumped-up Meg Syme who would dare to call a decent child lousy!"

Fannie was glad to see her father, but did not want to go with him. He found her dressed like a little lady, her locks growing well and tied with ribbon. She brought her slate, and her father, who had no lettering, was proud, and cursed his wife's foolishness, and left the child without a protest.

Harry went to Bunbilliko for a visit and came back with a rousing tale.

Peg-leg had died, so Mike and Harry re-explored the caves near the abandoned selection and in an inner chamber found two skeletons. The police were notified. The clothing indicated that the skeletons were not very old, though ants had cleaned the bones. The remains were those of Long Tom Bradford and Yorkie Driffield. All the Lillingstons recognized the projecting teeth of the taller man, and a glass eye rolled out of the empty skull. The men had been murdered by a heavy weapon—probably axed while sleeping. They must have been killed elsewhere, as one of the skeletons lay on a rough hand-barrow. Two people had been necessary to carry them there.

Peg-leg's hut was two miles distant. No evidence was forthcoming from the son, so long after the date. Mike and Harry's reconstruction of the case was that Long Tom and Yorkie had been overtaken by night on their journey from Cooma to Bunbilliko, had been refused a shakedown by Peg-leg and had gone on to camp at the creek near the cave. Peg-leg had killed them in the night and compelled the old woman to help him secrete the bodies. That may have been what Brandy Mary had tried to confess on the day that the old man had dragged her into the hut. That was why he

fiercely forbade people to visit his hut or seek for stock on his
holding. Also, he had lived on the money that the dealers had
been carrying. Nothing could be proved. Suspicions grew into
history. The spot became known as Murderers' Cave.

"I wish the money had not been lost," said Johanna.

"So do I, but what is there in a few hundred pounds compared
with the knowledge of honesty in men. Poor fellows! Came back
true to their word," exclaimed Danny.

Harry had a pleasanter story. He and Mike had accompanied
the Sergeant from Cooma to Gool Gool, as certain formalities had
to be observed in that township. One night they had put up at a
station renowned for its hospitality and the beauty of its daughters,
and here Harry met his princess, Josephine Battle.

"Ghost! She is the most beautiful woman I ever saw! A complexion like pink wax, and hair the colour of gold!"

The young lady was referred to as the Princess, a member of
the Royal Family. Harry was so romantic about her that Della
found him good material to further her own plans.

Township and district were entertained by Hennessy's marriage
finally—and to Euphemia Fitzhugh.

"Sure, I knew she'd come to it when her plumage began to
moult," said Johanna.

"A fool not to have taken him long ago. He could have had
children."

"Hasn't he always had Molly Macallister?"

The Township was long since a municipality, and Hennessy the
mayor. He had a bigger hotel than formerly, the blacksmithing
business, the leading general store and a flour mill. He was pros-
pering far beyond his needs and had much to lend him importance.
Even Johanna admitted that it was surprising that he should still
want, "that ould hairo, well over fifty".

"Sure, the attempt to win her was a habit with him, and at last
she caved in. 'Twill be entertaining to observe which will overcome
the other. They are both too long in the horn for the frictions of
double harness."

Euphemia had capitulated in a fit of despair. She was overpowering for governessing, and met no eligibles. Hennessy was her
last resource from the footless drifting around that confronted a
woman, whose man died, whom the law did not bury with him,
nor provide with a pension, and who refused to be a drudge in
the background. With mingled feelings Hennessy installed her in
a stone house near the Township. She was provided with a vehicle
and a groom; she had soft carpets and a rosewood piano, expensive

china, jewellery and silks, and servants to wait upon her, but attached to them was Hennessy—corpulent and sweaty. He was also vulgar. Euphemia had been well-seasoned to vulgarity in army days, and later among the squatters, but in nothing is there more caste snobbery than in the quality of vulgarity, and Hennessy's was not the swagger kind. He was bogtrotter Irish, in itself the lowest form of vulgarity. The way on earth of Euphemia Hennessy was not harmonious. Molly Macallister mortally hated her. She had long been cultivating her "uncle". Molly and her youngsters were his best root in life. Euphemia had nothing but fear of poverty, fear of the approaching abyss of mystery, which kept her clinging to the daylight called life, even as Mrs Hennessy.

She provided diversion for her district when personal gossip was the salt of human association. Every one knew that she demanded a separate sleeping apartment. Grandfathers, denatured by gentility, declared that Hennessy should seize his wife by the hair of the head and thrash her into subjection. If women were allowed to act as she, all wives would get above themselves, and what then would become of the sanctity of marriage and the family and the home!

It was Danny who observed, " 'Tis little compliment to the marriage state, if women have to be kept so tight for fear they'll lepp right out of it entirely."

Johanna put him to rights. "Ye men have no more logic than an eft about women. We let ye blather to keep ye out of worse mischief. Listen to min talking—and they don't need to have the grog in neither—and ye'll hear that women are wild for marriage. At the same time ye daren't let wan wife escape from her sleep being ruined by the grunts of a living tobacco or rum kag, but ye're all raging with fear as if an armed rebellion was disrupting the bonds of matrimony. Och, ye're such, that only that there's nothing else, ye wouldn't be put up with at all."

After that, when Euphemia's marital behaviour was dissected, Danny would exclaim, "Leave her to Sergeant O'Gorman to deal with if she's as scandalous as that; or let the Bishop be called in to adjudicate the moral question."

Hennessy, despite the snipe-bog beginning and the chain-gang finishing imposed upon him by society, was too much the natural man to babble of his affairs in public or to coerce his wife in private. Through his paid menials and those who listened to them, yarns seeped out and were lapped up by "the buckeens, who for lack of better think themselves the aristocracy", to quote Delacy— one of the few men in that region sufficiently outstanding to be quoted.

CHAPTER XXX

A YEAR passed without issue for Margaret and Robert. Della and Ned had decided to marry, and Della was nerving herself to confess, first to Robert, and worse, to her mother.

Robert, established, was as proud as his mother, but Della had stood by him and Margaret, and Margaret was now standing by Della. William was disappointed that Della should be a failure, his clever good-looking sister, so well educated! Her marriage, even to Ned, would relieve him of the humiliation of having in his family the only old maid he knew. Harry was warmly for his old mate, and everybody liked Ned personally, when the shock of the disparity in years wore away.

Della sent for her father, who was delighted by any call to the mountains.

"All that time away, she wants ye as the go-between to bring her home," said Johanna.

Della made her confession in the vegetable garden across the river, whither they had ridden for privacy.

"In the name of God, woman!" Danny burst out. "He's scarce done teething compared with you. You let Butler go to that squeaking beanpole of a Fullwood, and then to make a fool of yourself with a boy. God knows what his family may be."

"His family is good enough for the Urquharts. You were eager for us to marry there. This is next door, with both Janet and Donald married to Anguses."

Danny would not divulge that Janet, as salvaged material, had been compelled to lower her standard. "That's the Urquharts. Once there's a breach in the fence, the dingoes run in, but you have no call to get into the yard where they are coming. And what will you live on?"

"You might well ask, when I'm treated as if I were the black gin who was picked out of the bush. There was a fuss about Margaret Syme being only a free selector's daughter, but she came with cattle and horses and furniture and good clothes, and a shelf of books and some jewellery and a maid. And didn't you rush and make her a vegetable garden; another of flowers, and an orchard— mostly from the remains of my hard work in the valley when I was a girl? And didn't you career the country, like a Chinaman trading to the diggings, with crates of fowls and animals for another man's daughter? You can surely do the same for your own? And didn't you nearly kill a good pack-mare, and I attend her for weeks with venice turps, and you were going to shoot her, the smell was so bad. Surely I'm entitled to her for a start. Perhaps Margaret will spare me a clutch of eggs from the poultry you brought her. Wong Foo might give me a jar of ginger, seeing I spent years making a home for him to come to."

"Sure, if anny man ever paid his way by giving, it was Wong," interposed Danny.

"In that case, perhaps he'll give me a bag of seed potatoes to boot; when he was so generous to a strange woman he never saw."

"Arrah! Robert was the head of the family."

"And I have been the sides of the family for longer than Robert. You can't have the roof without walls, and I've worked myself old only to be overlooked."

"Why, Della, what's got at you? There's no call to bally-rag me to such an extent. You are entitled to the same as I did for Margaret, and a few head of stock are neither here nor there, but you can't disguise the fact that you're an old worn-out woman of forty wanting to marry a man so young that you'll look foolish."

"And how did I become worn-out but by slaving to make homes for others, and now have none of my own?"

"What home will Ned provide?"

"Ned built a house for Janet Urquhart: Harry helped him. Now he can help Ned to build one for me. I had no share in the property, but thank God, I have as much right to select on Burrabinga as a perfect stranger."

"Sure, there's no need to act like an inimy. I'm open to the argument that it's not meself who is to marry Angus. What do your brothers think about this?"

"When Robert was about to marry Miss Syme, Norah was consulted because she was a married woman. No one asked my opinion. No one took any notice of me then; I'll be obliged if they pursue the same course now."

"Och, you're soured by letting your chances go by, and having to take the unsuitable stick in the end. And what will your mother say, who had you all salted by for a nun?"

"Me, for a nun!"

Danny had a twinkle in his eye in contemplating the old maid, designed for the cloister, thus saving herself at the last moment by inappropriate marriage.

He needed more than humour, however, to face Johanna with the news. Della's outburst had been based on just grievance. Johanna was unreasonable. She accused Danny of being a nullity, and his children of taking after him.

"It only remains for William to run away with old mother Euphemia Hennessy and Harry to take wan of Bella Rafferty's sisters, to complete me joy and proide in me family, all established among the quality. Sorrow the day and God's blame on me, that I ever left me beautiful home of Cooley Hall to go to the furthest inds of the globe, with blacks adopted as part of me family, and a haythen Chinaman for a brother, to become a haythen and savage meself, with a bunyip and ghost as me main companions."

" 'Tis sad indeed, me brave Johanna, that you left the attractive Kevin O'Gorman, with the hair sprouting on him like kangaroo grass on the ring-barked flats, and all his well-grown children, and his few cows and potatoes running on a furze patch, to die in the famine beside a snipe bog, for such a pitiful picture as you depict."

"And it's ye that would reproach me, and attimpt to marry me best son on every streel. . . ."

"Och, the facts don't stand up to your allegations. 'Twas meself who rescued your supertoploftical Robert from wan string of a thing, and he's now got as fine a woman as ever I saw; and isn't Norah getting rich and visiting at The Plains and by damn, I like Ned Angus. He's none of your sour-bellies—always a fine laugh out of him—and Della has rights in the country that you and she civilized in the first place."

" 'Twill never be civilized. 'Tis only fit for dingoes."

" 'Twill be more sought than the Lakes of Killarney in a hundred years. Sure 'tis the water supply from here to Death-o'-Day and beyond."

"It's easy to blather what can't be proved for a hundred years. It's manny an ass-load of foolishness has assailed me ears, and manny the heart-scald since I married ye. Now the children are going the same road, me heart is killed in me bosom."

Her last hope of religious atonement was being smashed. She was humiliated. How could she tell Father Shannon that her daughter was about to marry an inferior, ten or twelve years her junior. Her natural supports were collapsing. Maeve was failing, and she was weary of contending with impudent colonial lasses. A wave of depression enguifed her, as it has many another at her age. There was no future. She lay upon her bed, and, like Hezekiah, turned her face to the wall. It seemed as if her early hardships and griefs had damaged her resilience. Night fitted hard on her like a cap. The curlews' wail came from the flats and the wind moaned in the casuarinas and grumbled in the chimneys.

The faithful Maeve crept in next day and watched her dumbly. Jane Hannon came, but Johanna refused to be tended or comforted. She lay listening to the rushing Murrumbidgee and its soughing oaks. The peewits scolded the cats who intruded upon their work in the garden, and a dozen other species joined in their protest. Butcher birds practised assiduously; scores of magpies filled the gleaming day with musical enchantment; the kookaburras raised their wild mocking laughter in the homestead precincts. Danny offered to bring Norah Butler, and was rebuked for thoughtlessness, for the Butlers were recovering from measles. So Doogoolook was despatched with a note to Della.

A pet wallaroo that Robert had brought in his pocket some months since, hopped in and sat beside the bed, his little forepaws placed on the coverlet of his dead clansmen. Johanna caressed the soft head. "Another of me outlandish adoptions." Her thoughts reverted to Maeve. "Poor lost thing, what has she to look to but meself?"

Johanna arose and went about her duties, but consolation was absent from the daily brew. She was never now, it seemed, to make any restitution to her Church. God's blame was on her. Della came home, her jaw set for stirring encounters, but Johanna was already defeated. Della waited on the rack with nervousness for her mother to open and was met by depressed silence. Della was forced to speak first. "Mother, aren't you well?"

"Well as ever an old woman can be who has nothing further to live for."

"I hope you are not upset because I'm going to marry Mr Edward Angus. He's some years younger than I am, but Mother . . ."

" 'Tis no concern of mine what age Mr Edward Angus is."

"But Mother, please try to understand."

"What is there to understand? Ye have the right to do as ye like at *ye'r* time of life. It is not as if ye were young and likely to improve in sinse."

Della tried conciliation, but her mother balked her by calling to Maeve about the turkeys, and in the weeks that followed, remained impervious to persuasion or attack. " 'Tis of no interest to me to discuss ye'r affairs. I have plinty to consider in me own," she would say icily, neither impolite nor sulky, but impenetrable.

Della would lie awake furiously resenting her mother's attitude, which she felt was deliberately cruel. Johanna too, lay awake, in a life denuded of purpose or nourishing emotions, and she could not attain peace because denied the ritual of her special creed.

William, who was at Bewuck, paid a Sunday visit to Norah to report. "There's no sense in calling attention to the bad match by this dust-up. Ned is a steady chap; doesn't even get drunk. He can't be worse-off than old Jimmy Fullwood, and his family stick to him in spite of Bella Rafferty and a big tribe of Raffertys in the district."

Stewart Butler liked Ned, and commented, 'With George and Susan married to Urquharts, the family is going up, and that is what counts. You can't blame Della for thinking anything better than being an old maid."

"It's terrible at home," William told Norah. "Like a death that doesn't get buried. Why don't you invite Della here?"

Norah sent a note by him.

A day later Della said, "I am going to Norah. I'll stay there till I am married."

"Please ye'rself," said Johanna.

Della said to William, "Mother is so strange, I don't know how to act, but I'm entitled to some things."

"Yes, of course. Ma will come round. Don't make matters worse by saying anything to regret. She's getting old, and had such ambitions."

Johanna ignored Della's preparations, and when she came to say good-bye, merely murmured "good afternoon!" and walked into her room. She could not give way graciously, and her intransigence was making her ill.

Danny's attitude served him better. "Sure, Della, I wish you well. I'll be up to make your garden; and I'll go gather fowls too. Do your best if your mother holds out the olive branch. She's feeling worse than you are over this. She started on too high a rung, and now, God help her, she can't climb down. Sure, I've always found it easier to cut the tail off pride than to go to bed with it and be strangled."

Margaret supported Della, even to her property rights. Margaret was so happy in finding romance, when she had put the possibility from her, that she blossomed generously that year, with little thought of self.

"None of us has pleased poor old Ma in our marriages," remarked Robert. "Norah did the best. Harry must make an alliance with this Princess of the Blood to pull things up."

Della was married from Norah's and rode to Burrabinga on her own Nullah-Mundoey, known as Fairy, whose proud foal followed her all the way, companioned by a colt of the pack-mare. That was four horses Della had for a beginning.

Ned's home, to be known as "Homehurst", was going up on a selection farther down the river. Della was to stay with Margaret until it was ready. Danny with a hen on his pommel, his pockets full of chicks, and a renewed zest in pioneering arrived to "tigrinize" in the gardens. He prepared the deep clean earth for potatoes—those efficient pioneers, who tamed to friability the most resistant clay. He procured from Robert's stable a bag of albinos with blue eyes and long white hair. "Sure, they're a trifle far gone," he observed. "They'll mostly be stags, but they deserve a chance to fructify."

He was invigorated in mind and body by the solitude amid the stately boles of the gums, resembling marble pillars. Sunbeams fell like searchlights through the roofs of sickle leaves on to the bracken and aromatic shrubs below. Magpies, black and white cockatoos, gang-gangs, tits, kookaburras, honey-eaters, wood-peckers, thrushes and countless other friends were with him all the day, as they had been over forty years earlier when Bewuck had been equally virgin. Across the river the lyre-tails flashed in the openings as they played hide-and-seek with their families, or paused to reproduce the sound of his axe. When first at Burrabinga he had been sure that some man had been near at hand, but one man, creeping quietly while the other worked had traced the sounds to the mimicry of Menura. Mimicry by pet magpies and other birds was an amusing parody, that of the lyre-birds a spell-binding recital. On misty winter mornings when all was damp and dripping, and fragrant as imagination with the sharp sweet tang of the dead leaves, when other creatures were still, then the lyre-bird's notes rang full and clear through the eucalypt aisles,

The swift water was to Delacy a companionable voice from unpeopled eternities. As he visualized the thronging generations to be, he pondered on the productivity of seed—animal and vegetable. Posterity of his own was a bulwark to set against the ephemerality of the separate life span. Satisfaction that Della still had time to perpetuate him outweighed the lack of property in the match: and he had never detected anything amiss with Ned's principles.

CHAPTER XXXI

AT the time of his marriage to Susan Angus, Donald Urquhart removed to the Riverine. Tom Angus was tea-planting in India. George and Janet held Birrabee. Ned and Della were at Homehurst, where Danny's garden flourished free from weeds and pests. All were behaving in a way becoming to an empty continent where population was in demand.

Johanna was impatient for Robert's son, and to ensure his safe passage, all the voluntary man power available in addition to what the Delacys could afford, worked in a bee cutting a gradient around the most dizzying pinch so that Margaret could come out by vehicle.

With several stout fellows to help, Robert could now drive out. Down the precipices the wagonette was steadied by a tree on the axle; around sidelings, men acting tug-of-war on ropes prevented a capsize. When climbing the pinches extra horses were adjured with whip and shout to do their utmost. To have walked might have been easier to Margaret in places, but it was "all in the moind", and the mind of the incipient nation was liberated from trudging on foot.

At dinner time the horses had a respite while Margaret was enthroned on rugs on a log. Fannie, her little maid, sat near. Appetites were unrivalled. It was a pleasant and distinguished occasion for all concerned. Parrots flashed by like flowers. Dozens of other species warbled or called. Lyre-birds escorted them all the way. The dogs disturbed hoppers of numerous clans that whirled around the hillside amid the tree-ferns and shrubs. The boles of the eucalypts pillared a far-reaching, echoing world, holy with emptiness.

Margaret reached Bewuck where she was made to sit down more than she enjoyed, with her feet on a hassock, and the men modulated their voices sentimentally when they addressed her.

When the child came, two and a half years after her marriage, it was nothing but a girl, a small object with black fuzz on her top. "All that time waiting and ye could have put it in a milk jug," complained Johanna, disappointed.

Boys were the fashion. Margaret had missed her chance of doing

a spectacular thing for the family. And there was that streel of a
Bella Rafferty with four strapping boys. They must have been
showing the breed of Bella's unknown father, the men ribaldly
declared. This was discouraging to the strait-laced women as it
seemed that virtue had little to do with virtuosity in motherhood.

Della's turn came. "Hurrying against time," chuckled William.
He was regarded as a confirmed bachelor and was an interested
and amused onlooker.

Bella offered to come to Homehurst to officiate, and Margaret
invited Della to Burrabinga, but in view of the fuss made of
Mrs Robert, Mrs Edward would not hide her epic in her own back
yard. She invited herself to Norah's, as a demonstration to her
mother—taking a woman not her own flesh and blood to Bewuck,
and ignoring her own! And all their grinning and criticism of an
old maid married to a boy! Della's fighting spirit was up to show
what a lucky pioneer could do, and all that swagger.

She took care of her home and husband until within six weeks
of her time. Then she set out on a side-saddle, and her horse
heaved and struggled under her all day like a canoe in rapids
through snow which lay as deep as the girths as far as Birrabee.
She was bruised and fatigued, but cheerful, as people are when
making a grand gesture. Her next stage was Keebah. Her appearance so shocked gallant old Urquhart that he drove her in his
dogcart to meet Stewart, who took her to New Glenties where she
arrived in high spirits.

Eleven months from her marriage day she was delivered of a *boy*!

She wrote to her mother—it was a command—to come and see
her *grandson*!

The carriage was beyond repair, the dogcart away at the blacksmith's, so William went a mucker and bought a double-seated
buggy to take his parents to see his nephew.

They brought him and his mother back to Bewuck with them.
No reference was made to the past, but Johanna heaped gifts and
indulgences upon Della and her grandson. She put a new sovereign
in each of the child's fat paws, whereas Margaret's girl had received
but one. Della knew that it was a complete reconciliation and was
happy.

In the confidence of her newly established state she sent to
Robert to bring his wagonette. Robert, without demur, came as
far as The Plains. This far Della was driven at her order by
William, with her father to hold the horses while William opened
sliprails or gates. Nothing could have been too high for Della in
her victory.

She called the son Daniel Cooley, which delighted the grand-parents. Ned simply laughed his deep bass laugh in his deep brown beard without advancing his own parents' rights in the case. He was the most agreeable man in the world.

There was rivalry for the next goal, and Margaret again produced a daughter. This time she dispensed with flourish, and went to one of her sisters. Della came only to Birrabee and with Janet for nurse, produced twins, a boy and a girl, each as big as Margaret's one. "What about an old maid now?" she demanded, a little delirious with such success, at the age of forty-two.

"Making the most of her chances before closing time," chuckled Danny.

William laughed until the tears had to be wiped from his eyes. The whole family laughed, none more generously than Margaret, whose sense of humour carried her unrancorously through the comedy.

Danny and William rode up to see the children.

"What can you do about this eclipse?" Danny asked Margaret, but with a twinkle.

All Harry's flames had been divinities to him, but Josephine Battle, whom he had courted for years, was a topnotcher in the class. Hennessy summed up the three men, "Robert is a divvil for women, and William is so afraid of thim that, begor, he must be sick to know what they could do to him wid the chance; but Harry is the owld man over again. He is as aisy wid an owld trull, and with a young wan too, be japers, as he is with the most innocent and schwell young gurrl in the counthry. He is that innocent himself that he thinks every one the same."

The whole connection was delighted when Harry went across the watershed to bring his princess home. They were surprised that the least of the Delacys had done so well for himself, but princesses need courtiers, and a disposition deficient in spiritual emotion found stimulation in Harry's poetic adoration.

A carpenter was engaged upon a house across the river from Robert. Danny was as busy as a wombat, and as much in the earth, making a garden for Margaret on her own side of the Burrabinga. The other had sometimes been inaccessible. A footbridge attached to the eurabbi trees was to ensure communication during floods. Wong paid rich tributes and grew mellow and noisy. He saw that it was customary for Europeans to imbibe much alcohol at wed-dings, births, funerals and miscellaneous celebrations, and also without festival, obviously for practice. To become drunk was productive of amusement and admiration among men, though the women pricked at them like gnats and tried to spoil sport, even as the women in his own country.

The "front room" of the new house was a source of pride. In it reposed the set of horsehair chairs, the scroll-headed couch and a pedestal dining-table, which William had sanctioned, and which Harry and Ned had brought by bullock dray. Teams had superseded the valiant pack-horses. To take loading up and down the passes required intrepidity from men and bullocks—in roadless days. Bullocks were undefeatable. Straight up the pinches they strained, all hands energetic as offsiders, execrating, flaying, belabouring, jabbing to ensure a simultaneous heave, inch by inch, until men and beasts were winded. Descending the precipices, the polers, staked down by the pole, bellowed in the agony of holding the load. Complaining but unrebellious, maddened but staunch, until their tongues lolled and the breath was crushed out of them, they held until time after time all hands had to rush to their release. Freed they lay down and chewed their cud, without rancour they came at call to submit their raw swollen necks to a renewal of the ordeal and again leant to haul with hearts that could not be soured or broken. In awkward places the down-driven weight of the clumsy yokes and bows forced them to toil for yards on their knees—penance enough to buy the district a place in Paradise, if vicarious expiation is ever efficacious. There are peoples with sacred cows; Australians could fittingly honour the memory of working bullocks.

It might have been less arduous in places to hang the merchandise on poles, but only the peasant laboured as a beast, forcing his ox or his wife to similar toil. The Australian, whether clerk or yokel, had taken the English county gentleman as his pattern and lifted his wife out of the furrow for ever: and though using beasts in some places was an incredible feat, it was accomplished with the swagger brewed by such feats and grew into the psychology of a people to blossom later in daring exploits in South Africa or on Gallipoli.

The Delacy bullocks had two trips on the bride's behalf, the second to her maiden home, and this one involved the traversing of country where no vehicle had previously gone. Every man was proud of the chief article imported, Josephine Delacy's piano. It established Burrabinga's social standing. Pianos were still rare. Norah Butler had not long had one. Even the bullocks had gained prestige through hauling the piano. Station bullocks in any case were the aristocrats of the trade and often reached great size and an honoured old age in flowery ways of peace unacquainted with the hardships of the carriers, who lived in perpetual hell; and on the day that Danny arrived to pay his respects to his new daughter-in-law, the unsmashable dray was gathering rust under the fairy shawl of a wattle while the bullocks luxuriated in the cow paddock, their intermittent trials forgotten.

Margaret warned Josephine, "You'll need to get used to old Mr Delacy. His wooden leg makes him odd."

The Burrabinga dogs hullabaloed the Bewuck dogs all across the flats, and Father was reported to be at the stables. Josephine and Robert, Della and Ned, as well as several remittance men as guests, were seated at dinner when Danny could be heard admonishing the dogs, and something else, as he stumped along the veranda with Harry in attendance. Josephine rose to meet a small figure in a soiled linen duster. His weather-beaten cabbage tree was buckled about his formidable pipe. Under one arm he had a peacock and under the other that gentleman's wife.

"Take the faymale, I'll be obleeged," he said to Margaret. He was then free to display the tail of the cock to Josephine. "Sure, me dear, I'm proud to welcome you as a mimber of me family. I've brought this beast as a fitting creature to celebrate such an evint. Sure, I could lepp over your head this moment with pride."

"If you are not careful, the bird will fly over your own head," said Robert.

Consternation was on the features of his sister-in-law. She was conventional, a twin soul of Johanna's in her desire for the elegancies of life, and her starched standards were more constricting than standards can be in the liberating Celtic temperament.

This the great man! That horrible Irish brogue!

Josephine had taken from the air the English notion that the Irish accent was socially beyond the pale, and came from a home where gentility and probity were equal. She concluded that Danny was intoxicated, and awaited the righting of. what was to her, a vulgar situation; but Harry's face was beaming. He had pictured peafowls as connected with palaces and princesses, and here was Father with one under each arm for the bride!

While Harry hung on further pronouncements, Margaret retrieved an awkward moment. "Josephine is so overcome that she does not know what to say. The peacock makes me feel like a fairy tale."

"He is magnificent, Father. How did you carry him over the mountain without a feather spoiled?" Robert sent Fannie, now quite sizable, to bring the rouseabout.

Josephine was terrified that the old man would kiss her, but he kissed no one but Johanna, and her only when he was departing on a journey. As lovers the Delacys were amateurs.

The rouseabout and Harry went to place the birds in safety in the salt room. Danny was free to make his speech. He removed his hat and the leaves fluttered about his shoulders like good wishes.

"The paycock to my moind is the most imperial of birds. 'Tis not only his tail that he spreads around him as the rainbow, but 'tis the carriage of his head with the mantle and crown upon it. And by that I consider him a proper gift of welcome to make to wan whom me and me family regard as a princess. Sure, I've brought a few other things as well, but this is the most advinturous. Me woife has sint you some token of her welcome, and she hopes ere another week has gone you will grace Bewuck by your presence."

Margaret had not been invited to Bewuck until she was to have a child. Josephine's evident distaste and embarrassment registered against her with Robert. There was resentment as well as jealousy and satire in his aside to her. "It must be an ordeal to have a morganatic bridegroom." (This had been Margaret's private comment earlier.) "Come Father, you need a wash," he said aloud. "Fannie, bring Mr Delacy my coat."

"Be the poipers, the birds have christened me! I'll disappear," said Danny, ignominiously stopped in mid-flight.

He reappeared with his mop of black silk—still without silver threads—combed from his noble forehead and cut in a pudding-basin crop. Robert's coat made his father a comical figure, but the torrent of welcome continued until it tailed off into political disquisition.

Later the whole family went to the new house. Billy, who had been a kid at Margaret's inception, was now a patriarchal and odorous personality. A king of Billies, he would send his family up a leaning tree and stand at the foot to protect them from dingoes. He mounted a pulpit of rocks and expectorated his defiance of all and sundry. Margaret had long coveted his hide for her floor, but Danny demurred, "Sure, 'twould be ungrateful to kill wan who has more against the dingoes than we have."

Danny asked the owner of the piano if she could sing "Those Evening Bells", and "I'm Sitting on the Stile". During the exhibition of her repertory he said, "Oh, moi, be all the poipers, Johanna will be pleased."

It was glorious to report to her, "You never saw a finer prospect than Margaret and Robert, and Harry and Josephine."

"Sure, I hope Josephine's first is a boy."

"Wan is no use without the other. Those women are no dolls,

but can take their place in opening up the country for future generations."

"A grave will be opened-up for ye and me before long, Danny-boy."

"There's no circumventing that, but we can't sit on our hunkers like the fox waiting for the time to arrive; but when you contemplate, why do we tigrinize so, when it all ends in a bottle of smoke?"

"Circumspection can make it ind in a fat banking account."

"But all the circumspection in the universe cannot take the banking account away with you, me brave Johanna."

CHAPTER XXXII

JOSEPHINE distinguished herself by producing a son at the end of her first year.

"A pity it's only a morganatic union," Robert sarcastically observed, but had too much style to omit due respect to his sister-in-law, and journeyed with Danny and William to the Battles' station to see his nephew. Though jealous of Josephine as likely to eclipse Margaret, Robert prized any connection worthy of his family. Such a judge of women made no mistake about Harry's wife.

William brought back glowing accounts of the skill of the house-keeping, the refinement, and order at what Robert derided as "Battle Abbey". Danny was eager that William too should marry a daughter of this house. The same idea invaded William. Here at last was perfection in a nest of daughters who would never be guilty of "looseness".

Danny reported, "The dayvil a finer child I never did see—as good as wan of those first wans of yours, Johanna; and the white skin of him, and big eyes. A robe on him to the floor. He's that extraordinarily refined he ought to have been a female."

"He ought not to be anny such thing! William shall take the buggy and bring Josephine down to show the district as soon as possible."

"Sure, Mrs Harry's brother is carrying him home on the pommel, and Elizabeth Battle,"—Danny winked behind William's back—"is coming to aid Mrs Harry till she gets strong . . . Moi, oh, moi! Before long the boy will be astride one of the finest Nullah-Mundoeys in the world. I must go pick a promising foal."

Johanna produced the rum jar. She even took a sip herself, and summoned Hannon.

Harry wished to name the child Daniel. Danny suggested Brian, but a name so vulgarly Irish was abhorrent to the Battles. Harry then constructed Johan from Johanna. "Sure, me brave Johanna, it is a fine romantic thought, and you deserve it," said Danny.

The boy's second name was Darcy, which slept until the old Delacys should have passed. "I'll call him 'baby' as long as I can," thought Josephine.

When Josephine came to Bewuck, it was Robert who drove her. "I cannot risk the heir-apparent's neck," he said. His brothers always deferred to Robert in this, as in business. Josephine felt safe only when he handled the reins. She admired his efficiency and authority, though she could never be sure whether he was humorous or sarcastic about the "heir-apparent". Elizabeth accompanied her. Robert brought Margaret out also, and her maid. He had an instinct for advertisement and would not hide his wife in the valley while Josephine in her glory, with her son and her sister, was being peddled around Johanna's radius.

Johanna had her arms open for both Margaret and Josephine, but Robert said he had business in the Township, and put up at Hennessy's with enough dash to fill the stable yard, and Euphemia's former suite, and overflow to enliven the main street. William's pair was outclassed by Robert's four big greys and the three unrivalled kangaroo dogs privileged to decorate his progress.

The dressmaker was called upon to outdo Josephine and it took all Margaret's height and personality to dignify her courageous attempts. Robert was elated by the result. Margaret would have been willing to concede the palm to Josephine and retreat to Burrabinga. "Let her have her day," she would say with a wan smile to Robert's urging. "Mine is probably coming. I feel sick enough for triplets—all boys!"

Johanna was shocked that Josephine had no maid to wait upon her, and set about training an unbroken "gurrl" into a "surrvant" and nurse-maid. One maid, aged five, had been discarded by Josephine, as such an infant only added to her duties. Some philanthropist had sought to find the child a berth because her mother was dead and her father the usual drunkard.

Never had the little lady at Bewuck been so proud, so near to happiness as in the acquisition of Josephine. She revelled in the young woman's beauty, her accomplishments, her family, her competence. Many women were as resourceful as Josephine, but the style of all her work set her apart and earned her the resentment of those who had to compete with her. It is difficult for superiority to be forgiven by those cribbed with it in a small community. Josephine was never rough-and-ready. She was always ladylike in deportment, even when building the hen house, or making her own furniture, which she could do with the skill of a carpenter, and in a high collar and steel-slatted corsets, without disarranging her long skirts. Her dresses inside and out had the finish of a fashion-plate, which she could reproduce without the aid of a model, no matter how intricate and elaborate the design.

Johanna commanded a rally at New Glenties because of Norah's piano. Neither Josephine nor Elizabeth had any more music than a budgerigar, but Johanna was not educated to discover this. They had been stiffly governessed and executed their repertory with precision, not a note missing in the "pieces", not more than two semi-tones flat in the ditties.

Johanna's pride and joy were touching. Her eyes sparkled as she dandled Johan Darcy while the young ladies rendered, "Fly Away, Pretty Moth"; "Jeanette and Jeanot"; "What are the Wild Waves Saying?" (duet); "By the Sad Sea Waves"; and "Annie Laurie".

Stewart shut his eyes and yammered, "Her Bright Smile Haunts Me Still", and "Juanita"; two songs with which he had courted Norah, as well as "Silver Threads Among the Gold", with which he still flattered her. Old Butler, with his sweet tenor, sang "The Harp that Once"; "Believe Me If All"; "Oft in the Stilly Night"; "The Minstrel Boy"; "The Dear Little Shamrock"; and in response to Danny's importunities, repeated "Those Evening Bells" and "The Irish Emigrant" until he was hoarse. "Just Before the Battle"; "Tramp, Tramp, the Boys are Marching"; "The Gipsy's Warning"; "Sweet Belle Mahone"; and "I Wandered To-day to the Hill, Maggie"; were sung in chorus by the company while the soloists recovered their breath.

Elizabeth touched all hearts with:

> Sweet dreamland faces, passing to and fro,
> Bring back to memory days of long ago.

And as an encore:

> Do you remember the paths where we met,
>   Long, long ago, long ago?
> Ah, yes, you told me you ne'er would forget,
>   Long, long ago, long ago!

The frail plaintive voice and tender sentiments drew relieving tears from souls nostalgic for the scenes of youth. The refrains escaped into the silver night, a minor chord to modulate the coarse maledictions lingering from chain-gang days, the reverberating laughter of aborigines, of birds, and of invading Europeans of the pioneering century—motifs awaiting release by indigenous genius.

Stewart was tactless in his admiration of Josephine. "Harry has found a real lady. It's a mystery to me how he collared her."

"Huh!" said Norah, indignantly, "She was never away to be educated in Sydney like Della and I."

"Lot of good Della's education is, buried at Burrabinga."

"Isn't Josephine buried there too, and glad to be married to my brother! And didn't Della refuse yours?"

Stewart stupidly reiterated his admiration to Robert, who was cynical. "You must remember to walk backwards from her or the marriage may be annulled."

Stewart and Johanna were able to revel together about the new connection. "Sure, Stewart, do all ye can to push on a match between William and the sister. Look at them now; does she look interested, do ye think?"

Elizabeth, a fragrant flowerlike presence, sat on a couch with William, who was as stiff as a sergeant in mufti at a court martial.

Danny adjured Josephine. "Sure, where would you find a finer young man than me son for your sister?"

"I'm not a match-maker."

"But you can urge it on."

Josephine knew her sister's tastes and her own—*now*. William had whittled away his lesson time by putting on the clock and possuming, and Elizabeth demanded education as a corollary of gentlemanliness. For her, no homespun worth could outweigh lack of polish in the intimacy of marriage.

Harry and his mother had the idea that both families should go to Sydney on a sight-seeing trip to provide general entertainment and foster romance.

The discomforts of the expedition remained in the memories of Mrs Robert and Mrs Harry for over half a century, the one through the nausea she suffered, the other because her infant would not stay with a nurse, and waked up and shrieked at every entertainment into which she smuggled him. Also the hotel was infested, and awful to Josephine, whose family not only were in the piano class but among the more select who kept insects out of their beds, a distinction unachieved by many genealogically arrogant families a generation later.

Mrs Robert envied Della who had remained at Burrabinga in charge of Margaret's children as well as her own. Della had retired on her laurels of two sons and a daughter and would not risk their health "to flash about the country in fine clothes". "It's a mere act of God to give birth to twins," she proclaimed, "but it takes a good mother to rear them both." She was reacting noisily against earlier slights, and levied upon her circle for admiration of her capability and devotion.

What William and Elizabeth got out of the holiday has been forgotten. The supposition was that William proposed and Elizabeth declined. Johanna and Danny were painfully disappointed that no engagement resulted from the grand visit to Sydney. They discussed it with Robert.

"William says it's because he is not educated, but surely Robert, you are well educated."

"Ah, but Elizabeth hasn't the opportunity to marry me, or she would probably rush it."

"Josephine married Harry, and he had no more education than William," persisted Danny.

"But Harry, most likely, deafened her by spouting enough poetry and history for a professor. William has always pooh-poohed that stuff."

"When it comes to family," said Johanna haughtily, "who annywhere can compete with me own? The Cooleys came from Kings and were beacons of culture when the English were paddling about in the woods living on acorns with the wild boars. With us, princesses and scholars were plentiful and equally honoured."

" 'Tis so, me brave Johanna, and out here whin we had a princess from a people as old as the Irish—if we only knew—a black princess given to us—what honour could have been higher and didn't we follow the swell proclivities of all those in the saddle by making a servant of her and letting her milk the cows and . . ."

William was in no humour for his father's two-edged philosophy. "Oh, that old talk!" he grumbled. "It's a drawback to be Irish."

This was hard on Johanna's pride, but she did not give in. "Elizabeth will come round by and by," she said.

William did not feel that way. The rebuff he had received, though gentle, hurt him deeply and hardened his bachelor shell.

"The day will come when she'll regret she did not marry William," Johanna would repeat.

Maybe it did. Elizabeth shortly afterwards married a man with slightly more syntax, but none of William's kindness, who neglected her. She died four years later, and her husband remarried within the year.

The Delacy pride had another jolt at that time.

Donald Urquhart, who married Susan Angus and went to the Riverine, was drowned. Sandy set out to aid Susan, but when he arrived at the home, near Wagga Wagga, found that she had gone to the town in Gippsland whence the Anguses derived. Sandy followed and called at the police station for directions. The Sergeant knew no one of the name of Angus, but the recently arrived widow was with her mother, a Mrs Farmer. Sandy concluded that Mrs Farmer had remarried.

"Not that I know of," said the Sergeant. Asked why her family should go by the name of Angus, the police officer supposed that they had dropped their own when they went across the border while the old man was doing his term for robbery under arms.

Investigation proved the truth of this. Urquhart's first grandson of the name! And Janet too, the wife of George Angus! Urquhart came near to violence upon his wife when she said placidly, "The thing can't be undone. The less noise about it the better. They are better than those with model parents."

"By God, woman, it's the breed "

"Good men have bad sons. This is the other way about."

Sandy was impelled to share his grief with his old mate, Delacy, and set out with Janet, also Jean who was still single. Bounding across the plains in a light buggy in which the passengers sat back to back, Jean was thrown out, had her arm broken and arrived at Bewuck in pain.

At daylight next day Johanna and Janet took her to the doctor in the Township. William drove them in his own vehicle. Janet and Johanna had an enjoyable reunion and Maeve and Mrs Hannon were left in charge of Danny and Sandy. The women remained overnight in the Township and during the evening of their absence Sandy divulged the scandal.

"By damn! Be the poipers!" The loosing of these oaths at intervals indicated Danny's emotion. "We who set such store on principle, to be married in with a robber who was doing time! Isn't that life all over for you!"

"I don't know what steps to take," said Sandy.

"You can't take anny steps but to keep it from the women, your Janet and my Della, and above all Johanna, me wife. I'm disturbed to think how she would take it. I kept the secret tight about young Janet and it was blown out when she married."

"It cannot be kept dark when old Farmer is out."

"If he'd take the name of Angus and keep quiet, the bit it would take to keep him would be neither here nor there."

"He's too much of an out-and-outer for that."

"Then we must face it with what composure we can assume. Isn't there a convict in nearly every family we know, but our own, and them mostly better than the rags of free men that succeeded them? Sure, Sandy, there's going to be a great levelling down of the consequential upstarts in this Colony, and an eruption from below of the bolder spirits. In another fifty years the sons of horse thieves may be slimy with rayspictability, and the rayspictable rayversed. Isn't it better to be coming up from a felon than going down to wan? Sure, there should be no brand put on the son for the father's crime. Otherwise, in logic, he'd be forced to be dishonest because his parents were, and the implications of that don't stand pondering upon, Sandy. And by damn! I can't help the situation annyway, no matter what disquisitions arise in me."

As the two old mates gathered comfort and whisky, Danny was ready to consider a son-in-law whose father was in jail an acquisition. "Why," demanded he, "should I expect the son of a bad man to stay clear of marrying into my family more than another? Put it to logic, Sandy. And sure, too often I've been made into a fool by me bull's nest exploding on me with Robert, to worry about this wan."

Sandy craved to kill somebody—anybody would do—to relieve his angry humiliation. Janet foolishly had left her holiday ration of good Scotch, and Jane Hannon and Maeve had no control over the old gentlemen. Danny feloniously ordered Doogoolook to track Johanna's cache, and with wide voiceless grins he soon produced the demijohn.

"Sure, we've enough to stiffen an army, or our own old bulls. We'd better go to the kitchen, where we can mix a sup of hot water with it. By damn! we'll drink the jail bird to consternation."

Doogoolook was served with a nobbler of each brand, which sent him on a walk-about for the night, but what the inarticulate exile found in the way of company, none knew. The clamorous silence may for him have been peopled with obvious magic which scientists will not unravel for another cycle.

Danny could have been heard to exclaim, "Sure, I'm so overjoyed by this reunion, without anny interference whatever, that I could lepp over your head in wan lepp."

"I'm a wee bit stiff for that, mesel'."

"That's mortal curious. You would think I would not be so soople as I was with two legs, but lepp—why man alive, lepp, sure, I could lepp over the moon this mortal minute!"

"That grog must be ower powerful," said Sandy, who could carry more at the beginning, but grew poisonous as the debauch ripened. " 'Tis not good to mix drinks, Sandy."

"Hoots! We'll mix drinks and whatever else we dom well please in this gey nicht of freedom from those tyrannizing besoms, though I'm no denying that Janet is good in her way."

An eavesdropper could have heard them swimming the Yackandandah in 'fifty-two and bottoming their shicers at Bendigo or Mount Alexander, and burying the digger murdered by the bushrangers. They went further back to the burning of Burrabinga hut-homestead when Danny had returned to desolation and tragedy.

"Sure, Sandy, we're the greatest pioneers, bar none. Anny man who thinks he surpasses us, 'tis calumny. Those fellows on The Plains had much clear country and no precipices to be climbed, and as manny assigned men as they could employ, and money, and a mort of other advantages. A lady could pioneer by watching others put their backs into it. But those that did are the rale men, and by damn, we're them! Those Camerons and the like only over-looked while the poor dayvils in chains were the rale pioneers—sure, there ought to be statues of them erected."

"It would never do to let the working man get above hissel' or the Colony might as well be abandoned."

That was a dangerous lead to the great open sore that Angus, Senior, was a felon. At this hour Sandy "had enough drink taken" to be downright nasty, while Danny was philosophical beyond even lunacy's licence.

"Sandy, acushla, the old mate of me great days of long ago, what does it matter? Do you know who your great-great-grandfather was, and who the dayvil cares? And these would-be dukes on The Plains—who are fine people aside from their little assumptions of gentility—in the old country would not have the pedigree of anny buckeen in the bohreen—sure, that's nearly poetry I'm wasting on you. Wait till the next generation scatters what we are gathering. All the slip-rails are down, and they'll be all boxed and never drafted, and you and me will have carried our hides to the tanyard—and carried them like men. Sure, we have good hides to carry. There's never a feather of use in worrying about old Angus *alias* Farmer. Let the tail go with the hide. Sure, my breed is so good that I can affoord to purify the Anguses. No blame to them that they want to rise.

"Maybe in less than a hundred years nothing will matter. In the immeasurable immensity of space, Sandy, 'tis beyond the furthest limits of moind to compute, will they know 'twas you and me who first civilized the Murrumbidgee? Even then you had others before you, and before me was the poor dayvil whose wife and child fell in the river. They say they cry there still, and though I'm not for encouraging such foolish notions, yet often I think maybe, that those who believe in ghosts have a case. What proof have we, Sandy, that they have not, and what does it matter when 'twill all be the same in a hundred years? And a hundred years is but the twinkling of an eye. And the bunyip and the banshee, sure they exist, Sandy, to them that can see and hear them. It's all in the moind. There are only time and the wind and space to last for ever. Time and space are the same thing in different dimensions. If our faculties were fully developed, we could maybe hear in the wind all that wint on here when there were cities like Babylon and Tyre. Think of the immensity of oblivion that enwraps this continent regarding what wint on in times when ancient Asia was young, and youthful Europe was a wilderness."

Urquhart had been as silent as an old bison, and the glare in his eye was that of a bison about to charge. Over-proof Jamaica on top of potent Scotch was working in him. He burst into a sullen roar. "You are havering, Daniel Delacy; blethering about nothing, like an auld apple-wife selling pears. My heid is reeling with the clack of your tongue like the clapper of a bell in your empty skull. It is what happens now that matters. If I did something because it would not matter in a hundred years, I'd be as big a fule as you are, which the Lord forbid. I, Alexander Urquhart of Aberdeenshire, and now on the Murrumbidgee, I do not tamely submit to my bluid being mingled with that of a felon."

"But what can you do about your fine blood, Sandy, avic? You cannot extract it. Sure, a lot of pleasure is quinched with age, but a lot of sting is also flattened . . ."

"You're a fule, Daniel Delacy, a blethering fule!"

"Sure, you are proclaiming it like a blast of wind from Monaro in me face. You'd talk the teeth out of a saw yourself, and as for a fool . . ." Danny laughed in alcoholic glee. He arose with the intention of slapping Sandy on the back, but he sat with a whack on the floor. "Sandy, give me a hand. I'm not so soople as when I broke it in the Yackandandah. 'Sure, I'm Denny Blake from County Clare, and ready at command to sing a song in praises, of me own dear native land . . .'"

Sandy fell upon his mate and they rolled together until Danny reached the leg of the table and went up by that, followed by Sandy. When they were reseated Sandy began to sing:

> Scots, wha hae wi' Wallace bled,
> Scots, wham Bruce has aften led;
> Welcome to your gory bed,
> Or to victorie!

"*Gory bed or victorie*, Danny Delacy, there's a model for you!"

"You're looking for ructions, Sandy."

"You're a fule, a dom' fule, Danny. Let the tail go with the hide, ye blether, but the foul tail is taking the hide."

"What can you do to stop it, Sandy, asthore?"

"Do!" he yelled, infuriated by Danny's laughter. "I'll show you what I can do."

"You can't show me that a few years will not put a flattener on the praytintious and heave up the under-dogs like a volcano."

Sandy brandished a tomahawk from the dresser while Danny watched with the pleasure of a child. Near at hand the retired cradle was full of eggs awaiting Johanna's housewifery. With a clansman's screech Sandy jumped straight into them for the ease their scrunching gave his drink-inflamed nerves. His Yackandandah mate roared a couplet of "The wearin' of the Green", and cried "Sool him, boy, sool him!" and nearly choked with laughter to see Sandy's trousers lepping so gaily in the cause of scrambled eggs. He longed to assist but to rise was beyond him.

"Sure, you have plinty for lashings of pancakes, Sandy Mavourneen."

"I'd dance on Farmer like this," he bellowed with a stanza of "The Campbells are Coming". "That is how I'd show my manhood!"

"I'm destroyed with amusement," gasped Danny. "But still and all, 'tis only the eggs that are killed. To slap it at him like that won't hurt Farmer, nor make his children unmarried to ours, nor put the grand-children back where they came from. And 'tis ungintlemanly waste of the hins' labour."

At this, Sandy leapt right out of the box with the eggs dripping from him. Danny thought his last moment had come, but met the brandished axe as steadily as he met a charging bull, and the blow fell on the table that was Johanna's pride. It had the flaunting elegancy of varnished legs and a top of white pine when kitchen tables were of hardwood slabs.

This deed sobered Danny and startled Sandy. "Begor, you've done it now. Sure that cannot be covered from me wife. Come get to bed! 'Tis we are to blame for swallowing enough grog to stiffen a cannibal; and how shall we account to Johanna and Janet for having it?"

"The besons! It is their fault for keeping it from us!"

Sandy reeled away, resentful of advice, and got into bed as he was, while Danny found his own mattress. His pipe burned a hole in a bolster, but the special pagan god—a male god—that broods over intoxication smothered the conflagration in feathers.

Hannon laughed heartily at the dance, which he witnessed through a crack. He saw that the fire was safe, took a swig of the two alcohols, and ignored the eggs. His ageing bones were craving rest.

Rumour was that the kangaroo dogs fattened on eggs and that

the family lived on pancakes for a month, but that was drollery. Hannon did not report what his wife said as she followed a dried eggy trail all over the carpet of Johanna's drawing-room through to the spare-room bed. The wallaroo robe and broken eggs; and the goose-down mattress which Johanna had made in the tradition of Cooley Hall!

Danny was completely subdued by the charred bolster. "If you'll put as good a face on things as possible, I'll give you a pound," he said to Jane Hannon. "The table can't be attributed to accident, but the eggs need not be dwelt on to anny extint. The kangaroo pups could be mintioned, but 'tis more honest to face it." Danny resisted temptation with a sigh.

Consciousness returned painfully to Sandy in the "ind room", in all his clothes, even his boots, and glued to Johanna's best bedding from the knees down. He invariably wakened in a dangerous mood after a spree, and now flamed with rage against Janet, though in sane stretches he upheld her, was sensitive about social mistakes and had a high sense of what was due to the ladies.

He laved himself, put on another suit and said grandly to Jane Hannon that he had taken some of Mr Delacy's overproof, and must have stepped in the egg box. Profuse apologies. If Mrs Hannon would rectify the damage he would split five pounds between her and Maeve. Mrs Hannon worked with a will after that, and the hens cackled all day long as if conscious of emergency. The hacked side of the table was turned to the wall, and Jane later reported that everything but it had been restored to normal.

"What table?" asked Urquhart, and the stupid woman led him to it.

"Mrs Delacy sets such store on it, sir; I only hope she won't blame me, sir."

Urquhart glowered in a frightening way. Craving for a "wee drappie" got the better of him in the afternoon, but Hannon had finished all that remained. Sandy therefore drove off in maniacal fury, hurling imprecations at his old mate Danny, asserting that that besom of a Janet would find the door shut in her face if she attempted to return to Keebah; nor would he suffer the other besom's tongue about her table.

William brought the ladies home at dusk. Jean had her arm bandaged mightily; the journey had tried her and she was grateful for William's kindness. The baying dogs, the carrying of parcels to the house, the rich meal awaiting, the stimulating presence of "company", and the adventure of Jean's visit to the doctor obscured Sandy's absence for the moment.

"Has any accident happened Sandy?" Janet asked when preliminaries had subsided.

"No accident." Danny took her aside. "Sure, Mrs Janet, he and I celebrated a little over-much last night. You being Sandy's old mate the same as I am meself, only on the inside of the bedroom door, know that he can be a little cantankerous next day . . ."

"And he's taken the needle and gone off?"

"Dayvil a needle! He's craw sick and gone to look for a sup of whisky."

"He'd make to the nearest pub, but we did not meet him."

"He went the other way."

"I can't do anything now," said Janet calmly.

Danny clutched this straw, and the cheerful meal proceeded. A great deal of attention was given to Jean, especially by William, who cut her food for her. Every ear was alert for Sandy each time the dogs barked, but they announced only possums or other marsupials invading the homestead.

Danny thought it better to inform Johanna before she found out. "Sure, me brave Johanna, Sandy was so afraid to meet you that he has cleared out."

"Is the drink still in your senses that ye talk a double ass-load of foolishness?"

Danny confessed about the eggs first. "They're nothing that can't be replaced by the hins, but Sandy got a bit beyond himself and cut your table. Whin he remimbered he was so ashamed that he took to his heels."

"And did he think he'd be ate up by me?" exclaimed Johanna with spirit. "Since whin was I a man eater? And what was ye'r part in this, me brave gladiator? Ye did not sit by like a son of timperance with a blue ribbon bow on ye'r beard."

"A man is entitled to a sup or two whin meeting an old mate who saved his life in the Yackandandah, and sure, it made me so sleepy that the pipe singed the bolster."

Johanna gasped. "The place afire! Have ye destroyed me best things, the workbox and the stuffed birds?"

"Not at all! 'Twas nothing. Think if the house had caught fire and I and Sandy to have perished in the flames."

"Ah, as long as ye had really perished—the pair of ye together— I'm thinking that Janet and I could have borne up under it very well entirely."

Johanna could track as well as Doogoolook among her sacred

elegancies and when she found that her secret still had been raided she quickly reconstructed the orgy. "Sure, they swam the Yackandandah and found gold all night and were the finest pair of marvels in the universe; but I'm distressed that poor Mr Urquhart should feel it upon him to run away, as if from an ogre."

"He had every right to feel upset. I'll have to be taken after him as soon as William can spare time," responded Janet, imperturbably. She knew what had led to such an outbreak, but with superlative discretion let it be attributed to mixed drinks.

The crisp day and the skill required to handle his pair cleared the fumes from Urquhart's brain and he thought better of running away. Instead he went to Queanbeyan, about fifty miles distant, and had a refresher at the Royal, and left his horses to the groom. At dawn next morning he was again rattling across the plains. Janet was relieved to see him and pleased with the tiny book cabinet, the walnut table and the brocade which he had procured as a peace offering to Johanna. Gallantry and friendship were both served, and the mutilated table, repaired by Hannon, still exists in one of the family storerooms, a refuge for spiders and empty flower pots.

Jean remained at Bewuck for her arm to mend, and so quiet a maiden was she, so esteemed was William, that he was permitted to drive her home later unchaperoned.

Sandy, subjugated by the eggs and table outbreak, agreed to divulge nothing of old Farmer, and in due time Mrs Farmer conveniently died and Tom did his duty to the family by taking his father to India to end his days respectably under the *alias* of Angus. The secret was nobly kept. It became known only to some of Danny's grandchildren fifty years later, when neither an Angus nor an Urquhart was left in the district.

CHAPTER XXXIII

ROBERT's children were growing healthily, as Danny observed when he went up for the shearing. Sheep had been introduced. Danny helped to muster with splendid yells, from the back of a Nullah-Mundoey. He could still burst through the scrub and descend sharp declivities with *élan*. William was also much at Burrabinga trying to reduce the dingoes. He and Harry were sometimes ill of cramp through long hours of sheep-washing. The Delacys began too late to re-adjust themselves to sheep. Where horses inspired swagger, sheep compelled a poking and slogging which irked the reckless caballeros. The paradox of mounted infantry was beyond them.

Surveyors had been busy for a decade. Much of the mountain country was now leased from the Crown. The rich squatters from Riverina and farther north built summer homes there. The Mesdames Delacy were hostesses to any amount of the best society, and were general favourites. They were smartly dressed and well mounted, had well-stocked gardens, and the social amenities introduced by Josephine were observed in their homes.

Danny had a gardening uniform of white moleskin with pieces of soogee bagging tacked on the trousers. He still wore leaves in his hat and a fly veil. Mrs Robert and Mrs Harry, both conventional, were deprecatory of the old man's eccentricities.

"If only he would keep in the background," would murmur one or the other, embarrassed to have him daubed with chocolate clay bursting upon the cream of the squattocracy. Danny found more entertainment in the foreground and his guests enjoyed him. His opinions on horse breeding were respected; he was known to speak the truth even in a horse deal, and that set him apart.

The children grew to need tutors. A supply of remittance men was still to be found at the hotels in the township, some of whom had been sent out for unalloyed uselessness, others because to this they added imbibing. Among them were charming and expensively educated gentlemen with documented family trees, and as Burrabinga was celebrated for its inaccessibility to pubs, the Delacys could pick and choose.

Little Clare Margaret, known as Clare for short, was the pride of the station. She had the blue eyes of Danny, with a darker tinge, and lashes that were early a snare, and had her mother to thank that the Delacy floss turned up in adorable curls. Her lips rippled with laughter. They had much practice as she was a merry little cricket with an equal sense of humour and of devilment. She held court with station hands, squatters, drovers, remittance men and relatives in her kingdom of eucalypts. So little of the bush had been driven back that from the house she could gaze down its aisles. They had no end, the big trees swept the sky and magic birds were as plentiful as flowers. There were kookaburras to laugh, leather-heads to fulminate, parrots and gang-gangs of gay colours, magpies and cockatoos of several varieties, honey-eaters, coach-whips, wag-tails, tits and robins, peewits, curlews, plovers, pigeons, quail, cranes, ducks galore, the ibis and a hundred other species, for some of which the bush men had onomatopoeic names. When Clare could escape to the hut, the men could tell her what the birds said, and she could watch the lyre-tails playing on the sideling across the river. The men often caught her one and tied it up by a leg, but it always died and then its tail was pretty on the shelf above the fireplace.

Peacocks as big as clouds flew high in the gum trees. They were swaggering fellows who descended as the reivers of old and wrung the necks of chickens, and cannibalistically ate eggs, or harried the hens until some had to be shot. Then their tails, like tapestried panels, beautified the corners of the sitting-room. Grandpa was proud of the peafowls.

A dog guarded Clare Margaret from forest or stream. Sometimes she would escape to a cleared space in the foal paddock to see the peacocks spreading their tails like rainbows in the sunlight until she clapped her hands with glee, when Rover would rush up with a "woof" and disperse the exhibitionists. Clare Margaret rode on Rover at the beginning but soon progressed to a Nullah-Mundoey of her own, and went to the muster or sat on the top rail and gave her opinions like the best horse-coper of them all. At three, and four, and five there were males slaving for recognition, and oppor-tunities for mischief were illimitable. Uncle William had the spancelled idea that physical freedom or any mental capacity beyond that of a hen would rob a girl of womanliness.

"Clare Margaret is as rough as a boy," he confided to Josephine. "Sitting up on the fence and knowing unladylike things about stock. I blush at what she says to the buyers."

He had a case when Clare, at the age of four, had shown-off for those assembled by following Grandpa with an imaginary wooden leg as she declaimed, "By damn, it's hot to-day."

They were all too concerned for the child's gentility to be amused.
Grandpa, himself, the awful example!

"By damn, me dear," he said to her, "You mustn't say what I
say till you have a beard like me and a pipe to put in it."

"Can I have a pipe at once, and when will my beard grow?"
demanded the adventurous child.

"I must bridle me tongue, and not corrupt the young before their
time," said Grandpa, joining in the laughter.

"By damn!" said Danny's parodist, with an inimitable guffaw.

William was in a fantod. He thought the child should be
reclaimed by segregation. This angered Margaret, with only Fannie
as helper and a dozen men to make work. She complained later
to Josephine.

It broke Clare Margaret's heart to be kept behind when men and
dogs moved back to the yards. To pacify her. Margaret put her
across the bridge to Aunt Josephine, Rover by her side. Clare
could do wonderful things with Johan (pronounced John), who
was as obedient as Rover, but Aunt Josephine was not pleased
when he ate mud-pies at his cousin's order.

A doctor of medicine, with high degrees but no resistance to
alcohol, was retained by Robert, who said he could come in handy
in case of accidents, and could tutor Clare.

The tutor diminished Clare's leisure until she promoted him to
be a glorified Rover and a party to her adventures. She loved to
visit Aunt Della, where she had three followers, but they mostly
followed into mischief.

The tutor at Burrabinga soon had a school of three. Another
remittance man resided at Aunt Della's, and it was his office to
ride with Daniel Cooley Angus each morning to within a mile of
Burrabinga and return for him in the afternoon. As often as not
he spent the day at Burrabinga. All were welcome at the Delacy
tables. There was ample food in the townships, any number of big
bullocks to haul it, and horses to sell to pay for it all, including
the bullocky's wages. If a bullocky were not forthcoming, William
or Harry acted instead, or Ned Angus.

The remittance men carried culture beyond the Murrumbidgee.
They patronized modern writers as well as the classics. Even Walt
Whitman and Zola were read (one by the men and the other by the
women), and some of the tutors could sketch, and some could play
chess, and all were appreciated for their company.

The school-house was away from the main abode. Through the
doorway Clare could watch the butterflies in her mother's garden.

She could see the cherries reddening in the orchard beyond, where she would climb to the highest bough as soon as lessons were past. She could also see the plovers and magpies assailing approaching horsemen and feigning broken wings to lead them from the direction of nestlings. Kangy lay on the veranda sunning himself, safe from strange dogs, and Cocky swore at him from the gate post, where he had come to rest after pulling the pegs from the clothes on the lines. A full and glowing life for a little girl in a natural environment and with but a minimum of restraint.

Doctor sometimes secured an illicit bottle. The children learned that the gentleman was ill, and enjoyed the results of these indispositions. There were other holidays connected with the post-office when the tutor made-up the mail bag and sealed it carefully as deputy for Queen Victoria herself.

On a certain summer afternoon when Clare Margaret should have been pricking her fingers and a sampler with a needle she was at liberty while her mother wrote letters, so she led Johan and Daniel Cooley to the foal paddock to play hide and seek among the mares. She could stoop under the flanks of the taller ones and holding on by the stifles, peer out from the ambush of tails that swept the ground. When the fat little boys came near she would skip on to another animal.

"God help us!" Grandpa looked over the fence of the vegetable garden and saw the danger. Those children to be running between the legs of treacherous mares with foals! "And not a hair of their heads to be hurt! Every wan of the Nullah-Mundoeys should be hung with a blue ribbon for their motherly conduct. Sure, the breed was always gentlemanly."

Reprimanded and cautioned, Clare Margaret was allowed to lead her men to the mice hunt. The hay shed had to be cleared for the new hay. The old hay was rich provender for the mice, and the mice made sport for the dogs. The men prepared for the massacre by chaining dogs at certain points to keep mice from the house. Others worked with the men who were active with waddies as the straw was pitch-forked out. Mice ran about like a disturbed ant bed, the dogs were delirious with excitement and the kookaburras gathered for the booty.

The children found many nests of baby mice and collected them. The intention was to have live lambs whose tails could be cut off.

The men shovelled the stunned mice into empty tar drums for despatch later. Their minds slipped off the children, who stole away dragging a can of mice. Clare Margaret knew of the drownings of kittens and puppies. Arrived at the river, she had the idea of swim-

ming races. The smooth hole was best for this, dangerous and deep
under the pulpit of Billy the Goat. Chubby hands set scores of mice
in the water. Small feet waded in to give them a start. Fannie
reported that the kitchen was invaded by bedraggled mice. They
had swum to land as the water revived them. They were traced to
the river. Margaret's heart lost a beat to observe the children's
danger. Then she was so angered that she plucked a quince switch
and went for them. Her switchings were aimed impartially at all
offenders, and Clare Margaret stepped aside and let her male
cousins take the stripes. They yelled so loudly that the men heard
them, and ran. Mrs Robert nearly laid the stick about them in
her fright.

"If you can't be trusted with children you should be in a fish
bowl for newts."

The men were meek, relieved to have escaped tragedy.

Clare Margaret was angelic for the remainder of the day. Her
mother had been so frightened that Johan was sent home immediately, and Daniel Cooley Angus's equerry went early with his charge.
Clare Margaret went to garden with Grandpa. "Sure," said he,
"such energy must have an outlet or it corrodes." She picked out
all the young carrots and parsnips which Grandpa had already
reset. Grandfather was not annoyed. He had a beautiful temper.
His idea of gardening of late years was to pick out everything and
then reset. This was less tedious than separating weeds from
vegetables. The Mesdames Delacy complained of the set-back to
the plants, but as Grandfather pointed out, there was such a mort
of vegetables that half of them could not be consumed. In any case
if he operated drastically in Robert's garden there would be plenty
left in Della's or Josephine's, and a rouseabout with a pack-horse
could fetch liberal supplies.

Danny Delacy was being sunk in Grandpa by young souls who
had known him as no other.

The Mesdames Delacy, aiming at style in the society of which
they were the summer centre, chafed under the tutelage of William,
the treasurer of the partnership. He kept such a string on the purse
that Margaret said, "He mistakes himself for an almoner."

"It is ridiculous that we cannot order a new saucepan till he
approves of it," agreed Josephine.

"Nor even a thimble, and his ideas are so old-maidish."

William, on his side, was shocked by the general extravagance of
Burrabinga, and particularly by the wastefulness of Mrs Robert.
Grandfather was corroborative.

"We'll be bankrupt before manny seasons, if something isn't

done to stem Mrs Robert's squandering—and she well-abetted by Robert. Sure, every wan in the world uses the place for a private hotel. Every Tom and Dick make there to camp. The kitchen is as crowded as the dining-room—like two tables at Hennessy's, only you have to pay at Hennessy's. I counted, Johanna, last Saturday night—there were twenty extras. There were squatters and doctors from Melbourne and Riverina, and you'd think the sitting-room was Hennessy's bar, with the smoke so thick you couldn't see through it, and the grog flowing grandly."

"It would be. Who took the grog there? Is it all put down to ye?"

"Whin I recall, the visitors brought some, except wan bottle that Robert swaggered in with, and that and its large family of brothers will presently be put down to Father—you're right."

"Sure, it wasn't I ever gave me sons an example in drink, except to keep from it."

Danny took another lead. "There were horse-buyers putting in time, and min pretending to look for work, and a genuine traveller or two. A stockman from Keebah and another young fellow from the dayvil knows where were sticking up to Fannie. There were the surveyors, and a fellow as agent for an American book—sure, I bought a copy meself for two guineas."

"Where did ye put it?"

" 'Tis to be delivered later."

"Two more guineas gone."

"Well, at anny rate they were all there. They thinned out a bit on Monday morning. Robert has a store-room—like a magazine for the army—bins set around to keep the goods from mice and ants. Be the poipers, it's the two-legged ants that walk in there. You can track them in a stream by what they drop as they go. Every man-jack free to replenish his tucker-bags, not only with a bit of flour or tea, but with currants and the like. Sure, Johanna, that can't last! No use in all me scraping to save at the spill and it going out at the bung like the Murrumbidgee."

Grandfather made many trips to keep his eye on the extravagance, with no result but his own annoyance. He and William and Della were for ever complaining of the spending, and Mesdames Robert and Harry were irritated by William's questioning of their every trivial requirement. The situation was unsatisfactory. Harry too had his discontents. He was tired of being the drudge. Robert was no longer his hero. An attitude of worship adopted in adolescent fervour had grown irksome. Margaret had her hands full in bearing a family, in making their clothes, in running a house that was used as a hotel, in raising poultry, in making jam and butter with only the aid of Fannie and occasional rouseabouts. In addition she managed to read and hold her own as a clever woman in the estimation of her guests from the cities, and this she could not have done had she cultivated penuriousness. She looked forward to the help of her daughters. Clare was already a marvel when housework could be presented as an adventure. Otherwise she took adventure out of doors. At seven and eight she could ride like a stockman in her pretty side-saddle, and she could sew and spell and cook, but she was for ever leading her devoted swains, Daniel and Johan, into trouble.

She was eight when a mail holiday fell on a splendidly rainy day and Johan and Daniel stayed overnight because the river was high and the approach to the footbridge under water. She loved to hear the ground sing after rain, and between downpours the children paddled about driving in sticks to halt the shrilling of crickets and frogs.

"What a lovely lot of water for the geese, let's drive them in," she exclaimed, as she beheld the river swollen to its outer banks.

Twenty descendants of the birds imported by Grandfather were sheltering near the pigsty. They had no liking for the fierce stream, but their resistance was broken by Clare and her boys with sticks and stones. The sty full of grunters was at their back, the flood before. They took the flood.

"They bob up and down like the ships in the poetry," Clare could mimic them exactly. Her inferiors laughed to see the geese riding so bravely. They could not land on the opposite bank for the castellated rocks of Billy's pulpit. The current rushed them away.

Margaret came out in time to see them in the distance. "Aren't they lovely? We drove them in," cried Della's boy.

Margaret plucked a sucker from the quince tree by the kitchen gate. Clare escaped by diving from the pigsty fence on to a big barrow, which flung her in the mire. The boys received the switch, and pink streaks appeared on fat legs. Daniel howled. Johan, though only five, bolted on to the swaying bridge through water above his middle, and home to his mother. Seeing that he was safely across, Margaret sent a horseman after her property. He followed for twenty miles but not one of the beautiful birds ever returned to Burrabinga, alive or dead.

Josephine was none too pleased to have her darling come bawling home at the risk of being drowned, though she recognized that Margaret must be weary of other people's children in addition to her own.

"If Clare Margaret can lead Johan about by the nose now, you can see how it will be later."

"It might lead to marriage," responded Harry.

The Delacys, themselves without cousins, thought of them as scarcely removed from sisters and brothers, and Danny had instilled into his family a nausea at the idea of marriage between cousins. This maturing danger and the gathering irritations of the ill-defined partnership led Josephine and Harry to consider removal.

CHAPTER XXXIV

WHEN removal was mooted, Grandpa was astounded; more, he was dismayed, grieved. Leave, after Harry and William had sweated to enclose the ranges with leagues of fencing! Forsake the kingdom which he and Johanna had squandered their youth in civilizing; now, when the lonely years were past and roads were making the area accessible! Even Johanna was aghast that Burrabinga should be abandoned by Harry now when it had grown desirable.

Nevertheless the Delacy partnership fell to pieces because of reasons indicated. Harry secured a place in the direction of Cootamundra and he and Josephine were both relieved to go, though regret also seared Harry. He had put more hard labour into the making of Burrabinga than either of his brothers, had spent more years immured in its solitude and had deeper poetic imagination to bind him to it. However, he wanted to be free.

The ordeal of surmounting the passes with infants was direful to Josephine and she was glad to escape. Her ideal was in parts that of her mother-in-law. Though she had spent all her life in the bush, Josephine never loved it. Her hunger was ever for the pavements, for city conveniences, city pleasures. She would have found more satisfaction with a conventional city man of English mind and habits. None had been available so she had accepted a fey Irish bush native, and in thinking she could change him to her mind, was as fatuous as Johanna had been in believing that she could woo the free-thinking Danny to her creed.

Johanna almost keened her lamentations. "He'll never collect a shirt to his back once he leaves his brothers. He's his father over again, only much worse. Danny had no heart to grasp and gather like those who became rich, but he was content to be thrifty. Harry is extravagant. Sure, Josephine, stop it, for the love of God!"

"How can I stop it?" said Josephine, who was aching to be free of the Delacy association, which she abominated. Hibernianism was to her synonymous with vulgarity. Harry would improve when he cast it off. Irish exuberance of expression she abhorred as lying, though Grandfather had never been known to misrepresent, and Harry was almost as foolishly truthful, while Josephine herself lacked tolerance and the judicial mind on which truth is dependent.

When she had Harry under her single influence, he should lead a different life. Burrabinga, as far as she was concerned, would remain literally Bunratty Castle thereafter. Only Johan Darcy wailed all the way to Birrabee. He cried to leave Clare Margaret, and for other causes beyond his understanding. He was a dreamy child and Grandfather's pronouncement that he should have been a "faymale" was apposite.

They remained some days at Keebah bidding good-bye to other neighbours as well as their beloved Urquharts. Then they passed away to a different district, and Johanna's prophecy of indigence was fulfilled over and over again.

Della and Ned Angus also left in the reorganization. Ned went back to Victoria, and his family, with Harry's, dropped from the trunk line of Delacys. Robert, the eldest son, the one Delacy who had been born at Burrabinga, now reigned there alone. Danny retained Bewuck, and William, the confirmed bachelor, remained with him. Hannon had died, and his wife gone elsewhere.

A year after the dissolution, Grandpa reported, "Sure, Robert is bursting into the heavy swell now."

"Why should he be climbing down into a wombat burrow like the rest of the Delacys? Who is more entitled to be a swell than my Robert?"

"As long as he can support it he can become a duke, but surely, Johanna, I can engage in a little descriptive conversation without having me throat jumped down? If I don't tell you the news, you say what use am I as a companion at all."

"Well, what is Robert doing?" inquired William, who never read a book, and derived his mental nutrition from gossip.

"The house is spread all over the place from wan ind to the other. That eldest girl is a treat to see. She is you over again, Johanna."

"She has blue eyes."

"That is an inconsequential detail in the main scheme of character. They also have a lady companion who teaches the little girls music. Bedad, I think the boys are learning the piano, too. They have an old lag living in Harry's kitchen, and he does the gardening. Sure, I thought I'd be eaten up whin I wint to help him."

"I wish ye'd be ate up whin ye pull up me best flowers."

Robert was happy in exercising his talent for organization and hospitality unfettered. He disposed of the sheep with the partnership. Sheep were subject to footrot and fluke, and the dingoes could never be stemmed, but the horse was still in his zenith.

Robert had ringers and fencers all through the hills. The rich river flats of mineral loam that had silted from the hills through centuries were free of timber for grazing paddocks, and some of the heaviest beasts that went to Sydney and Melbourne were fattened there. And the horses! A horse of the Nullah-Mundoey strain won at Randwick. Robert's breakers turned out saddle-horses which became known at all the up-country shows. His personal pre-occupation was a coaching strain of big fellows for Cobb and Co., and light harness ponies.

The animals that Robert bred for tandems and four-in-hands were famous from Melbourne to Brisbane. When Athol Macallister, late in the 'eighties, drove eight horses to show off to Lord Carrington, they had been bred by Robert.

Money came in a stream to Burrabinga, but it went as easily. An absence of skin-flint thrift characterized the *ménage*. Robert had a head on him; so had his wife to advise him, but both were more spenders than hoarders, and those who rise to great estates from small beginnings, are weft into legends of parsimony or tightfisted-ness, or sharp practice of some kind. If Danny had been known as Hungry Delacy instead of as Honest Danny he might have trans-mitted a strain to make his sons financial nabobs. Tales of the Delacys were all on the other side of the ledger. Burrabinga was called a free hotel, and it staggered its descendants to estimate how much could have been invested more profitably than in the unreturned thousands of meals, in the tons of rations distributed in tucker-bags, in horses lent that never returned.

"Sure, it's come-aisy, go-aisy," Grandfather remarked.

"And that is 'good-iron wingey!' till there's a stoppage in the come-easy part," added William.

Johanna hungered for Robert. He, of all her children, gave her the most heart-warming attention. Her sole pleasure, now, was visits from her grandchildren so that she could reward them with presents. Like Danny, she was a giver. She complained of feeling poorly the year that followed the dissolution of partnership.

"Sure, I'm past the allotted span, and that is the ind of the road for most of us. If ye want to see me, Robert, ye must come without waiting too long between whiles."

"The death of poor Maeve and the departure of Jane Hannon have dispirited her," said Danny.

Maeve had passed like a sigh in the chimney corner one daybreak—in the ashes, despite all Johanna's training. They laid her where she had for ever the susurrant lullaby of the Murrumbidgee released from the bunyip hole where her vanished tribe had come to feast on the cod, and later to accept the bullocks given to them as rent.

When Clare was nine, Margaret visited her sister near Bungendore to help with a family event, and Robert decided to take his eldest daughters to his mother, who was always asking for them.

One morning saw him pulling the tails of the four-in-hand to the correct outline. No one could thin a tail more expertly, nor so cleverly escape the lashing hoofs of the irritated animals. Robert enjoyed his family's credit in his mother's eyes, and took pains in staging this event.

Every one was assisting. Wong Foo had ridden in with a pack of gifts. Robert had taken over Wong's allegiance with the departure of Danny. Doogoolook also preferred Burrabinga when it came to settling down. He had a lair at the end of the stables, and, like Maeve, was addicted to the chimney corner, for its company as much as its warmth.

They set off with the usual routine of extra horses and a vassal sent ahead to boil the billy at Danny's spring at the top of the pinch where the top of the morning saw the sun enchant the mists to rainbow veils beneath the travellers. Robert drove with Margaret beside him, and Vida between them. Miss Hassell, the music governess, sat at the back with the two little boys. Clare and Mavis rode horses fit for a pageant. They had exquisite points and showy action, could walk away from normal beasts and cantered pneumatically. Their velvet mouths responded to the children's fingers; their bridle bits gleamed in the sunshine, the children sat with the certainty of monkeys, on hogskin saddles, which were the fashion at the height of the horse age.

These two girls were the joy of Robert's heart, but Grandma never saw them on their beautiful horses.

She lay down one afternoon, complaining of feeling queer. Danny suggested the doctor.

"I wish ye would fetch Father Shannon," said Johanna.

"Nonsense!" exclaimed Danny, a little sharply because he was startled. Johanna said no more.

On the following day she sat in the garden under a climbing rose that she had early planted, and seemed herself again. Later she was so strange that William galloped a swift Nullah-Mundoey to the doctor. Danny reported on his return, that Johanna had been wandering. She had talked of the bunyip, and the banshee, and the keening of the river oaks, and had held a conversation with Kathleen Moyna, though she had scarcely mentioned the little girl during the years that had gone since her tragic death.

She looked at the doctor quietly. "Ye can do nothing for me, doctor. It was Father Shannon I needed."

It was Danny—surprised to see it—who picked up the rosary on the coverlet and handed it to her.

"It does not matter now," she murmured, the nostalgia of life-long exile in her voice. "It is a long time Danny-boy that ye and me have been together. A long time and a long distance away from old Ireland we've wandered in this lost place; but I am going home now. They are all waiting for me—ye'r mother and me own, and Kathleen Moyna. . . . Is that the wind Danny, or is it the oaks crying for ever? What can be their grief, I wonder?"

With that she turned her head, as though weary, and left her old partner all alone with the little elegancies she had so gallantly accumulated—*at the furthest extremity of the globe.*

CHAPTER XXXV

The Delacy men were helpless without women—respectable women. Other grades were unknown to any of them but Robert.

Danny and William were as the abandoned on an island. William recognized that life had stopped until he could bring a woman to Bewuck. Jean Urquhart was reaching the no-man's-land of spinsterhood, and deserved to be rescued. The property that would later be hers was a bait to him, while Danny was overjoyed to have an Urquhart.

William was accepted without quibble after an awkward and prosaic proposal. When he had recovered from his stage fright, he joked about their swimming the Yackandandah together, and recalled the spree enjoyed by Sandy and Danny while he and Jean had been absent. Jean confessed that it was because of his kindness when her arm was broken that she had come to love him and had waited for him. William was contented to hear this.

They took possession of the main bedroom, and Danny moved out to the "ind room", where he was free, henceforth, to be a tobacco or rum "kag", with none to care enough to reprimand him.

The loss of Johanna finally defeated youth in him. Zest of life waned with the realization that he was alone, a supernumerary, that the vision that had led him forward in high-geared courage had eluded him by changing character and position. The beautiful mountain ranges no longer lured him; he grew indifferent to the extension of life through the medium of his children. The source of beauty and inspiration was as far away as ever, farther, and retreating still. His *aisling* was now in the rear; a young man sitting on a furze bank with a high-spirited girl entranced by his tale of the land of opportunity at the far end of the universe.

"Oh, moi, oh, moi!" he would murmur, and croon to himself old songs that he had heard at cabin doors. William said, in his hearing that he was childish, but Danny was not annoyed by that. His sweet temper did not fail him, and scandal and criticism went sick in his presence. He knew that his sons, except, perhaps, Harry, were too childish to attain any but mundane wisdom. Despite his years and wooden leg, he would mount an easy-paced Nullah-Mundoey and call upon those of the old squatters still above ground. Their misdemeanours were forgiven, only their companionship craved now.

"Arrah!" he would cry. "If I meet a man of fifty or sixty, he's only a boy who does not know what I know. He hasn't seen the Murrumbidgee as I first saw it."

The year of Johanna's death, two others of Danny's circle passed—O'Neill and Doogoolook. One of O'Neill's faithful dogs had to be shot before Robert's men could approach the corpse in the hut on Dead Horse Plain. Among the man's belongings was a packet, sealed and sewn in sacking, and addressed to Danny. Robert brought it to his father, who took it to the end room to investigate. Some stray literate had written for O'Neill the request that Mr Delacy, Senior—or in case of his death, Harry or William—should carry out his will.

"You must take me to Sydney," commanded Grandpa.

William said he would go alone, but his father demanded, "Am I to be shamed by a dog, who would not be cajoled from his trust? Shall I fail in a human act put upon me by a lonely soul who depended on me character?"

So he and William found, in a room in a terrace in Surry Hills, one Katherine Magee, who had lain nearly a life-time on her back. Delacy handed her O'Neill's hoard.

"Larry took me up wrong," she muttered. "I was only teasing him a little before giving-in, but he rode his fine horse over me, and ye see before ye the result."

"Wan result," said Danny. "The other was a man dead after fifty bitter years with no companion but a dog."

Doogoolook went in the ashes—like Maeve—the shadow of a shadow departed to rejoin his lost tribe. Clare Margaret staged his funeral. All the flowers from the garden were piled upon his coffin, and the children followed sobbing lustily. There were now two other graves in the enclosure on the hill above where the curlews wailed in the tea-tree. Burrabinga hospitality extended even to wayfarers who came there to die and to return to its clean deep earth.

Others of the early associates deserted Danny. Charles Fullwood had gone. James, husband of Bella Rafferty, remained, retrieved a generation since from cattle duffing, and now living in the old Heulong homestead. Mrs Charles was much with her sister, Mrs Hennessy. Both men's sons were hard-working bushmen. Some of both broods got jobs to fence or horse-break on Burrabinga, which was a refuge for all classes.

William became a father without losing his bachelor aridity. Jean was easy-going and kind. Johanna's standards of house-keeping were abrogated, but no word of criticism escaped Danny. Jean did not heel him from one retreat to another as a demonstration of her abilities, and he appreciated peace.

The children grew and murdered Johanna's garden. Grandpa saw the elegancies which his Johanna had earned so valiantly and treasured so tenaciously being spoiled and hacked. He was so wise that these things meant little to him now. He sat where the sun could warm him, and the Murrumbidgee gorges would disappear, and in their place would materialize the young Johanna and his mother and others, each detail of their environment in Ennis in old County Clare, as clear as though a spotlight rested upon it: Athlunkard Street out of Limerick, the ruined Abbey of Donough Cairbreach O'Brien, the Austin Priory, founded by the last King of Munster, where Danny had played as a boy. Ah, those roads to Crusheen and Kilrush! "Oh, moi! Oh, moi!"

William's interest in gossip shifted base as he became a family man. He had some of Johanna's pride, and looked forward to good matches for his nieces and nephews, with whom he kept in affectionate association. He was pleased with the Butlers, who were firmly in the stirrups of the highest squattocracy. Cooley Butler, of New Glenties, was one of the best set-up young men in the district, and the desire of all the girls of his circle.

Another interest to William was the Nullah-Mundoey stud. He did a little breeding and could still sit a buck-lepp, though he was like Danny in his lack of horse swagger. He neither betted nor raced. He had improved the Nullah-Mundoey stock and was always hoping for the perfect beast by a process dependent upon knowledge and selection, equine heredity and a sixth sense; and then when everything had been attended to, a fluke, as with the appearance of a great diva or a major batsman. The horse artist, as every other, is never satisfied. Still, William had the usual share of luck, and his picked colts and fillies were worth a lot of money.

He received a plea from Cooley Butler, in the 'nineties, a few years after the bank-breaking crisis, when pastoralists were beginning to return to normality. The Butlers, in continuance of early custom, were the hosts for a picnic race meeting on Boxing Day. On this occasion several good horses were coming, and Cooley wanted Uncle William to lend him a Nullah-Mundoey to knock the stuffing out of rivals.

"By damn!" said Grandpa. "Lend him the brown colt. The Vances nor anny wan else can't produce a beast to get within cooee of that wan."

Cooley (written and pronounced Coole for short) followed his letter and was allowed to take the colt back with him. William had an ambition for this nephew. He was to marry Fannie Vance. Old Vance, of Longview, was the rising wool champion of the district, a settler who had the qualities for enlarging fortune so conspicuously absent from the Delacy temperament. His only daughter was now twenty-one, a handsome girl with none of the dubiety of a siren. The Vances hoped she would marry a connection of The Plains— money to money. The Butlers were prosperous, but Fannie should command one even more prosperous than Coole. Fannie and Uncle William, however, saw eye to eye in this. The colt was being lent to Coole to add to his popularity. William had another match in view between Coole's sister, Laura, and Humphrey Vance. This young man was three years older than Fannie and did not squander his resources on any but useful horses, which among sheep, were of the moke variety. Laura was a sturdy girl, like the Butlers, and William felt that she would need some pushing to set sail on the best pond of matrimony. Laura and Humphrey, both big and ungay, would make a fine buggy pair, thought William, fallaciously, seeing that suitability as a pair or anything else, is rarely conducive to marriage.

Aunt Jean decided that she would be more comfortable at home. She could stay alone at Bewuck and keep an eye on the stock as well as the children, while she sped her men's departure.

Grandpa elected to ride to the races. This was opposed as childishness, but the pride of still being a horseman, at nearly eighty-two, and the prospect of meeting the remnants of the early settlers sustained old Nullah-Mundoey.

Shortly after his arrival, Robert appeared. The Burrabingas were spending Christmas with Aunt Nessie, near Bungendore, and Robert had cantered over to the races with Clare Margaret. She was now seventeen, tall and finely developed, a competent eques-trienne, who showed off to perfection the form-following habits of her day, with their absurd jackets with pert little tails weighted with shot. She had Johanna's complexion and features, and the willowy grace of the Delacy men. She was supple and straight as a quince rod, rosy brown, such as her mother had plucked for the impish escapades with mice or geese, and hers was the unusual beauty of the quince blossom. She was merry and witty. In serious mood she had the poise of a woman of twenty-three. Angry she was like a thunderstorm. Old and young livened in her company. Robert was vain as he walked in the wake of the sensation caused by her appearance.

Robert's advent created a stir. His dogs always ensured that. His kangaroo and cattle dogs and dingo-killers were more useful to their master than men, and a menace to every one else. He was usually to be seen about Burrabinga with a pack of pets, some of them pups, receiving their training. Fowls, food, clothing and other articles disappeared with them, but complaints were received by Robert either with satisfaction in the prowess of his champions, or dismissed as false reports.

His marauder, Prince, soon had a pullet. Aunt Honoria squawked as loudly as her bird, and rushed out with a broom. Clare Margaret skimmed to the rescue, seized the big brute by the collar, and with merry disregard of his growls, kicked him spiritedly until he dropped the bird, which was fit only for decapitation. Coole ran to help in chaining Prince and the cousins were immediately friends. Coole asked her to name the Nullah-Mundoey colt.

"Oo! I'd love a sprint on him, then I could choose a suitable name," gurgled Clare Margaret. Coole forthwith carried her saddle to the stall where the embryo champion was housed and they took a gallop in the sweet respite of twilight after a baking day. This was a horse as near perfection as the girl would ever feel under her—big with long elastic stride, intelligent and sweet-tempered, a thorough gentleman. When Clare sprang off him into her cousin's arms she turned and buried her face in the animal's sweet-smelling neck and exclaimed, "Oh, the love, the darling. I wish I could ride him in the race."

"I have his name," cried Coole. "We'll call him Truelove."

Coole went to slip this into the programmes, the top conceit of the occasion. Coole had procured a hand-press on which they were copied—on tawdry pink paper. In the interests of surprise, the press was hidden in Coole's bedroom.

"Lady Grey was so frisky that I'm tired," remarked Clare Margaret. "She stood on her hind legs all the way and shied at her own shadow."

"Flop on the bed and get your wind while I tackle this fakement," said Coole. Reared in the Delacy idea of cousinship, they had no amorous thought, but they were congenial. No one had yet awakened Clare Margaret, and Coole was half in love with Fannie Vance.

Uncle William saw Clare Margaret going into Coole's bedroom. He had known the girl was not safe, as soon as he saw her alight from Lady Grey. The way the young men, and the old ones too, were electrified, was proof of it. None of the women of his family would thus have entered a man's bedroom with him unless the man were invalided. Uncle William strolled past the door. It was closed! With convention to support him, he blundered in, "I thought is was Grandpa's room."

The scurrying to hide the press suggested guilt. "You had better go to your aunt." Uncle reserved the remainder for Coole.

"Lordy, Uncle, she was only helping me with advice."

"What advice could she give worth taking?" But what young man would take the advice of a seed onion when that of a quince blossom was to be had? "If any one saw this there would be a scandal."

"Oh, I say, Uncle, don't draw the long bow. She's only a kiddy."

When Coole next saw Clare Margaret, he remarked, "Whoop, there was a dust-up!"

"I'd like to do something to shock Uncle William properly. He's like a clucking hen."

"The name of the colt will stick in his craw."

"You bet!"

"Don't let him hear you say 'you bet'."

"Let's get Grandpa on our side about the name. He used to help me secretly when I couldn't do sums."

Grandpa had awakened and was being fortified with a nip of rum. Clare had changed into a muslin frock billowing with frills and a sash, and fresh from the iron. She had her hair up, hasting to be adult, and came to Grandpa with a girlish laugh and pinned a rose in his coat. "Grandpa, can you keep a secret?"

The old vision winged to County Clare on a May morning long ago. Here was Johanna, lovely as his youthful and aged dream of her blended.

"Johanna, me brave Johanna!" he murmured. Then half to himself.

"The place is little changed, Mary, the day is bright as then,
The lark's loud song is in my ear, and the corn is green again.
But I miss the soft clasp of your hand, and the breath warm on your cheek,
And I still keep listening to the words you never more may speak,
You never more may speak!"

Tears ran down the old man's cheeks. Clare Margaret was touched. Coole was awed.

"Grandpa, pet, am I like Grandma?"

"Sure, acushla, I thought she had come back again, no less. And be all the poipers, 'tis me old friend Clare Margaret grown into a grand young lady. Sure you should be grand too, seeing you had me brave Johanna as a copy."

To forestall fresh grief, Coole interposed. "Grandfather, the Nullah-Mundoey colt is yours as much as Uncle William's, isn't he?"

"Ne'er a Nullah-Mundoey at all would there have been if I had let them shoot the original. Sure, am I not Nullah-Mundoey meself, honourably named by the blacks? You've reminded me of what I have forgotten for years. . . . Sure, every one is dead but a few inconsequential boys."

"Then we can name the colt for the races?"

"Where could there be a prouder name than Nullah-Mundoey?"

"That's his surname. He must have a Christian name too."

"Sure, he is a Christian. Oh, moi, oh, moi! Then me love, call him something to please yourself, and we'll all be pleased."

"You will be on my side, even if Uncle William doesn't like the name?"

"I'll support you if you call him the Pope or the Dayvil himself."

"And it's a secret, mind!" The girl pranced away.

Grandpa sat on his bed and chuckled. "Begor, it's a secret as far as I'm concerned, for I don't know it. 'Tis safe that way, me little Johanna-over-again. 'And the red was on your lip, Mary, and the lovelight in your eye. *The lovelight in your eye.*' Oh, moi, oh, moi!"

On Boxing Day most of the neighbours and many townspeople assembled on the plain near the homestead, where the races went with zip. Humphrey Vance immediately forsook Laura Butler to squire Clare Margaret. Laura was a childhood's friend, but here was a thrill. Uncle William interfered. Clare had plenty of time, and Humphrey and Laura would be ideal. Clare went away, laughing back at Humphrey. Uncle thought it a wanton laugh, but it was the girl's ordinary chuckle at a male subject, and with such she had been surrounded in all ages and degrees of surrender since she had first arrived at Burrabinga. Inured to the admiration of men, she found no more danger in it than in the company of horses and dogs.

As she twitched her habit about her alluring form, Uncle thought she would look more modest in a dress. She was wearing her habit because she felt unfurnished without a horse, and she was so stylish in bearing that William feared a tendency to be "fast". Horrors, if she should be a menace to the families of Delacy, whose women were all as far above reproach as if embalmed!

The chief event for William was the Nullah-Mundoey's race. The pink programmes were distributed. Uncle, exercising his best conversational graces to impress Mrs Vance, unfolded his. He ran down the names. The colt was not there. He reread. Messrs Daniel and William Delacy were in the owners' column, and Coole Butler was up. This Truelove must be the Nullah-Mundoey. The peerless colt to be insulted by the sick effeminate name of *Truelove!* It was nauseating to Uncle William, who had never experienced any inspiring demonstrations of true love.

He hurried to correct the blunder. Too late. The horses were ramping, while Humphrey Vance waited to drop the handkerchief. The Nullah-Mundoey was causing the trouble. He had a fancy for galloping in the wrong direction. Clare Margaret was among the men, shouting superfluous advice in a voice shrill with excitement, and devilishly unladylike.

The horses were off at last, Truelove in the ruck, but when it dawned on him that the rabble was trying to out-distance him, he reached out and came in some lengths ahead. He was so undistressed that Coole put on Clare Margaret's saddle and let her have a run, himself in attendance.

The day was spoilt for William. The origin of the flash lovesick name for the colt was as evident as a toll bar. The girl was a trouble maker. William went to Robert. Did he wish to see his daughter making a spectacle of herself with a cousin? Robert swore that he knew nothing of the naming of the horse, and was proud of Clare's popularity.

"Your Uncle William is blaming me for the colt's name," he said when he met her.

"Grandpa knows all about it," said Clare.

Old Cameron, of The Plains, had arrived—a ducal honour—and wanted Clare Margaret to mount his horse too.

"If she would only do something there," mused William, "instead of making a mess in her own family." But alas, there was no eligible Cameron, merely a susceptible one.

"Did you know about the name of the Nullah-Mundoey?" inquired William.

"And what is his name?" countered Grandfather.

"Truelove!" snorted William.

"Be the poipers, that's fine!" Grandfather chortled with youthful gusto. " 'Tis easy to see how that was inspired And if it hadn't been, the young min of to-day would have been nullities entirely. That's me granddaughter," he said to Hennessy. "Dayvil if ever I saw a prettier girl. You must drink her health."

No youths in the throes of adolescence were more delighted with each other's company than Grandpa and Hennessy. "Sure, Hennessy, I'm so glad you've come that I could lepp over you."

"And sure, Danny Delacy, I could lepp twice as hoigh as that to see ye, me owld hopping beauty—owld Nullah-Mundoey himself—and his colt to be coming out as Thruelove at this date! God hilp us! The day that was impty as a barn in spring is now furnished for me loike a palace by ye'r prisince."

Hennessy was practically owner of Bandalong, and its perpetual mayor; Delacy the most interesting of its pioneers. The two old men were inseparable. Spread around them were the "improved" properties, the result of sixty years of war against the trees, and far away was the panorama of blue distance to liberate the eye and spirit with a calming foretaste of eternity. The for-everness, the wistful divine for-everness of the massed ranges strung the soul to nobility and to the understanding that eternity was there and then. The old friends leant upon a four-rail fence, after studying its timbers and the craftsmanship, as artists examine picture or book, and smoked with the distance before them while the stewards buzzed with preparations.

"Sure, Hennessy, there's a lot of country there that has scarce been seen and never trod upon yet. All me tigrinizing and dragging, what has it amounted to? I had more than twenty miles square to meself when I went there, and all I'll need now will be six feet by two. A power of people have carried their hides to the tanyard since I struggled through that gap." The sweet cleft prinked the blues of an atmosphere beyond description and awaiting a new school of painters. "And it's you and me for it next, Hennessy."

"Ye'r right, and we're carrying our owld pelts fearless and game."

Clare Margaret galloped up and tweaked Grandpa's beard. "You're a true love of a Grandpa. Uncle William is as scotty as a French hen with her feathers the wrong way. So please say that you called the colt Truelove after me, and I'll say I called him after you, and that will mix them up."

"Sure, they'd be efts if it did, but we'll play hide and seek, if it pleases you, me beauty."

"And if anny wan disbelieves, shure, I'll sthamp on him," added Hennessy, thinking that the girl had her father's dash without his sting. As she curvetted away he said to Danny. "There is wan that to be looking at makes ye think of ye'r youth and the pains and proizes of it. Some there are, Danny Delacy, that ye shake hands with, and others ye take off ye'r hat to and thrimble to contimplate. Oi'm thinking that all the young min will be standing in loine to marry that wan, and they'll have to struggle through the scrub of owld fellies that will feel young again to be looking at her."

"Sure, that is the sort that never picks the best match after all. She's the spit of me brave Johanna, and didn't she pick me."

"Ye must have had ye're points, no less, or she wouldn't have done it."

The Butlers had an overflowing house party and there was dancing in the evening in the biggest rooms. Grandpa was given a bedroom to himself, and he took Hennessy with him for company. Two dormitories were set up for the crowd: at one end of the house the school-room for women, at the other the billiard-smoking-room for men.

Fannie Vance was the belle, in a fussy ball dress, and Coole danced with her often enough to encourage Uncle William. Clare Margaret had to be content with the muslin of the previous evening, but she danced like a sprite and had every one dithering with interest.

"Give her a couple more years and there will be heart-burnings," said the men.

"Her mother ought to look after her, or there will be trouble," said the women, as she danced with Humphrey while Laura Butler looked on. She danced with every one, including Grandpa and Hennessy, and between dances played follow-the-leader with the rowdies of her own age, or charged down the orchard in search of booty—half-child, half-woman, wholly captivating.

William took his mind off her to prance about with Mrs Vance seeking to make a good impression on behalf of Laura and Coole. Around 2 a.m. all the non-dancers grew weary, and began to slip away one by one. Uncle William realized with a start that he had not seen Clare for a long time. He set off on patrol and came upon her in a side garden, where gooseberries were the attraction, though Uncle suspected Coole.

"Is the men's room this end?" he asked, to cover his presence, and pointing over his shoulder, but glancing past his niece to ascertain if Coole were lurking in the shadows of the bushes.

"Yes," called Clare Margaret, on the wing. Uncle William felt that he should wait about to see what mischief she was in, but sleepiness won, and he left her to good luck.

CHAPTER XXXVI

WILLIAM was unofficial steward of the proprieties, and the whole boiling of Delacy women was blameless. Technical chastity was obligatory for all decent women and had to be vouched for by watchdogs of sexual decorum called chaperons. Feminine frailty of mind and physique was sentimentally idealized, and, to complement this faked fruit of chivalry, masculine virility was so emphasized as almost to induce satyriasis. However, all the Delacy men were so civilized that none of those tragedies common to servant maids in the protection of gentlemen's homes had ever disgraced the habitations of the Delacys or of their in-laws: and Uncle William was the most correctly chaste of them all.

He awakened with Clare Margaret on his conscience. As he yawned he was thinking that he should have consigned her to her aunt before retiring. Sissy Vance, adopted sister of Fannie, was already out of bed and surprised to see a formidable black beard other than her foster-father's beside her foster-mother. She was only twelve but the code was embedded in her mind. Surprise ripened to startled astonishment. She was transfixed. So was the bearded one as his wits cleared. That was a big girl putting her naked limbs—they were not legs except to the vulgar—into her drawers! Her long hair was afloat about her shoulders. Sissy emitted an hysterical yelp, "Ma!"—which brought that person to consciousness. Uncle William and Mrs Vance sat up and confronted each other as though the Judgment Day had come and wiped out distinctions. Sissy ran out shrieking, "Ma and Mr Delacy are in bed together!"

The elder women said: "Ssh! Ssh!" too late. Suppression of the scandal was impossible.

"Shure, William must have been very dhrunk, though I did not see him take a dhrop," was Hennessy's comment.

A general summarily degraded at a drumhead court-martial could not have felt worse than William. He fled.

Mrs Vance, sensible, kind, placid, appeared, blushing but valiant, and said, "it was an accident. Poor Mr Delacy is so terribly upset that it would be nice to say no more about it." She had been asleep when William came in, and no light but the dimmest of lanterns on a high mantelpiece. The incident was the funnier because

William was almost a teetotaller. Mr Vance dug Robert in the ribs, "If it had been you, Bob Delacy, it might have been more dangerous!". Robert retorted too gorgeously for print in Australia, and nettled Vance.

"When old Hopping Danny dies the best of the Delacys will be gone," he said, and meant it.

"And when you go the worst of the Vances will be out of sight," returned Robert, throwing his legs about and departing.

The young gathered out of sight to giggle. The elders upheld their dignity by laughing when the young were not by.

The pressure of merriment speedily united both generations in ribald laughter. There was much laughter in the unexpected continent where even the birds chortled in derision and were mimicked by their own kind.

When some wag started a subscription to buy spectacles for Mr W. Delacy, that person demanded a scapegoat, in the person of his niece. He believed that she had purposely misdirected him to spoil the promising state of affairs between Coole and Fannie Vance. He insisted that Clare should apologize to himself and Mrs Vance, and that Robert should remove her from the meeting. He was in such a fantod that Robert had to take notice, though he thought his brother a number of obscene kinds of fool.

Clare was found by her father in her grandfather's bedroom, where she had hidden because her sense of the ridiculous was too immature to surmount the scandal in an affair for which she was blamed. She was furious with Uncle William's stupidity. Robert smothered a smile in his beard as he asked, "Why the deuce did you do it?"

"Uncle William mistook me. I did not do it on purpose."

"I should have been even more amused if you had," said Robert, and decamped with a swagger.

Clare Margaret's humiliation evaporated. Her smiles returned. There were cheers when she appeared on the racecourse.

"She's going to the devil straight," said William to Norah. "Does no one care that a girl with the name of Delacy promises to be looser than Molly Macallister was in her day?"

Norah was too busy to heed. "Tell Grandpa to speak to her. He was always very strict with us."

Danny roared with laughter when Clare Margaret came before him. William rebuked his venerable parent as both drunk and childish.

"Arrah, William, if only you had been a little of each, it would have saved you from being a whole ass-load of fools at wanst," retorted Danny. He had thrown off Grandfather, and become Danny again for an hour.

William walked from him.

"Och, Mavourneen!" exulted Danny, speechless and weeping with mirth. "That this should have happened to your Uncle William, no less. Years ago, it would have been good for what ails him. He's too long in the tooth, now . . . There's a five pound note for a new dress. Go forth, me dear, and pluck the flowers while they bloom. 'And the red was on your lip, Mary, and the lovelight in your eye!' " he murmured, as she sped away. "Och, Hennessy, if I could go home and find Johanna there to tell about this!"

"Shure, women don't look at things the way min do. Would she have seen the rale fun of this!"

"Maybe she wouldn't, but 'twould have been a satisfaction to tell her all the same."

They went and leaned over the fence again, with its sound grey rails, moss-patterned, of uniform length, well-shouldered into perfect mortice holes in stout posts sunk unshakably in the earth—a sample of the early fences set in undeviating lines, up over ridges and down into gullies, mile on mile, on mile. Danny, as ever, was tranced with that view wreathed in speaking silence and translucent light.

"Such a botheration! Sure, me son couldn't make more to-do if he was the Pope and found himself in bed with Queen Victoria. Have we the morals of the kennel, that we take this in such a way? There hasn't been another such hullabaloo since Sandy Urquhart danced in a hundred fresh eggs."

" 'Twould have been better had they been rotten."

"Maybe . . . Sure, Hennessy, me son William is always saying I'm childish. 'Tis himself that is not childish enough to permit anny wisdom . . . Sure, life is curious. Did we ever think we would ind up together looking over the fince here into—into—why, by damn, into eternity, Hennessy?"

"Begob we didn't, and with thim what wanst took dark glasses to protect the ois from their effulgence now so faded and shrivelled that a telescope is called for to discern thim at all."

"By that token, how is your wife?"

"She loikes more and more to get away to Sydney. Sure, Oi'd pinsion her and her sister, only for the look of it."

"Sure, Hennessy, now, on the last lap, it is never me generosities that I have regretted."

"No man could have less regret than ye."

"I've manny a regret to nag at me now that I don't sleep so

sound in the nights, whin I can hear the river like a wind, and the oaks for ever crying, as me wife said, with some unknown grief. There may be truth in the ancient fables that turned women into trees."

"In the name of wonder, Danny, ye, with a cleaner sheet than manny setting up to be holy."

"Och, me wife, at the end, craved a priest, and I did not bring him. It worries me for ever, Hennessy. It was meself was the bigot, for what harm could a damned old parrot—of anny denomination whatever—do, trying to interpose between a soul and its Maker? And 'twould have comforted me brave Johanna."

"Forget it, Danny Delacy. Thim fellies nevir took any throuble to support me whin I needed thim desperately. Now, they can follow after thim that can't see through thim."

"You were always an intelligent man, Hennessy."

Clare Margaret withdrew from her Grandfather, overcome with conflicting emotions due to her age and temperament. Humphrey sought her, and found her alone in a buggy. He elicited that everything was hateful, Uncle William the most hateful of all, and that she was ashamed to look Humphrey's mother in the face; only Grandpa was a dear.

Humphrey was an easy victim of feminine tears. Something had to be done to cheer Clare Margaret, who was talking of leaving to escape her notoriety. Hang the races! Humphrey suggested a spin in his new sulky ostentatiously silver-plated.

They were soon speeding towards the Township, where Mount Bowning stood like a blue dome on the horizon. The highway, undulating across the plains, whose ivory contours were dotted with contented live stock and birds, had known the early explorers. The ringing hoofs, the wheels crunching the fine gravel took them six or seven miles into that fair view, before Humphrey remembered that luncheon would be on, and that he had made matters worse for Clare Margaret.

"We'll take the track behind the wool-shed, and you can slip into the house and come from there later."

"Why?" demanded Clare Margaret.

"You're a grown-up young lady now, and should not be leading me astray."

Dimples beautified her cheeks. "I'd love to shock them. If Uncle William says anything, you must stand by me."

"I'll do that to the finish and back again," said Humphrey, elated to rollick into the picnic with the prize girl in his sulky, and the high-stepping trotter under it.

Again Clare Margaret eclipsed the races. Uncle William came at her as she went to the house to tidy her hair. "If your father hasn't the sense to keep you in order, you are old enough to understand things for yourself."

"Yes, Uncle," she said demurely.

"Then why did you, on top of the other ugly thing, go driving off in that flash way with young Vance?"

"He wanted a chance to propose without you all listening."

"Propose! . . . You are not old enough."

"Humphrey wouldn't mind waiting for—for his *true love!*"

"I'll speak to Humphrey."

Before she could warn Humphrey of the joke, he and Uncle had moved aside together. "You shouldn't have taken Clare for such a conspicuous drive. She is so flighty that she says you needed a chance to propose."

"Surely she did not say that?"

"It shows how rattle-pated she is, but she is only a child, and I want you to say nothing about it and be careful with her."

"You can trust her never to come to any harm with me."

"She was just poking fun at me again."

"More likely at me."

"She is very young."

"If a fellow didn't get in early with Clare Margaret, he might not stand much chance."

"Then I'll say no more now. She is so taking that she had better be married early. This is a pleasant surprise."

"Yes, indeed," agreed Humphrey.

William reflected that he would have to select someone else for Laura, but it would be a relief to have Clare tied up out of mischief with such a steady young man.

Humphrey, smiling fatuously and thrilled to the core, hurried to find Clare Margaret, but she had fled the field, as disconcerted as Uncle William had been earlier.

"Clare Margaret!" Humphrey repeated to himself. "Clare Margaret, you little pet! You must mean it. Clare Margaret Vance. *Mrs Humphrey Vance!*"

When he descried his love she was coming from the house with a young man who was leading a hard-ridden horse in poor condition. Her embarrassments of the last twenty-four hours were all forgotten.

"Humphrey!" she called, with beaming face. "See who has come all the way from Cootamundra to see me."

"And Grandfather," added the traveller. Humphrey was relieved by his youth. Not a suspicion of down on the lad's lip! He was made known as Johan Darcy Delacy, son of Harry, who had left Burrabinga at the dissolution of the partnership.

"His name is Johan, after Grandma, because she went mad with joy because he was not a girl like me. As Grandma is dead and her feelings can't be hurt, I'm going to call him Darcy. Don't you think it the prettiest name you ever heard?"

"Rather girlish."

"It's ever so stylish, like a book."

"But we're not in a book."

"Darcy! I can't help saying it."

"I like Clare Margaret."

"A silly name—as long as a wet week."

"What about Humphrey?"

"Too much like Humbug," said she, with a twinkle ripe for her years.

"It's you who should have it then. How do you like the sound of Mrs Humphrey?" This an aside.

"I'm deaf," she laughed. "Come on, every one is dying with curiosity about Darcy. We must find Grandpa."

Humphrey walked on one side of her, Darcy on the other, leading his intrepid beast. Grandpa was found. "Oh, moi, oh, moi!" he exclaimed. "Sure I'm glad to see you, me boy. You've grown like a gum tree. What age are you now?"

"Going on for fifteen," said Johan—now become Darcy—which meant that he was just fourteen.

"You look eighteen." Grandfather had said the right thing, and Darcy thought him a "real nice old clip".

"He's three years, all but a week, younger than I am," said Clare Margaret. She introduced him possessively, and he was welcomed like a hero.

"You've come to stay with us?" said Aunt Norah and Uncle Stewart.

"You must stay at Bewuck," said Uncle William.

"You are coming home with me to Burrabinga," was Uncle Robert's interpolation in his grand-seignorial manner.

Clare Margaret answered for him, "Of course he is."

Darcy was impressed by Uncle Robert, his leggings and spurs, his tall striking carriage, his condescending air, his enviable dogs.

"By damn! He should have been a faymale!" observed Grandpa to Hennessy. "The eyes of him like an owl, with the lashes like the reeds around a pool, and the gentle expression,"

"Shure, only that ye had a beard loike a billy goat from the first minute I beheld ye, this youngster remoinds me of ye."

Darcy was both Danny and Harry on their imaginative side, with a plus of his own, and he was homing to his own place and people after exile. He looked towards the wreathed blue ranges that lay as a glory on the day, and was impatient to complete his journey. Only the presence of Clare Margaret enticed him to delay. The day, the occasion, were enchanted for him; all that he had expected, could he but return to that delectable region. His horse, Deerfoot, had a reception matching her rider's. She, too, was a relative. She was by a famous polo pony, and mothered by an old Nullah-Mundoey that Harry had taken away with him, a tireless beast as free from vice as an unborn child. Her daughter was the delight of the boy's heart. There had been prolonged drought in his part of the country, with awful losses in stock. Every rib could be counted in his filly, but this could not rob her of beauty; the points were hers. She was lined with sweat, showing her weakness, but she had done the eighty miles to Bewuck in a long day. Darcy had arrived late on the previous evening. His Aunt Jean had tried to detain him. Failing that, she had offered him a fresh horse, but no, he set off again next forenoon on Deerfoot.

"She's a clinker," said Uncle William, "but it doesn't do to break their hearts at that age."

"I'll coddle her up a bit," said Coole cordially.

Clare went with them. "I want to show you Lady Grey and Truelove."

"Clare Margaret," called Grandpa after her. "You go get me the Nullah-Mundoey mare. Johan can have her to ride while his own spells. I'll go home in the buggy. I feel a little stiff." A wave of sadness, of relinquishment, bathed the old man as he looked towards the hills, that had so long bewitched him, and realized that he would never ride thither again with the wide sunlight casting its spell all day until he came at evening to the valley he had tried to tame.

"Remember the day we ran the geese into the river?" Clare was heard to ask young Delacy, as they went away with the filly.

The field of Venus was left to Fannie, Laura, and the other grown-up young ladies. Clare Margaret reappeared with her hair in a plait, and a manner in keeping. She had returned to childhood with her old playmate. Humphrey found the boy a nuisance, but hoped that he would guard the girl from others as well as himself. Even Uncle William saw no danger in so young a cousin. Humphrey noted the boy's mended bridle, and gave him a prize on the score that had the filly been in condition, she would have won more than a bridle. "Your old bridle will do one of my men for poking about . . . I want you to take care of Clare Margaret. You are an older friend of hers than I am." Darcy thought Humphrey one of the nicest men he had ever met.

Aunt Norah gave the boy a sovereign for his birthday, "Just as if you had been here for it."

There were other presents. Darcy had not dreamed of such riches. A letter to his sister Isabel, reflecting his delight in his reception and the events, was a masterpiece for a boy in the midst of an active campaign. Every one was described in character as well as person. The judgments, glowing and youthful, but discerning, were a revelation when long afterwards the letter came out of hiding.

CHAPTER XXXVII

DARCY was not to be diverted from Burrabinga. His visit among the affectionate Bandalong relatives was merely the prelude to his homing. Uncle Robert agreed that Deerfoot needed a spell before tackling the mountains. "Supposing I leave Clare Margaret to show you the way," he said.

"That would be spiffing," interposed Clare Margaret. "Then we can stay with every one who invites Darcy."

"Can I trust you never to take your eye off her?" Uncle Robert's smile escaped from his beard, but Darcy was serious.

"It wasn't necessary to say that," said Aunt Norah later; "he follows her like a spaniel."

"Good job he's so much younger, or there might be a case of cousins," remarked Uncle William, and every one laughed.

Darcy rode Grandpa's Nullah-Mundoey to Bewuck. Coole drove Grandpa in the Butler sociable. Uncle William led the colt with the disgraceful name. Clare Margaret and Darcy careered ahead on their perfect saddle hacks.

Uncle Stewart put another sovereign in Darcy's pocket. Aunt Jean gave him new boots. Hennessy pressed him to stay, an invitation which delighted Clare Margaret. She and Euphemia were warm friends. Clare admired her elder's luxuriousness. Darcy was uneasy about all the gifts. He murmured something about paying back by and by, which made every one smile. He was a true Delacy, for they never could take. Give. Give. They needed no exhortation to give to the poor. They gave indiscriminately to rich and poor the fortune which could have been theirs had avarice walked with industry in their pioneering epic.

Gerald and Mrs (Grace Fullwood) Butler took the young people to their home. Mrs Butler said, laughingly, "When I was like you, Clare Margaret, your father used to ride about with me as Darcy is doing with you now." Thus was an old incident translated—at least for publication.

Darcy's coming created an interest out of proportion to his worldly prospects, but his satisfaction in the people and places was that of a child in fairyland and cheered every one. Though manly of physique and bearing for his age, there was nevertheless some illumination of spirit, a gentleness which made Grandpa call him Johanna right out, to the amusement of William, who had no delicacy in dismissing Grandpa as childish.

"Childish, by damn," said Grandpa, imperturbably. "It's you who's too childish to see what's there. Sure, the boy should have been a faymale; then the visions that are in him would not get so much in his way when he has to drag about after money."

"What are you going to do? You should study for a barrister," was said to him, but Darcy was proud of the certificate, which at thirteen had entitled him to escape from the little bush school to begin life on the plane of a man.

He and Grandpa enjoyed each other. The old man took him over every paddock of Bewuck and told its history and grew voluble about the bunyip hole and Delacy's Crossing Darcy adored the sighing she-oaks. Mounted on the Nullah-Mundoey of rocking-chair paces, Grandpa rode up on to the plateau to explain the landscape.

"Oh, moi, oh, moi!" he cried, suffused with emotion as he beheld that holy of holies, that chapel of his soul, as remote and witching as when he first beheld it. His eyes glazed with memories. They could see so far and so much—the roads leading to Limerick, and to the Atlantic beyond Cooley Hall on a May day when a beautiful girl awaited Danny Delacy in the coomb; the long, lone trails that he had blazed, extending to eternity, and foreshortened until Ennis and Burrabinga coalesced. To his inner consciousness, the scene was glamorous and haunting, plangent with silent voices of past and present—future or past—which was which, in the bewildering circles of time and space? He could only repeat, "Oh, moi, oh, moi!" The boy must grow to it himself.

The lad gazed, his dreams coloured by youth. He listened rapt to the story of Burrabinga being tamed, and without murdering the blacks. How Grandpa came by his wooden leg, and how he swam the Yackandandah in 'fifty-two, were grand yarns. Darcy wanted so many others that Aunt Jean gave Grandpa a toddy of rum when he came in, he looked so white and old and illuminated. The alcohol loosened his tongue again so that he tried to explain to Darcy that in the aura of Australia were a thousand mysteries awaiting those with grace of understanding, but that most human beings were inferior in insight to the quadrupeds. "Be the poipers, the lad's meself over again. He has the vision of posterity in his eyes."

Uncle William rapped out, "Posterity, be damned! He seems

just like Harry, a damned fool that will never know a shirt to
his back."

"Sure, there'll be somewan always to see that he has a shirt."

"Leave Grandpa alone," said Aunt Jean, and promised him a
second toddy if he would go to bed.

Glad of the excuse to see Clare Margaret, Humphrey Vance
brought Deerfoot at the end of a week. The filly's condition was
a certificate of special care. Humphrey was frank about his predilection for the girl, but agreed with William that it might be
unwise to force her emotions for another year.

At the end of January, Margaret called Clare Margaret home.
Grandpa confirmed the gift of the Nullah-Mundoey to Johan, and
added a ten pound note. He was giving practically his all. Care was
exercised that he should not have too much to "strew around".

Clare Margaret pooh-poohed Uncle William's suggestion of accompanying her, so he showed the short cut through Old Glenties, by
which Keebah could be reached the first day, and thence to Birrabee
and Burrabinga in old-fashioned stages. No prince had more poetic
exaltation in regaining a kingdom than Darcy upon returning to
this region.

His relatives gave him a warm welcome. An extra bed was placed
in the boys' room, an informal apartment where the cracks were
stopped with strips of tin. The slabs were whitewashed, the ceiling
was of calico. The possums often came in at night. The floor, also
of slabs, was softened with splendid skins. The bedsteads were of
rough wood. There was a shelf on pegs, and a stool or two to complete the furnishing. There was not even a mirror.

After the qualities of his mother's house-keeping, Darcy was a
little shocked, but to one who had never been called a pet name,
the atmosphere of this family, with the careless freedom and livelier
life, was exciting. Clare Margaret and Mavis were his elders; Syme,
Vida and Roger followed. What Clare Margaret decreed was law.
Darcy became a leader in enterprises demanding imagination.

The younger ones were still slaves to the school-room for the
greater part of the day. After that, there was a young lady to instruct
in piano, sewing, fancy work and dancing at a wage of £13 per
annum, plus unrivalled opportunities for marriage.

Josephine wrote at the end of a month calling Darcy home, but
he asked to stay a month longer, and then another month. He then
pleaded to see the snow, which covered the ranges in the months
of July and August. When the snow came, the rivers were swollen
and prevented his getting out for weeks.

There was a dreadful drought all down the Bland. A springless spring gruelled Murrumbong, with not a blade of grass in the locality, and all but eight of Harry's horned cattle died. Life could barely be kept in his horses. Half a dozen faithful friends lay down under the brassy skies and breathed their last. Harry was mortgaged to the limit, and in debt everywhere. Josephine kept the house going by rearing fowls and selling eggs. There were three other children besides Darcy, but Grandma Battle always had one of them.

In the circumstances, Darcy was allowed to linger at Burrabinga, though not without misgivings on Josephine's part, one of them because Robert derided teetotalism. He boasted that his sons should grow up to be men of the world, who could take a drink and meet other emergencies like real men, and not like girls in pants. Chief and Chieftainess were little for precepts of correction. The children learned by imitation, and grew to be resourceful and so lavishly hospitable, that, in a predatory society, they must eventually beggar themselves.

But those fell days were not yet.

The Burrabinga youngsters were enjoying a life of experiment, which filled Josephine with another apprehension in regard to her beautiful boy, than whom she would have preferred to see all her other children dead in one sweep. In Darcy's letters to Isabel, which Josephine had fished from the girl's secret cubby, there recurred the swear-word *damn*. Josephine never went farther than d— in indicating such an oath. Harry was not allowed the relief of it in her hearing. "A foul mouth indicates a foul mind," she observed, firm in her understanding of what was purity.

Margaret did not read her children's letters unless requested to do so, and at that date the Burrabingas were effervescing in the adolescent swagger of oaths tacked on to their speech for ornament, while their parents remained unaware of their reputation as "foul-mouthed young rips". They were merely in advance of the fashion in smart expletives.

As the terrible seasons at Cootamundra did not mend, Darcy was allowed to linger indefinitely at Burrabinga. Harry could not send him a penny. It did not occur to Robert to give wages to one so young, though he acknowledged that the lad was as useful as a man. He had his own horses and gear, and a few pounds in his pocket to begin, which quickly went into the young people's common store. Darcy was not a hoarder. He made something from the price on dingo pelts and the sale of possum skins, and for the remainder was in love with living and ambitious to become as good a rider as his associates. He was that from the beginning, but they jeered at him for a townie because they knew the way down a few precipices which at first made Darcy pause.

Life was a tournament and a picnic, spent largely in the saddle. If Robert was harassed by the Bank overdrafts and the mortgages, which piled up during lean years, he did not pass his worries on to the young, beyond developing his gift for sarcastic comment. He was a silent man, and indeed, when had he opportunity to talk? During meals he looked down a table which held twenty eaters, and where the minimum was ten. All had to be served before he could take a bite, and third helpings were common at that generous table. Talk was for those with leisure.

Great days for Burrabinga, to be remembered with regret and affection!

Darcy and his cousins were growing up.

Robert caught his son Syme in the kitchen trying to kiss Mimie, one of the successors to Fannie, who had long since married and retired to a selection beyond James and Bella Fullwood at Cherry Tree Hill. Robert recalled Molly McCathie and the hotel girls to whom he owed similar education, and said that girls in the kitchen would be a constant menace. A Chinese cook was substituted, a man who did wonders in the garden and laundry, in addition to the kitchen. Lady-helps were engaged for the house.

It was the day of the lady-help by whom the housewives were saved from a shortage in household drudges. As a sign of the times numbers of young women had the need or the desire to escape from their mothers' homes. Some went as governesses. Those not smart at their lessons—none had any education—served at lady-helps. They found domestic tasks in other women's houses more endurable than in their mothers' so long as they were not menialized. Housewives could offer £13 or £20 per annum with aplomb, where before they had had to give female servants more than £26 as a minimum. Then lady-helps, as equals, could be expected like daughters to keep on until all hours, but unlike daughters they had the adventure of flirting with the sons of the house as well as others—adventure and openings in the career of matrimony. Their mistresses were freed from the moral care which had to be extended to menial females. Social equals were not so preyed upon by those of exaggerated virility as were the girls on the lower social rung.

Time drifted along in the remote station life, idyllic and sufficing. Neither Darcy nor his cousins went as far as Sydney. There were thousands in the same untravelled condition. Out in the world of the capitals women like Catherine Spence, Ladies Jersey and Windeyer, Rose Scott and Annette Bear-Crawford, with Vida

Goldstein as the young and lovely subaltern of the regiment, were leading women towards political enfranchisement. They provided a popular subject for caricaturists, one well within the grasp of all, from the city slums to the Never Never, and there was no fear that revolution would grow from a demand so amusingly in opposition to what Nature had decreed for the feminine brain.

A more tangible revolution, and which was to end the supremacy of the horse, was vested in the bicycle. The "penny farthing" velocipede had been superseded by well-proportioned pairs of wheels, which multiplied like mushrooms. The bicycle became the instrument of sport. Bicycles were the rage. Bullet-headed varlets, with all their power in their thighs, pedalled like demons around banked tracks and were the heroes of envious crowds of congenial mentality.

The bicycle became a bike and an epidemic. The craze infected women, who went a-wheel amid shrieks of disapproval and prognostications that the race would be endangered by such unsexing of potential mothers. The bar on the bicycle was let down so that women could cycle without freeing their torsos from steel slats, or their legs from several skirts flapping to the soles of their shoes. Thus was convention confused with Nature's differentiation, and "womanliness" preserved. Nevertheless popular journalists frothed about complexions being spoiled, skins wrinkled and expressions becoming hard under the strain of cycling so that feminine appeal to men would disappear; but men, as ever, accepted the girls available in their decades, regardless of the vagaries of fashion, and without establishing a reputation for sexual abstinence.

There was lively intervisiting with other stations. Uncle William would rave from one visit until the next at what he observed. "Harry, of course, is a born fool. He would give away what he had not got, but Robert was supposed to have a head on him, but is it sense to work as hard as he does and then squander it all in keeping a private pub for every loafer than comes along?"

"It's as bad at Keebah," said Jean placidly. "I was tired of always slaving for callers."

"Sure, wasn't I always telling you that everything is as free of charge as if it was this Utopia the agitators talk about." This from Grandpa.

"Ah, but that was poverty camp compared with what it is with all the youngsters grown up and acting independently."

"Keebah has become nothing but a half-way house for those hurrying on to take up residence at Burrabinga," added Jean.

"The Governor's aide-de-camp was there, and two lady-helps, and the old tutor who looks after the post office, and a Chinese cook. The fellow from Government House is one of those flash dolls out from England who must have olives to eat. So one of the girls ordered a whole case by mail—cost pounds. Did you ever try olives?—not fit for pigs—I spat them out. They are going mouldy because some pup wanted two or three, and if they met him in Sydney, he would look the other side of the street."

"Snobbery!" interpolated Grandpa.

"It will give the girls a chance to make good matches," suggested Jean.

"More likely to give those lady-helps the chances. Robert's girls will pick up some useless crawler in the end. . . . They are too swell to make their own candles now. That Syme—as flash a young black-guard as ever was foaled—took a whole sperm candle from the piano and melted it between the logs until the blaze started. Too lazy to get stringy-bark or even to throw a log on in time. And tools or a new saddle are dropped where they are used. Like the blacks!"

"Queen Victoria couldn't afford that," said Jean. "I've been told from Keebah, that they all, from Margaret down, put on a new dress and wear it regularly instead of keeping it for Sundays."

"They have orchards enough to supply the Township, but I saw a dray load of tinned jam going in. There were three leading doctors there being run after like gods—there for pheasant and kangaroo shooting—and if Robert got a belly-ache in Sydney, they wouldn't take a bob off the fees."

"Such extravagant habits are shocking—shocking!"

"Arrah!" said Grandpa contemplatively, removing his pipe for emphasis. "It's difficult to do annything with children after they get out of arms. Didn't I elope against me parents? And did Robert ever perform wan thing that his mother had laid out for him? And now, maybe, Robert can do nothing with his family."

"Bosh! You are childish! I shall never let my children have these extravagant notions."

"Huh, be the poipers! Robert and his family have the pleasure of squandering in company. You may drag yours up like a lot of gomerils in moleskins, and before you are cold in your grave, William, me brave warrior, they may have started to scatter what you leave."

"You're childish!" grunted William.

"That boot is on your own foot," retorted the old man with humorous good temper. "You are too narrow-minded to observe the facts of life, and when you are bowled out you call me childish."

CHAPTER XXXVIII

BICYCLES caused no uneasiness at Burrabinga. The precipices were against them. A few far-seeing horse breeders were alarmed, but the parrotry, clacking that no new invention can influence the existing order, remained undisturbed. People who rode bicycles were graded as flash townies. Squatters and selectors had a feeling of wholesome superiority over the town-dweller as a parasite. The male townie was on a lower grade of manliness generally; his female was suspect in virtue and home-making ability. In the incipient Australian nation the parasite had not then become as a whole more important than the person who supported him.

The system of profiteering and business rationalization, under which every man finally naïvely expected to live by usury at the expense of his brother, had not yet induced world paralysis of trade, nor so universally grafted the artificial fruit of poverty on to the tree of plenty. The regulations of trades-unionism were still being resisted as anarchy by those subscribing to the doctrine that slave labour is imperative to maintain a prosperous state. A world strike of workers for the limitation of the hours of the working day with an increase in wages was extreme among postulates for reform. Recurrent minor strikes in various trades—shearers, dock labourers, building workers, or workers in manufactories—were the nightmare of employers.

Banking cycles moved in irregular but inevitable tides. Hard times came, but there remained enough slack in the manipulation of world resources for them to pass. The Colonies, with plenty of elbow room for mistakes, had recovered from the panic of 'ninety-three, and the Empire was drifting towards eruption in South Africa. Spectacular imperialists glittered there. In huts or in smoking-rooms from Burrabinga to Brisbane and Ballarat men read of the parties given in Mayfair. The newly-arrived remittance fraternity were as popular and as ribald as Scheherazade with tales of noble ladies as mistresses of charm and of Princes of the Blood— lovely females decked like Arabian nights by the South African millionaires. Diamonds bribed the ladies who were the link to association with certain Royalties.

'Strewth, they were appetizing reports!

Men, so red blooded that unless tanned to the colour of shoe leather they looked like trussed beef, swore bullockies' and squatters' oaths—in which there is no difference—as to what they would do if any prince, king or "Gawd-Almighty Himself" tried to have the loan of their wives. They felt themselves superior to the effete fellows in London Society, but the ladies protected their complexions, and dreamed of going Home to be presented at Court, to appear at the opera at Covent Garden, and at the Derby, and of having illustrious and clandestine lovers. Either royal or diamond swells would have been equally satisfactory. Many went, but few had courtesan luck.

The "moind" plays tricks with perspective, and London was near to Sydney and Melbourne, while Australia remained a terrific and uncouth distance from England.

All this scarcely touched the Delacys, except in the enjoyment of salacious stories. They had no hankerings for England. Danny and Johanna had not transferred to them any desire to be, nor any sense of being other than Australians. At that time, too, young Australians awakened to a sense of nationality which is inevitably fostered by poets. Native balladists were interpreting Australia's magic in an inspiring and satisfying form. Rhymed stories and challenges were recited in every school or Church, concert hall, drawing-room, hut or camp.

For Australia was a vital slogan.

Then war with the Boers was definitely proclaimed. Australians were wild to go. Here was a congenial adventure for those whose lives approximated a cavalry campaign since ever they could sit up and say "gee-gee", a word as early in their vocabulary as "dadda". There was some talk of the foolish waste of money involved in sending men all the way from Australia when the mighty General Buller and his forty thousand men—the undefeatable English cavalry and infantry—would have Johnny Boer back in his place before the Australian contingent could land in Africa.

Still, the gesture must be made. One people! One flag! Britons never will be slaves! There is life in the old bull-dog yet! The British Lion cannot have his tail tweaked without the Kangaroo giving the tweaker whatfor!

Chamberlain would accept only a handful of colonials, and seemed to think they would be a nuisance. The rush to get away was so great that men were selected as carefully as offerings to the gods—which indeed they were.

It was splendid for horse-breeders. Men came through the land offering good prices for military horses. Burrabinga rejoiced. The still-dominant horse was refurbished with cavalry swagger.

Grandpa was disturbed by the prospects of war, he who had been born in the year of Waterloo, and had heard the drums all through his childhood. He did not feel so lightly about the outbreak as did the young fellows reared on a continent too distant for war to reach. He knew the wreckage and poverty inseparable from military glory.

He had not been on a horse for more than a year, but he insisted upon a visit to Butler at Old Glenties. The old man was valiant, mounting a little stool to a chair and thence to an old nag's back. His grey beard was long on his chest, his exquisitely fashioned hands, frail with age, were small as a girl's upon the reins. Sophie, William's eldest, went with him to open gates.

"What does the war matter to him?" said William as they went. "I'll get a better price for those horses." William had never fathomed the man who was his father, had early regarded him as a fool, but despite a wooden leg, old Danny, in the neat suit and bowler hat, bought long ago to impress his Johanna, had dignity and distinction. He could be recognized as a man with culture behind him—a personality, whereas William remained an honest, uninspired bushman to whom all flights of imagination were insanity.

"The poor old man wants a yarn," said Jean. "He is lonely with all his mates gone."

The visit was disappointing. Butler never had had any mind beyond his own runs, and had prospered on sheep. The reviving effects of war were not so readily apparent among the jumbucks. Butler was for smashing the Boers without argument—low ruffians that they were. Delacy had looked forward to discussing the Boer's side of the fracas, where lay his sympathies. After a few nobblers on both sides, he grew so noisy and was so trounced by Butler that Sophie was excited by the scandal she would have to report.

Mrs Gerald Butler—Grace Fullwood that was—lived with her father-in-law since the death of Grandma Butler. She intervened at length. "He is sorry for the Boers, and so am I. Why should any one want to tear off there and interfere with foreigners—in their own country? They might get shot themselves, too. They would be safer at home minding their own business."

This snuffed the wrangle. Butler was above arguing with females, who invariably raised some trivial point outside the subject at issue.

The nag's aged action jarred the rider, who was in pain from fatigue and bruising when he returned to Bewuck. William had to undress him and put him to bed, and he gave the old man an unfeeling lecture for thinking he could ride at his age. Old Danny could retreat beyond his son's animadversions, not merely forgiving but free from the rancour which needs the purge of forgiveness. He was a week recovering, and then complained anew of loneliness. Women were gabbletraps. He ached for an intelligent political discussion of the war, or a yarn on horse-breeding with an old mate. He asked Sophie, who was precocious with her lessons, to write to Sandy Urquhart inviting him to come down for a good conversation.

"Nonsense!" said William. "The war is of no interest to any one."

"But a little conversation. . . ."

"Conversation! Blather! It won't pay the taxes for any one but the publicans, who set a trap of conversation for the windbags."

Grandpa refuged in the store-house of memory—those days when the larks sang loud and high. One of the children fell over Grandpa's foot and howled. To divert him Grandpa sang, "I'm Denny Blake from County Clare."

No one would analyse the implications of the war though it speedily became more personal to the Delacys than a horse fair. Syme Delacy and Jimmy Fullwood joined the Light Horse and let the mustering go to attend drill and go on cross-country cavalry picnics.

Uncle William chuckled with relief. "It would be grand if the war would last until Syme got there."

"I think of his mother," said Jean.

"So do I. She'll have something worse to face than a hero killed at the war if that fellow hangs around town much longer. If he got out of Burrabinga he would be fit for nothing but horse-breaking; he has an evil tongue; he'd be good enough to shoot Boers."

Syme had his father's gift of satiric repartee, and no discretion in employing it. He was the *bête noire* of his uncle, who could not discern the charm he had for women, and who considered him a flash jackass with no more brains that a turtle. He was however a smart horseman, with more than his father's swagger at the same age. His uncle had observed him in Bandalong where he was led by Jimmy, one of Bella Rafferty's sons, and where though so young, Syme was to be seen pursuing a vital part of his education with servant girls in embrasures at midnight. William knew that if he spoke to Margaret she would take to hysterics and Robert would tell him to put on Mrs Grundy's drawers. William, in avuncular anxiety, grizzled to Grandpa.

"Moi, oh, moi!" he commented. "I was given no instructions, and Robert had to go to Molly McCathie for enlightenment; and now Robert's son has to depend on some ignorant streel for knowledge essential to his manhood."

William regarded this as further evidence of Grandpa's senility, but the days were glorious for Syme and Jimmy. To the deviltry of reckless horsemanship was added the cavalry swagger—war danger—acclamation of heroes—all the swashbuckling sentimentality of bugles and uniforms. They were a gay pair of cockerels in olive green, and hats to match, turned up at the side with chookie feathers.

Margaret was thrilled with the look of her darling. "It will keep him out of mischief," she said.

The impression still was that the Australian contingent was a mere gesture of empire, and that a war against a few untrained farmers would be ended before it could reach the front. It was unlikely that a second contingent would embark.

But the war ripened. The Australians arrived and were absorbed into various British regiments. Methuen's check at Magersfontein, with great loss, the Colenso disaster, where Buller suffered a humiliating defeat at the Tugela River by a force much smaller than his own, were incredible. The superciliousness concerning Australian and New Zealand troops had turned to a special call for volunteers who could ride and shoot—"shoot a mosquito at three hundred yards and live on fresh air and exercise as long as there were holes to pull in their belts."

"Moi, oh, moi!" moaned Grandpa. "Going out to shoot colonists like themselves, to uphold a few blood-suckers in their debaucheries in London!"

Kitchener and Bobs were taking command. There was a call for 20,000 men to fill the places of those cut to pieces in the first engagements.

A second contingent was to depart after the New Year, and Syme and Jimmy were trying to get into this. Some of the lads from the land were so humiliated by military rejection that they would not return to their own districts. The Delacys and Fullwoods were puffed with pride when Syme and Jimmy were definitely accepted because they could not be thrown by a horse, unless by a miracle, and could top the score with rifle, carbine or revolver. Also they were each presented by their parents with a superb Nullah-Mundoey. Women are always exalted to sacrifice sons to Moloch, and fathers believe that war is the thing to make a man of a lad.

Hurrah for adventure!

The idea still was that Syme and Jimmy were lucky young devils because this detachment would never need to land in Africa, but would go right on to England for a jamboree. The Queen would be so pleased with the whelps from the far Southland, who had rushed to her aid, that she would invite them to Buckingham Palace. They would go up to London to look at the Queen. Lucky young beggars, indeed!

The family went to Sydney to see Syme embark. His youth and the willowy Delacy grace and sensitiveness of feature attracted attention as the marchers struggled through the embracive crowd delirious with imperial fever. Margaret walked on the pavement. Girls threw so many handkerchiefs at the boy that he was covered. He thrust them across to his mother with his rifle. "Here, Ma, souvenirs."

The excited crowd collected them and handed Margaret the spoil at the wharf where she put it in a cab—three hundred handkerchiefs. There were paragraphs in the papers. Margaret was extolled as the magnificent type of Australian woman who produced heroic sons to serve the Empire. It was said that if every one who had enjoyed the generous hospitality of Burrabinga could have thrown a handkerchief, Mrs Delacy would have been smothered and the traffic blocked.

Thus the departure of Syme at the touching age of seventeen, and a heavy bill to be met at the Grand Central, and for the cabs the family had constantly occupied during the festivities.

After that the war settled into its stride, and enteric and other allies of Mars did their part. Grandpa continued to grieve. "You'd think the war was a personal affair with him," grumbled William.

Finally, in the interests of harmony, Grandpa suppressed his peculiar ideas and contented himself with dreaming in the sun. As the days shortened, the cooler atmosphere tempted him to walk about the homestead. One afternoon when autumn held the scene in delicious stillness, he took his ancient hat and staff and called to Rover, the last of a long succession of the name, and with him went up the cutting. The day was full of birds, many of which had come down from the mountains for the winter. Among the arrivals were the grey magpies, making a raid on the quinces, still hanging like golden lanterns in the orchard. Grandpa's unfailing friends, the kookaburras, sat low on snags, feathers fluffed, and meditated on the imminence of winter, or occasionally laughed furiously from higher branches. The wag-tails accompanied him closely, revolving their fan tails. Robin red-breasts and many other tits and wood-peckers were present. Rover intermittently dispersed the more intrusive with a "wuff!", and the peewits and soldier birds repri-manded him like viragoes. The magpies showered their mellow notes into the charmed air, and the cockatoos rent it with their screeching when, at the warning of their sentinels, they rose in a snowy cloud from the cultivation paddocks. Bright parrots passed in spasmodic flight or tarried to indulge in small talk. Down by the stockyards the crows were holding a corroboree of mourning and resentment over the discovery of a dead comrade. Grandpa observed many other forms along the track that resolved themselves into feathered friends, and he joyed in their companionship.

He sat on a boulder now and again and rested. He had plenty of time. He was realizing that he was free of eternity, that he was at its centre, that it flowed all about him. It was a vast realization, but he had no one with whom to share it, except perhaps Harry, and Harry was such a fool by the rules of common sense, that he would not have a pound note to bring him for so momentous a conversation. William would flout the necessity as a symptom of mental senility, and as for Robert—the old man chuckled to think how Robert would receive such a revelation. "Moi, oh, moi! The moind! The moind!" he murmured, his soul refusing to surrender to Robert's and William's standards. In the illumination of Hy-Brasil there was assurance that somewhere, some time, not Robert, not William, but Harry, had the superior wisdom.

Near the crest of the cutting he sat on a grey log. He remembered felling the tree more than half a century gone; it remained as sound as a stone and was decorated with beaded lichen. He watched the Murrumbidgee tumbling from the bunyip hole into Delacy's Crossing, and heard the complaint of the casuarinas mingling with its sigh as it ran from out eternity into eternity, crying Husssssssssssh! to the sun or stars. There was mystery for you! Danny liked to ponder on mysteries, but the twin mysteries of time and space were overpowering.

He went on his way with his staff and wooden leg, a figure firmly etched into the consciousness of the district. His object was the point from which he could see the panorama of plain with the mountains stacked behind. Short of breath at the top, he sank down to recover and grew tranced with the view. Between gorges he could still see the river coursing from the dark hills past the homestead which he and Johanna had made. Equally near, since his realization of eternity, was the land he and his Johanna had renounced on that May day long ago when they had plighted their troth and planned to elope. Did Time flow forward in a straight stream, or in circles, or were there two streams passing each other?

Far away was the timeless, illimitable blue with the mountains prinked upon it and a presence palpitant with a thousand centuries of oblivion, behind which the sun was going down to Riverina to rise on old Ireland, now so near at hand. Poor Ireland! So scourged by conquerors and usurpers, that at best she could have afforded him room for a goat and the operations of a spade, but here was the glory of wide horizons, sublimely empty. He worshipped the pregnant peace of the piled ridges with their lore unlegended. Potential revelation hovering just beyond capture gave the locality its haunting magic.

"The moind! The moind!" he spoke aloud to himself, in the way of a poet lacking an audience.

When the evening meal was prepared, Grandpa was missing. With an imprecation, William hurried up the cutting, one of the men with him. Old Rover, who loved Grandpa, barked at their approach. The April air was nipping after sundown for old bones. Grandpa had grown so stiff against the stump that he was unable to rise, so they made a chair of their hands interlaced. William was startled because the old man did not speak. He was fey as one who had been out all night on the hill-tops with the Little People, and all the host of elfin spirits, which in his native land retain their identity. He seemed to see things beyond other vision, to hear voices to which other ears were closed.

William scolded him sharply because he was uneasy. They bathed his foot in mustard and hot water to guard against chill, and put him to bed. He refused a toddy by a headshake.

"He's had a stroke," said William. "Either that, or his mind has completely left him."

Danny lay for a time looking into the night and pondering on posterity. His urgency for future generations was tempered by what he had gathered on the hill-tops. Liberated, as he now was, from the time limitations of the earth-bound, he recognized that posterity should not be in haste to squander its dwindling heritage of unpeopled spaces. There was endless time for posterity. The more time and the less posterity, the better for posterity. Posterity could afford to wait.

This thought was his lullaby. In the morning he did not rise to make the fire, as he delighted to do. Jean went in to him. He spoke in his usual resounding voice, though it was husky. "I would like to see me family, more particularly Harry and Della, that I have not seen these manny years."

"Aren't you feeling well, Father?"

"Never felt better, nor worse neyther."

"We can't get Della here, unless he is very ill. We'd be blamed for useless expense."

The doctor arrived on the following day, and could find nothing wrong. The heart was weak, but not more than to be expected in a man of Danny's age.

"Sure, doctors are wasted on me now. It's me family I'd like to see for a little conversation about important mysteries."

"He's gone really childish," said William behind his back. "Della and Harry could not afford to come."

As though he had heard, the old man remarked, "We never can afford to go see each other while we're alive, but when it is no use, money is strewed in foolish show. 'Tis a pity, but it does not matter now. Sure, I'd like to see me old friend Hennessy."

"Hennessy is too old to come out these short days."

"Sure," said Danny resignedly. "Johanna wanted Father Shannon, and I was too benighted to bring him. This makes it square. Human ignorance will keep on repeating itself till the end. When we come to carry our hides to the tanyard . . . yes, old Danny Delacy from County Clare can step up with his wooden leg with manny another scar, and say *adsum*."

William was sure the old man was wandering. However, he dropped asleep after saying that he felt as well as ever he had been.

Little Danny shared the "ind room" with Grandpa because the old man liked his company. In the morning the boy ran to report that Grandpa was not sitting up and smoking as usual, that his pipe had fallen on the floor.

Danny's pipe had gone out.

CHAPTER XXXIX

No expense was spared on telegrams or other arrangements.

Harry rode through as Darcy had done three years earlier. The mother of Deerfoot, thin and old, did not founder in the long day. Harry too was thin and old and shabby. Every one thought he had grown unnaturally quiet. He spoke of the iron drought in his region and said there were scores of others in his plight. He was never a grumbler.

He felt as though the roof had been lifted from life and he left unprotected against the elements as he turned from the figure which lay in the "ind room" in the still dignity of death. As he wandered alone by the bunyip hole he pondered on his inability to conquer destiny, and acknowledged his father's single-handed achievement as considerable. He could not recall any lie, any ignoble action or cowardice as emanating from that being, and now realized how much his father had been to him. He could have gazed all day upon the wreathed ranges that had engulfed his adolescence. The keening casuarinas were a voice from another life and drowned him in emotion. Gone, all gone now, Danny and Johanna, and many another, and he alone in the world of arid facts and insurmountable difficulties. Nevertheless that other magic—the nobility, the spiritual exaltation—were a man's birthright could he but attain it. He had inherited, in intensified degree, Danny's sensing of the spiritual potency of his continent—that *aisling* sense of his forebears which personified Ireland as the Dark Rosaleen.

William was in charge of the funeral, and barred women, though Clare Margaret had ridden out with her father and Wong Foo and other Burrabinga retainers.

"There won't be many at the funeral," remarked William.

"No," agreed Robert. "Father could have left us a fortune, if he had had any sense."

"Every one could put a hand in his bag."

"He was harmless. That's about the best that can be said for him."

"Old Butler and Heulong Fullwood and Urquhart are all that's left: Father really died when he retired from partnership. He's been childish for years."

Drought was making horse-flesh precious: only a few people followed from the bunyip hole and the haunted crossing away from the homestead and up the cutting down which Delacy in his prime had brought the first Nullah-Mundoey. Turning at right-angles from the panoramic background, which the guest of honour had loved so well, the neighbours took the crisp road along which Johanna's carriage had bumped home to surprise her.

The highway was marked now with split-rails and wire. Gates and mail boxes denoted the homesteads, and from every one came a representative. William was surprised by the buggies and pairs of the squatters, the sulkies and spring carts of the smaller graziers, and the numbers of horsemen.

"It's out of respect to us and the Butlers," he remarked to Robert. "Funerals are for those that are alive to see."

Robert was sure that he had most to do with the increasing congregation, but Harry had more credit in the bank of spiritual understanding. He knew that the demonstration included men who hardly knew William and who had no admiration for Robert, and was entirely for old Danny, the ineffectual pioneer, who had bullocked to tame a wilderness with more thought of posterity than of personal gain, and who by courage and generosity over-topping that of his fellows had salted existence with drama.

Old Nullah-Mundoey; Fearless Danny; Honest Delacy of the Murrumbidgee, was taking his last journey over the way that he had travelled first of those assembled, and the news had spread.

"How the devil did they get to hear of it!" exclaimed William, as place after place yielded its tribute.

Danny had outlived funeral tears, but Hennessy, the publican, heavy, old, known to all, let his loss have way. Two women wept as they peeped from the shrouded windows as the procession went along the main street to the graveyard. Bella Fullwood and Molly Macallister, both now blousy and elderly, recalled the lance that old Nullah-Mundoey had broken for each in her youth, with a generosity and innocence that had not been repeated in their experience of men, and which that day was passing into legend.

A bullying autumn wind thrust the tails of the horses far aside and mocked the *cortège* with little whirlwinds of dust that rose in the road and danced away across the bare dry ridges. The buggy pairs could not be held to William's sense of decorum. Their drivers withdrew occasionally for a smoke in sheltering knots of scrub. There was talk of drought and prices and of the war, and anecdotes of Nullah-Mundoey, which had emanated from Hennessy. William and Robert did not appreciate their father's fame being invested in this Boswell, once a convict and always a publican. William was overly respectable, and Robert respected genteel respectability.

There was a bell to toll for Danny, as he passed the new church, and a railway line to be crossed along the track which he and Johanna had followed sixty years earlier in Mr Moore's bullock dray. They laid him to rest on the wind swept hillside above the Township with Mount Bowning as a sentinel on one hand, and far on the other the adorning ranges which he had worshipped as a fountain head of the continent.

Harry returned to Bewuck with Robert and William. There was no will. Danny had given away his personal effects long ago. Harry coveted some memento of his parents, but sighed as he realized that Josephine had her own conventions in elegancies, and lacked tenderness towards the past. Harry felt that life was defeating him. Robert urged him to take a turn to Burrabinga, but Harry had no heart for this, now, when old Danny's passing had left the universe so unaccountably blank.

He was surprised to see how Darcy had grown, and noted his sensitive features and the willowy Delacy physique. Josephine had commanded him to bring the boy home. Darcy asserted that he would return only for a short time, and stipulated that he should first get his possessions from Burrabinga. Harry said it would be a pity to expose his Nullah-Mundoey and her two promising foals to the drought at Murrumbong. Clare Margaret then promised to care for Darcy's belongings and send them after him if he did not return in a month. Her pretty oval face, where the dimples played when she laughed, was swollen and red as she wept with abandon at the prospect of losing Darcy, even temporarily. Uncle William, scandalized, thought it time that the cousins were separated. The girl's emotion saved Darcy from heartbreak. He too wept, out of sight by the bunyip hole, screened by the sighing casuarinas while he and his Oread staged one of the colossal partings demanded by young romance.

Among the younger members of the Burrabinga family, news of the big muster at Grandpa's funeral was eclipsed by the sudden withdrawal of Darcy. They straightway made a cult of the absent one with Clare Margaret as its priestess. They hung his pack-saddle on the rafters to gather hornets' nests, and the Nullah-Mundoey and her progeny became sacred. At Burrabinga romantic tendencies were free from parental curiosity.

Margaret asked why Darcy had disappeared. "Harry said something about the danger of cousins. Josephine wants him to go in for teaching."

"Cousins, pshaw! Familiarity would be the best way to counteract that. I'll miss the boy."

"I reckon Josephine is not going to run any risk of a morganatic alliance for her Prince of the Blood. That poor old devil of a Harry is looking terribly down on his luck.'

The elders had much else to engross them with the interest to be met at the Bank. The war with the Boers was providential in this connection. Drought had not scorched the well-watered valleys of old Danny's kingdom, and stirring horse musters continued. Fine profits but little of the grief of war reached from far-away South Africa to farther-away Australia.

Strangely, the war had not finished before Syme arrived in South Africa. The few, who, at the beginning, were concerned with the ethics of the case, had been silenced by the noise of drums and "The Soldiers of the Queen". People had come to have a lower opinion of the Boers. They shot from behind rocks instead of swaggering out into the open in the glory of martial etiquette where they would soon have been settled by the expert soldiers of the Queen, my lad, in the fight for England's glory, lad.

Syme was the current hero. His letters were splendid, and he sent his mother a ring he had cut from the finger of a dead Boer. It looked like a worn wedding ring. It was perfectly sound, so the family said the cutting must allude to the finger. Clare Margaret thought that the finger might have swollen when the man died. The rigours of war were beyond their visualization.

Darcy and his father scarcely spoke on the way. The boy's heart was behind him in the lively routine of Burrabinga, the man's in that life which old Danny had taken with him to the grave.

Arrived at Murrumbong, Darcy felt cramped. The thirsty stricken paddocks were hideous to him. He lived only for the mail from Burrabinga, ten days distant—an eternity—and fell to work with feverish energy so that no task should block his return to his cousins. He whitewashed the dairy and cowbails, cleaned the vegetable garden, topped the fences, and started to plough the dry paddocks, which had been months waiting for rain. Harry procured seed wheat on credit.

Josephine quickly discerned that Darcy's life hung on the mail. Her children were denied sanctuary: she had no urgent spiritual needs herself and her suspicion of inner retreat was that of the crime psychologist.

Clare Margaret's first letter came as the breaking of the drought:

DARLING DARCY,
We nearly all died when I got home without you. You must have heard me howling all the way from Murrumbong. I've packed up all your dear things. No one shall break in your foals but myself.

There followed pages of the doings of the family. Each member added a postscript expressing ardent affection, and a merry anecdote against someone. There was an oath here and there. Clare Margaret said she had swallowed a stiff nobbler the first night to drown her sorrow; and that Roger had got drunk, and it was terribly funny.

Darcy read with passionate nostalgia, reliving the past with sick longing. "This day fortnight I was with Clare Margaret. This day month we were . . ." and so on. At Murrumbong he could not enter without being reprimanded for some omission. Coming weary from work he was nagged to perform some extra chore to spare his mother. After the careless freedom of Burrabinga and its village of buildings the compact house was a cage in which there was no escape from the stings. One day he burst out that it was hell, and the issue was raised.

Josephine rebuked him for being coarse and rough. She was ambitious to see him in a clerkly position with meek manner and well-laundered linen. " 'Evil communications corrupt good manners.' You moon about, and I know the reason. You wait for those indecent letters from Clare, full of vile swear words and vulgarity—dreadful enough in a man, but unthinkable in a girl. A grown-up woman now. I don't know what her mother can be doing to let such stuff pass through the post."

"Aunt Margaret and Uncle Robert never pry."

"It is high time that they knew what is going on."

He hurried to the spot where he secreted the letters. They were missing. There was no place from floor to rafters in Josephine's house where so much as a spider or a speck of dust would dispute cleanliness and order. She projected herself upon her circle as an unsurpassed manager and housekeeper, and her technique in motherhood was equally brilliant. To break a child's rebellious spirit was parental sport—part of parental dictatorship. Children's duty was obedience and gratitude to the authors of their being.

Darcy returned with blanched face and blazing eyes. Josephine had no intuition of error in pursuing an established course.

"Where are my letters?" Darcy was perilously near to tears.

"I haven't finished reading them yet."

"You have no right to read them at all!" He could not have believed such outrage possible.

"Don't look like a madman! Who has a right to read a boy's letters if not his mother? Who is the one in all the world best able to advise him: who has his best interests at heart, but his mother? It is disgusting for a boy of your age to get letters like that. I demand to know what you said to her—your cousin too. I don't know what your father will say. The evil influence of Burrabinga is glaringly evident."

"I *love* Burrabinga and *hate* here," burst from him in all the passion of his being.

"People always love sin and hate what is good." Josephine was unacquainted with such intense emotion, and attributed it to bad temper and the Irish strain.

"Give me my letters!"

"That I never will. I shall burn them. I would not defile my house with such rubbish. If you don't turn over a new leaf, you'll find yourself in terrible trouble—with a creature like that. She can have no shame. I pray that evil practices have not already gone too far."

Darcy rushed from his mother, quivering in every fibre. She called after him in scornful parody " *'Darling Darcy, I got drunk. Darling Darcy.'* Ha! Ha!"

She was shattering beauty and innocence, so that afterwards, had the boy a holy of holies, he would employ any subterfuge to protect it from his mother. There is sadism in motherhood as well as in *amour* and the boy felt that his mother enjoyed his wounding. She had had no mercy on his sensitive writhings as a child, had called him silly. He shrank from further mention of the subject by her, as added profanation. Nothing was left for him but to flee—no matter where—to be safe from further inquisition. He disappeared for the day, unable to face the ordeal of others knowing what had happened to him—not simply the spoiling of his adolescent idyll, but that the spoiling had been done by his mother, with evident satisfaction. His mother, whom he had been taught, by that mother, enthusiastically supported by his father, to honour as a priceless pearl among mothers, had done this thing to him, had put complex shame in his soul, because to question a mother's holiness was blasphemy. He walked all day among the soldier birds and crows and cockatoos and whistling jays and scrub wallabies and hares, gathering a shell on a festering wound.

He had come from the ploughing, leaving the horses a meagre ration of straw—the only fodder available. When he did not appear for dinner, Harry grew uneasy, and rode around the paddocks where the boy might have met with an accident among his rabbit traps. He speculated until Josephine had to explain.

Harry listened in silence. "I wish you had told me first."

"Why, pray?"

"There may have been no harm in the letters."

"No harm—after what I have told you! It looks like the low Irish coming out—drinking and swearing—and now immorality!"

"That's not Irish particularly, but all human nature."

"Nonsense! Every publican in the country is Irish. Your own father made no bones about saying d—— in front of little girls."

There was much that Harry could have said, and all of it would have been so unavailing that he merely sighed and went to continue the ploughing, glancing in every direction in the hope of seeing Darcy. The girl and boy next in age were with Josephine's relations, the younger girl at school.

Darcy returned with her in time for the evening meal, and kept with her so that his mother could not renew the attack. He went to bed when the little girl did. Josephine remarked that he was sulking, and that she despised moodiness.

She insisted upon Darcy facing her next morning when his sister had gone to school. "It's time you thought of doing something now and helping me with the younger children. Your father can't make a living. The right kind of young men take an interest in helping their mothers, who sacrifice everything for their children."

Pupil-teachers were in demand, especially males. Darcy had been unusually quick at his lessons, and Josephine's design was that he should return to school and study for examination. His academic education had been obtained in a tiny bush school-house, three miles from his home, one of the many which had sprung up in accordance with old Henry Parkes's beneficent Education Act. In the growth of closer settlement, following Robertson's earlier Land Act, this resulted in school-houses occurring every five miles or so, wherever a dozen or a score of children could be mustered. The demand for instructors, had, at the beginning, provided genteel careers for men and women with a little lettering and the ambition to escape from the plough or cow-yard. Darcy's instructress had had more ambition than knowledge. Elderly and weary, her fierce canings of stupefied frightened louts who had not the mentality to learn by rote the multiplication tables, or chunks of the *Gazeteer*, or dates of English history, had been a nightmare to Darcy. He had prompted his less gifted school mates and this had brought harsh canings upon him too. His delicate hands were often so swollen and bruised that his home tasks—especially milking—were painful. His sensitiveness which made him fear that he might involuntarily withdraw his hand before the cane descended was a nervous trial equalling the pain itself.

Thus had he gained a conception of the teaching profession, and his mother asked him to return and sit among little kids under the scotty old woman in order to take her role. He would rather be a navvy.

"Then what are you going to do?" demanded his mother.

"I'm going back to Burrabinga."

"That you shall never do. I shall write to your uncle and aunt." This was ordeal piled on ordeal to the hypersensitive lad.

"Don't you dare write to them!"

"It shows what you have come to to talk to your mother like that. There is only one condition on which I'll consent not to warn them, as I should."

"What is that?"

"You must keep away from Burrabinga completely."

His choice was instantly made Anything to block his mother from writing to his uncle and aunt. "All right, if you'll keep your word."

"What right have you to suggest that I shall break my word? I leave that sort of thing to the Irish."

"All right then. Give me back my letters."

"I burned them. I hope you will try to forget every silly indecent word that was in them. Clare Margaret must be a horrid girl."

Josephine had shut him from Burrabinga effectually. She felt him shamed yet thrilled by the awakening. Like a drought blast on fruit she had forced his adolescence prematurely to manhood at seventeen. In the same stroke she had made Murrumbong uninhabitable. Henceforth his foremost emotion toward his mother was dread of her power to desecrate. He must guard against this danger by flight. He would remove his dream to the Diamantina, or the Cooper or Roper or the Paroo or the Never Never to keep it safe from profanation.

Harry had gone to plough. Darcy walked down the hill to him. That his father would understand did not enter his head. Stroke by stroke, unceasingly, Josephine imbued her children with the fact of their father being useless as a parent or a provider, and Harry had not counteracted this either by self-assertion or practical demonstration. Darcy strove to make his announcement as one man to another. "Father, I'm clearing out. Mother and I have had a bit of a row. I can't stay here any longer."

Harry's insight and kindness prevented him from probing. He

said quietly, "Better give it a week's thought, my boy. Your mother has a great deal to worry her. It will pass." He did not mention Burrabinga, which was healing to Darcy.

He remained with his father for some days. His mother recited the opportunities for pupil-teachers. There were numerous examples of men in public affairs who had begun as school-teachers. Darcy shuddered. Relinquish Deerfoot and all the tribe of Nullah-Mundoeys, retire from swinging neck and neck after wild horses, or from catapulting down precipices after cattle at the musters, to sit inside like an old woman, with a few kids!

He busied himself in secret preparations. His saddle was given more stuffing. Deerfoot got stout new shoes. His father noted the ominous signs, while his mother thought she had brought him to her way of thinking.

He asked his father for a pack-horse, for which he would send the money as soon as he had it. There was no danger of Harry requiring money from the boy, though he had not a penny and did not know where to raise one. He could never drive any one, but all could squeeze him. He asked Darcy what he was going to do.

"Go droving!" He pronounced the words as a challenge.

"Hard work. You want to get with a decent man."

"I've written to Donal Geraghty."

"Have you told your mother?"

"Not till I'm ready to start."

"Her idea of teaching is all right, you know."

"Walloping helpless kids all day! I'd rather blow my brains out and be done with it."

"You'll want a good dog."

The boy's eyes softened. "I'd like to take old Barney. He's a champion heeler."

"You can have him. I have little use for him here."

Josephine railed when she was informed on the evening before Darcy was to leave. She commanded Harry to detain him. Harry said that he had been contemplating a droving contract himself until the drought should break.

In the morning the boy took the possum rug for which he had himself shot and tanned the skins. He had some extra shirts and socks. Harry contributed his own old oil-skin coat, his quart pot and tucker-bags. Josephine produced a pound note from her hard won store.

The boy was sad when departure was upon him. He said good-bye to the little girl and to his parents. He mounted Deerfoot, pulled Blackie's halter, and whistled to old Barney, the only being involved who seemed to be pleased.

Bound for the outer Overland, where the roads were still unfenced, the youth rode down the rise from the house among the messmates, and crossed the cow paddock amid the briars to gain the track that led to the Great Stock Route that fed the Riverina and the Lachlan and the Bogan. As the stage to restless girls, as the sea to European lads, so called the Great Stock Routes to Australian boys in those decades. To go a-droving had glamour. The drover, idyllic, comic, tragic, manly, was a sentimental subject for the balladists who were fostering a new nation and portraying its unwieldy place in the sun.

Harry was dejected to see his boy go thus. He understood, but was powerless. In the great days of Tara, he might have thriven in giving richly as a *seanachie* through his endowment of memory and poetic imagination plus physical courage and skill. Born out of his century, he had nothing but spiritual gifts to offer, gifts which in his environment, were spurned as foolishness bordering on lunacy. Deprived of any outlet or income spiritually from which to renew courage, hope seemed to wither. He was sickened by his helplessness in an economic system in which, as his mother had expressed it, he was as unprotected as a plucked goose in a snow storm.

There was no one to understand him, though he understood Josephine's bitterness to see her son spurn a sensible suggestion and depart as a mere casual labourer or station "hand". His was a double agony. He blamed himself for his own failure and what it was bringing upon Josephine. She went into the house out of sight. She suffered from an angry sense of obstruction by the futility of another, heartily despised that other's incapability, and was not free from a desire for revenge upon him.

Harry glanced around the arid landscape, stricken by the white glare. No green anywhere. An empty watercourse gaped at the foot of the homestead rise. A brazen sky oppressed the shabby earth—bare dusty paddocks, dead standing timber, ragged sombre scrub and the pitiless bleaching sunshine from dawn until dusk. Ugly, sordid, poverty-stricken.

The road, upon which the two horses and the dog were becoming specks, uncurled its grey tape to the crest of the ridge, where it dropped out of sight in the blue. There was always romance in a road, beauty in the way it lay across the horizon, suggesting something beyond the rim, even if only at the furthest ends of the globe.

The roads led up and on and away, with a promise of liberation. Highways of hope—adventure—possibility.

Harry's thoughts lay upon old Danny, who had blazed his way where roads were yet to be. A boy with Danny in him could not sit like a barnyard fowl sifting the dust through his wings.

Harry continued to stand as if petrified, gazing along the road where his son had disappeared, and on which he was never to be seen again. Distance and the magic light cast a patina of exquisite blue on the suffering land, and wove a spell of beauty to lure the traveller beyond the rim. Only advancing age and horny experience could hold a man to the realization that the beauty of distance was a mirage.

Johan Darcy, grandson of Daniel Brian Robert M. Delacy, had disappeared into the distance with two horses, a dog, and a pound note, to follow, by droving on the Overland, the double mirage of adventure and romance.

CHAPTER XL

THE best of the Delacys may have gone in old Nullah-Mundoey. The most impressive remained in Robert, whom the astute Wong Foo had early elected as head of the family. With rare exceptions, all stations were centres of sociability and hospitality, but Burrabinga was known as the most hospitable of its region. The Delacy personality gave that hospitality charm. If Harry was a misplaced *file-seanachie* of the time of the *Ard-Righs*, or High Kings in Erin, the Delacys in general were reincarnated *brughaids*, those honoured officials of hospitality, of whom it was written that they warned off no person of whatever shape, that no company was refused, and no account kept by the hosts against any person, no matter how often he came.

William continued to rage at the madness of such unbridled hospitality. Both Margaret and Robert were generous and careless. The family grew up more so, in keeping with the increasing availability of commodities. Putting the brake on became impossible.

The war dragged on. The continuing demand for horses was all to the good. The chief danger seemed to be typhoid fever, but Syme, so far, had weathered everything. No one any longer discussed the rights of either Uitlander or Boer. The gentleman who had lost his job at Sydney University because of unpatriotic talk, spent months at Burrabinga, but did not debate the ethics of the war. Just as well. No one but C. P. Scott of the *Manchester Guardian*, and old Danny, would have understood his views, and the first was removed by distance and the other was mouldering in the grave.

No one knew if Robert had views. He had voted for the sitting Member for years, and was free from profundities of thought, a silent man in his sixties, with a spanking overdraft at the Bank, and a family that took little notice of him, or he of them, except when there was a crisis. Instead of commanding his son and keeping him into the collar, he rode the ranges himself. Though stiffening, he was still slim and straight as a reed, and with his aquiline features and height, a striking presence. He could not now swing on or off a horse in motion, but he was always a-horse, rode magnificent animals, and the excess of vigour, which had had an overflow in swagger in youth, still lent him grit and grip.

There were many leagues of fencing now. The knolls and lesser hills around the homestead were dotted with stately trees, spared by the axe, and had the appearance of a park wrested from the wilderness, but much labour was necessary to keep the scrub at bay.

Young Darcy had been months on the road towards the great north-west "where all the rovers go". He was bringing cavalry remounts from Queensland. The days on the Warrego Tracks, the nights with horses, the drovers' purgatory, were hard on his young frame. but his shattered dream was reshaping itself in the grand unpeopled-ness of the Route.

He had denied himself to send money to his mother. There! That was better than miserable school-teaching. Barney and Blackie were still with him. He was getting letters from Clare at odd corners of the Overland. Clare had sent him Grandpa's Nullah-Mundoey by a drover who had stayed at Burrabinga—most men would go out of their way to serve Clare Margaret.

Darcy—plain John on the Out Back Overland—was horribly tanned, and lines were already chiselled by the sun around his eyes. He was learning to take his grub like a dog, and to lie down and sleep like one, in snatches, with little between him and the earth, but there was nothing at all between him and the full glory of the inland sky at night—a free field for the visionary. From the Leeuwin to Cape York, from the Great Bight to the Gulf of Carpentaria, the eerie land ached in the sleep of oblivion, but poets increasingly sensed her dreams. Often, in the night, young Delacy could feel the startled silence throb with magic.

Otherwise he was growing hardened to many things, but he was also growing a moustache, and on that his plans depended.

With a moustache he would return to Burrabinga—to Clare Margaret—a man.

In time the Boers surrendered. Among those who left their bones on the veldt was Syme Delacy. The living heroes straggled back into the old life, where most of the population worked for a living, and soldiering was healthily out of fashion as soon as war ceased. Slogans about badly managed troop ships were shouted at political meetings, and had reference to experiences which acquainted warriors with the actualities of war as well as its licence and adventures. At intervals, since the incipient nation had outgrown its garde-major character, there had been attempts by certain cliques to re-impose military snobbery, but without success, and contingents which, during martial fever, had been lionized, found their military doughtiness forgotten as they returned to normal citizenship. Federation and political enfranchisement of women had slipped on to the country unaware. Excepting Margaret, the Burrabinga people took little notice of political statutes. More interesting to them was the death of Wong Foo, in his hut at Bullock Gap, whither Clare Margaret had galloped to nurse him, but too late. He was brought in by a fellow countryman to be buried in the station graveyard with family honours. He had made a legal will leaving his selection—now paid-up freehold—to Robert and his heirs for ever.

Roger was turning out as good a whip as his father. He drove four coachers in the family sociable, which could accommodate six dignified sizable people and many more if they were undignified and squeezable. Among the guests would be staid members of the medical and legal professions, and various young fellows who imitated vice-regal *aides*. When any of these needed horses they sent to the Burrabinga Delacys. No others were known. Harry was obscured by poverty in a cockatoo-farming community. William rendered his family inconspicuous by a routine imposed to counteract the "flashing-about" of Robert's family. His prediction of Burrabinga, "It can't last," was complemented by other people's, "How on earth does it last? The banks will fetch old Robert a gutser one of these days."

William's girls were not so gay and captivating as Robert's. The Burrabinga girls were tall and slim and as supple as eels; they and their horses seemed one. William laid his daughters' lack of dash to the fact that Bewuck was primarily a sheep station. "Sheep put the comehither on flashness and all that swagger," he said to Jean.

"A good thing too. Girls can't spend all their lives riding about on flash horses to show off their figures, or in making fun of other people."

Everybody extolled the Burrabinga girls and predicted great matches for them—those merry, curly-headed, dare-devil minxes bubbling with witty ridicule of each and all, but also warm-hearted, who could make a pie-crust or a ball dress as well as they could break a filly to lady-like paces. They had opportunities of marrying city wealth, but William was astute as well as envious. "I'd like to see them going up in the world," he said. "But they are likely to be snapped up by some useless fellow with an eye to the main chance. All the no-chop bankers' and clergymen's sons are mustered there, as horse-breakers, or to sink post-holes, and because they set up as swells they are taken inside, and make themselves so familiar that the desirable men are shooed off."

"Has Humphrey Vance gone back to Laura Butler?" inquired Jean. "Clare Margaret ought to think of someone else if he won't come up to scratch, or she will be an old maid."

"Humphrey will never think of any one else while Clare Margaret is free. He goes up now and again. She is a fool to hang off. She will never catch a better young man anywhere—and the property too."

CHAPTER XLI

LATE one afternoon Darcy reined-in to note the changes that had taken·place in Burrabinga during his absence. Some of the nearer slopes had been ringbarked and burned; trout fishers had denuded a reach of the river of its fairy shrubs. The orchards obscured the low-set house. Old Wong's grave was new in the little cemetery.

Clare Margaret had planted a drive of poplars and clumps of pampas grass, and the leaves of the trees shimmered as beaten gold, the white plumes of the grass waved like the crests of a medieval crusade against the setting sun. Pale blue wood smoke from the autumn burning-off was incense to the traveller's senses, and the cool, familiar song of the river poured between day and night like eternity whispering *Hussssssssssh!* to the mundane disharmonies of man. Darcy felt that he had come home. The western country could not be what this was to him. It was like entering a deep, cool castle after the heat and glare, dust or wet or cold of unrelieved night and day. He rode forward to the announcement of the dogs, which brought some of the family to the veranda. He was breathless in thinking of Clare Margaret. Would she know him?

"He has the Delacy figure," said Margaret, turning pale and withdrawing because of Syme.

Clare Margaret sped between dahlias and chrysanthemums, thence through the orchard and her pride of pampas plumes, and the horseman sprang to the ground as she came. They met. They had kissed effusively at parting, but Darcy could not go beyond a hand-shake now. She saw the joy in his eyes, the emotion on his sensitive features, and his capacity to feel quickened her pulse as it never quickened for Humphrey Vance.

Darcy was a man. He had a "mo". That "mo" gave him confidence as his eyes caressed her. She was adult. Darcy thought her curly hair lovely in the new fashion, straight out of *Madame Weigel's Fashion Journal.* How tiny her waist in the exacting blouse and belt, a style in which the Burrabinga girls were experts.

Darcy went about investigating the changes. The girls had remodelled and rearranged the house to accord with their ideas of elegancy. One of the tradesmen, that were for ever dropping anchor in the sheltered cove of Burrabinga, had been commissioned by

Clare Margaret. Her father had protested in view of the overdrafts, but the man, depressed after D.T's, was comforted by the young people and glad to work for nominal wages. He added a smoke-room or den, and another broad veranda, such as dignified the old bush homestead to their uses. There were splendid pelts from descendants of Billy, the tanning of which cost little but time, and the Delacys would have been amused to put value on their time. There were shelves for books; a roomy sofa was softened by cushions of bright "crazy work" of pieces of Burrabinga dresses, a piano was weighted with showy photograph frames—an informal room held in fond remembrance by its friends.

Later in the evening Clare Margaret and Darcy had the school-house to themselves. There were so many guests that their absence went unnoticed. They lighted a fire and feasted on apples and quinces and pears. Darcy had forgotten that such cosiness and so much luscious fruit could be his.

Clare Margaret spoke of the soldier of the Queen who had not returned from the veldt. "It was terrible when word came. That was what made Ma so grey. Then she and Pa began to pet Roger, and he began to play-up and think he was the Governor. He's smitten on a barmaid in Cooma and she is threatening breach of promise. Pa says it will blow over because Roger is under age, but Ma gets so upset over things since Syme went."

Clare confessed that Roger got drunk ever so often, and that his state had to be hidden from his mother. Nosy old Uncle William had come up once specially to tittle-tat about Roger, but Pa had squelched him.

"If the boy does take a glass now and again, I want him to. I could always take my glass among men. Harry was kept in a coop, but as soon as he got away from us he drank like a fish. I don't want my boys to be like him."

"But I was reared like Harry," William had contended, "and if it came to real assets, I might be ahead of you."

"A young man can't carry his liquor if he is kept on a feeding bottle too long." Robert had walked off with his defiant swagger, which William called "throwing his legs about". He had turned back for a last word. "I reckon you remember the false accusations that were brought against me when I was Roger's age. It will take more than hearsay to put me against my own flesh and blood."

"It is to be hoped that Roger has your luck in crawling out of tight corners," was William's parting thrust.

There was harness and saddle repairing to keep Darcy busy for weeks, and with Syme gone and Roger so erratic, there was need of a stockman. The war had cleared away the sons of lawyers and bank employees who had sown their ne'er-do-wellism around the station. Robert said, "If you are wanting a job, you might as well go on my books for the present."

A night or two after his arrival, when he was in the kitchen writing labels for Clare Margaret's jam pots, he observed with some confusion, "You are not married yet?"

"Who would I marry?"

"One of these fine swells for everlasting eating the place to beggary."

"The lady-helps don't give me a look-in; and," she continued with a provocative smile, "Humphrey is like a policeman and sees that no one else has a chance."

"Are you engaged to him?"

"I might have to take him yet."

"Then you don't care for him so dreadfully much?"

"Not so much as I wish I did."

"What do you mean by that?"

"Oh, you know. Uncle William says he'll be able to buy and sell every other man who comes here before long."

"Pooh, money! What good is that?"

"You'd know, if you saw poor old Pa and Ma so worried about the Bank. Scissors, it was awful just after you went away. The Bank would have foreclosed, only the war saved us . . . but it took poor old Syme."

"You know why I came back, don't you?"

"Every one loves to come back to dear old Burrabinga."

"That's true. I reined-in the nags on The Plains and looked and looked for half an hour at the mountains. I thought of what Grandpa told me that time I rode Deerfoot to the races. He said the mountains had beckoned him always. It seemed as if the silence were speaking, if you can understand what I mean."

"I know."

Another generation or two and Danny's breed would be indigenous to the soil which they had awakened from fabulous fallowhood, its primeval virginity scarcely yet ravished from timeless sleep.

After a silence, Darcy continued, 'If you were going to marry Humphrey, I'd saddle the nags and make back to the Diamantina." Then his heart gagged him. From the den floated a waltz medley: The Indies—Weber's Last—Myosotis—Blue Pacific—The Isis—a string of favourites, banged out in accentuated rhythm. The voice of the Burrabinga rushed like wings into their personal silence.

"So now you know," said the youth haltingly.

"Yes, I know," responded Clare Margaret, without a trace of coquetry.

"I suppose I must go away to the Paroo or the Roper."

"You mean because of the cousin business?"

"What do you think about it?"

"There would be the father and mother and uncle and aunt of a row."

"Is that all!" exclaimed Darcy, suddenly elated. "You mean that you wouldn't object, yourself?"

"Well, lots of cousins do marry, from Royalty down."

"That's what I want to tell you. I met a man out in the Never Never—fellow with a university education—talked real hee-haw like the old parson. Cripes! it was funny to hear him swearing at the cattle in that brogue. Told me about the Ptolemies—Cleopatra you know, and Pharaoh. They married sisters and brothers."

"The worst trouble is that I'm old enough to be your mother."

"Don't be batty,—it's not much over two years."

"You mean a few days under three years." Then Clare Margaret, the plucky, the actual manager of the homestead, broke into sobs and said irrational things. She was a wild creature. Parental discipline had been skipped, and life itself had let her run as untamed as a high-spirited Nullah-Mundoey, which knew neither bit nor tackle until fully grown. She was maturing with the loss of Syme as her only experience of grief, and Roger's lack of self-control as the major trouble of her days.

"We can never think of it. I couldn't marry a boy. If I wait till you are old enough every one will say I took you because I was an old maid and could get no one else."

"Aunt Della and Uncle Ned were as happy as Larry."

"Uncle Ned wasn't a cousin," sobbed Clare Margaret. "I wish you would go away where I'll never see you again, because I can't bear you being my cousin."

"I can't bear it either," said Darcy, equally distraught. He had learned much in the hard days of drought, in the pitiless sun, in the restless nights under the frosty stars, or in the dreary sodden rain, but nothing that enabled him to bear up under Clare Margaret's tears. "It would be best for me to go away at once and get it over. I'll never think of any one else as long as I live."

Clare was so moved that Darcy had to clamp down his own excitement and comfort her. "Don't go away at once. I could not bear it. I'll ride all the outlaws and try to break my neck."

Darcy was weary of camp food and a bed on the ground and

the endlessness of roads—of sand or dust, naked of grass, without water, or else boggy or deadly with poisonous herbage. The prospect of sojourn where Clare Margaret was could not be resisted.

The saddling took a long time, as he was so often called out to the mustering, or to deliver stock. He could drop into the breach when Roger failed, and when he spoke of going, not only Clare Margaret but his aunt and uncle would inquire what was his hurry.

His mother heard with disquietude that he was again at Burrabinga. She harped on the cousin danger, though others were more alarming to her. Harry sought to minimize uneasiness.

CHAPTER XLII

A YEAR passed: Darcy was still at Burrabinga. Robert and Margaret were unaware of the quality of his and Clare's affections. The others were engrossed in their own affairs. Their life was lively with bouts of hard work interspersed with picnics or attendance at the agricultural shows or charity bazaars in the surrounding townships. Clare Margaret was left more and more to superintend the homestead. On her depended the regulation of supplies, the sowing of vegetables, the harvesting of the orchard.

Mavis married. The third daughter, Vida, announced her engagement. Mavis's husband was the son of a barrister, and following his father in the law. Vida's affianced was supposed to have wrecked his health in the war, but his father was able to give him a liberal allowance, and his idleness was envied.

Clare and Darcy might have drifted indefinitely in the morass of cousinly *amour*, only that Humphrey Vance appeared and remained at Burrabinga until he could define matters. He sought opportunity one Saturday night by manoeuvring Clare Margaret away from the people singing in the den or dancing on the veranda. Robert was resting in his own room with Margaret. It was increasingly their habit to withdraw.

"I don't believe you care as much as a tobacco tag for me," said Vance when alone in the school-house with his love.

"Oh, yes I do. It's only that I haven't time to get married. If I didn't look after things, we'd be on the rocks."

"If you cared, you'd think of marriage first."

"How do you know?"

"Because I care."

Humphrey forced himself to go on. He was a straightforward man with less feeling and imagination than the Delacys, but more ballast in worldly affairs.

"I've been doing a lot of thinking this last year. You are wearing your life away here for nothing—just keeping a free pub for all and sundry. I want you now while we are young, to have some fun."

"Marriage always looks to me like the end of fun."

"Well, what is your idea—working like ten for every loafer that comes along to take advantage of your soft heart? You'll be eaten out in the end, like the people in the back country with the swarms of rabbits."

"We have the Wong Foo estate," laughed the girl. Wong's estate was a family by-word like the Yackandandah.

"You might be jolly glad of Wong Foo's thrift before long," said Humphrey with a touch of rebuke. Flippancy about money matters savoured to him of half-wittedness.

Clare was silent. Humphrey had to re-open the question. "I could give you everything you want."

"Yes, but I'd have to marry you," flashed the girl, partly in return for his financial superiority.

Humphrey winced. "You won't mind if I speak plainly?"

"Fire away!" she said brusquely, to cover her apprehension.

"It has been hard on my vanity, but I have to face it. You like me as a friend, but you are dead in love with Darcy. He's the dreamy sort of chap that girls like to coddle."

He was shocked by the effect of his words. Clare Margaret blushed to her ears, then paled as if fainting, and broke into sobs, equally disconcerting. She had always been the most high-spirited creature of Humphrey's acquaintance.

"There! There!" said he, attempting comfort, but determined to straighten out his emotions in a business-like way. He was too common-sense to waste his substance in providing a free resort for spongers—some of them supercilious. "I did not mean to hurt your feelings, but I have been living in a fool's paradise. Cousins are the devil. They have an inside pull and you can find yourself in deep water with them before you know where you are."

Clare Margaret continued to cry, but softly, so that Humphrey recovered his composure. "Now, you are soft on Darcy, aren't you? He means more to you than any one else in the world: 'fess up."

She said no word of denial, for which he hungered, however false. With stern effort he continued. "That would not matter: I could help you to overcome your infatuation for the youngster, if he did not care for you, but he loves you like a girl in a story book. I can see that now, from that day he came to the races. You turned into a different person to play with him. The familiarity of the cousin business blinded me."

"We tried," said Clare Margaret, with a sob.

"Ah!" breathed Humphrey, and was silent so long that the river imposed its *Hussssssssssh!* upon the ephemeral fret of man. "Well," he said at length. "You can't go on for ever as you are now. What are you going to do?"

"How do you mean *do*?" asked the girl.

"You can't marry him."

At that Clare Margaret demanded, "Why?"

"He's a cousin, and I know how the Delacys look at that."

"Lots of cousins do marry."

"Yes, but how would he keep you?"

"Like Uncle Ned keeps Aunt Della, I suppose."

Humphrey's face went blank. "Then you are thinking of marrying him?"

"It seems to be you who are thinking that."

"I've thought of nothing else but marrying you since you were seventeen: and I'm just waking up to see where I stand."

"Right in front of me in the middle of the school-room," said she, very Clare Margaretly. He was incited to seize her wrists and hold her where he could look into her eyes. Her femininity excited him as wine, and she enjoyed his male strength, but his nose looked too big, his eyes too small. He was broad and heavy—like a coacher. Her ideal was the thoroughbred.

"You can waste your own time if you like, though it's a terrible pity when you'd make such a lovely little wife; but you have no right to waste Darcy's life, and mine."

"I don't want you to hang around."

"But you let us hang around. If you don't want Darcy, why don't you send him away? On the square—which of us do you want?"

"Oh, I wish, I wish Darcy was older." She began to sob again.

Humphrey was tender to the indecision of such a beautiful girl. He decided to have a talk with Darcy. He liked him in spite of being jealous of him, but, as a man able to add to his property, he felt mighty superior to any male Delacy. He went with Clare to bathe her face in the river, opposite old Billy's hustings, and then they returned to the den, where dancing was proceeding as usual. A Sydney man insisted upon a turn with Clare Margaret, which gave Humphrey his chance with Darcy. They went out on the pretext of letting a horse out of the stable. It was not easy to begin, but Vance was direct, not complex.

"I wanted to talk to you about Clare Margaret." He made a good deal of lighting his pipe, though there was no wind. The stars blazed in a clear dark sky. Darcy freed the horse. This accomplished, he stood with his back to the stable door, waiting for Vance to continue, and thankful that the night hid the commotion in his senses.

"I've been talking to Clare Margaret. She can't make up her mind: we ought to do it for her. You know what I mean?"

"Go ahead."

"Well, hang it all, I've been telling her that she doesn't want to waste her life; and I don't want to waste any more of mine either, just hanging around. It's this way: I think she would be fonder of you than she is of me, if you were not her cousin and so much younger. But those facts can't be blinked, and I think it would be a good thing if you would go away and let me see what I can do."

"Did Clare Margaret say that?"

"No. I think she is between two fires, but if one went out she could turn to the other to boil her billy."

"Did she say who she liked best?"

"No. I'm telling you that she can't make up her mind, and if one of us went away she would be satisfied with the other."

"Are you going away?"

"Damn it all, how could I, and take care of my property?"

"I see," said Darcy helplessly. He had no property.

"Excuse me for saying this, but I'm a bit older, and could provide for her better than you can, but if she really wants you, and you have the guts to go through with it well, I'll keep out of sight. I have no more time to waste. After all, Clare Margaret is not the only girl in the world."

"She is to me."

"To me too, of course, if I could have her, but if I can't, I don't see any force in mooching about as an old bachelor for ever."

"Whether Clare Margaret marries someone else or not there could never be any one else for me."

Darcy said this with an intensity astonishing to Vance—of different mould. The Delacys were like that, he reflected—emotional—*Irish*. It was attractive in the girls. They seemed to feel so keenly that beside them other girls were wooden and dull; but in men—damn it all, such sensitiveness made them girlish. That was what had foundered young Syme and Roger. Their company was so sought that they had been spoiled. And two of a kind would never do. An outsider might be charmed by Darcy, but surely Clare would be repelled by the Delacy qualities, which led to waste. He had to acknowledge, however, that Darcy showed none of Syme's or Roger's tendencies. He was as steady as a girl, but it was doubtful if he would ever have any property. A man could no longer acquire land by sitting down on it as the Anguses and others had done years ago. There would be nothing of Burrabinga left for any of them. He wondered how old Robert hung on as he did.

"If she means all that to you," said Humphrey, picking his way. "And—well—if you mean as much to her—I reckon the difference in age and the cousin business will have to go."

"But you point out that I can't give her a grand home, so I'll up and clear out." His mother's tribulations because of his father's failure as a provider came across the screen of experience as a warning.

"Will you?" said Humphrey, with a throb of hope.

"Straight wire, I will. I had a letter from my old boss this week asking me to join him on the Overland to Adelaide."

"I reckon that will let us both know which of our cakes is dough."

They lingered affecting interest in general matters. To both came insistently the swift river singing on the way to old Murrumbidgee Big Waters—a susurrant thoroughfare of sound accompanied by the yelp of a dog, the neighing of a horse, the cry of the curlews and plovers in the tea-tree swamp, the crickets chirping for rain. All sounds flickered out against that melody, constant as time, untamed as the wind.

"The river is so loud it promises rain," said Humphrey.

"Doesn't look like it," said Darcy, glancing at the sky, velvety black and crowded with stars. Both were impatient to return to Clare Margaret.

On Monday evening Darcy announced to her his intention of leaving Burrabinga again—this time permanently. She saw by his manner that something had decided him so she took her life in her hands and voted for love and poverty. Darcy tried to stand by his principles. They were together in the laundry on the bank of the river, the girl "folding down" for the morrow's ironing in the light of a hurricane lantern. Darcy helped.

"I thought you cared terribly for me—you pretended."

"I do, but I'm trying to save you. I have no property. Vance will have the whole of Longview."

Clare Margaret was practical. "You could take up that selection out by Bullock Gap, where Wong Foo used to fossick, on that ferny creek. I can do everything in a house. Look at this wash, piled to the rafters—a first class hotel couldn't have more. Most of them act as if they were conferring an honour on me to come and eat us out. That old swine who came with Dr Christopher on Saturday actually complained of fleas in his bed. He took them there from that mangy old dog he put inside the flower garden. He broke off my dahlias."

"A fatal accident is sneaking up on that dog."

"Goody!"

"I'm getting full of these old culls too. They smoodge around Roger but they order me like a rouseabout. One had the cheek to offer me a tip last week."

When all the linen was folded they sat together on the ironing

table and swung their feet and talked to the lullaby of the river
until the lantern went out for want of oil, and all the household
was in bed. They had caught a gleam of the light of life and were
exalted by the radiance. In it they ripened and laid plans within
the fortress of their preference for each other for a partnership
against the world at large.

Storms followed. Robert was proud, with Johanna's social values,
and had dreamed of Clare making a splendid match. Inconsistently
he had not employed the least stratagem to ensure this. His training,
or absence of training, by Danny, had not fitted him for such
diplomacy. He could not manipulate people to his will. He was
growing to be a lonely, if distinguished figure, resembling one of
the stately river gums among a scrub of saplings and underbrush,
but still unbowed by fate. He denounced Clare's intention on the
grounds of consanguinity, her seniority and Darcy's lack of property,
and said that Vance would be more satisfactory. He discussed the
matter with Margaret.

"It's a case of propinquity," she remarked. "I cannot understand
marriages between cousins on any other grounds. They lack
romance or novelty."

"It's as disgusting to me as it would be to think of marrying my
sister. Josephine and Harry will make an uproar."

"They should have kept him away."

"I like him, if it wasn't for this." Robert wished that Roger
promised half as well, but he was jealous as well as proud, lacked
his father's passion for abstract truth, and would not permit such
heresy to escape him.

There ensued a period of strain for the old people and Clare
Margaret and Darcy. Mavis, Vida and Roger welcomed the prospect
of Darcy to keep Burrabinga going. They wanted the dear old
homestead to come home to, and Darcy was one of themselves.
Clare Margaret had done more for the place than all the others
together, and felt that she had a right to the status of a son, but
women's rights had little of such logical results despite the political
enfranchisement granted some years before to Australian women
and applauded by the progressive throughout the world.

With signal wisdom Josephine and Harry refrained from public
comment on a marriage that was distressing to them.

"Marriage between cousins is revolting to me," said Harry.

"Cousins or strangers don't matter so much eventually as having
to drag along in poverty. With the publican taking the bread out
of the children's mouth, it is worse."

"As old Hennessy used to say," observed Harry grimly, "old Danny was the best of the Delacys. There doesn't seem to be any promise among the rising generation."

"It is a bitter thing for a mother to be helpless to do anything for her children. I knew that Darcy was gone just as much as the poor boy that was drowned, that day I watched him ride away. Heaven knows I tried to save him from questionable influences and this scratching on the land, but he would not listen to me."

The marriage took place six months later at Burrabinga. Mavis and Vida did not come from Sydney for it, and no one was invited in the neighbourhood. There was no pack of guests to gloat on a bride decorated with satin and orange blossoms: the principals were almost as modest as illicit lovers. The swarms of visitors to Burrabinga were relieved by Clare Margaret's self-effacement, which enabled them to say later, "You should have let your friends know so that we could have sent presents."

Humphrey wrote a letter of congratulations to Darcy and offered to be godfather to his first son. Coole Butler and Fannie (Vance) sent a present. Four years since they had married, much to Uncle William's satisfaction. That was one solid union of property with property in the family.

Following the wedding Darcy and Clare rode to Keebah for the night. Old Sandy and Janet were still living, but piteously old, and there was also one of the sons to extend a welcome. A special dinner had been prepared and Clare was given an egg cruet, which so touched her that she wept.

"That's her grand match, to her boy cousin," sniggered Uncle William to Jean. "A nice child, but as damned a fool as his father."

"Poor things. They have to make the best of it now."

"If they had some of the money they've squandered on cadgers and flash showing-off, they wouldn't be starting in the scrubs with their bare hands like our fathers and mothers did over seventy years ago."

"Clare Margaret won't have so much time to make fun of others now." Clare's entertaining ridicule found unfailing material in Uncle William's and Aunt Jean's peculiarities, but considering that Clare was now extinguished, Jean added, "We had better send them a wedding present."

"That flummery of silver plate to put on airs above themselves won't be any good at Bullock Gap. A cheque will be handy."

Clare—she dropped the Margaret in the struggle of marriage—

wrote Uncle William and Aunt Jean a grateful note and felt less
critical of the Bewucks.

She and Darcy selected on a creek abounding in tea-tree groves
where a horseshoe of ranges rose in tiers against the sunset. They
lived in a tent during the summer. Darcy and two men, plus Jim
the Carpenter from Burrabinga, worked to have a shelter before
the sleet of winter. To conform to the residential requirements of
the Act, the main house was Clare's, the kitchen and store-room
Darcy's, with the boundary line between. The home was of slabs
as the first hut at Burrabinga had been. Clare, however, insisted
upon two progressive features: all the floors were boarded and the
roof was of corrugated iron. The bark roofs of the early pioneers
had retreated to a lower social level, and Clare and Darcy clung
to their squatter grading.

Darcy had to guard the poultry from prolific native cats, and
lessen the marsupials on whose runs he had settled. He tanned
skins and sold them; the capable and tireless Clare made rugs of
more to be used as blankets. They made their own furniture and
displayed one or two "elegancies" collected in addition to the egg
cruet. After all the arduous and unflinching pioneering they had
less than Johanna had started with seventy years earlier. There
were no longer any friendly gins to wash for Clare.

On moonlit nights Darcy scarcely went to bed at all, but spent
his time in clearing while Clare helped him with the firing, as
Johanna had helped Danny at Bewuck. They had a start with horses
and cattle and began to collect a flock of sheep. They made a
garden and orchard in the deep pure earth of the flats, free from
weeds, blight or insects.

Their ceaseless endeavour to wrest an estate from the bush left
them no time to be lonely. They were glad to sleep during the
abbreviated nights and on Sunday afternoons. There were no
hordes of tourists to eat them to bankruptcy as at Burrabinga.
Their nearest neighbour was the son of Bella Rafferty, who, with
one of his Heulong cousins, was bringing forth a large brood in
James Fullwood's old homestead nine miles distant.

Bella was still living at Heulong. James, Charles and his wife,
as well as her sister, Euphemia Hennessy, and Hennessy himself,
were now all dead.

Towards the end of the first year Clare had to slacken her labours.
Darcy increased his—if that were possible.

All their thrift was needed to offset the descending rhythm of
trade. The demand for horses declined and declined. Bicycles had

banished horses in thousands from the towns. The progress of the horseless wonder was further alarming.

"Horses will soon be two a penny," the breeders said.

A few years more and the motor car, which had excited such derision at the beginning of the century, became a commercial reality—the final challenge to the horse, and all the swagger of his acolytes. Most people were still assured that the motor car could never be anything but a toy for the wealthy. The cost would keep it above the ordinary man, who would have to depend on the horse.

Other changes came. The district had been triumphant in the provincial and acrimonious rivalries for the site of the Federal Capital. The Plains were to be adorned with an ideal city scientifically planned. People in other countries found the name of Canberra in the cabled news and gave it a new mispronunciation. In the image of Washington, D.C., U.S.A., Federal Capital Territory was resumed.

Numbers of old pioneers were swept away as rubble before progress. It would have been an act of grace to leave undisturbed a few old identities, so soon to join the aborigines, whom they in a recent day had unfeelingly ousted, but a young and impatient democracy could not loiter. The old folks—all gone these twenty years—had to pull up their stakes in the sunset of their days. Birrabee and Keebah were resumed. This finished Sandy at something above ninety. He died of a stroke and left with a long *cortège* expressive of sympathy. Janet—only five years his junior—went with George and Janet Junior to Victoria. She was valiant and uncomplaining, but when the boundary gate of Keebah closed behind her she was shorn of all that had been her and hers through seventy years, and became a piece of displaced furniture, superfluous and with but one wish, to be brought back to rest beside her Sandy.

Their headstones dignify the pioneer graveyard where the wide day lights The Plains. Few remember them to-day. All the settlers contemporaneous with the first Delacy generation were too hard at work, too unschooled to leave written records. The shelters they erected against the blazing sun, the sparkling frost, the deluging rain and the wild winds sweeping without obstruction across a quarter of the globe, have decayed or been reshaped to other uses. The occupants have vanished as last year's snows from the frore highlands of their old time runs, their bodies returned to the comfort of the earth which their burial disturbed from an oblivion of cleansing fallowhood.

Robert Delacy, of all his coterie, was left for a time to reign alone at Burrabinga, the most tangible result of the dreams of the young Danny, who at eighteen sat on a stile one May day in old County Clare, projecting adventure and plighting his troth with his Johanna, with the lovelight in her eyes and the hardihood to elope with her Danny-boy to the "furthest extremity of the globe".

CHAPTER XLIII

Motor cars had conquered the Blue Mountains by 1905. Delacy's Peaks protected their realm a little longer but *decrescendo* was written under the high-spirited rhythm of blood horses' hoofs, and brought dispirited years to Burrabinga.

Old Robert's silken thatch still had no white threads, though there were some about his jowl. Mavis and Vida, when he visited them in Sydney, insisted upon Pa submitting to the King Edward clip, which had long been in vogue for squatters with any sense of style. Those who clung to the possum formation in whiskers had been relegated to farce, and ridiculed as Dad Waybacks, successors to the earlier bushwhackers.

Robert's flesh, in the Delacy way, grew less and less with age. He alighted gingerly at the end of the day, though he still rode spirited beasts of the old strains, and he and his dogs were about the runs all day and every day. He suffered at intervals, but Margaret's embrocations kept the wolf of decrepitude at bay. They were both feeling their age, with the whole elder generation departed as last season's leaves, and themselves on the outposts as the oldest hands.

To the oldsters the world never recovered from the passing of Victoria. King Edward had not time to sink his life-long role of Prince of Wales in that of King, ere he had gone, and his son had taken his place. That was better: King George and the new Queen had made themselves actual by a visit to open the first Commonwealth Parliament. Australia owned a social share in them.

Robert was the only Delacy, who in the false phrase, could carry his liquor. Alcohol was his constant resource in heat or cold, fatigue or depression, but no one ever saw him fuddled. Grog was forbidden to the lads at Bewuck. Uncle William was able to say, "I told you so," with reference to Roger, who patronized the hotel of Gool Gool because no reporting relatives were there. When he was ejected by some publican he would make to Ferny Creek and implore Clare to shelter him until he was fit to reappear. Margaret had never seen him in the trough of his bouts. As Johanna with Robert, she refused to be aware of anything that belittled her son. Robert accepted this as natural from a mother. The police and the publicans had early informed him, however, and his haughty spirit was hurt that he had to be grateful for their lenience.

Enlivenment came from the grandchildren. As soon as they could lisp they all plumped for Burrabinga. Adventure lingered in its orchards, its river, its domestic animals in the fascinating processes of multiplying. A boy could collect eggs from a score of species, or find an eerie or bring home baby possums and wallabies. There were no bird lovers or animal protectors to give him a bad conscience. And there were always horses. No Delacy walked except to catch a horse.

Another of Josephine's children died of chill after influenza. The tragic Delacys again! William said that Harry's brood were weeds. One of his own daughters, Sophie, was distinguishing herself. She had persuaded her father to send her to Shirley, a school conducted by two advanced Englishwomen, where she won scholarships and other prizes which diminished her expenses and earned her a reputation. She had begun pedagogic training at the University. William exulted in her. There were paragraphs about her in the local paper, and her picture had been in the *Town and Country Journal*. Hitherto no Delacy had been mentioned in the *T. and C.J.* unless he died.

" 'A live dog is better than a dead lion,' " said Clare at Ferny Creek, criticizing the picture. "One Delacy promises to be worthy of old Danny, as Hennessy would have said it. I must congratulate Uncle William."

William was not without uneasiness lest his prodigy might be "strong-minded", and shut out of matrimony, the weak-minded *per contra* being more fitted for that exclusive field for women.

Clare's boy had blue eyes and hair like black floss from old Danny. Clare taught him, and he could write a letter before he was six. He was also a dare-devil. Punishment was no deterrent to shinning the highest trees after birds' nests or to riding as recklessly as all the Delacys in one. He also had a tendency towards machinery and disgraced his tradition by preferring a bicycle to a horse. Josephine claimed his mechanical genius, as she was the only one of the fraternity "handy" with carpenters' tools.

He had been christened Brian Daniel, after Danny, and Franc-Alleu, after Johanna's mother, with reversion to the old spelling. Josephine deplored the hideous names, but Harry cherished the naming.

Clare was determined that the child should have the highest education obtainable. "It is time that one of the Delacys knew more than to be a drover or a boundary rider," she observed.

"They rack themselves delving about the ranges, just for loafers to cadge from them. We need a few Delacys with fat tummies to spread gold chains on, and to sit in town while others take a turn tigrinizing in the scrub."

She was thin and prematurely wrinkled and brown from hard work. Her wit had sharpened in the struggle, but her pride and the unfailing devotion of Darcy kept her up. Darcy seemed like an old man, not a peck of flesh on him, but people contended that emaciation was schetic of the Delacys. The weariness of his bearing wrung the heart of his father when he came on a visit.

Darcy attributed his state to having wrenched his back when fencing. Such work with the Delacy physique was the relegation of a racehorse to a wool wagon. Harry reported that the homestead was a wonder. He did not know how Darcy had managed so much grubbing and fencing.

"A pity it is such an out-of-the-way hole," observed Josephine. "Why the Delacys buried themselves there in the first place, puzzles me."

"The easy land was grabbed by the big fellows with capital, and influence with the officials. That region is one of the fountains of Australia."

"Lots of men started as convicts and left fortunes. The Delacys were free, yet came to nothing."

"To become rich you have to grasp without principle."

"Lots of rich people have as good a character as your father."

"I have never seen as great a character as my father."

"A man is not great who cannot provide for his family and attain some prominence."

"Criminals can be prominent. My father had a vision of the future. He opened a region without bloodshed among the blacks: Doogoolook and Maeve confirm that: and without convict slaves, or any ill-gotten gains."

"But he got nowhere. No Delacy has ever been a member of Parliament, or even the Mayor of Bandalong, or anything but a wasteful nonentity."

"Perhaps when all our hides are in the tanyard, it will be difficult to say who were the failures and who the successes." Harry was dispirited by his financial helplessness. Josephine had much to endure because of it and did not allow him to forget it.

The twist in Darcy's back did not mend. Clare had to bring him to the doctor all the way around by Heulong. Those living in the direction of Ferny Creek lacked the influence to obtain a bridge. One had been thrown across the river to transport materials during the building of a weir, but this was on the Learmont property, and Learmont threatened to shoot trespassers. Other landholders tacitly supported him. Opening the road would entail expensive fencing and the loss of acres now used in grazing.

The doctor said that Darcy had been dying on his feet for two years. Hard years of droving, followed by racking effort and frantic industry to provide a home for his Oread—beautiful as a quince blossom—had wrecked his sensitive frame. He was to be given all the peace possible. Nothing else now mattered. He craved to return to Ferny Creek. The litigious Learmont contesting the right of way to a bridge without approaches and high as a gallows in the air, was in the minds of Darcy's friends when they advised him to stay in Bandalong. Soon the rivers would be swollen with winter, and communication cut off.

"If I was home you could look after me better than all the doctors and nurses put together. If only I could have a rest I would be all right. Ghost! I'm tired."

Clare did not fail him. She choked back her grief, her warm heart all indulgence. She borrowed a buggy and drove him home. They had to ride from the Murrumbidgee. Trees had fallen in a recent gale and great holes had been washed in their bush track, but Darcy uttered no complaint. When Clare laid him down at the end of the journey, he was a waxen shadow, but the sapphire eyes thanked her with a look of contentment.

During the autumn days—soundless, still—Nature held her breath. The comfort of return lent Darcy a little strength, and soon he was able to sit in the sun. Clare was fortunate in old Dunlop, who could turn his hand to any task. As with many a homeless middle-aged man, his mistress was alcohol. He was an occasional boozer, who might once a year obey the craving, but Clare did not think he would go while responsibility braced him. Roger promised to come for some weeks after the autumn mustering and branding.

Darcy was free from pain and talked of being well when the cold weather went. Clare was feverishly happy those days, and her strength equal to the calls of housewife and nurse as well as the field work. She toiled and scraped with no one but young Brian to aid her. From early extravagance she had changed to hard thrift.

"Doctors are often mistaken," she said to herself, and recalled hopeless cases that had recovered.

Only Dr McKenzie was surprised that death delayed. During this reprieve old Dunlop's will collapsed and he departed for Gool Gool on imaginary business, where he began to drink himself to verminous emaciation in a pub beyond the township. Roger had gone in the same direction with butcher's fats, and camped in another pub.

The cold weather was a strain on Darcy, so Clare had his bed removed to the largest room, with the deep fireplace, in which the logs could be piled until they roared. When the crisp frosty weather was broken by grey skies and the portents of storm, she persuaded him to rest all day.

Darcy continued to complain of the cold, though the logs glowed white as a blast furnace and hissed as a rising gust whirled rain drops down the wide flue. As darkness approached and the animal world took shelter from wind and rain, Clare reheated the bed until it was an oven, but still Darcy shivered. Then Clare's heart missed a beat as she recognized the visitor who had come through the barred hard-wood door on the wings of the furious night and waited near the threshold. "No! No! Go away!" cried her heart in anguished resistance.

She knew nothing of death, despair unnerved her, but courage even as fear, is sometimes an entity beyond the volition of its host. Darcy began to talk, and she placed him comfortably on his pillows.

"You know, Grandpa was a dear old man. He gave me that beautiful Nullah-Mundoey with no more fuss than if it was a kitten. He was the most wonderful old man I ever knew—all those wise things people tell of him. When we're youngsters, we don't understand. We make fun of the old instead of finding out how they did things. It's too late by the time we have enough sense to know how wonderful they were."

"Are you warmer now, pet?"

"I don't know. I've forgotten. I wish I could talk to old Grandpa now. He could tell me what I wanted to know. He knew all about Ireland, but we never asked him about it. . . . Think of that time he lost his leg."

"Yes, and those spiffing yarns that old Hennessy told us about how he acted with the carriage, and when old Grace Butler wanted to get up a breach of promise case against Pa."

She talked with forced gaiety as the hour approached midnight and the Reaper drew ever nearer while Brian slept, and the wild wind was lashing the sleet on to the roof, tearing the vines from the veranda posts and laying low many a forest giant.

Darcy roused after a doze. "I'd like to be buried near old Grandpa! I'd like to do something friendly to him. He was such a friendly old man. He didn't mind us being only kiddies."

His head fell sideways, he gasped, a look of unutterable weariness passed across his features and left them calm and without expression.

Then Clare Margaret knew that she was bereft of her dearest, her richest anchorage. No miracle had spared her this ordeal. No miracle but that of fortitude would support her or extricate her from the finalities.

Numb with loss, she suppressed the desire to run sobbing to the child in the farthest room, and turned to prepare her beloved for his last sleep in her presence. The storm continued to shake the house and lash the big trees to frenzy as it rushed up from the vast south with a voice like the wrath of God.

When everything was in order she wakened the boy, who came wondering-eyed from his nest under the possum fur to the light of the kerosene lamp and the sinking fire.

"Is Father worse?"

"No pet, he will never suffer any more."

A sob stifled speech so that Brian, terrified, demanded, "Is he dead?"

His mother calmed him and said he could sit beside the bed and keep Father company while she arranged the cold room for his lying-in state. At daybreak she said, "You must go for Charlie Fullwood." This was Bella Rafferty's son, nine miles distant.

Brian departed, enjoined against galloping, or jumping over logs lest his sure-footed friend should slip in the water-logged tracks.

Fullwood set out immediately, leaving Brian to escort Mrs Fullwood. When she was ready she clambered on to an old neddy and the baby was handed up.

Charlie had arrived with a drenched horse, but Clare, working inhumanly, had milked the cows and was attending to the other animals. She was too tense for speech, and Charlie was relieved by his wife's arrival. He then went to inform Burrabinga.

The approaches to the foot-bridge had been washed away during the previous spring. Many things were in need of repair since Clare and Darcy had left, and Jim the Carpenter had gone to his rest in the station graveyard.

The river foamed past as on the day the mischievous Clare had rounded the geese into it. No one attempted the Burrabinga in flood. Hydraulic pressure would have swept the most dauntless horse off his feet or to some spot where there was no bank to land.

The dogs brought out the household. Roger was still in Gool Gool, Robert away on the run. Intuition told Margaret that a "bad turn" had to be reported. Nothing more could be done. The river would run down quickly if the rain ceased, but the dense snow clouds did not promise fine weather. If the river did not fall,

Margaret supposed that it would be necessary to bury Darcy at Ferny Creek.

Fullwood rode away to get a prospector on the Gool Gool road. Rain fell, steady and windless, warm and with no signs of clearing. When Fullwood returned it was time to dig-in for the night. They would go at dawn for the pine flooring-boards of Fullwood's dining-room.

Mrs Charlie reported Clare's intention of taking her husband to Bandalong. "We couldn't get round the sideling to Heulong bridge. Ferny Creek is washed out in deep holes." He repeated this to Clare.

"His last words were that he wanted to be buried beside Grandpa Delacy, and I'm going to do it."

"If only the bridge were finished," murmured Charlie.

"Surely to heavens!" she broke out passionately, "When I think of all I did at Burrabinga—went miles and days out of the way to care for people—any tramp or Chinaman was always looked after—there must be. someone to help me now, or they are a beggarly lot."

"How can we get to the bridge?" said Fullwood, but merely while he collected his wits.

The rain roared on the iron roof and trickled down the chimney and hissed in the fire. The augmented voice of Ferny Creek could be heard in the distance. No other sounds came from a drenched world. Beast and bird had sought shelter.

"My poor darling is so wasted, he can't weigh eight stone. Up the stiff places we can carry him. I can sew the coffin in bags so that it can be hooked on."

"Learmont wouldn't think twice about a charge of shot."

"We'll go at night."

"All right, Clare. We'll be ready."

Fullwood went out to talk with his mates. Decent men near to primeval Nature, to balk a woman exigent for her young or her dead would be blasphemy to them.

The old Fossicker took off his hat to think. "Christ!" was the most printable of his expletives. "We'd be a lot of old women if we couldn't do what she wants. Child's play to what I've seen on the diggings."

CHAPTER XLIV

THE lowering skies did not lift. It was one of the wettest months remembered in Danny's kingdom. A spring broke out in the stable. Water gushed up if a stick were thrust in the ground anywhere about the premises, but Clare was not to be deterred. Two more men had mustered from beyond the Fossicker's. No word had been allowed to seep to Learmont, a mile below the bridge.

As soon as Darcy was in his box they set out. The coffin was slung on an old salt lumper. The vast saturated bush was voiceless save for the patter of rain and the music of rills filling a hundred channels. Every gully had a creek swollen to a river, each hillside its cascading bridal veil. The horses sank to the hocks in mud or waded girth-deep through swamps and creeks. The hills and side-lings were the most difficult, as the earth gave way in greasy slithers.

The silent traveller lay through the first night in Annie Full-wood's best room. The party arose by candlelight and departed at dawn. The rain had ceased for a brief interval, and along the ridges the lyre-tails could be heard singing anthems in their arboreous transepts. The returning rain silenced the heavenly choristers who still accompanied the procession for some distance, and then fluttered across the track and disappeared down the precipices.

"I don't expect Learmont will give any trouble in the circumstances," Charles Fullwood whispered.

"The circumstances are just the ones he'll fight, if he knows anything," responded the Fossicker, who had seen life undecorated on many goldfields and knew that superstition was stronger than law concerning a corpse conferring the right of way to a place of burial.

"I'll deal with Learmont," said Clare, overhearing. "Darcy goes to Grandpa as he wished."

Brian shinned up a pole with a rope. Getting Father over the bridge became an adventure to him. "Here comes someone," he shouted.

"Old Learmont," said one of the men, halting in his task.

Clare nerved herself for combat. The rider approached, blazing with rage, until he noted the woman and that other malign shape.

His reaction was immediate. He dismounted and came on with uncovered head in the rain.

"Clare Margaret, I am very sorry for this," he said in earnest neighbourliness. He and the elder Delacys had been boys together. "I'm in time to lend a hand."

Clare broke down at that, while Learmont joined the men.

"You should have let me know."

"We hadn't time to send so far," said Fullwood.

"We thought you might run us off as trespassers," observed the old Fossicker.

"Circumstances alter cases," Learmont admitted.

At the farther side of the river the burden was carried to the bank by the men waist deep in water, who then took Clare and Brian. A horse and cart were fetched from a settler: messages were telephoned.

"A pity we had no time to let Burrabinga know," remarked Fullwood. "They might get out by the Keebah punt."

Clare's response was bitter. "I'm glad they did not know. Pa and Ma are too old to slop around in the sleet and get rheumatism. Every one else can go to hell, and stay there. No one came to our wedding. My poor lamb died on his feet slaving. After seventy years of pioneering we still had to start with our bare hands because we were mad on hospitality."

"But that is how the country got settled," murmured Fullwood, "by helping each other and sharing."

"I don't want any flash cadgers gloating now," snapped Clare.

Nevertheless telephones rang with the news of Clare Margaret. She had become Clare Margaret again like a princess resuming a title. Forgotten since her eclipse in a poor marriage, she now, in flood and storm, re-emerged with the silent Darcy and opened a thoroughfare.

Tales were revived of old Delacy's honesty and fearlessness.

"His deaf and dumb blackfellow on one side of him and a full blown Chow, as flash as a white man, on the other!"

"Started those horses from a colt that he stuck a wooden leg on."

"And scattered peacocks and billy-goats from Goulburn to Cootamundra."

"Any youngsters?"

"One boy, about eight."

"Old Danny's breed on both sides ought to produce something."

"Fullwood says he was like an engineer getting the coffin on to the bridge."

People met the mourners. Danny Delacy was a living legend,

and scarcely a soul in the district but had enjoyed the hospitality of Burrabinga. Many remembered the vivacious girl and her prancing horse and glittering gear, her pranks in all the gay swagger of the 'nineties, and this tragic reappearance stirred the imagination. A squatter between Butler's and the bridge met her with a buggy and pair, and the rough box rested in another drawing room for the second night with the winter flowers of the station garden laid upon it.

The rain held up at dawning as they left for the Township, but the sky was heavy and the wind had asperity. Fresh contingents of sympathizers followed for an hour or two and dropped back when others took their places.

Uncle William came to meet the procession with the Bandalong hearse. On, on, across the rolling grey plains in the biting cheerless day. The Township had not enjoyed so interesting a funeral since old Nullah-Mundoey had enlivened the route. Brian whispered to his mother, "All the people to see Father buried! They must think a lot of him."

"It's too late," said his mother grimly. "It doesn't matter what they think now."

Uncle William's plan for his niece to remain at Hennessy's with her Aunt Jean died when Clare Margaret looked through and beyond every one. Silent, tearless, stern, showing the ravages of hardship, she stood by the graveside, for the first time in her life careless alike of appearances or opinion while the sodden clods drummed on the coffin. The prelude to life with its flowery morning and perfumed zephyrs had passed: she had learned that life was an isolating monster; that those worthy of maturity—the givers—must ever meet it separate and alone.

The top boots which had been Darcy's one scrap of wedding finery, showed under her shrunken skirt. Her bare coarsened hands were blue with cold. She had lost her gloves at the bridge. The soaking rain had come on again. Someone held an umbrella over her. It was Humphrey Vance. He had looked at her across the grave but she had not acknowledged him.

He remembered the lilting girl on the blood filly, the budding woman in frilly gown, a-bubble with high spirits, and now, though she was a sombre and weather-beaten widow of thirty-three, in a battered hat and shabby coat, he knew that his heart still was hers. The quince blossom girlish beauty had left something of gipsy defiance in her unheeding despair as she stood by the filling grave, a sorely smitten woman, but clearly of fighting mind.

Vance would have stood by her to a greater extent than the

umbrella, but was too aware of his environment to bring gossip upon her. Also, she had not wanted him long ago and might resent his intrusion now, though he was nominally godfather to the boy. Later, he might assume some responsibility, but action involving expenditure needed deliberation.

He relinquished the umbrella to Harry Delacy, who had arrived in time for the burial. Financial helplessness was stamped upon his clothes, but he had Danny's wholesomeness of disposition, and neither defeat nor bitterness looked from his eyes as he acknowledged old friends. A cough racked his thin form, and people were relieved when the Vance umbrella shed some of the drops off him.

William tried to lead Clare Margaret from the grave after the first clods, but she would not move. All perforce had to stand with her. The shovellers worked furiously to shorten the ordeal and soon the mound was shaped. Still she stood.

"I'll bring her presently," Harry whispered to William, as the crowd withdrew to Hennessy's hotel to take nips against incipient colds and to discuss the widow, past, present and future.

"Vance can have her now," said one of Vance's employees. "She still must be sticking in his craw."

"Good iron wingey! Wouldn't it be a lift for her."

"My oath! She's a fool if she doesn't nab him now."

"Big streak of fool in all the Delacys—riding horses no sane man would back."

"Yes, and spouting poetry without being drunk neither."

"They were eaten-out by loafers—worse than rabbits."

"My oath, yes! The Vances started later and now are the nobs of the district, and the Delacys are going to pot."

"Old Vance never gave a meal away, even in the early days."

"Showed his common sense."

"Old William has enough savvy to sit like a clucking hen on what he has. Old Robert's overdraft must be a boomer."

"Hear the kid ask if they were going to cheer his father?"

"By cripes! she deserved a cheer, bringing him out like she did."

"It put old Learmont's pot on properly. Have another?"

"By oath, I will. It's so flaming cold it will turn to snow."

The bar talk eddied to the price of wool and live stock.

Brian's question about the cheers had issued in a clear treble. His only other gathering had been a football match at The Plains where the hero of the game had been hip-hip-hoorayed.

Harry and Clare lingered by the grave. The large attendance at Danny's funeral had inspired the sons to replace Johanna's modest headstone by a pair of more elaborate design. The cost had fallen on William. Robert had not yet sent a cheque for his share, and Harry rarely had a penny.

The horizon was obscured by a veil of slanting rain that soaked the mourners in spite of the expensive umbrella as they read the epitaphs, and Harry then and there informed Brian of the great qualities of his great-grandparents.

CHAPTER XLV

UNCLE William hurried them to Hennessy's, to dry clothes, a big fire, and nips of grog. Harry made light of his cough, which had persisted since the whooping cough contracted on the roads with the wheat when a boy. He suffered keenly his inability to aid his daughter-in-law, but as Josephine constantly pointed out, he could not give his money to the publicans and still have it for his own use. He had been twice rescued with advances on Josephine's expectations, but this had not prevailed against droughts and the mismanagement due to a lack of bargaining proclivities. He was now meditating a loan from William.

"Don't take it too hard," said Uncle William to Clare. "I'll take a look around myself. A few pounds is neither here nor there, if you're wanting it. We can spare it."

"Of course we can," said Aunt Jean.

Clare appreciated this liberality, but her pride was wounding her. William was generous to his relatives, also, since Vance's action with the umbrella, Clare's stock had begun to rise again. She always felt the necessity to stress friendliness with Uncle William since maturing to understand the depth of the affront she was supposed to have put upon him long ago. He, on his side, had come to see that it had not mattered.

"You are a strong young woman yet, and time does wonders," he said, bent on cheering her so that he could show her the wonderful photograph of Sophie in her cap and gown. Sophie was the only one of old Danny's stock achieving any distinction. William could afford to be bountiful to the once-gay and merry Clare Margaret now a sorrowing widow. His boys promised to be capable of holding what he had accumulated—something for thanks when one of Robert's sons had been killed and the other was thriftless, and Harry's were so delicate that they had early disappeared.

"I'm glad that Sophie has struck out and got education," said Clare. "If I drop like a bullock in the chains for it, I mean to give Brian a chance. Only fools drag at this pioneering. The fat slugs who never soil their hands come and sit in the places we've bursted ourselves to make."

When the rain lifted William drove her home by Heulong bridge. Harry had delight in little Brian, and Josephine invited Clare to bring the boy to Murrumbong, but she was eager to be at Ferny Creek, where the old Fossicker was in charge.

Josephine was not softened towards Clare Margaret by Darcy's death. Clare had lured him from home; she had won. Josephine remembered her last view of the boy riding away across the dusty paddocks in defiance of her plans. Had he listened, he would now have been in a comfortable school instead of having bullocked himself into an early grave; and that he would have been wearing good clothes was in Josephine's subconsciousness. Old Johanna had struggled until the end for the elegancies through which Danny had charged like an antelope at a horse fair. Josephine, in her turn, longed for the sleek city man, and the pavement parade for herself instead of the shaggy bushman and his isolated home. The mating instinct brews a delirious spring, then follows a long summer and autumn, frequently of incompatibility.

Roger had got as far as Ferny Creek to find the Fossicker alone. Dunlop appeared later and the three were there when Clare returned to reflect bitterly that any of them could better have been spared than the light of her existence.

Before the river was safe to ford, Robert with the hardiest of his dogs came to ask Clare to return to Burrabinga. But Clare refused firmly. Ferny Creek was all that she had for her boy, and she meant to hold it.

Disappointed, Robert turned to execrate Roger. Roger in turn, accused his father of neglect to instruct his sons regarding the need for sobriety, and laid the blame for his youthful surrender to alcohol on the fact that it "was everlastingly shoved under my nose". Outsiders thought Robert obtuse to his son's delinquencies, or that he had lax standards, but that was due to his pride. He rode homeward with William's early warnings—so contemptuously dismissed—bitter in his recollection, while Roger raged about the slack way he had been reared.

"Nothing but New Guinea will pull you up this time," said his sister dryly. "Queensland will be too cool to keep your indignation at boiling point. You can't blame Pa for what you were doing while Darcy was dying and I was alone."

This pierced Roger's armour. He abjured alcohol and returned to Burrabinga to rebuild the foot-bridge far above flood level.

When the river was safe Margaret rode out to add her persuasions to Robert's.

"It is kind of you and Pa, but I could never go back to waiting on a lot of tourists for nothing. Mavis and Vida had stacks of useless wedding presents, but I had nothing. I mean to educate Brian so that he can escape to the city and have everything to his hand. The Delacys have done their share of tigrinizing for others to reap the benefit. It's time some of the city people worked a little of the corporation off themselves. Grandpa and Grandma, then you and Pa pioneered like navvies, and yet Darcy and I were not a bit farther along. The poor darling had to be hauled out to be buried like something from the North Pole."

"What would be a pity would be to leave the benefits to outsiders after doing the slogging. You must do as you feel best." Margaret turned to other subjects.

"It's a pleasure to see Uncle William's pride in Sophie," said Clare with a flash of her old humour. "He has the copyright on the only Delacy that isn't a dud. He's so pleased with me now as a down-and-outer that he's forgiven the night he got to bed with Mrs Vance."

"I hope William will never know sorrow or loss. We shall be grateful if his children carry the name to the top."

Clare was well-off for man power while her loss was fresh. Every neighbour offered to carry a load of supplies or to mend a fence, and so forth. Dunlop had straightened up once more and was due to give a term of excellent service. The Fossicker too, was glad to ring-bark or do odd jobs during the winter in return for his keep under a sound roof.

"She can't carry on there with nothing but men," said Robert. She did though, for a time, preparing to part with Brian for his own sake. She was willing to mortgage the property to assist one bright Delacy intellect to something other than bushwhacking, and in this was part of the general revulsion against bush life that was infecting the people.

The city lured. Young men who had slogged from dawn until night in fencing or grubbing, hilling potatoes or ploughing in the dust, or tending sheep, or who were tied to a dairy, thought that to drive trams, or guard the lunatics in the asylums, or work in the gardens of such institutions, or to stroll about dressed-up as policemen in shifts of a mere eight hours, was girls' play. To receive for such service high and sure wages with no loss of sleep through fear of frost, or drought, or blight, or a slump in demand, which reduced return for produce to less than its carriage to market—well, only woop-woops would longer endure bent backs and grunting effort to support city parasites. It was the bushman's turn to rest while others carried the loads.

Times were hard. Burrabinga was in a sad way, less two males and the most stirring female Delacy, and with the market for beef and horses steadily declining. Bank foreclosure was postponed only in the hope of recovery.

Clare was safe at Ferny Creek. She had a picked flock of merinos. The place was dog-fenced and cleared on the rich deep flats and on some of the slopes.

Brian was sent to school in Sydney. Mavis, who lived at Burwood, took him, and he attended the public school there. He was a long way behind other boys in his subjects, but he applied himself to study and settled happily to his changed life. His mother's hopes were on him. For his sake the days were all too short. To throw a sop to convention she acquired a gentlewoman whose husband had led her a dog's life and finally abandoned her while he retired to Darlinghurst Gaol. She was pleased to retreat from censorious tongues and more relieved than touchy that the *alias* of Mrs Thingamebob generally hid her real name.

Humphrey Vance found business to bring him to Ferny Creek. Clare was able to spare her outer paddocks for agistment and thus earn more for Brian. She was indebted to Vance for equitable pay for her grass, good prices for her live stock, inquiries about his godson, and the example of his close-fistedness.

Harry was dogged by ill-luck as well as mismanagement. The youngest girl passed in an epidemic of diphtheria. Only Isabel survived. She was a sturdy, opinionated woman who met Josephine in full combat. A final battle-royal had resulted in Isabel training as a nurse and disappearing into the Orient with a medical mission. Josephine denounced her as an ingrate, but Uncle William laughed merrily about her, and Clare said she was glad to see her making a profession of the Battle self-righteousness instead of wasting it on the family.

Margaret and Robert were like two ring-barked gums, stripped but not yet struck to the ground by lightning or wind. Roger had his uses to his mother. Because of him she had no trouble in securing "jineroos" to fill the place of her departed daughters. The ambition to be established in the squattocracy lured many a subaltern lass beyond the Murrumbidgee. City girls still had the illusion that it was necessary only to reach a station to enjoy easy wealth and a continual picnic of adventure.

Roger had all the Delacy charm, which none of the family had so far been able to market as personality. He was not one who absorbed from others, nor who shoved both fists in the bag when perquisites were being distributed—ah, there was the family weakness. He had sweethearts in all the townships of his operations— Cooma, Bungendore, Bandalong, Gool Gool, and farther afield, but showed no disposition for the fetters of marriage.

Old Danny's breed was lying fallow as far as any distinction in his descendants was discernible.

CHAPTER XLVI

THUS the Delacys and other integral units of the populace drowsed along until one fine day they found the world at war. From Chicago to Baghdad, Tokyo to St Petersburg, Canton to Canberra and Rio de Janeiro, and back again to London, wiseacres were assured that it could not be real. Just some mad scare: the dogs of war would be back in their collars again in a twinkling.

Kitchener was predicting that it would be a three years' job, and was regarded as a war-monger, talking in character. War could not last with all the modern appliances. Europe would be blown to smithereens in two weeks. The doctrine of "frightfulness" to make war so terrible that men would shrink from beginning it, had mesmerized the masses.

France had no illusions.

The war continued and spread. Nation after nation became infected—"got hysterics", as an old lady remarked in Chicago. Australia heard England's bugles "blowing o'er the sea, as they had called a thousand years". That calling, calling, across the wintry sea, aroused England's outposts. Once more the lust for adventure in beef-fed men was fanned to imperial uses by sentiment conducted through the umbilical cord of quasi-nationhood.

Australia will be there, will be there!

The Australians swaggered up again to fill contingents as for the Boer War—cavalry, too, though the rhythm of horses' hoofs was but a dying echo far down the road to yesterday.

Ethically progressive mentality and engines of war are incompatible.

The war for votes for the Uitlanders had with time assumed a different complexion to the veterans of that campaign, but the saving of gallant little Belgium was a brand new cause to ignite the idealist in Youth—a glamorous war cry to disguise the lust for blood, the lunacy of general havoc.

Margaret winced to recall the going of Syme. She could still hear the thunder of the farewell salute on the last day she had seen him. She hoped that Roger would not contract war fever.

Station people were hopeful that the price of produce would rise and set the pastoralists and farmers on their feet again: the country would be cleared of a lot of wasters and braggarts as in the Boer War.

The Delacys were not war-minded. Danny's contempt for arms and braggadocio had made them indifferent to soldiers and all that they stood for. Still, there was one Delacy who heard the call of adventure. He had respected the Germans, having heard that they were people who could amass property, and were up-to-date in trade; but Sophie was a stout jingo, and informed her family to the contrary. The news that the Germans—unlike many natives and imported wasters—did not look upon Australia as a "beastly hole", soon began to tell. The *Emden* incident was near home and put pep into the whole performance.

Young Dan from Bewuck enlisted.

Clare was so startled that she spoke of bringing Brian home.

"There are plenty of wombat holes at Ferry Creek for him to hide in," said Uncle Roger. "If the whole Australian contingent hid in them instead of going overseas to shoot Turks, it would be better business."

Dan's family went down to see him embark, much to the amusement of the Burrabinga girls in Sydney. Their letters to Clare Margaret were full of merry ridicule of the antics of the Bewucks in town. Aunt Jean, it was asserted, was lost in George Street and sat on the edge of the pavement until the police took up her case. Uncle William meanwhile was wrapped around a lamp post in King Street and coo-eeing so that she would know his whereabouts. Rescued from this predicament they rode all night in an automatic lift where help could not reach them.

Little Brian, however, took his cousin seriously. He had the adventure from the schoolboy angle. Dan from Bewuck, sweating along to Woolloomooloo, and then climbing the rigging of the ship, was a hero to him. Brian was proud of Dan and hoped that the war would last until he too could go amid cheers and crowds, and the thrilling thunder of a military salute across the harbour. He wrote to his mother that the jokes of Aunties Mavis and Vida about Aunt Jean and Uncle William were mostly taradiddle. Brian liked Sophie. She was the only one who took an interest in his lessons and helped him to win a prize.

Kitchener and Bobs made a popular come-back. Some of the horses and bulls named after them and Oom Paul, Cetewayo, Umslopagaas and Lobengula were still remembered. Anticipation of the newest atrocity made the newspapers more exciting than a detective novel. From lurid propaganda hungrily absorbed, grew the belief that the Allies were a race of God-fearing crusaders saving heroic little Belgium, and that of these, the Australasians—speedily become the glorious Anzacs—outstripped every other breed of men at five to one. Through the restricted channel of the cables the news could be kept pure and undefiled by reason or the truth of the criticism voiced by the thinkers, and war glory made a resounding din from pole to pole.

In the absence of the picked men, all kinds of persons, super-annuated, superfluous, or flawed by God, found in the war resur-rection and liberation, and accordingly revelled in it. Fear of financial depression was speedily removed by inflated prosperity.

Wool! Wool! Wool!

Wool was crowned king anew. The big sheep men became local kings. Every cockatoo farmer entrenched himself as a thriving wool squire by the aid of sacrificial dogs ruthlessly bred and ruthlessly trained as a substitute for slave labour.

The Robert Delacys had not run to sheep. The poking quality of the industry had repelled such caballeros. Burrabinga, however, had lands to let, and endless horses and dogs, and no men knew the area as did Robert and Roger. Robert had hopes of catching up with the interest on the mortgages.

Roger was kept away from the townships because all the girls were hysterical about the glorious heroes, and continually demanded of him to enlist. He was goaded to try but was rejected for physical disabilities, of a nature to rob him of any swagger in the eyes of the ladies.

Good fortune came to Clare Margaret with the boom in wool. Her flocks were first class and she was well-off for man power. Old Dunlop continued to soak at intervals, but was glad to crawl back. The Fossicker also was happy to work at Ferny Creek without recourse to Wages Boards for the fabulous gold which he was certain remained in the gullies. Indeed, he found plenty to supply his simple needs. These retainers were permanent because Clare left them alone. They could combine the freedom of hatting with adjacence to a home and did not make off as formerly from any community where women appeared.

Clare Margaret's wool brought a high price at first and later was purchased by B.A.W.R.A., or the great British-Australian Wool Syndicate. She banked money. Her property increased in value, and was entirely at the service of Brian's education. There was to be no retirement among the dingoes for that young man.

The war went on and on, draining even far-away Australia of first-class man power. Europe had become a shambles. As war fever progressed from initial hysteria to chronic paranoia, there arose a clamour for conscription. The Australian boast of fighting as free men was to be challenged. Australia mustered crusaders, who, from hustings up and down the Commonwealth, and at the risk of personal assault, strove to publish the facts of the war that was wrecking European civilization. Among these were a few independent thinkers devoted to truth, and many more who believed that here was an opening to pay off an old grievance against England. The crusaders were branded as cowards lacking the spirit of a louse; perverts who combined with irreconcilables—traitors—to let down the glorious heroes in the trenches. Recrimination and vituperation reached furnace heat, and then the heroes on active service themselves rejected conscription.

No imputation of slacking could have held against the battle-scarred features, the virile appearance of a big fellow declaiming in Hyde Park, while his mates upheld him. No one dared to interfere with his sentiments, as the men wore on their sleeves the letter "A", emblem of the sacred Anzacs, extolled by Press and public as the equals of the gladiators of old. "You see, it was this way, we came over here as free men to fight, and we've had a bellyful of war—a double-dyed-damned bellyful, with all this saluting like a monkey on a stick. We came to save Belgium and end war, and all we're getting out of it is to be made lick-spittlers like the people here. Instead of saving any one, we're being made like them, and we'd be damn' cowards to force the other poor young bastards out home to come by force, now when we know what it's like."

"For God's sake vote to keep young Dick out of this," was the type of admonition in scores of letters from elder brothers in the trenches. The day was saved, symbolically or actually for a shred of freedom. There were people, with names great in the humanities, who graded this as the outstanding distinction won by the Australian warriors, and one of the most heroic incidents of the war. "The Diggers," exploited *ad nauseam* by military propagandists, in this took a stand magnificent in its isolation and independence. Other armies could tell of battles held or won, and flaunt the trophies taken with mad heroism equalling that of the Australians, but only these men from *the furthest extremity of the globe* had volunteered to fight as free men, and, in the midst of world hysteria, coolly maintained their right to do so. For what it might mean, there it was, a lone banner unequivocally unfurled in a demented world.

Advance Australia Fair!

The Delacy women in Sydney—capable needlewomen—sewed, sewed, sewed; knitted, knitted, knitted, on those bales of pyjamas, those bales of socks, those bales of baby clothes, famous from Monastir to Belgium and to London's slums, so many of which went to the decimated Serbs in Macedonia, and so many to the haunts of the fishes *en route*.

That was as near as the Delacys, except Dan from Bewuck, got to the war. One of the Butlers had taken a commission and was rising to glory as a major.

At the end of 1916 Humphrey Vance created a sensation by enlisting. Every one said that he was the last man of whom it was to be expected. Clare Margaret was really responsible. After two and a half years of renewed hovering he had definitely asked her to marry him. She as definitely refused. The glamour of her love for Darcy remained. She could not put this heavy, middle-aged man in her darling's place. And there was Brian. He was her life work. She had managed alone in the impossible years: she would not share him with any one now when money was easy and the way clear.

"Oh, well, then, I might as well take a look at the way they are coming along in Europe," announced Humphrey.

Clare Margaret expressed regret that he should endanger himself. He laughed comfortably. "I've no ambition to run around butchering Turks with a bayonet, or bombing Germans. I shall get into the remount department. They want men who know something of horses."

This made him a new butt for the bright Delacy wit. What could he know of horses, poking about on open country after sheep? To the highly specialized Delacys, his knowledge of horses might have been fifth rate, but to the officers who were wont to come to New Glenties or Longview to blunder after rabbits or wallabies on over-fed crocks, he was a marvel of practical knowledge, and readily given a commission in Egypt.

Young Dan from Bewuck never came back. He never walked the home way from those gates at Woolloomooloo, through which he had sweated so gallantly in quest of adventure—never, not even as one of the nerve-shattered or mutilated, who are still serving their sentence to Mars.

CHAPTER XLVII

WAR gripped the world as a chronic state wherein people ceased to realize any other kind of existence, and were devoid of any other pre-occupation.

Then suddenly the slaughter ceased. The word *armistice* took the place of the word *war*. Brutalized and exhausted peoples, destitute of leaders of vision or followers of faith, groped in a limbo of shattered ideals and discredited philosophies. Nevertheless the welcome home celebrations were flattering to the survivors, and a relief to the spiritual lesions of the non-combatants who organized them.

Bandalong turned out to honour its returned heroes, led by Major Butler, who had not suffered a scratch and was covered with glory and medals. His mother—Robert Delacy's rejected adorer— was the only Fullwood who had done well for herself socially and financially. Her son, the Major, was companioned by Captain Vance.

Later, Bandalong erected a monument to its soldiers, fallen or standing. The dedication took place during the holidays, so Brian and his mother came in a sulky driving a Nullah-Mundoey who could do the fifty miles from Ferny Creek and go home next day undistressed, though she was seventeen. All the progressive and prosperous now had motor cars, but they were not used in the procession, because horses had not yet accepted them and there was the difficulty of combining the old pace and the new. Brian was vain that one of the heroes was his godfather, though Vance had been merely nominal in the office. All the living Bewucks were present, and Dan's name was in gold on the granite column. There was pain in their glory, but Dan had bequeathed his family a gratifying importance for the holiday.

"It's like Daddy's funeral," said Brian. "Only it is not raining and there are more people."

"It's a funeral sure enough," responded his mother. "All the poor fellows who never came home to be buried."

Every one greeted Clare Margaret and her son. She recalled the day that her boy's father had come riding on his heroic pony,

Deerfoot, and her heart was desolate; but no one else remembered Darcy. He was not mentioned.

"Brian is the living image of my father," said Uncle William, and added, "If he's as good a man, he'll be harmless."

"A great old pioneer!" remarked someone else.

"I'm glad there's no pioneering for Brian to do," observed Clare.

"Oh, but I want to be a pioneer," chirped Brian. Someone laughed.

"He was luckier still to miss the war," volunteered another.

"Plenty more wars to get into as soon as he is ready."

"I thought you fellows went over there to end war."

"More like the beginning of dozens by the look of Europe."

There was a band to drown such banal babble; as well as the Member for the Constituency, the Mayor of Bandalong, and others to make speeches. There were, as show pieces, stifling in their uniforms in the blazing sunlight, a few of the surviving Anzac heroes of France and Flanders and Egypt, who were receding so swiftly from public interest, that with the dedication of the Memorial that day, they became a memory.

When the ceremony waned, Clare drove to the cemetery, where northerlies, searing from the equator, southerlies, blustering from the pole, blow on the high point beyond the Township, and the roads cross and run away to Monaro and Melbourne, Riverina and Bathurst and Sydney.

"Every one says I'm like Great-grandpa," said Brian, reading old Danny's inscription, "What was he like?"

"I only saw him when he was a grandfather, but you have the blue eyes and silky black hair, and Grandfather was smallish, like you."

"Why was he called old Hopping Danny?"

"Because he had a wooden leg."

"Was he a soldier?"

"No. He was a pioneer."

Brian was invited to all the family places: to old Glenties and New Glenties, and Longview, Bewuck and Heulong. At all he asked questions about his great-grandfather. He was eager for an ancestral hero like the splendid war heroes, and Great-grandpa Danny was the most promising material.

"Why was he called Fearless Danny? Why was he called Nullah-Mundoey? How did he get the wooden leg?"

These questions called basic and satellite yarns from old tongues. Clare Margaret too found pleasure in reconstructing her grandfather. Upon the demand of Brian he reappeared as a personality big in heroic as well as humorous stories, a man who could emerge larger than life from ridiculous anecdotes. He had talked much with Darcy during that first visit when the boy had been captivated by the gift of the Nullah-Mundoey. Darcy had constantly repeated his knowledge to Clare Margaret and she had a full store to draw from.

"Tell me about the time Grandpa Danny brought the peacocks?" Brian would demand. He would question his Burrabinga Grandmother, another gifted raconteuse, rich in tales of Great-grandpa, and humorous. He would gallop off to Burrabinga to get the rights of the story of Billy the goat, or of the finding of Doogoolook and Wong Foo. "Tell me again about Great-grandpa and the Yackandandah. Tell me about the time he brought the carriage home to Great-grandma."

Clare sent him to his Grandfather Harry, settled at Bowral. From him she knew he would come to know much that he might otherwise miss. The visit was bliss, and renewed hope in Harry. Josephine was pleased with the lad's "handiness". He returned full of ambition and lore and an increased interest in old Nullah-Mundoey. "I'm sorry there is no pioneering for me to do," he would sigh.

"You must turn pioneering backsy-fore and be the first Australian Delacy to go to the old country and do something there—something better than leaving your bones in the mud like poor young Danny and Syme."

"I'm afraid the kid will be no better at money-grubbing than the rest of us," said his Uncle Roger.

"That's why I'm arming him with every scrap of education I can get."

Brian's mechanical gift grew with him. When a motor car penetrated to Ferny Creek and broke down, he righted the trouble. He decided to work with motor cars forthwith, but his mother persuaded him to continue with his studies, just to please her.

"You must swim the Yackandandah of those exams," she said with a twinkle. A sense of humour was a bond between them. Clare Margaret's idea of education was to pass examinations so brilliantly that the result was letters after the graduate's name. She lacked acquaintance with any other view of it.

At Burrabinga, foreclosure by the Bank cast its shadow. "It will kill poor old Pa and Ma," they all agreed. Every one was aghast at uprooting the fine old pair. Bank officials and influential friends presented a plan to capitalize the hospitality of the homestead. If Clare Margaret would return and run a guest house there would be little difference excepting that guests, instead of eating their friends out of their home, would help to eat them in.

"Your friends would rally to you," said the Bank manager.

"Yes, like they did to me when I married," said Clare.

"A lot sent kind letters when Darcy died," remarked Roger.

"Yes, when it cost them only a stamp and a bit of paper."

"You don't want to let yourself get bitter."

"And you don't want to let yourself get bitters," retorted his sister. "If you kept off the booze you could save Burrabinga yet. I could if I was let at it without interference."

The decision was to adhere to agistment. Flocks were priceless, there was brisk demand for grass country, and the boom had every prospect of continuing. The guests were dropping off with the old people's increasing age: expenses could be cut in many directions, and Roger was blithe about pulling the place together. Clare would not risk the loss of her hard-won independence. Mrs Thingamebob gave thanks for the preservation of a situation wherein the energies of a mistress, usually directed to making a house a place of petty persecution and unrest, had to go to the superintendence of remunerative flocks.

The Vances had progressed to the champion class of sheep breeders at the Sydney Show, which meant that they led the world as growers of fine merino staples. Their wool attracted the notice of foreign buyers to other growers in the district, and Clare Margaret benefited. Her brand was sought and her neat bales went to market by way of the bridge which Darcy had opened.

With a year or so at Ferny Creek to delay him, Brian advanced to the University. Clare Margaret had been wise as far as she knew concerning the relation of examinations to education. Brian's facility in imbibing knowledge won him one scholastic prize after the other and attracted attention in the Faculty of Arts. He had inherited old Danny's wiry speed on his feet, and prominence in games made him more important to his fellow students than if he had discovered why men were born. His interest in machinery was diverted for the present into a delight in maths.

He arrived home on his first vacation in a motor car. By bargaining and exchanging he had a machine that could be nursed to go for miles at a stretch. He also had money in hand.

"Whoop!" exclaimed Clare. "Perhaps the Delacys are going to produce a financier at last."

"Old Danny will never be dead while he is alive," said those who remembered old Nullah-Mundoey. Brian wore that as his panache and took his great-grandfather as his standard. In a difficulty he would recite the old man's exploits. "If," thought Clare, "I can only get him to follow Grandpa's lead in other directions, he will be safe from one kind of woman."

For the present girls had little interest for Brian. He thought more of the conspicuous pipe he was cultivating in imitation of his progenitor. He loved the Murrumbidgee area as deeply as old Nullah-Mundoey could have desired. The influence of his grandfather Harry had also to be considered. The region was being dredged from oblivion by the projection upon it of human personality. A land beloved, as a being cherished, garners spiritual identity.

Brian was skilled in handling horse or car, but he said the horse was dead commercially. "He's staggering on his last legs now, except for pottering about on rough country. Next it will be the aeroplane everywhere. Golly, I'd like an aeroplane for travelling and a car for small errands."

The daring had long been risking life and limb in motor car races and by stunting in the air. The air suggestion terrified Clare Margaret, but this danger was out of the question financially, and the desire died down in Brian when he was half-way through his University course. Having wasted a year in the transition from pupil to student he became a glutton for studies.

"I'd tremble to think how she'd take it if anything happened to him," said her family.

"There's a lot to come out of him from others as well as old Honest Danny that might throw him off the rails," said old Dunlop, who had worked about the district since Brian's granddads had been in their prime.

During the bold boom years that sprang like giant nettles from the humus of havoc, young Brian, with not a care, was a worthy object of parental and national pride. In due course he achieved his Bachelor's degree with honours, and his mother, exhausted by excitement, went to Sydney for the graduation revels. There were friends among the University staff who insisted upon the acceptance of their invitations, and did much for her pleasure. These were hold-overs from the palmy days of Burrabinga, who had lapsed from association through gathering age rather than because of Burrabinga's moth-eaten finances, as Clare was touchily inclined to think. It was placed to Brian's credit that he had not swanked about this intimacy with the dons.

"Pooh!" said Brian. "My great-granddad, Nullah-Mundoey Delacy, was a greater man than all the professors glued together. You should see where he took the first bullock dray beyond the

Murrumbidgee. I'd like to see old Prof. —— confronted by such a problem."

Pioneering had become a passport to social importance. Young people swaggered about having the greatest number of Australian forebears possible, and the more bullocking these had done the better.

The country regions had an epidemic of centenaries, marked by festivals of remembrance in the banal little towns, which drowsed in arrested mental development. Even Bandalong had a Boomerang Week to celebrate the arrival of Mr Moore, who had settled there some years before he had come back from Ireland with young Delacy. Sophie was an eminent daughter who honoured her native town and was proud of Brian.

Clare Margaret was able to say to Uncle William, "There are two Delacys able to distinguish themselves, at all events."

William was happy and proud. He had long since forgiven Clare's flightiness and respected her as one able to hang on to her property. They could talk of wool and markets as twin souls. "What is Brian going to do with his grand education now that he has it?"

"He's hankering for the motor car business."

."But isn't he educated well enough for a doctor or lawyer? It would be a waste of money if he did not use his education."

"At any rate he has it. I was determined he should not be like all the other Delacys, feeling clever enough to be Attorney Generals, but with only a rabbiter's education."

Others were curious about the purpose of Brian's "flash education". The land was in favour again with the boom in wool. Weird little selections of hop scrub and wallaby runs, far back on barren ridges beyond Goulburn and Gunning, Bandalong and Yass, which had been the retreat of casual labourers, now commanded extortionate sums.

One fine day Clare Margaret grew hysterical with pride upon receiving the news that Brian Daniel Franc-Alleu Delacy had been awarded the James Gawler scholarship. This carried £300 per annum for two years at one of the leading universities of Great Britain, with the possibility of a third year, if so recommended by the authorities of the chosen university. Brian was brilliant in a number of subjects, including philosophy, history and economics, and had a talent for applied mathematics which should have put him in the Engineering Departments if this ability had not been jostled by his hunger for academic subjects.

This award set the seal on his excellence in scholarship and character. There were those to point out that it took life to test what was real talent, not this cramming at universities; but this was not the point of view of the prize winners, nor of their immediate families, especially outsiders like the Delacys for whom a university retained its prestige and superiority.

All the families consented to be proud of Brian. He was easy to lionize. He had the physical health of his progenitors and the Delacy humour, in its broader, kindlier aspects of liberated personality as distinct from the carping ridicule of those suffering inhibitions or a sense of failure. He was claimed by the squattocracy as a bush boy, and his residence in Sydney had broadened him into an all-round Australian. Tales of old Danny gained him the ears of the reporters. The members of his family, accepting a strong lead, recalled Grandfather as an original and extraordinary character with manifestations in keeping, rather than as an oddity with an Irish brogue. Clare Margaret pasted this fresh notice in the scrap-book with the obituary tributes to old Danny. "At last," she exulted, "There is a Delacy who is something more than a waster throwing away opportunities of fortune by supporting spongers." Old Harry was similarly jubilant.

People warned Clare Margaret that she would lose her boy by letting him go to England, that all the geniuses stayed in England or were grabbed by the United States, and Australia had to be content with the ordinary natives or importations of small calibre.

"If I lose him, I lose him," said Clare Margaret. "He shall have his chance without any strings. I'd rather lose him to England or the United States than have him wasted as a dingo here."

People suggested that she should go with him.

"No. I stay right on Ferny Creek. I'm only an old wombat, but I'm a queen wombat on my own run. I'm not going forth to be exhibited in a circus or a zoo. I see ship loads of remarkable creatures all off to London—much queerer than our marsupials. I often wonder what is thought of them on the other side."

"Used to 'em—most of them are pommies taking a trip home."

"Thanks for such a feasible explanation."

She went with Brian overland to Melbourne, big travel to her, who had been no farther than Sydney. She was unwavering in gaiety and comradeship until the bell clanged for her to go off the ship.

"You'll come over, Mum, just as soon as I get the hang of it? We could live like fighting cocks on £300 a year. It's a fortune."

To hear this was almost as sweet as the days of her youthful love. It sustained her going down the gang-plank and during the long wait on the wharf on the end of a paper ribbon until the ship moved out of sight and across the Rip for the voyage. It was with her on the return to Ferny Creek.

"That is the end of him for me," she said to Mrs Thingamebob, a sympathetic confidante, now of years' standing.

"Why should you say that?"

"He never can be the same again. He will soon belong to some other woman, and even if she had two heads and cauliflower ears, I'll never take the bloom off his love affair when it comes, and hurt him as Darcy and I were hurt. No. The only chance of companionship in life is a real mate, like Darcy was, and if he goes, you are alone."

"Or at peace," softly interposed Mrs Thingamebob, thinking of her mate who had died in Darlinghurst Gaol.

CHAPTER XLVIII

THEN to look for letters.

The first two came from the home ports, then a blank until the third from Colombo, and a long wait until the first from England. At length the regular report once a week. Eagerly awaited, these letters were at first full of description. Clare Margaret's in return, so detailed, were eagerly devoured, until in the increasing momentum of life at Oxford, they were scampered through and kept for re-reading, which rarely took place.

Brian found it harder to compile a letter. Much effort would be necessary to inform his mother of a life to which she had no key. The interests of mother and son drifted apart. Clare Margaret continued to write fully from her centre and was frequently disappointed that Brian omitted to answer her questions. She adhered to her work. The property was now her habit, her life. She left the care of the house to Mrs Thingamebob and tended her sheep and cattle, her cultivation paddocks, her orchards—her beautiful estate, which she and Darcy had made in partnership. Darcy had left his share to her to be halved with Brian on his twenty-first birthday, if worthy. Ah, he had been worthy: she had helped to make him so. Now he was a junior sleeping partner, and she faithful in stewardship. Brian was to have a property as well as an education: he should not be cast out naked and unprotected into the world as she and Darcy had been by incompetent parents. Brian's letters were the sweetest expectation of her days. That other woman had not yet intruded, so far as she could judge. Her mother pride and passion could be indulged unchecked. Sometimes a personal paragraph in the newspapers further rewarded her.

That was Australia's share of her Brian for years, Australia's usual share of her gifted ones; the inevitable share of the inhabitants of a distant colony of an Empire whose core remains, a vampire to attract all the ergs of scientific or artistic genius, long after its outposts have ceased to provide an outlet for its physical adventurers.

Clare Margaret lacked the spiritual or intellectual equipment to project herself into Brian's life, though the Delacys were humorous and informative letter writers. As time passed Brian told less and less of his daily routine and filled his page with comment on what his mother wrote. This too dwindled. Those mail days which brought no letter were agony: Clare did not know how to cover her humiliation from the Fossicker, Dunlop and Mrs Thingamebob.

As the first year ended there were honours to report. Clare revived and proclaimed that Brian had had to stick to his studies, without time for letters. Lo, here was the result. And still there was no woman to dispute her ownership. There was much to hold her attention at home. The boom in wool subsided during the year of Brian's departure, and with it the value of land. The Bank officials saw that there was no possibility of Robert and Roger redeeming Burrabinga, and were desirous of realizing before further decline. This had to be put to Robert, and he did not in life leave the old place where he had reigned as the last of the pioneer squatters of the district.

The stroke which prefaced his passing was attributed to shock. Fortunately he did not linger more than a few months and these were passed in the old home. Despite his great age, he partly recovered and was able to sit in an easy chair on one of the verandas in the morning sunlight within sound of the river, and three or four of his faithful heelers would find their way in to regard him with worship and snooze at his feet. The burdens of the present were blotted out, his memory slipped back to the past. To all and sundry he continued to offer the hospitality which had distinguished his establishment for half a century. He would look up, his once piercing eyes glazed and uncertain, and stammer, "Turn your horses out and stay the night. The cook will give you a feed for your dogs."

The cost of that hospitality, hoarded, would have given him comfort and freedom from worry at the last, that hospitality so free and generous for which his only return had been the pleasure in dispensing, and the final worry of poverty.

He who had been born at Burrabinga should have lain there or have come out with a spanking four-in-hand, but the horses were gone; a pall of debt as well as of death hung over the valley.

William waited in Bandalong for the funeral. Harry, still slim and erect, came up to Burrabinga. He wept tears of age-weakness and sadness to see the old valley again, and Robert for ever asleep to the Burrabinga's anodyne lullaby, while a fierce old dog howled mournfully like a tolling bell.

"Poor old Robert," he quavered. "You've carried your hide to the tanyard, and carried it well. I won't be long following you."

"Death—time—just a breath or two—and all our swagger, where is it?" he observed to Margaret, and relinquished the scene that had known his shy lonely youth, the strength of his thews, and his still-born dreams. He was now living in Bowral, rescued from final destitution by his efficient Josephine's inheritance.

Burrabinga was shortly to be sold by order of the mortgagees. All those rich deep acres watered by creeks that had never run dry in the memory of white men, and the white men of Burrabinga were all of old Danny's providing! Long years of loneliness and stiffening slogging were represented by its extensive freehold. Three whole generations of bone-racking, neck-risking exploits had gone in wresting Danny's now curtailed province from primeval fallow-hood and taming it to Europe's service, and the last of those who had waged war against resistant Nature would not reap the harvest of their despoiling.

Roger was bitter, but Clare Margaret said, "If you hadn't the guts to hold on, you can't blame outsiders. You have to thank old Wong that you have a cubby to retreat to."

They hoped—Roger and Harry—that by some fluke Burrabinga would still be Delacy's. The world until recently had been booming; all the money could not have disappeared overnight. Roger expected the mortgage to be realized and the Bank to retain him as manager.

"A pity that none of the Delacys had any business sense," remarked Josephine. "Fools tame properties for the wise to enjoy."

Harry's hope was that Clare Margaret would pawn Ferny Creek and her merinos—the lesser to retain the greater. "If they could have Burrabinga without one old cow or so much as a fowl to stock it, surely to God, it's a fortune. Motor cars to bring it near. Think what it was when my father went there with his bare hands and a few head of cattle, and the blacks to be conciliated. His own axe the first to blaze a tree, except those holed by a black after a possum. I wish I had my strength."

His strength was gone. All that he had from Burrabinga, where it had been wasted, was an irrational love of the place, and that in Josephine's estimation was foolishness. Not hers to feel that it was spiritual tilth of a people, which in the potent circle creates the place soul to inspire a people. Harry worshipped this land which had lain fallow of love or hate since before time, or, had it the love of the shadow people, who melted as wraiths before invasion, that love—unrecorded in archives or architecture—lay so lightly, was so tenuous that it was beyond reach of man's working senses.

Old Harry as he dreamed in the sun, to warm old bones, was so near the end of the blind alley of life in the physical body that miracles for him had now to embrace a new dimension.

It had been clear for some time to the financial manipulators that world trade was on a perilous slope and beyond their control. Clare Margaret never speculated. What she had had been won by inhuman industry. She would take no risks. Also she was strapped for ready money. She kept her secret, but Brian, overseas in that superior removed life, that earthly paradise, was a drain on her. He was constantly requesting money on the ground that his £300 per annum went nowhere in England; as an Australian a fellow was marked.

Burrabinga was a bargain for the British-Australasian Properties Limited, many of whose clients lived on the Riviera, where the sunshine was so bright, and the franc, following the war, was so cheap. Some of them did not know a merino from a corriedale or a comeback, nor a brigalow from a swamp gum or a kurrajong, and they abominated the Australian accent. They were conscious of Australia as once a convict colony and still a retreat for a proletariat over-proletaneous since machinery was making so many men super-fluous in industry. The place was a store-house of gems, minerals and other raw materials, and now that British capital had been blown out of Europe by depreciated currencies and other results of military glory, Australia, by reason of its umbilical connection, was the safest investment for British usurers as it had been a hundred years ago the ideal dumping ground for spoiled or unruly British subjects.

"Usury must reap where it can," observed old Harry. "It has to shun both ethics and philanthropy, but when investment can be applied to taking in the family washing, it booms its own self-righteousness till its ears are full and the devil laughs out loud."

Roger was offered a job as boundary rider. No one knew the fences so well, and the points of invasion by the dingoes and wombats which refused to be dispossessed. Old Mrs Robert was informed that there would be a jointure for her. A letter from the chief panjandrum of the B-A Properties Ltd stated that she was welcome to reside at Burrabinga until the end of her days.

Upon reading the letter, Mrs Robert rose to her full height and her full dignity. With her ancient grand manner, which had sat well upon her as hostess there for half a century, she thanked the Manager-in-Chief of the Company, who was there taking stock and awaiting the arrival of a resident manager.

"I have made other arrangements, thank you."

The conversation was left dangling. The Manager, a decent man with heavy responsibilities, did not know how to proceed for a moment. Her anger would have made it easier for the "business is business" patter. "The storm that was promising seems to be passing off," she remarked urbanely, with a far grand glance at the familiar heavens.

The Manager wiped his forehead with his handkerchief as he agreed with her, and looked at the mighty clouds moving out by the source of the Burrabinga on the way to Bunbilliko where Robert and Harry had ridden when young with the Lillingstons.

She turned to Clare Margaret when the man had escaped, "I'll go with you for a visit, as you have so often asked me."

Clare Margaret had designed apartments for her during the Fossicker carpenter's remodellings. She had a private collogue with the Company's representative. By law Margaret was not entitled to so much as a tea-spoon or a pillow, but there are times when even the financial law of the hawk to the chicken, would lose more by taking its fill than by leaving a crumb. The Manager had risen to his present position from pioneering selectors. He was a success, and though business success is not won by Delacy characteristics of sharing and giving, nevertheless he was touched to see the old lady thus shorn at the end of her days. He was more sympathetic towards her position than towards that of the usurers overseas who had classified his accent as common Cockney. No inventory was to be made until Margaret chose what articles she wished from the sprawling dwelling. By all canons even those of usury, she had earned them at a thousand per cent paid up. Roger was allowed an old horse dray. No more drays for Burrabinga. On all up-to-date places drays were falling to pieces under the shade of some tree. The last of the horse wagons dwindled with Robert's final decade. Clare Margaret would send horses to take out the load.

Roger was left in charge until the resident manager could arrive, and his mother decided to stay with him. This was a reprieve for Roger. To send him from Burrabinga was like turning an old horse from his foal-hood's stable.

"The Manager must have perspired with relief," chuckled Clare Margaret, "when he heard that Ma had other arrangements."

Roger railed against the swindlers who turned people out with nothing after generations of pioneering labour.

"The Barbara Frietchie part suits Ma to perfection, but it looks rather silly on you," said Clare Margaret. "I'm not going to antagonize the Manager, and I'll take everything he offers."

"I wouldn't take a stick. Let the busy swine take the tail with the hide."

"Rubbish! He is not the one who is driving you out penniless, but all the cadgers for the last forty years—and the pub keepers. You ought to be thankful that old Wong paid his way."

CHAPTER XLIX

"It is strange that Brian never sends any word about the old place." Old Harry harped on this as he sat chopping the fuel. He knew the qualities of each block intimately, and handled it with artistic relish and affection, his mind reverting to the undesecrated forests of his youth and the dreams he had dreamed to people them.

"What could he say?" Josephine would pose. "The Delacys never had a business head among them. They got too big for their boots, and this is the logical outcome."

"Yes, but," Harry would counter, "young Brian felt differently about things. He was like his great-grandfather."

"That would not help him to get on very far."

Harry would abandon the argument. He was a man of peace.

Clare Margaret also wondered why she heard so little from her son. She had sent him all the spare money that came in, and was more than ever determined not to cripple Ferny Creek. The final illustration of the need for avarice was before her.

At the close of Brian's second year of absence there was a blow. Brian was not recommended for a third year's study, and as far as his mother could deduce, did not seem to have any definite profession. He told her that he was going to work, and he was sick of sitting about among books, which a girl could do and thereby "lick the Senior Wrangler". (Clare Margaret took this as a tilt at the nagging propensities of women.)

He further confessed to having been swindled, and that he was in debt, and would be disgraced unless she could rescue him.

She hastened to the Bank in Bandalong. Anything, everything, to save her boy.

Brian was thus released from debt, but loose in a hostile world without a paid position. He asked for his patrimony to start in business. His mother asked what kind of business, and he wrote that it would be something in the mechanical line. "I've been fumbling around wasting my time on academic subjects when I should have been in an engineering works. That has put me back years, but with a bit of income I won't be so hipped as if I had to cringe for a job."

Later he wrote of his arduous days in an aeroplane factory,

where he was starting from the ground up. "Tackling the dungarees again after lolling about like a swell soon took the fine lady out of my fists."

Clare Margaret did not divulge that he was not doing the third year at Oxford. There were a few, more conversant with the world than she, who asked what Brian was going to do when his term at Oxford had ended. What was he to pay in results for the capital spent in making him a graduate of two universities? Fortunately such "sticky-beaks" were few. Most of Clare Margaret's acquaintances were as naïve as herself, and looked upon Brian's scholarship as an Elijah's chariot which had lifted him to a region far above the Murrumbidgee.

Clare was pitifully uneasy concerning him and determined to face secretly whatever might come from that source. She reflected despairingly that the Delacy breed was certainly destitute of acquisitive proclivities. Nearly a hundred years since Johanna and Danny had landed, and no outstanding successes to show for all the struggle and honesty and heroism! Other families, started by lags, had amassed fortunes. New arrivals within the present century had made the environment subservient to their success; whereas the most distinguished Delacy was Sophie of Bewuck, headmistress of a High School, who educated the daughters of others, having none of her own, nor so much as a niece or nephew worthy of her. Since 1914 crowds of people had made war fortunes and ordinary fortunes and departed to splurge in Europe, but none of these were Delacys. The Delacys, who adored Australia, could not make her pay dividends—to themselves.

Della's children had dropped out of sight in Victoria as minor pastoralists and farmers. Honoria's family—the New Glenties Butlers—included Coole, who was a rich man, but not nearly so wealthy as the Vances, who had progressed to championship ranks in wool with social obligations in keeping. They had half a dozen rich properties; the sons played polo; the daughters had their photographs taken in the act of looking on, and appeared in what *Society* had become since the war and at the *furthest extremity of the globe* from its London origin. It was a cocktail rather than a cocktailed affair, inadequately furnished with distinction or intelligence. Its bright young things displayed their fine physique on the democratic beaches which made Sydney a paradise, or cavorted at charity functions where they followed trivially the procedure and fashions prescribed for them by Europe.

Clare Margaret always spent a night with Uncle William on her way to the Township and he was one of the inquisitive. They had grown close together with the years, and to him she confessed with a smile, "Like your Bob, I think Brian is wiping up grease with a dirty rag these days."

This was a family gag. Bob, one of the few Delacys to "chuck" the bush, had landed in a motor garage where he was set to clean the cars and was there found, to his father's consternation, "Wiping grease off a car with a dirty rag."

"Why, damn it," exclaimed William, "the money spent on Brian since he started to get this fine education would secure a tidy property." He was sorry for Clare Margaret. His own family too, except Sophie, were disappointing. "It's a pity his flash promise isn't coming to anything. He wants six months on the axe to make a man of him."

"Those who had six years on the axe aren't so wonderful."

"But he could have been an aeroplane mechanic without all the expense of one university education after another. If he takes to flying, you've as good as been at his funeral already."

"Oh, well, I shan't bury him till I have to, and then I shan't ask any one to help me cry." Uncle William knew when to desist.

.When Clare Margaret was leaving in the morning, he said, "I hope you get good news from Brian next time. It seems that you and I are the only Delacys with head enough to hang on to our property."

"I'm only a brumby compared with you. Bewuck is a beautiful property—six times the value of Ferny Creek."

"And six times as many to scatter it as soon as I am cold."

Those were his last words to her. She never saw him alive again. His tombstone stands head to head with old Nullah-Mundoey's where the unfettered winds fan the fleckless days.

Roger and his mother were finally ejected from Burrabinga. The new Manager arrived—without his wife until he knew how the dispossessed were to act. Unnecessary precaution. Margaret was too strong, Roger too gentlemanly, Clare Margaret too full of common sense for hostility.

Clare brought her car. The journey, which, in the era of the horse, would have taken the best part of a week, was made in the day. They stormed up Delacy's Cutting, through Delacy's Gap and down past the remains of Birrabee and Keebah without pausing, had dinner at the Hotel Canberra, and away towards Bandalong for Darcy's bridge and home to Ferny Creek at warm dusk in October. A cheery fire burned in the new room, for old bones. Margaret's smaller things were in place.

"It is all very nice," she said, in her grand way. "You must have waved a magician's wand."

"It will be better when all your own things arrive from dear old Burrabinga."

"Dear old Burrabinga, my Burrabinga, has gone with your father and Syme and Darcy, and William and old Danny and Johanna, and Norah and Della and Stewart and Ned. I never want to hear the new Burrabinga mentioned."

Thus she closed her life and turned with dignity and fortitude to its epilogue.

"We are lucky to have escaped the rain," said Clare. The storm could be seen approaching as on a screen far across the valley. Soon it was beating on the house, rattling the spouting, chasing any loose vessel of tin, tattering the soft young garden, and turning spitefully cold.

Wild hours always took Clare back to Darcy's passing.

Roger, with the aid of old Dunlop—now very stiff—had his belongings loaded as night was falling, and the wild wind intruded upon the spring scene. He was compelled to borrow a tarpaulin—the Delacy tarpaulin, now no longer his.

They had pulled the dray against the high palings of the little graveyard where lay Doogoolook and others. They sheltered under the end of the tarpaulin, Roger too depressed for further action, while Dunlop made a fire and boiled the billy.

The new Manager expected them at the house when they should have made all snug, but they did not appear. In an improvised bed under a dray with a few sticks of furniture, the last of the Burrabinga men spent his outgoing night. Danny, Robert and Harry had often gone out and soaked themselves to bring in wayfarers out of such weather, but not by such brotherliness are stations retained to pay dividends on far-flung investments.

At midnight, when the storm had ceased, and a waning moon showed through ragged clouds, Roger was aroused by a delegation of Wong Foo's compatriots come to remove Wong's bones to China now that Burrabinga had passed from Delacy ownership. They were furnished with a permit from the authorities, and this procedure was in key with Roger's mood. He and Dunlop assisted as by "the struggling moonbeam's misty light, and the lantern dimly burning", like a reversal of a famous burial, Wong's remains were disinterred.

The head board remained, the mound was carefully remodelled, and the Manager a week later reported to his wife, "All that trouble to clean up a Chinaman's grave—no wonder they lost their property!"

Old Harry, warming his bones in the sun, wept bitterly when he heard that Burrabinga was really gone from the family—that no miracle had saved it. Until the last moment he had expected something from young Brian, who had gone abroad in a cloud of glory, but he had not sent so much as a post card.

Josephine laughed that he should take it so much to heart. "What does it matter to you now, when your time at the longest must be very short?"

He felt that she did not understand. "It was the motor cars that ruined Burrabinga by killing out the horses. Stinking machines that eat Yankee oil," he quavered.

"A lot of Delacy money went to maintain the publicans in luxury."

"Even that was better under our economic system than keeping foreigners, as you'll find presently. . . . But it's strange that none of my father's progeny was worthy of him."

"He never taught them to do anything but tigrinize among the native dogs, as your mother used to say."

"My father was a great man," persisted Harry. "The day will come when his power will be seen in this young Brian or his issue, and it will be more for Australia and the race than a dozen of the usurers who have accumulated filthy lucre in the banks. My father's vision will be bearing the fruit of life when the money-bags kind of success is suppressed as out-of-date barbarism."

"It is as well for you to think so," cackled Josephine, and bore with his vagaries because she considered him childish.

Clare found her mother a comfort. Her mind was still keen and they always had had a sense of humour as a bond. Clare confessed some of her uneasiness about Brian. "With all the chance I gave him to get above rabbiting, he is only working in an air garage."

"Perhaps these things are dictated by fate. All sorts were of use at the start of colonization because they were scarce, but it is different now."

"Yes, but Grandpa had something notable about him, and as Uncle William said, the last time I saw the poor old man, the only difference between Ferny Creek and Bewuck was that there were more scatterers at Bewuck."

"Brian has not found himself yet," said Margaret, too tactful to fan anxieties. "At any rate he can still come back to you—not like

Syme and Dan. I see in the paper that Aunt Jean has gone to Sydney for some ceremony at the gates where Dan embarked."

Sophie, instructress of the young, whom the years had not disillusioned regarding patrioteering, took care that her mother and she had their places on the official dais at the ceremony of commemoration when the wharf entrance was christened the "Gates of Remembrance" nearly a generation after young Dan and many as likely a lad had disappeared that way never to return; but the soldier lads had been replaced by oncoming youth and the gates neglected—forgotten—by all but a dwindling company of ageing women who assemble there on Anzac Day with rosemary in their hands and a hurt look in their eyes that they are no longer acclaimed as the givers of men to Moloch. They are disgruntled to learn that the promises of Mars are as false as those of Don Juan when despoiling a maiden, but they remain incapable of instructing the rising generation that the glories of Anzac are as empty as all military glory down the centuries, symbolized by a tattered flag or a suit of rusty armour in a silent museum.

The memorial service fell on a beautiful afternoon and the clergyman denounced those who desecrated the day by football or tennis, with never a solemn thought for the men who had given their lives in a noble cause, but the cause, half a generation since had been discredited by ethical thinkers, and the exhortation was sanctimonious and dreary.

Jean could not stem her tears, so she walked down the pier. No one had thought of war when she was young, but now it was on every page of the newspapers, and these silly memorials were everywhere. Why did not the clergyman honestly say that the soldiers had got what they deserved for being such fools as to go, instead of scolding the young people for snatching their holiday play while they could?

The harbour so grand, so blue, so restless, awed her, and she was fascinated by the great ships steaming directly towards her. She asked a man sitting on a bollard what ships they were.

"War ships, lady. Getting ready for the next war."

"Getting ready for the next war," she echoed stupidly. "But what are they doing here now?"

"Been outside the Heads firing off for practice. Love the crows, Mar! ain't you heard the windows rattling fit to split, and the houses shaking, and all them cows feeling as if they were God Himself blazing away?"

Jean had the impulse to ask him more, but he looked like a wicked bolshevist, and Sophie kept her family informed of the danger of Russian ideas. The man had turned back to his paper, numbed by the news that the Imperial General Staff in England were exercised by the difficulties "of training a new generation of officers who have no personal experience of war". The General Staff, faced with such a problem for the successors of those who had given their lives to end war, favoured staff rides over the battlefields of France. While the English army benefited by its nearness to the Western Front battlefields "the United States Army is not so fortunate, but the same problem of training officers who were too young for the last war is likewise being pondered at Washington . . . the keynote . . . is to make officers 'psychologically fit' to face the mental stresses of war."

"Gor' damn me, can you beat that!" muttered the man as he read. He would like to tell those —— young fools of the actualities of war. He could open their eyes. "These old women too, with their remembrance, and the old cow of a parson working them up to think they are heroines when they are b—— fools, who ought to be . . ." He took an explosive turn towards the old lady who was gaping at the ships. But no, she was a fool, and might have him arrested for assault or something . . . What was the use? What was the —— use?

Jean continued to gaze at the ships. She recalled what Dan had said when he enlisted, what Sophie had said, and was bewildered by the way it had worked out. Dan had gone to save Belgium and to end war, and she and William had given £20 to the fund for Belgians, but still there was no peace. Everybody was mesmerized by armaments. The ships compelled worship in their resistless might, and rode straight from battle practice up the bay, though she was there specially to commemorate the spot from which her Dan, long ago, had gone away to die in the big brave war to end all other wars for ever.

Old Harry, dreaming over book or newspaper, still pinned his faith on Brian with reference to the continuity of character through the generations. "It stands to reason," he would say at such times as Josephine was amenable to listen unrancorously. "A great spirit like my father's could not go without results. It might not reappear for a generation or two. Breed is like that. But in the immense age of the human race, if a great spirit appeared every five hundred years, think what that would mean. All the same, I should like to see someone worthy of my father's breed, and it can't be in my time unless it's young Brian. Get me pen and paper. I'll ask him what he is doing."

His letter was so foolish, in Josephine's estimation, that she wrote an explanatory note. "Your grandfather is too old to write now. His fingers ache when he tries to hold the pen, and he is not clear in what he wants to say, but he will be waiting for a reply as if his ideas were of importance. He is always longing to see you, but you must not expect to see him here when you come as the doctor says that his organs are quite worn out."

"A dream, a vision of what is to be, is greater than all the money-bags in the world," Harry remarked, when the letter was safely in the envelope, and he set out to the post office to deposit it. Old and frail, a financial failure, isolated from his spiritual equals, his winged spirit nevertheless continued to resist the conclusions of materialistic common sense as stupid and wasteful.

"If I hadn't hung on to something, we'd be in a pretty pass to-day. And if my poor Darcy had had a money-bag or two to start, he need not have killed himself in that silly pioneering without any reward. There is reason in all things."

"There is one kind of reasoning that never does anything but fill its belly from the store-house after the other fellow has pioneered to build and stock it."

"But what is the sense in piling up for the other fellow? I'd rather be the other fellow for a change."

"Pioneering in thought—making the vision come true—uncovering the wonders for the use of man, that is the pioneering that never ends. 'The moind! The moind!' Flying, wireless, radios, all these things are the outward and visible signs—as the old parson used to teach us by the bunyip hole—of pioneering in the mind, but without integrity of the soul these discoveries will only destroy us. Now here I have to sit waiting for a reply from Brian, and it may not come until I'm dead, and if the cables and wireless were made to serve man instead of mammon I could hear in a day."

"You want some of the money-bags you despise and then you could send cables as long as letters."

"It is the criminal worship of money-bags that is depriving me of the right to use the cables."

Josephine ignored this as wicked communism which he talked because his mind was gone. "There would have to be laws to stop bolshevist agitators from using the cables for their purposes," she said.

Harry floated on the knowledge that Josephine was spiritually barren. Her disparagements provided a saint with a hair shirt, as her young beauty had once furnished a poetical romantic with a princess; and saintship is enhanced by hair shirts. With leisure he had cultivated the spiritual ecstasies, and the dismissal of his discoveries as symptoms of dementia had given him intense mental distress. Dreams cannot be secured by entailment, and he had been too visionary to grasp and to hold and thus impress himself upon a primitive community. For a time, he, the giver, had come near to withering at the root because his offerings had been derided. His ordeal finally drove him to a sanctuary of amateur yoga built upon the comforting thesis that pearls should not be thrown in the mire, and the gentle thought that his would be the lack in ethical understanding to demand fruit from nettle bushes.

Josephine was indispensable, efficient and unceasing in her duties and care, and habit is stronger than passion, and outlasts it. He was a one-woman man; none but Josephine had known his virility, and such a man, when of fine sensibilities, is bound to a woman for ever by his own virginal conception of her, plus his dire male need. To such a man the romantic adolescent ideal of his wife as a superior and extraordinary being can co-exist with his experience of her lack of spiritual integrity; also, subconsciously to tincture the most liberal masculine thought is the phallic content that, after all, women are weaker beings, who only of recent generations have been conceded the possession of a soul.

Not so long after posting the letter, Harry slipped away one morning to enlarge that presence palpable but intangible which is the aura of places where human association continues from generation to generation.

Of Harry's own family only Clare Margaret came to see him laid away.

Josephine consented to return with Clare for a week, but she was unendurably restless. She hated the district. The distance from a physician in case of sickness, and the lack of elegancies and entertainments had always been insupportable to her. She turned eagerly to her own life at last, the heroine of long years of incompatibility and the loss of all her family but Isabel, who was never mentioned. Her indomitable prosaicness exposed her to the discovery that she was lonely without Harry. He had given her much, though not of those things for which money-bags are the symbol. Long in advance he had provided illumination on many issues that arose, so that by comparison ordinary people were sadly uninformed. What had been dismissed in Harry as eccentricity now showed up glaringly the mediocrity of those who had submerged him without wrecking his spiritual genius.

CHAPTER L

THE hegira to Europe furnishes experiences so removed from those open to the home-staying Australian that Brian was able for a time to harvest his blunders without exposure to his native runs. Achievements conspicuous in Bandalong and Yass, and which lent him brief distinction at Sydney University, attracted no notice at Oxford. There he was merely one of the colonial students, who were of all persuasions, complexions and nationalities.

The national heritage, the man-made beauty of centuries of ancient glamour and still-living tradition had at first intoxicated him, and had involved the metaphysical experience of fusing his dream of old places with their actuality. Greedily he had tried to swallow all of life. First came the acquiring of knowledge in accordance with the curricula, then the stimulation of his thinking powers by association with mental equals and superiors in the movements having political platforms and affiliations. A diplomatic tolerance grown wily and mellow in the handling of resurgence and insurgence—any intransigence from colonists—ignored much, but twice Brian narrowly escaped being sent down for activities with subversionists.

He also excelled in sports, which enlarged his social contacts, and these flowered in the major biological initiation. For this a number of Brian's relatives had been indebted to the ancient and generous school of serving-maids. In England, in Brian's decade, the faculty had widened; social equals were available in a fairer educational exchange, and Brian's experience on this front proceeded without volcanic disturbance. Many more extensive dossiers are available in the novels which in the post-war emergent period provoked attention by their unreticent details of bodily functionings and provided capital sport when flung in the face of *fin de siècle* wowserism. The lack of variety in all normal biological processes reduced such case histories to unendurable dullness as soon as such confessions were accepted as part of modern behaviour.

Sufficient to record that Brian Delacy graduated in the Faculty of Sex without spiritual or physical accident, largely because his predilection for women older than himself saved him from the enticing flappers or vicious demi-mondaines.

His dismissal without the third year of the Gawler Scholarship drove him to cover, tortured in every fibre of his being, in which there was some of the sensitiveness of his father and his grandfather, Harry. For days he floundered in humiliating reflection that he had wasted his chances at Sydney and at Oxford. He had lost the rewards of both the careful and talented and the daring and gifted. He must flee from the scene of his immediate defeat; nor could he face return to Australia with empty hands and no definite profession, seeing the flourish with which he had departed.

He was loose in a world where to drop from a post was as hazardous as falling off a liner in a high sea, for all the hope there was of getting back to a berth. To such a pass of futility had Big Business Dictatorship brought the human race at the beginning of the fourth decade of the Twentieth Century. However, Brian's mother had rescued him from debt and was sending him a small income, and the isolation of Australia from England enabled him to make a new start without the derision of former associates.

Talents, dormant during his pursuit of academic arts and philosophies, now re-awakened. In any case he would not have remained drugged by ancient glamour. Mechanics. As he had rallied to the filibusters in the political line so he would be in the van of mechanics, and to him that meant aeroplanes. He turned with a will to Coventry. Those were the days when he wrote of dungarees, which in the real sense were a passing incident. His personality was worth more than a university degree in the acquaintances it brought him.

"If aviation attracts you," said Sir Coverley Benedict, father of a fellow collegian, "I'll get you into the Royal Air Force." His own son was working off headiness in this avenue, and Brian seized the chance to join him, though he was temperamentally unsuited to military organizations.

His ambition to master every branch of aeronautics combined with his talent for mechanics quickly made the air his element. He won his wings with expedition and wore them with the dash with which his grandfathers had clanked their silver-plated spurs.

He and young Benedict went often to the Duchess of Tilbury. The Duchess was divorced, but traded under her old title. She was a man-eater of air officers, and herself a notorious aviator. No airman was too young for her, and she specialized in those from overseas, and found their lack of ceremony amusing. They sometimes found her food and other things "rotten", and it was after a midnight supper at her apartment that both Delacy and Benedict were smitten with gastritis. Brian, who considered himself gastronomically as invincible as a goanna, was kept in hospital for a month, at the end of which the official physicians declared him permanently unfit, and gently dismissed him from the Service.

It had been a relief to inform his mother that he was in the Royal Air Force, and to sprinkle his letters with the names of the swagger people—many of them with titles—who petted flight officers, while his mother's fears for his safety in the air had speedily given way to pride in his stylish career.

To be discarded as unfit was as staggering if not so painful as his retreat from Oxford. He spent terrible weeks of depression in lodgings, and sent no letter to Australia during the time. Then he sallied forth to tell the Duchess what her supper had done for him.

The Duchess's ambition in aviation outstripped her means now that the Duke had a practising as well as a cast-off duchess to support in the style to which she had been accustomed. That was why her lobster salad had been poisonous. Her refuge was Americans with money, preferably the *nouveaux riches* who had the illusion that any of the British titled were "the best people".

Brian found her Grace preoccupied with his successors, but one Lola Bradley, a miss from the Middle West, glamour-struck for Europe in general, and aviation in particular, was kind to him. She was older than she looked, and had but lately seized her freedom. She had money, though was "not so lousy with dollars as some", to use the Duchess's classification. Lola's was that she was "just plumb crazy about flying". She was won by Brian's friendly Australian manner, and was a good listener, so he was soon telling her that he felt like making an end of everything. This resulted in Lola's suggestion to escape before he was again poisoned by the Duchess's "muck", and spend the remainder of the day with her. She persuaded him to remain a couple of nights and later to fetch his possessions from his attic in Bloomsbury and accept her care until he was fit again.

Lola had dazzling teeth, but at school had been called pop-eyed, a state arising from her enthusiasm, and which time was tempering. Good-natured and easy, she restored Brian's *amour-propre*, and freed him from a threatened fixation concerning "the tragic Delacys", which had arisen after the second mishap to cloud his sunny outlook. She confessed to being six years his senior. When he, sun-lined and tanned, said that he would not have thought her more than thirty, she regretted that she had not proclaimed herself that age. Her companionship, ostensibly as nurse, was wholesome. Brian's emotions were affectionate, and promised something more.

Lola had broken away from home determined to have an *affaire* ere the years should have superannuated *amour*, and pursued her purpose without hesitation.

Brian consented to go with her to recuperate in the south of France, and for a time she relinquished her ambitions as an aviator in favour of love. They dawdled along the beaten track, forgetting which was Arles or Nimes. In Avignon they stayed at the Grand-Hotel d'Europe and inspected the Notre-Dame-des-Doms Cathedral with its "richly decorated interior". Owing to Brian's reversals, romance was inhibited until Lola noted in the hotel register the name of a physician from Chicago. She called on him and begged him to examine Brian, which he consented to do, and testified with confidence that Brian was as sound as an ox.

A young man renewed went from the physician's presence.

Inquiries later convinced Brian that the real reason for his removal from the R.A.F. was that at Oxford he had embraced a set tainted red, and that his manner had not been sufficiently conforming to superior officers to be tolerated in time of peace. His Duchess had been of the wrong bouquet to protect him, where there were so many young fellows who could more safely be moulded to the pattern of "an officer and a gentleman".

"I'm tickled clear through that you are free," exclaimed Lola. "Let's do all the stunts right away, darling. Cape to Cairo first, for practice. Then we'll fly to Australia and see that Uppamurrum-badgeree you talk so much about."

Continually Brian's thoughts reverted to the Murrumbidgee because he was shut therefrom by failure of two kinds. Now himself again, his nostalgia was the spring of inspiration. Avignon, capital of the Department of Vaucluse, sent his thoughts to Vaucluse House in Sydney.

Australia so far away! England had once been a mere five weeks from Australia, but in the Anglification of his perspective Australia had come to be at the furthest extremity of the globe. Yet a year since a girl had upped and flown to Australia in a matter of days. An English girl. The world had buzzed with the miracle. Its full significance came to Brian now.

Strolling in Railway Square he remarked of the statue of the inventor of the flax-spinning machine. "By Jove, it would suit me better to be doing something to win a monument in my own land than to be paddling around here like a poodle on a string looking at the round towers and machicolated battlements. You should see the battlements at Burrabinga! All the blah like that about Francesco Petrarca seeing Laura de Noves in a nunnery church, and the old popes living here in thirteen hundred, and the glamour of distant days is woven into a sentimental camouflage and hides the present squalor and lunacy of Europe. Romance needs adventure at the start, and the start of tradition is adventure that gets recorded. I'm for starting something glamorous concerning my own wide open spaces. Whoops! that's a filthy cold wind."

"That's the famous Mistral," contributed Lola.

"Huh! even their old wind is given a title! You wait till you feel the Monaro wind across Canberra; it would shave a gooseberry as we say . . . These religious artistic works are a bit frowsty, and the incense like soup. I wish you could smell the bush about Ferny Creek on a summer night. I reckon it's holy. The earth here cannot work off the continual contamination of human contact, like lice for ever on it, and fertilizers and battles."

Following this outburst Brian walked alone on the terrace with its view of the Rhône and the Cevennes and the Alps, majestic in the waning light. The splendour drove him, as his great-grand-father, to ponder on posterity, his contemporaries being inadequate to people the eternal grandeur of the globe. His spiritual and intel-lectual harvest from the history piled before him and from the glory of the past as exemplified by Oxford was realization of the potentialities of his own anciently empty new land. He compared his own double heritage with the circumscription of those who possessed only Europe, and exulted. He had inherited Danny's and Harry's dreams.

Far Australia was brought near if a girl could fly there over the week-end, so to speak. In a flash he saw his future. Aviation. Aviation not for mere aviation's nor adventurous stunt's sake, but for Australia. The caballero would transfer from the horse to the aeroplane. He was impatient to be winging his way by Rome, Vesuvius, Athens, Damascus, Baghdad, Basra—names mossy with legend, but which in his present mood had not the liberation of the mellifluous lullaby names of his native beat, plucked like the echo of an echo, the shadow of a shadow from a wraith-like people who had left undefiled and undespoiled their disdainful, capricious land.

In the profound suffusion of emotion which transcends thought, and but for which the intellectual absolute would be too arid to prevail, he sat upon the hotel bed that night and harangued Lola, as the young Danny had spell-bound his Johanna in the coomb in Clare a century earlier.

"Beggar it all!" he exploded. "I'm glad I came to Europe, and more glad that I didn't fit. It has just come to me—the indignity of crawling home to Europe and drawing on what has been made here—mostly made a mess of—and rehashed, and polished and traditioned and precedented for centuries, when we have a whole new country still clean and free—free—*Free!* Do you realize its freeness? The freest social and sociological conditions on the globe, and empty. Think of the glorious emptiness of it! The purity! Here you have the treasures of art and architecture of the ages, but as well you have accumulations of pollution. Do you grasp, woman, how clean we are in Australia?"

"I hadn't heard any big noise about your cleanness."

"Talk about incense! The heavenly perfume of Australia used to waft far out to sea before it was civilized. You've never known a rapturously pure smell until you have been in a eucalyptus forest. There's not even any damp smell of rot from vegetable humus. It's antiseptic with cleanness."

"But you'll find it kind of different from what you expect when you go back. You won't be able to stand it after Europe."

"How d'you mean? Stand what?"

"You miss all the contacts—you know, the culture."

"Culture, bah! I'm beginning to see that culture makes a poor return for the time it has had and what it has cost in blood and slaves. I've been up against men dripping with culture, and what is called breed and education, and it did not save them from being crawlers who had no semblance of manhood. The highly cultured can be the lowest perverts. The cultured can be contented amid gross injustice. Culture be damned! Culture is not enough, we need decency and goodwill in brotherhood—common sense in opportunity and in distribution of the world's products—ethical ideals in control of man's inventiveness.

"Culture, Huh! Filaria, hookworm and leprosy are samples of ancient culture of the East that were introduced into the Australian garden of Eden a century ago. It would take a lot of Ming vases and artistic prints and flowery proverbs and polished manners and underhand subtle diplomacy and military glory to outweigh those scourges. Culture! Europeans haven't the common business savvy to live without war, and they spread their Kelly gang tactics through all the world. Europe should be boycotted to stew in her own juice. Asia's somnolent ignorance is preferable to her wakening and speeding-up to Europe's general lunacy and inefficiency!"

"Yes, but I've been back to the Middle West, and it was a bit crude after Europe," interposed Lola, when he stopped for breath.

"Crude, be blasted! I pray that Australia may remain crude and

empty as the last refuge for the doomed of Asia and Europe. . . .
How do you mean *crude* any way?"

"Unsophisticated, I guess—that's what they call us Americans
when they want to be polite but . . ."

". . . superior. Crude people always do better for their fellows
than the sophisticated. If you analyse sophistication it explodes as
a nasty stink. Sophistication is a green sickness that feeds on
decadence. I'm off back to first principles. One of Europe's biggest
crimes is to drag her descendants back from Australia and America
to gather diseases and to die in her tribal racketeering."

In the manner of women, Lola was giving him one ear while
with half her consciousness she pursued her own thoughts. She was
ten years older than Brian. Like him she had come to the hub of
sophistication from an outpost; similarly at first she had been
shocked by the poverty, the servility, the flagrant assumption of
superiority by caste. She had grown homesick for Michigan, but
upon return to a tortured sojourn among her early associates she
felt that the women trading upon domestic womanliness, the
standardized college professors, the exalted pants-pressers cried
aloud for debunking, if not indeed for elimination. On her second
escape to Europe she had become selective of congenial contacts,
as one could in the old-world centres. Class or caste could be used
for one's comfort. In this reorientation, poverty and servility had
ceased to distress her. She was not responsible for her own state in
life nor that of others. History demonstrated that humanity was
unchanging despite its new gadgets; experience taught that there
was more profit in getting the best out of the world than in
attempts to reform it, though men must gas about something. This
was rather a safe hobby for Brian as long as it did not go too far.

She could companion him in his activities but not in his dreams.

"The most important thing about Australia at this crisis in
civilization is its emptiness," Brian was saying.

Australia's emptiness added to its isolation did not appeal to
Lola, but she listened satisfactorily. A trip to early scenes was the
only cure for childish illusions about the home town. Lola would
follow. One track was as good as another to the aviator, for whom
death waited daily. Aviation was not for old age. For the present
there was love—the pleasures of sex—Brian the indispensable instrument. She gazed at him indulgently.

"That emptiness sounds kind of lonely."

"Lonely, bah! Population hasn't saved Europe or Asia. Even
America isn't able to provide for or use all her population since
machines have triumphed. Fly! Fly! Air ships and their speed solve

the problem of communication and physical association and could preserve the glory and cleanliness of splendid distances.

"The profits expected from inducing people to multiply and populate the empty spaces have disappeared with the failure of the brave new magic of good salesmanship and business rationalization. George, it's laughable to examine the breakdown of the practical fellows who have been licensed as Caesars of human destiny! Their shebeening antics have ended in the race suicide of wars and have created nothing but a world bout of constipation in trade . . . When you think of warrior he-men submitting to tightening their belts and stinting their families in the middle of plenty to maintain a worn-out system . . ."

"It's surely a great demonstration of matter over mind."

"Yes, the whole world is paralysed by the mumbo-jumbo of banking jargon, like a binghi 'boned' by a medicine man. Australia is the sole remaining uncluttered frontier for a better experiment in civilization, with none 'debauched by slavery, or corrupt by power'. The idealists of the world should be mobilized to ensure that good old virgin Aussie is not wholly raped and squandered merely to alleviate the backward and undeveloped human products. Under the exploitation and profiteering of their masters it would soon be another Asia or Europe. It should be reserved for peoples who as a minimum of sanity will agree to abandon war and poverty and do something substantial to diminish disease."

"Promising when you say it quickly, but kind of an overtime job to bring about."

"The only thing needed is intelligence and the courage to scrap outworn systems. Intelligent brotherhood is the formula, but it would have to be camouflaged as something new. Intelligence has never been tried yet on a big ethical scale. Aviation has come in time to preserve Australia from the mess of over-fecundity which has been preached as a religio-politico doctrine to fill up countries to make consumers for trade that is manipulated by bandits—*alias* leaders—shysters—quacks, who allow people to starve while they throw fish back into the North Sea or burn wheat and wool or coffee or cotton from China to Peru just to regulate prices for the exploiteer. Such tomfoolery can't last."

"It has lasted a fair time."

"But not much longer."

"It's digging itself in stronger than ever. Look at Europe, and they're going to be a whole heap worse yet before they're any better is my guess." Lola's voice was ironical.

"The last struggle! We are faced with the choice between the annihilation of civilization as it exists, or a universal reorganization of ethical forces. Even stupid folks can see that, if it's put in simple catch words. *Try intelligence!* There's my slogan when I get into the Commonwealth Cabinet as Minister for Air Transport."

"Fine courageous young idea when you say it quickly, but the bone-heads and mugwumps will be hard to convert."

"You must never raise your doctrine too far above those who have no way of rising from the dust except in an aeroplane. A continent with population thinly sown but of better quality, now that the old idea of hordes being necessary to police manufactories or feed cannon has gone phut. Nearly time we did something about the racial crime of breeding from the unfit, and the race suicide of wars that waste the best and strongest."

" 'In that day blessed are the paps which never gave suck.' " quoted Lola, yawning and flicking a piece of cigarette from her lip. "Great opening for the debunking of motherhood. You'll have the women with you provided that you can wean them from their witch doctors, and the men against you if you advocate sex-control instead of birth limitation."

"The old pagan gods must laugh till the spheres crack. Wait till you hear the kookaburras laughing all around the sunset. Their chortles must have been transmitted from lost gods. A whole continent still unruined! No middens of the offal called history. Talk about European precedents! Ours are colossal!"

"I'm waiting to be led to this land of promised hope and glory. It sounds a pretty swell dump."

They began their joint career that night. Lola had the means to provide a plane, Brian the mechanical skill to keep it at concert pitch. Her ambition was his. Life was good again despite the financial paralysis which had crept outward from the core to the extremities of the world.

At Ferny Creek Clare Margaret was alarmed by the declining value of wool, though the first two years of the slack had not hurt the Australian workers. They let the motor cars go, then the gramophones, the player-pianos, the time-payment houses, while the so-called poor turned up their noses at the clothes cast off to them, and others with money sense collected them and sold them to the ol' clo' merchants.

At this stage had come the second blow through Brian's removal from the R.A.F. His mother cabled his fare. The money was useful to Brian in Europe. After weeks of silence came his statement that, to gain strength before the sea voyage, he was going to the Riviera to look for the sun. After further anxiety his mother was rejoiced by the verdict of the Chicago physician and accepted Brian's decision to return to aviation.

Families that had migrated to the cities from bush holdings now felt that evacuation had been a mistake. Those on the land could at least be sure of food and shelter. Interest on mortgages mounted to startling figures among the big men, but Clare Margaret's thrift kept her solvent while the financial crisis went on and on—ripened to a "chronic". Though the land was bursting with plenty, Australians began to feel the pinch. They had no gold. Britain relinquished the gold standard in banking while the U.S.A. collected gold and awakened the jealousy of the world. Despite this the U.S.A., another country groaning with produce, plus almost human machinery, was in a worse plight than Australia, because it had gone farther in industrial artifice before reaching the impasse.

No new theory advanced to banish this ludicrous scourge of poverty in plenty was acceptable. Russia's experiment aroused terror in the boss classes throughout the universe; besides, it was not applicable to those countries which had in their barns and warehouses more products than could be consumed under an inadequate system of distribution. Financial manipulators clung to the current economic organization, refusing to recognize that parasitism when too robust kills its hosts, and that the "cornering" of markets was no longer compatible with world peace and sanity. Attempts to graft new patterns of living upon the existing confusion revealed that the old virtues of thrift and industry were no longer rewarding, but those who still had possessions continued to decry new designs as anarchy and to demand of their experts the re-establishment of pre-slump normality.

The voice of the doled was dolorous in the land. Idleness enervated the adolescent generation as war had brutalized its predecessors. The only hope of betterment, of release from constricting poverty for the great masses of people in the mightiest empire on record was a lottery chance or gambling on the racecourses. All waited. For what?

For a miracle, in the ancient way of mankind, from out eternity, and to eternity; the miracle of leadership that would be accepted; some ingenious formula, to save people from starvation in the midst of abundance; simply that.

Brian proceeded healthfully with his career, confident that the thinkers must before long impose intelligence upon stupidity; otherwise some major explosion would wreck the present forms of civilization.

Lola was described as a brilliant American woman aviator, able in all departments, including wireless. Brian combined mechanics with aeronautics and wireless, and his partnership with her was filled with instructive activity. They took private persons on flights, competed in air races, gave some attention to aerobatics and put up a record on two of the authorized air routes Their performances gained the attention of leading makers who engaged them as test pilots. The owners of a new style of machine, partly of Spanish origin, which, through numerous metamorphoses, and because of its special construction, had come to be known as the Multiple-Vertical-Gyro, invited the Delacys to attempt the Atlantic in their product.

Lola opposed this in favour of Australia for the simple reason that in her own state Brian would discover her real age, and she loved him more consumedly with each month. She had as much nerve as he in the air but lacked the hardihood to confess that she was ten years his senior. So long as her youthful appearance remained she would conserve her romance.

The Multiple-Vertical-Gyro Company were agreeable to this as their product had already been exhibited in New York.

The Middle West held probable embarrassment for Lola; the Upper Murrumbidgee would be equally uncomfortable for Brian under certain conditions. He had absorbed enough of the sophisticated she-man point of view of Europe to accept Lola's gifts in *amour* while in London and France. It would be another matter to appear in Australia unmarried to his female partner. One aviator had been thus libertarian, an innovation which, on the Murrumbidgee, had eclipsed her achievements in flight—as Brian knew from his mother's letters.

He was too fond of his mother to subject her to such a trial, and spoil all the triumph of his return, for which she had so loyally worked. What he desired was a share in making Australia an avian Commonwealth as it had been an equestrian Colony in the days of the earlier Delacys. As with old Nullah-Mundoey, personal aggrandizement would not mean so much to him as the development of his incalculable continent where a spiritual legacy lured him home like a siren. His waywardness would be against other forces than Mrs Grundy. To protect his dreams from disharmony, his schemes from obloquy, he was willing to observe the most barnacled family conventions.

"If we flew to Aussie together, we'd have to get married," he said to Lola.

"Why, how perfectly ridiculous! I thought it was a new country with advanced ideas."

"There's nothing new about living in concubinage."

"How crude to put it that way!"

"It wouldn't be put so politely among the old pioneers on the Murrumbidgee. Not a single solemn simple simon one of my aunts or great-aunts was so much as breathed upon before she was married. Even the men had to be quite decent because there were so few women to be indecent with."

"I guess that was the only reason. Oh, well, I understand. I was raised in the same kind of bourgeois respectability in Jackson, Michigan, but I did not lie down under it."

"Well, what about it?"

"About what?"

"Our tying up."

She was aching to hear him say that he loved her, not merely to suggest marriage to maintain his respectability. "Maybe we'd better. I guess I can stand it as well as you, but I don't want to be taken for your grandmother."

"My grandmother's cat! I reckon I *look* as old as you *are*; and there's no need to tell all we know. Knock a couple of years off."

"All right. Let's. Then when I want to go home to Michigan you can divorce me for desertion."

"What in thunder for? I thought you 1— cared for me?"

His blank look was comforting. "Yes, but if you're marrying only to be respectable enough to carry out our flight to Australia, I don't want to hold you."

"Beggar it all, I'm fond of you, and would like to marry you if we did no flying at all."

"Then no backing and filling about the difference in our ages later. I've always said I'd never be such a fool."

"I'll forget it, if you do."

"That settles it then." Joy suffused her to have her Brian plus respectability. There would be no need to stick to him for ever if the union became impossible.

Brian regarded marriage as inviolable. He was subconsciously disappointed that he was not transported, but this he laid to having anticipated the legal partnership by "living in sin". As with his great-grandfather, his vision of life itself was more seizing than his amorous abandon to it. Marriage was the completion of a man's person. Now that this was achieved he could push forward as a bridegroom of Australia—the attitude held by all great men, perhaps, towards their country, their people, their art, or career.

AUSTRALIAN MARRIES WEALTHY AMERICAN AVIATRIX

It was crack cable news in Fleet Street, so full of Australians.

A freelance some months since had dispatched a photograph of the American aviatrix and Australian aviator, which was now unfiled and widely reproduced in the Australian Press. The newly married pair were credited with planning an air honeymoon to Australia in a new type of machine.

The photograph had been snapped in a bleak March dawn at the end of one of Lola's long-distance flights. In it she looked, as she expressed it, "Like something that never happened unless in a nightmare after eating an English boiled pudding."

"I think she must be a multi-millionaire," smiled Margaret.

"She looks a thousand, and old for her age," agreed Roger.

The oversea correspondents had delighted to cable her age, as given in the marriage declaration. Clare Margaret had had a joint cable from the pair which sustained her pride under the blow of the other woman's possession of her boy. She spoke now with a challenge in her voice. "It's that silly way they are all taken, showing their teeth like sharks. And she had just come off a killing flight."

"He has married a very old woman," wrote Aunt Jean in a letter of congratulation to Clare Margaret. "But the Delacys like to marry people older than themselves. I hope Brian is not killed before we get a look at him and his rich American wife. It is good to have someone bring money into the family at last."

"She could not be called a beauty by any stretch of the imagination," wrote Josephine. "She looks very old, but your Aunt Della married a man with a greater disparity in years and it made no difference in the end. A pity his poor old grandfather did not last till Brian came. He had such faith in him doing something great some day."

Clare Margaret began to work for the day of Brian's arrival. There were "kags" of paint, now distributed in tins. She looked with satisfaction at her property (and Brian's) in a bend of the stream, with the trees that made it resemble an English park, a condition ensured by Darcy's love of trees and the education of Clare by aristocratic English tutors. Beyond Ferny Creek, the enfolding ranges, still crowned with timber, rose in tiers. Comforting roads wound across the horizon towards the bridge, and Burrabinga and Gool Gool.

Humphrey Vance immediately offered to drive Clare Margaret and her mother, and also Roger, to Sydney for Brian's arrival.

"He's my godson, and that entitles me to a bit of a splurge. I've had a hankering to own a plane for a long time."

Clare Margaret's tense driving mood had eased with the prospect of happiness and success for Brian. She suggested taking Aunt Jean too. "The three old ladies, each well on the way to a hundred, will be an encouragement to the bride," she chuckled. "A certificate for the Delacy men as husbands that their wives all outlive them, whether they started at scratch or behind it."

When paragraphs appeared concerning the renown that this sprig was bringing to the pioneer family of Delacy, Clare Margaret slyly remarked, "Only that I disgraced myself by marrying a cousin it wouldn't have been the Delacy name at all."

"Lucky for the old man's memory," said Humphrey, "but you know the name you should have."

"You say that because you know you are safe."

"No fear! You could make it right yet."

"You'd die of fright if I took you at your word."

"Just try me."

"It would burst up our habits. Better if I stayed at Ferny Creek and you at Longview."

"I might consent to that."

"Would you, really?"

Vance looked dubious. "I might come to it if I could not get you any other way; but we wouldn't be able to stand the talk."

It was well that Brian had bowed to convention on the tracks that Danny had blazed.

The day came when the cables bore the news of Mr and Mrs Delacy's hop-off from England in a Multiple-Vertical-Gyro christened *Nullah-Mundoey*. The route was that which a slip of a girl had traversed alone some three years earlier, and three years were a generation in air-ship progress. The interest in this flight lay in the new type of machine. It was the first England-to-Australia flight of a man and his wife linking the two English-speaking nations of the Pacific. A point stressed in the recent Italian flight was that Balbo, the leader, had allowed none but bachelors to take part, presumably so that they should be unhindered by legally accredited feminine fears and tears. The terrors of illicit ladies had to be kept out of the public eye and ear, or presumably were an inspiration to virility rather than a softening of manly fibre.

Brian, with the Delacy sense of humour, turned this point inside out merrily, and started well with the Press. Old Danny had come immediately after the explorers Sturt and Major Mitchell, and made a home for wife and babies in the wilds. His great-grandson's announced ambition was to forward the family era in aviation and thus to banish Australian loneliness and isolation, internecine or international.

"We must take to the plane as the early settler took to the horse and the camel. We must all fly as a matter of course."

Lola knew him for a superb "mixer", and he was too normally of his nation to frighten it with wild ideas. He hammered on those already half-accepted, over and over again, a few genial slogans that grew familiar.

A winged continent can be mistress of her own sea-line and sky-line; a wingless Australia is prey for Molly Hawks.

"A few slogans pile up publicity and make fame—too many smother it," said he.

CHAPTER LI

CLARE MARGARET was filled with an exciting sense of unreality to be at the good old Metropole, the favourite hostelry of many of the squattocracy. They were still the squattocracy, though their stations were widely merged in syndicated ownership.

Aunt Jean and Margaret called the roll of the old timers, so few of whom could answer *adsum* as their names arose for review. Aunt Jean was forgetful and repetitive and a little deaf, but that was her complaint of Margaret. "Poor old thing, she must be nearly a hundred, no wonder she is as she is," she would remark in Margaret's hearing. Luckily Margaret's sense of humour was as mellow as her years. Josephine was also persuaded to come to the hotel. Hers was the final triumph. Neither deaf nor forgetful, erect and free from bulges, she was of striking elegance.

"You might take me to the theatre," Clare Margaret suggested to Humphrey, "I shall go mad with nervousness waiting here for news from the Timor Sea. There are three chaperons—more correct than the picnic when poor old Uncle William lectured me because I went for a drive in your new sulky; spoiling sport when he had you ready for Laura Butler." Clare laughed mischievously but was thankful that she had not married this "stodgy old cow".

Near midnight, the hotel buzzed with the news that the *Nullah-Mundoey* and its pilots had safely reached Darwin, and broken previous records with ease. Congratulations met the relatives of the fliers at every turn.

The M-V-G had proved the claims of its makers by resisting the sand storms of the Near East and the heat of the tropics of India, and by refusing to misfire in the monsoons which sluiced upon it over Rangoon. Mrs Delacy had done much blind flying and had taken the watch over the Timor. Delacy was in fine fettle, but Mrs Delacy was feeling the strain so that the passage from Darwin was to be taken in short stages.

Arrival at Mascot was timed for ten o'clock one August morning. A stubborn drought prevailed even as far south as Gippsland. The young day was pallid with the southerly which roistered up from the Antarctic to make heady going for the Nullah-Mundoey. The wind sausages bellied as tightly as boiled puddings. Whirlwinds of dust soiled the air, freezing to Sydneysiders, but mild to those from the Upper Murrumbidgee, where Monaro winds have the shrewd rasp of purification.

News came that Delacy had to land for an hour after leaving Narromine because of Mrs Delacy's indisposition, though she was finishing the flight with her husband. Old-timers shook their heads and stood to reason that women were not meant by nature to fly. Men of outmoded thought, who still felt that whistling was blasphemy for women, and politics beyond them, had a nourishing revival.

"Oh, why doesn't he leave her and come on," said Adrienne Butler, an aviator kinswoman of Brian.

"Too much like old Nullah-Mundoey," said his mother. "Grandfather always took Grandma with him everywhere until she jacked up."

Adrienne was a conspicuous figure among those milling around in the dust for an extra hour. The baby of the family of Coole and Fanny (Vance) Butler, she was Brian's second cousin and awaited him with feverish enthusiasm. She strained to be upon the minute or ahead of it. Roger Delacy described her in domestic society as a chain-smoker and a married-man chaser. In other congregations more pungent tributes circulated, which though unsubstantiated, rescued Adrienne from the obscurity which would have been hers had her deportment won approval from Roger. She was frequently the subject of Press paragraphs, and familiar to the public through the pictures of her opening-up the fleeces of her Uncle Humphrey's champions, or leading-in her father's winners at picnic races. She was a pet with her uncle, and regarded as his heiress, and much courted for his sake as well as for her own liveliness.

Coole was President of the Bandalong Jockey Club, and Adrienne among the dwindling number of girls who could ride. She boasted of the Delacy blood there. She could even play polo, on ponies of the old Nullah-Mundoey strain. Also she had an "A" licence as a pilot. A plane of her own had been postponed by the subsidence of wool profits. Adrienne had tried to wheedle her uncle into providing one, but a lot of the troglodyte lingered in him. He thought that flying had made Adrienne just a little "loud", though it was hidden from him just how far she had advanced beyond girls too genteel to whistle. She was eager for adventure with her cousins, and when she saw the pictures of Lola, felt sure that Brian would be an easy conquest.

"Married to an old scrag like that, he will be rabid for a little understanding," she observed to her confidante, as she retouched her pillar-box red lips. Her cheeks and finger nails were also lacquered with a flaming tint. Upon an endearing mass of curls, like a poodle's, was perched a *chapeau*, constructed from a piece of stockinette, to resemble the cap of Reskemeer's "Cornish Gent", and she had a fashionable coatee known as a "bum freezer", which outlined her anatomy apropos.

"In my young days it was the bosom that was upholstered to the shape of a plum pudding," chuckled Clare Margaret. "And to-day it is the b-t-m. You never got such a boomer from the Delacy side of the house."

"A great deal depends on it," said Adrienne, exercising her muscles like a hula-hula dancer.

"I'll say all depends on it when you have nothing else on which to depend," said Clare Margaret with an indulgent chuckle.

Adrienne was noted by a Press-woman who signed her social gossip "Ercildoun"—a distant connection of the Delacys—who had consorted with Brian and Lola in London.

"Absolutely, *mon vieux cheval*," said this person softly. She knew the European and American originals of Adrienne, and dismissed her as an unworthy graft on old pioneer stock.

"Why do you call me that?" demanded Adrienne, as they shared Clare's sandwiches and thermos of coffee in the last hour.

"Because you are so conspicuously *vieux jeu, mon enfant*."

Adrienne could not be sure of Ercildoun, but courted her. To be written-up was a criterion of success; Adrienne was no blob or woop-woop. Clare was amused by the disapproval of Adrienne by the old-fangled. Clare herself had been a shocker when younger than Adrienne, and now applied the yard-stick of experience.

"Pooh!" she said to Roger's complaint. "What's wrong with her? She's only going with the times."

"She's over the odds—a bit of a b——."

"Bah! Men always think dirty things that they manufacture out of their own minds about women. Noah took a pair of that fashion into the Ark and they have multiplied ever since."

Adrienne quickly discovered Clare's sanction and kept in the limelight by sticking to the celebrity's mother. Adrienne overheard someone say, "She ought to be thankful to Clare Margaret; she's the dog-in-the-manger who keeps Humphrey from some flapper who would make his money fly."

Clare Margaret took the girl as easily as she used to manage the spirited Nullah-Mundoeys, and with such handling Adrienne purred. She threw her arms around Clare and whispered that she loved her and wanted to help by lending her Humber with herself as chauffeuse.

At length the avian *Nullah-Murdoey* and its escort of twenty planes were descried. Clare and Adrienne embraced each other and wept with excitement. "I know he's lovely," exclaimed the girl. "I am so proud he is my cousin. I'm sick of so many blobs and woop-woops for relations."

The Press representatives were photographing the three ancient graces. "I should be in too," said Adrienne. "I'm the only other flying Delacy."

"We owe her the front page for carrying the ads," said a good-natured veteran. "Come on, Miss Aviatrix."

"The old bungs are very proud of my cousin," she remarked. "With his education he might have merely turned into some sort of old professor."

"It would be better though if he were bringing home the Davis Cup or the Ashes," said the veteran.

"That would be too much to expect," said Adrienne.

"Quite!" interposed Ercildoun. "We must be thankful it's flying. He might have obscured himself by producing a serious exposition of Commonwealth politics."

The earlier gale had blown the day clear, and eased a little. The wind guides slumped to the outline of big white caterpillars. The sun sparkled on the plain where a decade earlier had still flourished a garden of fairy shrubs and unique flowers. The world ran clear and flat to the distant bay, beautiful with the special magic of Sydney waters, the sea as Cook had first beheld it foaming about its promontories.

Roger and Humphrey re-tucked the old ladies' wraps and offered them alcoholic sustenance. The watchers eddied for positions in relation to the sun. The unemployed from adjacent suburbs and congeries were present in numbers, but there was no such muster as called up by Amy Johnson. These arrivals were becoming a commonplace, and no man could outdo "Smithy", whose constant achievements made him a classic.

The M-V-G machine neared speedily, gave the airman's curtsy *in excelsis* and rose to remain buzzing overhead.

"Stone the crows! A beetle or a windmill." exclaimed a spectator.

"A new fakement; haven't you read the papers?" demanded another.

"By cripes! it's a rum looking contraption."

Loud guffaws as at a clown among air ships.

"You can laugh, but it's the only machine that can hang about in the air. Aw, what's the good of talking to —— bastards that haven't as much machinery in their heads as a tin hare."

The *Nullah-Mundoey* was fairly overhead demonstrating her dragon-fly stunt. Then she alighted vertically, according to claim; she had really arrived. Her pilots were getting out of the cockpit. The crowd was prevented from shredding the plane for souvenirs by squads of police who pushed every one back to a place of safety from the planes alighting on the drome. The Pressmen acted as guards to the relatives who went to meet the pair, Lola looking her age—any age up to a hundred, as someone kindly said—and exceedingly white and drawn, in spite of chic make-up. She had been a passenger only from Darwin, but there she was as Brian's mate.

Cheers from swirling knots of people. Police regulating movement. Brian was caught by one camera in the act of kissing his mother. Then came the three old aunts. Adrienne pump-handled Brian's hand and omitted to embrace Lola. People strained on tip-toe to catch a glimpse of the pair, and stood on one foot and another and ached with apathy while the head of the Aero Club, the head of the Chamber of Commerce and others welcomed the flyers, and business envoys on duty pushed their commodities. A municipal authority put forward the claims of the spot, as an imperial drome. Here was a square mile of level plain, right at the city's side door, as yet pre-empted by little except the bedraggled skirts of a slum and Chinese vegetable gardens—a glorious opportunity awaiting people of vision and taste. The microphone was thrust before the flyers. Brian beamed and began. Fine popular pieces welled spontaneously from his overflowing zest in being an Australian. Everything was for Australia. His cheering pronouncements were direct descendants of old Danny's visions of posterity. Here was posterity fulfilling Danny.

Ercildoun made her way to Lola, whose eyes lighted to recognize a friend and ally. Lola whispered, "I feel as if I'm going to die. I'm so air-sick, and it does not ease off when I land. Oh, if only I could lie down somewhere and sleep for a week! They'll take dreadful pictures of me looking like something the cat left on the mat."

"You need a dragon. Ah, Adrienne, *mon vieux cheval*, here's your opportunity. The only member of Lola's sex in the tribe able to meet her on some sort of equality. Excuse me—excuse—please excuse—thank you so much. Splendid, so kind of you—just let me pass." Thus she made her way, with Adrienne commandeered to the service of Lola, and reached the Humber while the crowd pressed around Brian, warmed by his humorous tones.

The reporters beset him with busy pencils as he turned from the microphone. "Fly, that's the order of the day. My old great-grandad—all his kids went from the bottle on to a horse without a pram between, and my kids and yours—if we have the luck to have any—must go from their mothers—by George! they must go with their mothers straight into planes. We'll build hangars and dromes instead of roads. Instead of the old shanty-keepers with stables and nose-bags, we're going to have bowsers and skilled mechanics with spare parts dotted about from the Roper to the Paroo and Ayer's Rock, and from the Leeuwin to Cape York. It's the greatest flying land on the globe—the best sky—blow it all, we've got about the biggest sky there is all in one piece, and that's without any bolony. Here my wife and I are linking-up America. It is due to my wife's superb navigation that this flight has been so successful. She has a sixth sense of direction, like our ornithorhynchus. She can show me the way to Aussie in the dark, and the only condition upon which she would marry me was that I'd bring her straight home to see you all. She will now say hullo!"

"Your wife has eloped," shouted a voice.

Brian joined in the laughter. "She has a big heart for Australians. She's too modest about her achievements, so I thank you on her behalf for this magnificent welcome, and promise that she will talk later to you all on the air."

Fellow pilots carried him for a few yards between lines of curious people and then put him down. The three old ladies were cheered as they progressed under the care of Roger, Humphrey and Clare Margaret.

"Can't I get into the thing and see how it goes?" demanded Josephine.

"Would you, Grandma?" Brian shouted his excitement.

He was surprised and delighted by the stylish and youthful appearance of this grandma in her rich fur coat, her Parisian chapeau, with her feminine earrings and fragrant posy of boronia and violets.

"And what about you?" he turned to Margaret and Jean.

"I suppose I might as well end that way as any other," said Margaret. She was not to be outdone by Josephine in the last lap.

Jean refused to risk her life. She could never be prodded into family rivalries. The two old ladies were placed in the machine.

OCTOGENARIAN LADIES IN FIRST FLIGHT

Meanwhile Lola arrived at the Hotel and was taken upstairs to a back room, while the suite on the front, decorated by a Committee of Welcome, was left to decoy the bothersome.

It was Ercildoun who compiled the interviews loaded with cute and popularizing American opinions of Australia's gorgeous girls and vast beaches, she who set in motion the conception of Lola as so modest and feminine that she left all speech-making to her husband, though she could fly blind for leagues and take the watch over the Timor without a tremor.

Lola had to be excused from all the officially arranged welcomes. Such a pity, said someone, but Clare Margaret thus had Brian to herself, and Adrienne wasted no sympathy on the indisposed airwoman.

"She doesn't look so bad as her photo led us to expect," said Margaret.

"She's better looking than he is. He has that Irish mouth like old Grandpa Danny," said Josephine.

"Terrible pity he didn't take after the royal side of the house," muttered Roger.

Clare was so happy that she said, "Let her have her head. She's a show piece, and what Brian doesn't know won't hurt him. Humphrey is another ready to cheer now that the battle is won, so I'm letting the tails go swimming with the hides in this Yackandandah."

Clare decided to abrogate her unforgiveness. Humorously she realized that it would never occur to the unrelenting old lady that she could necessitate forbearance; always her own heroine, no tinge of remorse had ever tarnished her self-confidence.

During a family rally held later Aunt Jean remarked, "All that Brian needs to be exactly old Grandpa Danny is the big pipe and the long beard."

"And the wooden leg," added Roger.

Josephine asked what he would do with the *Nullah-Mundoey* at Ferny Creek. "It will get tangled up in the trees."

"You might drop something on the dingoes—plenty of them there yet," contributed Aunt Jean.

"Oh, the *Nullah-Mundoey* can land in its own space. That's how it will revolutionize flying."

"Rather early for a revolution; I thought flying was hardly rooted yet," observed Roger, whip and horseman, beached by change.

Lola remained so weak and nervous that she soon withdrew, followed by murmurs of these flights being unfit for women, but

Margaret said, "I don't suppose that flying is any more wearing than being in a hut surrounded by hostile blacks with fire spears, or than having a baby on a tarpaulin under a dray on a flooded stream bank among the flies and ants, as the women did in my mother's day. Women can stand more than men, and outlast them, as far as I have seen. Something else could have upset Lola; there is a lot of gastric flu about."

Clare Margaret was eager to have her daughter-in-law at home to smother her with attention. Eventually they went together in the car placed at Brian's disposal by the Oil Company, whose product he had used on the flight. Brian remained in Sydney to pluck opportunity while interest in him was awake. He was full of unction that he was representing Lola as well as himself. Only Lola was feeling more resentful than grateful to him.

His Grandmother Josephine was a rich find to him. Darcy had rarely mentioned his mother. Silence had been the only way to evade Clare Margaret's criticism of her mother-in-law. Not so long after Darcy's death Brian had gone away to school, and Clare's habit of silence about Josephine thus enabled her grandson to make her acquaintance free of the ancient jealousies and incompatibilities. Though verging on eighty, Josephine retained more vigour and beauty than the average woman of sixty, and could outlast any number of the flappers. She dressed expensively and stylishly. Women clamour for outstanding men, no matter how eccentric, but the most exceptional man would rather a stylish and handsome female relative than a successful genius, or one who had saved his life, if lacking in style of dress or person. Despite all Clare's devotion Brian, because of her weather-beaten appearance and uncompromising speech, found more satisfaction to his vanity in his grandmother's feminine grace and dignity. In addition, Josephine had the ability to take a practical interest in the *Nullah-Mundoey*, and with Brian on guard soon could manage the controls. She confessed a desire to have a plane of her own. Brian was equally a satisfaction to Josephine. She would at best have tolerated an acclaimed artistic genius, provided he could make money, but mechanical skill she could understand and in air science take pride. From all her marital disappointment, including the early loss of all her children but the stiff-necked Isabel, here at last was a shred of recompense. Her implacable disparagements of family members amused Brian. He attributed them to her great age. Also he was not at her mercy, and there was a precipitate of her own harder prosaic grain in him to rescue him from the visionary and sensitive Delacy temperament, while he retained the Delacy winsomeness.

He felt indubitably Josephin's kin and dramatized her strain in himself.

She was a prodigy for which he was thankful, as Adrienne said, "among the crowd of blobs". A born mechanic, she revelled in her grandson's skill, and in having her own recognized. She did not have to insist that Brian inherited his gifts from her; he loudly proclaimed his debt. Throughout her married years she had heard poetic interpretations of life and of nature, or dreams of posterity, which had irritated her as the delirium of incompetence, while the door of the stable might be hanging on one hinge, or the spouting escaping from the veranda, and she herself compelled to attend to such repairs. Men who could not make money were contemptible in her eyes. She was never tired of driving or flying with this young man, who belonged to her, and she put helpful sums in his pocket. The belated outlet for her mechanical skill in flying was an excitement to banish the *malaise* of old age.

Adrienne remained in Sydney, supposedly in the charge of her Uncle Humphrey, and attended functions on the invitations intended for Lola. She had much notice as the intrepid young aviatrix, Brian's cousin, and was described without reservations as beautiful. Brian accepted her and liked her as a kid who had an infectious excitement in her experiences. He needed advertisement; Adrienne was a fine publicity hound and a tireless honorary secretary. She took a palpitant interest in the *Nullah-Mundoey*; flew it with confidence, and gave her views on its coming supremacy. This was all attributed to cousinly interest. There lay the danger.

Awaiting the completion of the bigger M-V-G, Brian was compelled to take people on joy rides and to grab any odd job. Lola was not wealthy as rumour said. One after another of her father's enterprises had run dry since 1928, and she had spent her available assets with Brian in aviation. Brian spoke before every group that asked him, regardless of its size or politics. He had old Danny's sociable attitude toward his fellows, and was careful not to be too far above the crowd except in an air ship. He reinvested platitudes so that he was inspiring, and Adrienne toppled into amorous infatuation for him as only a girl of twenty can, and was heady with the anti-social delusions of the state. She was sure that Lola had taken advantage of Brian through her money—an old woman who was strangling his personality. Adrienne had embraced modernism and imagined that she had jettisoned the conventions. She was plaguing her Uncle Humphrey to float her as a Trans-Pacific flier, and dreamed of taking Lola's place.

Lola thought Ferny Creek the dearest, cutest place she had ever

seen as a week-end summer resort, but to her it had the primitive-
ness of a camp, with less of comfort and conveniences than many a
summer cottage of her childhood at Charlevoix or Harbour Springs.
To that was added a sense of isolation from the world which
Pitcairn Island might have given to Clare Margaret. Not even one
modern picture on the walls! Nothing but enlarged photographs—
and of what looked like hayseeds! Not even radio!

Lola could not ride, and hated the bush roads for the automobile.
She was not a nature lover. The strange elfin spring meant little to
her, though she obligingly tried to gush over the mimosa which
afflicted her with hay fever. She made no discoveries for herself.
She was a worshipper of machines, especially of the carrier that
could scour the skies and speak between continents. She was no
raconteuse to gain entertainment in entertaining others. Her social
equipment was in her ability to listen. During six years or more
she had been a mental sponge saturated with all the advanced
politics, isms and ologies of art and science of the capitals of
Europe and of the United States. Her indisposition at Ferny Creek
confined her to the housewives who called on her mother-in-law,
and their gossip of cake and knitting recipes was stupefying. A letter
from her ally, Ercildoun, provided escape.

Ercildoun had summed-up Adrienne's cousinliness to a milli-
metre. Neither trouble-maker nor alarmist, she simply said it was
a pity that Brian had to take the lionizing alone as it put him in
a false position, especially with women.

Lola was frantic to escape from Ferny Creek, and suggested to
Clare Margaret a descent upon Sydney in company to surprise
Brian. This was agreed upon and Ferny Creek was left to Mrs
Thingamebob and Roger.

Up and away at the first hint of dawn in the powerful car to
do in half a day what had taken Danny and Johanna weeks to
cover with bullocks and dray. It was lovely weather but Lola
scarcely deigned to cast her eyes back at the panorama which had
enchanted Danny and Harry.

Upon parking the car, Clare Margaret hurried to Neutral Bay
to see Josephine, who had hurt her foot and was confined to her
apartment. In accordance with her design, Lola went unaccom-
panied in pursuit of Brian. She walked into the Metropole without
luggage, and took the key from the attendant but brought it down
again to the office so that Brian could come up. "Don't mention
that I have come," she said. "I want to have a rest."

"Good-o," said the man, and forgot all about her. The lift
operator did not recognize her.

Brian's things were flung about with his customary disorder. Lola was orderly. She took a coat from the back of a chair to transfer it to a wardrobe. Letters fell from the pockets, an inscription uppermost. "Darling, dinkydi Brian." What followed was in the same vein, and signed "Coz Adrienne."

"Indeed!" mused Lola. "So that is the how of it."

She then read all the letters. They oozed mush from a variety of fair-weather admirers. Lola had had her own share of this, and knew how little the recipient was to blame. Adrienne was different.

"If Uncle Humphrey would finance you, you would not need poor old Lola's money any more."

Lola's nausea was replaced by a pain like a knife in her being. She read on, "It's no use. If I couldn't see you again, I'd kill myself and leave a letter saying why. I don't mind so long as I can see you every day. I count each hour when I don't. I don't care about my character. Perhaps if Lola knew, she would get a divorce, and then you'd be free."

If Lola knew what? How far had this gone? Lola pondered each phrase. The suspicion grew that Adrienne would not have gone on without response. Was Brian posing as a martyr tied to an old woman? The sentence about poor old Lola's money stung.

A box of powder and a perfume that Lola did not use, were on the dressing table, feminine garments in the wardrobe. The girl must be running a disgusting affair right in the hotel, which Lola had thought to be as respectable as the leading hotel in Tecumseh or Dowagiac, Michigan. It was nearly as primitive in her point of view. Was such behaviour countenanced in a family hostelry?

She went downstairs and made herself agreeable to the office staff, finger on lips and honeyed words underneath. Was her husband at Mascot? He was. Would she like to get through on the telephone? Oh, no, she was going straight out by car. She was expecting her cousin, Miss Butler—had she arrived?

"She is in and out with Mr Delacy. They are usually here to dinner, but go out to dance afterwards. There is some mail here," said the attendant, handing a sheaf of cablegrams and letters. "I hope you are feeling fit again, Mrs Delacy."

"Yes, thank you. I am glad my husband is getting some dancing. Don't mention my return as I want to beat the game by an hour or two. There is the key."

The key was in its place, evidence of her departure, but at the door she doubled back behind an influx of pastoralists and escaped upstairs, where she had left the door unlatched. Some of the cables were greetings and congratulations, but others informed her of further decline in her industrial securities. In fact she had over-drawn, and was practically without resources. She was so depressed by this second shock that she craved to lie in peace in the dark. She got through to Ercildoun on the telephone and confessed that she was feeling queerly and did not want any one to know that she had returned to town. Ercildoun recommended a doctor, to which Lola consented. She then crawled on to a corner of the bed under the motor rug and hat boxes and other disorder, and, placing something to keep the light from her eyes, drifted into sleep. It was the ability to sleep when under strain that so stood to her as an airwoman and preserved her youthful appearance.

CHAPTER LII

SHE was awakened some time later by the entrance of Brian. Adrienne was with him. Lola remained quiet and it speedily became apparent that Adrienne was entering surreptitiously to dress.

"I'll go down to the lounge till you come," said Brian. "The room next door will be ready for you to-night. Old Fullwood from Heulong has it and will be leaving after dinner."

"It's going to be gorgeous to-night. The *Monowai* has nice long decks. Ta-ta, darling!"

The sound of heated kissing inspired Lola to pop up and say, "Too cousinly!" but that was not sufficiently annihilating. She lay stricken while Brian departed and Adrienne changed her dress, posturing before the mirror as she hummed happily, "You Will Remember Vienna," and tossed her discarded garments on to Lola.

At the end of ten minutes Adrienne cautiously opened the door to a knock. Brian, in the aperture, began, "I say! They tell me downstairs that Lola came to-day and went out to Mascot to meet me."

"Damn! Spoils all our fun. Jump into your things and let's escape before we're stopped."

"I couldn't do that."

"Are you frightened?"

"Rot! No. But I shan't have so much time for you now. I'll have to take Lola about. I don't want her to get a wrong view Australia."

"Aren't you going to tell her about us?"

"What about us?"

"All we mean to each other."

"It is you that has worked up the vamp stuff. I have no time for it now."

"Yes, but we have a right to love. We are young and strong. Lola is too old to fly, that's why this has broken her up."

"I wouldn't say that. She can give me points yet as a pilot, though I beat her in knowledge of the engine. I use scientific knowledge; so does she, but she has intuition or something in addition."

"Every one says she is too old for you."

"Rats! All the others I tried were too young! This boy-and-girl mugging business soon palls on me."

"But you would never, never have thought of her if she hadn't money. That's true, isn't it?"

"It's true that she wouldn't have been able to afford me only she had money."

"If you only look upon it as boy-and-girl *mugging* business, I'll die. Why did you let me think you cared?"

"Hell, I couldn't stop you! You'll get over it. A year from now you'll be wondering why you felt like this. It's only puppy love."

"But there could never be any one the same again. Don't you care at all?"

Tears and hysterics were adumbrated. Brian hated such manifestations as the plague. "Yes, yes, of course I care in a way, but Lola is my wife."

"What difference does that make, if she is an old thing you couldn't love; besides, she is a Yankee, and the Yanks never stay married to the first husband. If they want a man they just horn-in and take him without worrying that he is married, like in both those talkies we saw last night. If you had your choice . . ."

"Yes, if you had your choice," said Lola, who had squirmed noiselessly from her position and stood up behind them. Her voice was as startling as a pistol.

"When did you come in?" asked Brian.

"A little while before Adrienne."

Adrienne was aggressive. "Well, now you know!"

"Yes, I know," said Lola slowly, and as if very tired. She felt as though her voice were coming from someone else, and that her limbs had turned to lead. As a novice in the first stages of intoxication striving to keep control of himself, she resolved to say as little as possible. She stood looking at them.

Brian was confounded, and enraged with Adrienne for putting him in a foolish position.

"You listened!" Adrienne accused shrilly.

"I surely did . . . and I *heard*."

"Well, what are you going to do about it?" proceeded Adrienne, defiantly, but her heart was pounding madly, and her knees threatened to collapse.

"About what?"

"About Brian and me loving each other."

"Why should I do anything? I have so many important issues chasing me that you and Brian must settle these paltry disturbances between yourselves."

"Adrienne is a nice little cousin, and only a bit sentimental," offered Brian.

"Are you trying to crawl out, and pretend you did not mean it?" flashed Adrienne. "Coward!"

"You'll learn that men are always cowards or brutes when they find themselves in a fix between two women; what else can they be?" Lola knew that she loved Brian to agony, but something at present made him so distasteful to her that she could have thrown him away like an old glove. "You can have him. All I want is a plane. I'll need that, as I have no other resources now. I have just heard that my Industrials have declined to nothing, so I can't be useful in the way of money. . . . If you don't mind, I'd like my room. I want to rest. You can decide your future elsewhere."

Brian signed to Adrienne to go. "It's useless making signs for me to clear out. Didn't you mean what you said? Was it all hooey?"

A man can accept a girl's offering as easily as walking into the sunlight, and Brian had not until that moment realized the intensity of Adrienne's predilection for him. He saw in a flash that he had been culpable—careless of the furnace at the end of *amour*. He could have wrung the girl's neck, but there was in him too much of old Danny and Harry and Darcy to be brutal. "I'll be likely to break my wooden leg in this Yackandandah," he thought, suppressing a grin. The women would not forgive amusement in such a crisis.

"This is a hell of a mess, Adrienne. I must say, I never thought you were interested in me for more than the flying racket, and being a nice little Delacy cousin."

"Are you beginning to crawl down?" demanded the girl, intransigent.

"Don't mind me. I'm only an old thing married for my money." Lola threw this bitterly into the controversy.

"Come now, Lola, we had the whole business of age back and forth before we started to swim the Yackandandah of marriage. It's not like you to nag about it now."

"But I've lost my money since then; and Adrienne wouldn't have used that line of talk to you if you had any respect for me. You'd have told her that my age was not her business."

"I have as much right to him as you have. I love him. Love has first right."

"You'll find it has second and third and no rights at all, when you've had as much experience as I have. You always have to be pulling a man away from some kind of creature—old or young—

tripe out of the gutter can seduce most of them. You can take on the job if you want it. I'm tired and sick."

She swayed and leant on the footrail of the bed in a determined effort against fainting. Her face was ghastly—sallow, puffy under the eyes. Distraught, she suddenly shouted, ' Get right out of here, this instant, both of you!"

"Oh, I say," exclaimed Brian. "Really, Lola! No harm has been done. I can swear . . ."

Angry expostulation broke from Adrienne. The chambermaid knocked loudly and said, "The doctor has come, Mrs Delacy."

A doctor of medicine is a sacrosanct official of society. In Australia he is naïvely an aristocrat to boot. This one was an imposing, authoritative female, one of the cleverest gynaecologists in the world. Even Adrienne could not buck a personage of such standing. It would have required a debauched outlaw to gainsay Dr Hester Augarde, and Brian *au fond* was of Murrumbidgee respectability and family discipline. He was also disturbed by the state of Lola's health. Her indisposition had continued for weeks.

"Good evening! Are you the patient? . . . I see you are," said the physician, moving towards the bed and Lola, who had now lain down. "Are you the husband?" she inquired of Brian, as though he were some kind of spider, and placing him then and there in the centre of the diagnosis. Adrienne was relieved to slip away. The adventure had lost incandescence with this commanding official regarding Lola stretched on the bed, though Adrienne clung to the flattering delusion that this collapse was due to jealousy of girlish charms. It would be miraculous if Lola had appendicitis or something similar and died under the operation.

"I'll remain in the hall in case you need me," said Brian.

"Thank you. Close the door," said Dr Augarde.

Adrienne descended to the lounge, where she met one of the polo heroes straight from Cobbitty—young Rodney Lillingston of Cooma. He was elated by the prospect of such a listener for a recital of the day's play, but speedily came to the conclusion that flying swank was deranging Adrienne's brain.

Brian walked up and down the corridor in a whirl of emotions. The doctor was so long that the husband had time to cool—to freeze—and to think. Blast Adrienne! He had been a fool, but he reckoned all men were when a woman was young and pretty, and eager. She need not be pretty so long as she was pressing. A succession of tripe, Lola had said in her bitterness, and the evidence was on her side. A man needed sentinels to warn him, or he was in a bog before he saw it.

He recalled how Lola had stood by him in his defeat and depression in London, and in the long watches in the air, the latest over the Timor. She had been none too fit before they hopped off, but would not hold up the flight. Now she had lost her money. He was happy to find that this reverse endeared her to him. His affection had roots in comradeship. Lola was generous and kind and the best pilot he had ever worked with. She seemed to possess some harmonious power over the machine, as women used to have over horses that were dangerous with men, and when she had to fly blind she held to her course as straight as a sextant. He hoped that she was not seriously ill.

Dr Augarde came out and closed the door behind her. "You are Mr Delacy, I suppose?" Assured on this point, she said with authority, "If care is taken, there is every hope of saving the child."

Brian went so white that she led him to the drawing-room at the end of the passage. "Does this come as an unpleasant shock?"

"The greatest thing that has ever happened in my life. I had no idea. Poor little Lola! May I go to her?"

"Yes, but rest and quiet, mind, no excitement. No celebration . . . Marvellous! My first aeroplane case. Three months and she took that flight. Madness!"

Brian's eyes flashed blue flame, reflecting such excitement as, generations past, Johanna had seen in young Danny's when there had been no resisting him, when she had had to follow to the furthest extremity of the globe, and from there farther still into the wilderness. This was something greater than himself, greater than *amour*; it was the extension of himself, a link in an unbroken chain—immortality.

"She never told me," he stammered.

"She had her reasons doubtless," said the doctor dryly.

"The fourth generation of Delacys to fly!"

"You must be careful—no strain—no excitement."

"Shall you send a nurse?"

"A sensible friend to seclude her for a month would be better. Absolute quiet for the next forty-eight hours—mind!"

As Brian escorted the doctor to the door, he saw Ercildoun approaching, and ducked to the florist's counter to escape her. He seized an armful of wattle—not so much as his forebears had sheaved-up to make wattle-and-daub shelters or sheep folds, but he ascended the stairway draped in perfumed fluff. He burst into Lola's presence, a golden cloud. She saw his expression and knew his mind.

"Some wattle, my love."

"I thought it was mimosa."

"That's its trade moniker; it's home name is wattle—good old wattle! God, is there anything so ethereal in the world!"

He stood by the bed, then went to her, tender and exalted, curbing his urge for corroboree.

"Congratulations, darling!" he said, kissing her gently. "This is unbelievable. I'm mad all through with joy. It's the most tremendous and symbolical thing that has happened in the history of Australia since Cook landed. A flying son! Flew before his birth, like I and my father and uncles and aunts and cousins went on horseback with out mothers before we were born. That's the way to have a nation of airmen."

"Or an airwoman."

"Oh, yes, forgive me. Too much phallic bumptiousness on my part, eh? We can have an air son later if you'd prefer one of your own sex to start," he gallantly amended.

"One may be plenty for me to produce and you to raise. I'm not so tickled as I might be about the loss of my income. I chose a bad time. This will put the kibosh on my flights for some time."

"A glorious time! Plenty of room for us all in the skies above Aussie, the biggest skies in the world over our own back yard. Never mind about the flight to America in the new plane. It is off for the present. The M-V-G Company has some new safety improvements and wants the *Nullah-Mundoey* over there . . . Humphrey Vance has been wanting me to stay here. There is a project to map out the unknown parts of Australia properly, and old Humphrey wants to fly, and will fork-up for that. Civil aviation, air mail—all sorts of leads. This settles it. Humphrey can be godfather to the kid as he was of me. You wouldn't mind, would you?"

Lola raised herself with effort. The feeling of unreality persisted. "I'll make a bargain with you. Mr Vance can be *one* of the godparents on *one* condition."

"What's that? It's granted anyhow. The kid is yours, of course."

"You must be more dignified about my age. If you had the right attitude, or any respect for our union, you would not let these flappers get balled-up. You are to blame somehow, or they wouldn't write you those sloppy letters."

"I never read their cows of letters."

"Maybe you don't, but if you can't control the situation with more dignity, I can't go on with the wear and tear all my life. I'd rather end it now."

"I never think of the damn flapps at all—only to dance."

He saw his mistake, but could not recall his words. Lola was not a dancer. She would be ungraceful on a dance floor—angular and big-boned. She had her ascendancy as a goddess of the machine. Up and away into the skies, she was glorious, an albatross, enduring, courageous, inspiring. She came to earth, like an albatross, awkwardly.

Fortunately for that forbidden excitement, Ercildoun knocked on the door. Lola called, "Come!" and welcomed her in such a way that Brian was glad to obey doctor's orders and give place. The caller sent him on an errand.

"So the murder is out," she laughed, to Lola. "Took a long time, seeing the clues were as clear as a wagon track on the Black Soil Plains after rain."

"I guess they never dreamed I would be on a big flight—that fooled them."

"Yes, they thought you were too modern for this business."

"This modern business gets my goat."

"Are you glad?"

"More worried. I'd go mad if I had to go through this among those women around Ferny Creek. They're darlings, but they don't know a thing about anything that's happened since our Civil War. How the heck do you put up with them?"

"I leave 'em, as you left Michigan."

"But Michigan has a few gadgets that Ferny Creek does without."

"Gadgets don't finally satisfy the mind, and you have to pick your clique in London to escape the fundamentalists or the 'spit and polish' imperialists and such. There are times when I know that one whiff of a Ferny Creek is worth all the intelligentsia of London and New York and Paris and Moscow put together."

"That could be true too, but there is something else." Without reserve, Lola gave the facts of the Adrienne complication. "Do you suppose the girl is neurasthenic? I don't know how Australian girls take things. Here, in this very paper, is a case of a girl in England who took poison when the man had to choose between *chère amie* and his wife—and chose the wife."

"I forgot all about Adrienne in this issue."

"It is to be hoped that she will forget."

"This will cure her. She's of good prosaic old stock. I recall my disgust when I was Adrienne's age. A man cavorted before me with caterwaulings of deathless love, and I found out that at the same time his wife was within a month of her time."

"That was pre-Ark delicacy. Girls are more advanced to-day."

"Advanced where?"

"Oh, well, it is considered smart to chisel-in on a married woman now. You're only entitled to a man while you can hold him. In my case the darlings have to rescue the martyred hero."

"Adrienne will be all right. We folks that were reared on ferny creeks are not so neurotic yet, thank God. I have telephoned for Clare Margaret. A word in her ear and she will prick the whole mess like a toy balloon."

Brian had gone to telephone "old Humphrey" about his godfathership to the first air-born child of the coming air-born race. He was so excited that he could hardly hold the receiver.

As he came out of the booth, Adrienne was waiting for him. He had forgotten her, but he had a stupendous alibi, as Lola would have expressed it. His thoughts were of Australians in the air, of children to be born in aeroplanes as they had been born in hulks or in bullock drays in the early days. He was impersonal, detached, as Danny of yore when the far blue peaks of his kingdom enthralled him.

"Oh, Adrienne, old scout!" he exclaimed, "Such news! A miracle—an air miracle. Come, I'll tell you."

The girl's heart leapt. Heaven knows how she interpreted that miracle in relation to her own infatuation. Brian's culpability had been passive; he did not think of Adrienne as a disappointed *amoreuse.*

"It's immense, Adrienne! You must be godmother," he concluded. "The only other flier of old Nullah-Mundoey's breed."

Adrienne turned a ghastly colour under her flamboyant lacquer. Her romance, her drug was being torn from her without warning or alleviation. "I don't want to be an old cow of a godmother," she protested shrilly.

Fortunately there were only one or two people present. The hotel had emptied for the picture theatres. While Brian had been in the telephone booth, Ercildoun had been giving Clare Margaret the facts. They both now came forward to blanket a scene. Adrienne had been through too much on her nerve with an unseasoned frame, fed on excitement and modernistic notions of securing thrills; and they had all been too preoccupied for dinner. Ercildoun put her arm around the girl, who strove to hurl something denunciatory at Brian, but it foundered in sobs.

"You go to Lola, I'll take care of Adrienne," said Clare Margaret to her son.

"Of course Adrienne will be godmother," said Ercildoun over her shoulder. "She's the right person, the second flying Delacy."

Brian was glad to bound away up the staircase. The women entered the lift.

"As soon as it is decent to mention it, I'll put it in the papers," said Ercildoun, as they reached the empty drawing-room. "Another honour for the popular young airwoman, Miss Butler."

"He made me love him desperately, and then he doesn't care," sobbed Adrienne.

"Don't let any one know that," advised Clare Margaret.

"They all ought to be told what he is."

"Never let a man know how much he has hurt you."

"Why not?"

"Oh, perhaps so that he can hurt you some more," she replied, with a humorous chuckle, and cynicism that was merely an echo or a subconscious recognition of the amoral quality of *amour*. Her own husband had adored her from his birth until his death; her father and mother had been congenial comrades as long as the partnership lasted. "Never let a man get under your skin. The more he hurts you, the more cocky it makes him—and you become a laughing stock." Nevertheless she was concerned for the girl's wan face, and put an arm about her. "Come on, old hard-timer, this is a Yackandandah that millions of women have to swim, but this one is only a creek, and you know how to fly. You can say 'ka-poop' and thumb your nose to the whole blinking lot."

It was a woman's night. Clare Margaret attended to Lola's wants and ensured the prescribed quiet. Ercildoun had full charge of Adrienne, and fortified her against making a fool of herself. She took the girl to her apartment in Darlinghurst, fed her, confessed to having survived crises of her own, so that Adrienne emerged her admirer for life and on the way to recovery.

A sense of satisfaction was mingled with Lola's recoil from the restricting and tiresome stretch ahead of her. She would avoid all risks. Other women should not be able to assume airs of superiority towards her because of mere motherhood, a detail she would take on the wings of her career. It would also mean more security of sexual tenure. Brian would be forestalled in a common excuse for paramouring. Even among the liberated of Bloomsbury a familiar eulogy of a woman was that she was a real mate who had given her paramour a fine son, a form of self-expression denied him by his wife. Well, she was giving Brian a child to assure his virility. Men were so hysterical; impair their sense of sex in this particular and they collapsed. Her secret out, her status with Brian re-defined, sweet relief sent her to sleep for the ensuing twenty-four hours.

Brian found himself superfluous and was thankful to be dismissed. The urge was on him to commune with the invisible, so he arranged for a plane to set off for his home region.

It was glorious weather in the heart of spring, warm and soft, the winds asleep. Up, like a god, from the drome carpeted with dew-sopped grasses, which had come when plentiful rains followed the winter drought. The works of men shrank as the machine climbed into the rosy dawn. The receding dwellings resembled verminous incrustations flat upon the soil, the movement of traffic that of insects. Only the Pacific, blue abeam, and the roads stretching across and beyond the wide horizons retained their dignity. Along the best of the roads, old Danny and his Johanna had crept for weeks like ants under the mighty timber. To-day, in an hour, their great-grandson sped the distance in the eagles' domain, a spot upon the sun. Below him a million acres cleared and paddocked danced in waves of light where scarcely enough trees remained to lend graciousness.

Before him lay the destined land of Daniel Brian Robert M. Delacy, in its aura of palpitant silence, enchantment welling from its ageless mystery. From that pregnant oblivion, glittering free of humanity to the Pole, shimmering broadly to the equator, might come the revelation for which man was toiling upward from the abyss. There a man had space to escape from the limitations of his outer shell into the boundless freedom of his inner consciousness. There the sun rose as the promise of God and set as His benediction.

Brian alighted upon an emergency drome in an early holding in the Gap, long since cleared except of wattles, and commanding a view of the far piled ranges beyond Canberra, that lie dreaming for ever in blue forgetfulness. The hills were an altar, this a vigil of oblation in the worshipper's private chapel with a choir of magpies, kookaburras, warblers—each after his kind—filling the invisible transepts with music.

The prospects of perpetuity through his child liberated the young man to that which has ever been found upon the hilltops; which some must miss, and which those who seek to condition by explanation, must lose. Brian, as Danny long ago, was realizing that he was free of eternity in the present, that by the release of spiritual emotion man transcends intellect and gains a glimpse of the kingdom of the unconditioned and unexpressed, with exaltation vested in its remaining unconditionable, inexpressible. The consciousness of infinity in such rare moments adds knowledge and experience to mere acknowledgment of immortality.

The son of this soil and sunlight thrilled to his destiny as guardian of an unspoiled habitat for the human race. Here lay a sensitive land protected by phantom qualities that would return her to desert to rid herself of the plague of too dense a population: an elusive land whose suns and floods could cleanse her, a land of elfin flowers and animals, an eerie land not to be bludgeoned but wooed from a vast oblivion wherein past history might for ever remain in the realm of conjecture.

Such was his land.

Wanted, a race worthy to possess her, a new race by developments in communications and transportation to be liberated from the primitive and panic trade compulsion of squalid gregariousness and proliferousness. Why not a people selected from the world's best?

Australia had sent him abroad to the best in the old world, had welcomed him home effusively. Here he was. He stretched himself on the warm clean earth and exulted in the fact of being born to this when he might have been dropped where the very stones were worn with the footprints of countless generations, so that a man was paralysed by the realization of being only one more leaf to fall on the humus of history.

Through disregard of the impossible men had come to fly. The aviator and humanitarian pondered upon the inconsistency of men who could dare and harness the elements and yet submit to physical want in the midst of abundance. There upon the hill-top in the crest of vigour he laughed aloud at stupidity which could so easily give 'way to sane employment of the resources at man's command. This ludicrous system of exploitation which wasted food while people wearied in bread lines had long since been brought to judgment and condemned and was being superseded despite all the false briefs, all the specious and special pleading and lethal armaments of the brigands who still clung desperately to key positions.

To every youth worthy of human estate the readjustment of the human comedy to the pattern of sanity and happiness appears immediately practicable; all the old men are doomed, when choked with experience, to see that readjustment deferred to posterity.

He took a letter from his pocket and tenderly unfolded it, happiness playing upon his features. The paper was patched at the folds, the faint writing in pencil, but Brian valued the document as the deed of his inheritance. It was the last letter that old Harry had written, which Josephine had covered with apology. Brian treasured both letters, felt in himself the qualities of the two writers and their divergent understanding of character.

The trembling sentences ran:

"I can see it clearly now at the threshold of everlasting life; believe me boy, the new conceptions of time and space will knock man's present superstitions sky high and liberate his mind. The infinite immortality is with us always. Future and past are words that can be used one for the other. Man presently will be able to look round time as you fly around the globe. Man only needs to give intelligence full play and fair play to own the potentialities beyond the frontiers of present human knowledge in the Never Never and the Never Yet of the mind.

"Australia is the most wonderful country in the world, but new ideas must be freed to save and develop it. Australians must do something better than copy any one else on the globe. There has been too much pioneering of destruction, trying to force Australia to the mistakes and achievements of Asia and Europe. Science must learn to take Australia on her own lines and let her remain different.

"A dream is the highest possession of man. I can see in a vision the pioneering that is to be done in the mind. The mind! your great-grandfather used to say. He was a great man. Your father was a delicate link, but he held the chain. I was a failure by all accounts, but I held the torch for you and will finally be a success if you are worthy of old Fearless Danny of the Murrumbidgee. His vision of the future and the past and his contentment with the big mysteries was a greater possession than all the money-bags in the banks because he could both take it away with him and leave it behind him too. In the eras which are coming it is not the felons, who can grasp at the expense of their fellows, who are to succeed in the fullness of living but those who . . ."

The frail hand had here failed its master but there was enough for Brian. And it was all true. He gazed across the blue-green ocean of ranges which Danny and Harry had seen as the vitals of the continent. There nestled his stake in the soil—as much as a man might retain in the choppy seas of evolution. Had old Danny been a grasper instead of a dreamer, what might have been his descendant's position to-day? Doubtful.

Danny, Harry and Darcy had given him vision. What had the financially successful achieved? From The Plains spread before him they had been dislodged by an urgent democracy, and had left no distinguished representative. Had any of the old squatter clans of Danny Delacy's kingdom done so? A noted Greek scholar and one or two literary men and women of the region occurred to him.

The merely predatory or acquisitive now went in terror of the nascent ethical order which might mulct the hoarders of their money-bags. (Old Harry's term served.) In such event hoarders would be nonentities; whereas Brian felt himself equipped to meet whatever the changing tides of behaviour might bring—even the repudiation of hoarding. No political party could rob him of his aspirations and ambitions; and he gloried in that alloy of ruthlessness—horse-sense—to armour him amid the wreckers and pluckers. For that he thanked his mother and Grandmother Josephine. His mother had definite suspicions of the motives of her fellows, a biting ridicule of their persons, but Delacy qualities also left her sympathetic and vulnerable.

Grandmother Josephine! He chuckled to contemplate that masterpiece. How she had worn! She must be the most beautiful woman of her age in Australia, and undefeated still. First-class material throughout was there, and no lyrical sensitiveness to betray her into weaknesses. Grandfather Harry had been a real man to lure her into marriage and to stand up to her through all those years!

"I'm glad you have some of my character, boy," she had said. "I do admire character." There was no hedging in her judgments. "You want to guard against the Delacy weaknesses—blathering poetry and ranting like red-raggers against money-bags while the thieves plucked them bare; or else giving away all they had. All that pleasantness and talk about a sense of humour, and that hawhawing at silly jokes, cannot make up for a lack of back-bone. I do respect a man with character, one who can make his way in the world and rise to something substantial for himself and his family."

Conspicuous results on the concrete level had been achieved by the operations of character as she conceived it. Babylons and modern empires had arisen at its will, and passed because of its lack of spiritual ascendancy. His grandfather had had another conception—character as mind—the spiritual man as of more importance than the physical. He was right. The pathways to the shrines of the saints remain smooth from the feet of pilgrims long after the tombs of conquerors are smothered by the jungle.

At the opening of his farewell letter Harry had exhorted his grandson of the new generation, as an aviator and man of vision, "To surmount the clouds, to woo the moon and dare the sun." To his grandmother, what a typical example of Delacy poetical blather! But Brian could distil exaltation from the hyperbole. Without such dreamers men could not have achieved even mechanical flight. His grandmother might have been of those to pile a faggot on the blasphemous inventor of the Middle Ages, but she could, even at eighty (by gad!), keep a machine in order and subject it to her skill. He understood both progenitors, and gloried in the temperament that was his by such a combination of qualities.

"I'm a new style millionaire. At any rate I would not exchange with one of the blobs with all the property of the McCaugheys, Kidmans and Tysons rolled together. Granddad was right. He was a success. Old Danny was a great ancestor to transmit the inheritance of an outlook to fit me for the uncharted future. Let it come. I'm ready for it, no matter which way the wind blows. I'm a two-headed kangaroo."

All too swiftly the day ascended and declined. The shadows lengthened from the cropped tussocks pimpling the hillsides. Perfume of wattle bathed approaching evening in delight. The bright landscape danced in air translucent and dazzling. The westering sun laying vesper offering on the rim of day, melted sky and mountains into a glory of filtered light and retreated to the core of a continent over which as yet man has no sure dominion. A land of distances, a land dependent upon distances for preservation; a land gorgeously empty and with none of the accumulations of centuries of human occupation; a continent surveyed, fenced, patrolled and policed by the nucleus of a nation analogous to a patriarchal family with unwieldy wealth.

"Australia, the incredible feat!" he chanted, with old Danny's habit of talking and laughing aloud to himself when lacking an audience to his mood or depth.

He returned to the plane and set the engines running. An old mare and foal frisked up to inspect him. Their points denoted his great-grandfather's breeds. Brian could see in memory his grandfather Robert riding on those plains with his dogs seeking sport and pillaging as they went. All the roads far and near had rung with the music of equine hoofs, which now echoed along the currents of past Time, and lingered in actuality west and north on stretches of country still held by a handful of men with their interminable leagues of fencing, their immortal horses and dogs, their intrepid and lonely women and children, awaiting the reinforcement of aircraft.

Airman Delacy pondered on the extension of his being back to his great-grandfather through living memory, and on to his own great-grandson—with luck. The pert foal frollicking up to sniff the machine illustrated the revolution in transport. He was part of the transition and had the good fortune to be in his prime at this stupendous parting of the ways. He recalled his youth a-horse, the companionship with spirited quadrupeds. Horse and man had laboured together, the man the lord, the horse the generous unrewarded collaborator, who had transformed the yokels of Europe into a nation of cavalry. In step with change they must now graduate as bird-men in vessels which could attain the stratosphere.

Critical days ahead with the machine as master, looming as the destroyer if manipulated to Satanic ends!

But it was inconceivable that men would hurl themselves into the abyss when the way out was as clear and wide as the shimmering track of the departing sun.

"I must have my eye on a promising Nullah-Mundoey for the young beggar that's coming," laughed the aviator. "A Nullah-Mundoey of the air."

The engine shuddered and hummed, moved, ran, ascended; roaring, it rent the upper air, drowning the rhythm of ghostly hoofbeats, swiftly was gone above the ranges, while on the silver screen of night appeared the spectral forms of bullock transport and receding Delacys moving against ancient unfamiliar apparitions on the palimpsest of Time.

Australia, 1933.